Coeptus Awakes

Being the fifth and final part of
Lake of Dragons

E. Michael Mettille

TMR Books
PO Box 510886
Milwaukee, WI 53203
www.themikereynolds.com

All images provided provided by Deposit Photos and Adobe Stock

Cover Artwork – © 2024 L.J. Anderson of Mayhem Cover Creations – www.mayhemcovercreations.com

Published by TMR Books 4/1/2024

ISBN 978-0-9975571-9-0

DEDICATION

For my grandmas, Beverly (Grandma Bev), Patricia (Grandma Mettille), and Grace (Nana Bear), three women who have inspired me throughout my life with their caring natures, spunk, love for life, and the stories they tell. They are joy personified, and the world is a better place because of them.

CHAPTER 1
THE TREES

The forest was cooler than usual. A dampness hung in the air and clung
to Hagen's cheeks as he carefully made his way across a trail grown
over with vines and interrupted by twisting and gnarled roots jutting
from the soft earth. The trees, ancient and mighty sentinels standing
tall against time, stretched into a cloudless sky and reached for one
another with their girthy and bent branches to block out any sunlight
which might prove bold enough to reach down toward the moss and
vines on the forest floor. Hagen loved all forests, but this one held a
special place in his heart. The trees of this wood were cunning and
wise. They had neither the time nor the patience to suffer fools or
mischief-makers. He could tell they recognized him after a few steps
in. The change in their demeanor was nearly imperceptible, but he
noticed. The path grew wider. Vines slipped away from it, slithering
back into the darkness while thick roots sunk into the soft earth. They
found his company as pleasing as he found theirs.

It seemed odd at first, the scrutiny. The trees of the Sobbing Forest
had always been very particular about which guests they would allow
to visit, but he knew they enjoyed his company and their chats. Of
course, the trees didn't speak. Instead, they hummed out melodies.
Some folks only heard sobbing as ominous as it was troubling, but
folks with a mind for knowing could pull meaning from those
melodies. Hagen had a mind for knowing, and he could tell right away
they hadn't recognized him when he stepped into the darkness of their
keep. He couldn't blame them. The last time he'd strolled among the

timeless creatures he had appeared a bent old man. The vibrant youth he'd become since Antopy reminded him who he was, was anything but that. At least seventy summers must have passed since the last time they would have seen him looking so young.

"I've missed you, old friends," he smiled up at the canopy with the truest joy he'd felt in far too long.

They hummed a happy response back. They had missed him too.

He'd been born there among them. Of course, he couldn't remember being born, but his mother told him the stories of how the trees helped her cope with the pain. Father wouldn't help. He was a good man, wise, but he believed in allowing things to happen as they will and refused to intervene. The trees helped in his stead. They hummed her soft melodies and lowered balmy branches thick with soft leaves for her to rest upon between contractions. They even bubbled fresh water out of the soft ground for her to drink and cool her forehead. She loved the trees and told him that story over and over again.

They hadn't stayed long after he'd been born and, though he had returned frequently over the many summers which had passed since then, the visits were always too brief. Breathing the fresh forest air, he felt he could stay among them for the rest of his days. The trees vibrated happily at the thought, but it could never be. He had too much to do. A new king perched on the throne of the greatest city of men, and that man needed his help. On top of that, Mother and Father had instilled a restlessness in him. He hated it. Most times he could ignore the call, but something always got him. It wouldn't be long before he'd have to hit the trail again. A great power lay dormant, sleeping in a tower at the edge of time and understanding. At some point, it would wake. Once Ymarhon had wrangled enough control over his subjects in Havenstahl, Hagen would need to investigate that great power.

Hagen's smile faltered as he got back to the business at hand, "I wish the goal of my visit was to share stories and reminisce. Alas, I am on a mission to find wickedness hiding amongst your glorious shadows."

Confusion swept through the trees as the canopy rustled with discontent. The trees liked to believe they knew vastly more than the dense and stiff things occupying other forests. They were correct. As far as Hagen knew, the mighty trees of the Sobbing Forest were the only trees in any forest who knew anything about anything. He also knew they could only know what they could know, and that was only what the birds flittering about their branches or the furry critters scurrying about their trunks would tell them. News traveling in that fashion was rarely news any longer by the time it reached their leaves.

"Forgive me," Hagen proceeded cautiously, careful not to bruise the collective ego of his old friends, "but beasts have sailed across the Great Sea to lay waste to these lands."

Of course, the trees knew all about the giants from across the Great Sea and the other monsters they brought with them. That wasn't news at all. Havenstahl had stood tall against that invading force.

Hagen's smile widened, "You are quite wise and quite right, as always. Most of those monsters have been destroyed or turned away, but not all of them. I have been hunting one of them who has been causing much trouble for men who fall under the protection of Havenstahl. Laenkishot Kil hides among your shadows, and he is the vilest of creatures."

The trees knew he was there. He hadn't caused them any trouble. They were skeptical of him at first, but he looked at them with awe and reverence. How could any creature that saw them as the glorious things they were be anything but pure?

"I mean no disrespect," Hagen pressed on as delicately as he could, "but the lands from which he hails are cracked and barren. Not to mention, the trees from Biggon's Bay to Mount Elzkahon aren't near so magnificent as the glorious host surrounding me here. Nor do they sing such mesmerizing songs. Of course, he admires you for the exquisite works of nature's art you are, but he is wicked. The five vicious trogmortem who follow him are the same, vile monsters with no love for anything."

The trees weren't convinced. They were probably no more dubious than any other moment, but they were dubious, nonetheless. They challenged his accusations. What had these peaceful creatures done to earn his ire?

"They have been raiding villages all around these lands," he frowned. "They hide among you, because the men of Havenstahl—even the fiercest among their ranks—are terrified of your wisdom and strength. They hear all these horrifying stories of the trees ripping men to shreds or suffocating them until their hearts cease to beat. They would never venture into the darkness of this place."

Their moaning increased in volume until it was almost a wail, the kind of shrill sound a starving baby might make.

"I know," Hagen huffed in mock shock. "How could anyone think such things? But you know men are strange. They fear things they do not understand. Sometimes, they fail to see beauty where it clearly exists, and thus, they fear you."

The blaring cry dulled again to a low moaning. It was almost a murmur, really. Hagen hated pointing out that they'd been duped by such dull creatures. The trees of the Sobbing Forest saw most other sentient life as beneath them, at least in intellect. The idea they could fall victim to something as base as flattery was difficult to admit.

Hagen allowed a mellow smile to rest between his cheeks as he held out his hands, "You cannot blame yourselves. I haven't met this giant, Laenkishot Kil, but I have searched his thoughts. He thinks very highly of himself, and he has an odd charisma about him. It is very disarming. Had I not the benefit of creeping around his mind and analyzing his intent, I would find him as pleasant and endearing as you. We can't worry about that. I bid you please take me to him, and I will rid of you of his vile presence in your sacred lands."

The trees parted toward the east bringing a wide smile to Hagen's face. The smile dimmed quickly. They weren't quite threats dancing among the rhythms of the humming vibrating off the trees but close kin. The wise and ancient creatures had sensed the change in him. Bolts of lightning blasting about the woods could cause quite a bit of hurt for a forest regardless of how wise its trees might happen to be.

"I would never think to unleash something so reckless while in your midst," Hagen smiled up at the canopy. "No harm will come to this glorious place."

The trees remained skeptical but made no move to hinder his progress. Despite the wide path they made for him, it was clear they refused to entertain any destructive forces unleashed beneath their leaves.

The path Hagen followed shifted slightly south. He could tell he was getting close. The trees' humming steadily grew as if a warning to alert him of his proximity to his adversaries. By the time he could see the faintest outline of shapes through the thick trees off to his right, the humming could have been the chime of a loud bell but sustained at the same volume and pitch as the moment it had been struck.

He sidled up to a massive oak and listened. The trees recognized his need for stealth and reduced the volume of their song.

It was difficult to see much through the thick trunks and brush growing around them, but Laenkishot Kil appeared to pace back and forth before five shapes that were seated in a semi-circle around a small but crackling fire.

"You threaten me against using lightning, but these invaders can enjoy a blaze?" he shook his head slightly as he glanced up toward the canopy and smirked.

The trees hummed out their answer. Laenkishot Kil and his group only burned what the trees allowed. Creatures like giants and trogmortem need the heat of fire to stay warm, and the trees had nothing to fear from them.

"So, you say," Hagen smiled wide. "Now, please let me listen to what they are saying. I need to know if they intend to depart for their homes or continue terrorizing the lands around this place."

"The army at Havenstahl has seen its ranks replenished," Kil complained to his companions as he paced about.

A trogmortem Hagen couldn't see clearly replied, "All the great cities of men answered the call from what I hear."

"There are no great cities of men," one of the others quipped.

"On that you are correct," Kil agreed. "However, those armies together represent a force far too great for us to battle against."

"Why battle at all?" one of the other trogmortem asked. "I am comfortable in this forest, and the men of Havenstahl seem to fear this place. We get all we need from the surrounding villages. We can remain safe here as long as we like."

Hagen had slowly been working his way closer to the clearing as he listened. By the time the last words left Gorban Khan's lips, Hagen had slipped around the tree he'd been hiding behind and into the flickering firelight. He recognized all the trogmortem in the clearing but one. Gorban Khan was probably the most gruesome of the bunch. Not because he was more vile or vicious than his kin. He had survived a battalion of dwarves during the battle of Fort Maomnosett. They had left him for dead with his nose split down the middle and deep gashes crisscrossing his massive face. Hanol Jo, Bancle Hig, and Lonac Yan were the other three he recognized. There was nothing particularly striking or unique about them, aside from Bancle Hig's size. At seventeen feet tall, he counted himself among the tallest of trogmortem. The last one was a mystery to Hagen.

After gauging the level of shock on the six faces looking back at him, the wizard looked toward the one unfamiliar face and said, "I know all the souls occupying this clearing with me except for you. How is it I do not know your face?"

"He claimed he was guarding the ships during every battle, but I think he was afraid," Hanol Jo chuckled. "Only came to shore when the bay got all angry and frothy. He jumped right into the drink and swam for shore when the first wave splashed against his ship."

"Shut up, fool," Laenkishot Kil growled at Hanol Jo before crouching closer to Hagen and sneering, "You are a bit far from home and obviously a fool to stand so close. I will grant you leave to depart this place if you do it quickly and never return."

The giant's breath was foul like rotten meat. He had been eating men. There were probably bits of villagers' flesh stuck between his teeth. Hagen winced slightly before replying, "I will grant you the same, Laenkishot Kil, mightiest of giants. Leave this place, and no harm will come to you. Stay, and there will be no place in these lands where you will be safe."

Lonac Yan lost himself in a fit of laughter that lasted long enough for Kil to snatch him up by the throat and pin him against a tree. Kil looked back at Hagen as Lonac's eyes bulged from their sockets. After a few moments of listening to the trogmortem struggle for air, he said, "Today is the day you die. I would like to know your name before I end your time in this world."

"Of course," Hagen smiled at the threat while removing his hood, "I am Hagen of Havenstahl, and I will be the one who sends the lot of you to the Lake if you fail to heed my warning."

The giant's eyebrows dipped toward his nose as he released his grip on Lonac's throat, cocked his head to the side, and said, "I have heard of a healer who goes by that name, but he was a very old man. That is not the creature standing before me."

"One and the same," Hagen's smile widened as he spread his arms out to his sides.

"Hmmm…I won't pretend to know if you're up to some trick or if you truly believe yourself to be that famous old healer, but I'll eat you just the same," Kil shrugged, "And, since I'm feeling generous of late after enjoying the bounty of your lands, I will grant you some knowledge before I swallow you down. We could not leave if we wanted to. Our ships were destroyed by a violent storm. Three escaped the bay. Ours was one of them, but she was in no condition to make the long journey across the Great Sea. We beached her farther down the coast and found our way here. This is our home now."

"Wait," Hagen raised an index finger as Kil took a step toward him, "What if I told you I could give you a ship stocked with all the supplies you would need to make that journey if you agreed to leave in peace?"

Laenkishot Kil laughed. It was a horrible sound, something like metal grinding against stone. After a few moments, the rest of the group joined in. They all laughed at Hagen as his smile faded in favor of a shallow frown.

"I would prefer not to hurt you," the wizard finally sighed, "but I fear your laughter is the only answer you will grant me on this day."

Kil's laughter ceased as quickly as it had begun. He leapt over the fire toward Hagen with his mouth wide and menace in his eyes.

The slightest hint of fear coiled around Hagen's spine as the monster's massive face lunged toward him howling a breeze of that rotten breath in his face. He had promised not to attack. Perhaps the trees felt more affection for this pack of beasts than they'd let on. There could be no clean way out of the situation. He hadn't the might to battle the monsters with his fists, and any spell he might conjure would enrage the trees. A battle with those old sentinels was one he wasn't sure he could win even with magic.

The giant's fingers were inches from his face when Hagen decided to try his luck with the trees. He couldn't just let the monster eat him after all. Perhaps the forest would understand.

The words Hagen would use to focus his intention on the spell that would cause the ground to erupt in a massive mound and launch the giant high into the canopy died at the back of his throat before they could be born into the world. He couldn't tell if it was a vine or a branch. It happened too quickly to identify the weapon, but it fired out from deep in the trees. Then it wound itself around Kil's neck and squeezed while yanking him back into the fire.

The giant screamed as the fire caught hold of his boots and flames licked up at his trousers. A vine whipped out and wrapped itself around his neck from the other direction. More vines came. They snapped out from the darkness faster than an eye could track them, each latching onto one of the giant's limbs.

Hagen almost felt pity for the giant as the vile thing struggled to get air while the fire finally caught a firm hold of his trousers and flames began licking up toward his shirt. The poor creature's face was red with effort as a soundless scream poured forth from his wide-opened mouth.

The sound the trees made when they yanked the monster apart wasn't any kind of humming. It was a guttural howl dripping with malice and revenge.

Hagen covered his face as Laenkishot's insides spattered the entire clearing. He and the five trogmortem were covered in meat and guts and blood as the vines raced back into the darkness carrying the giant's limbs with them.

"I am sorry," one trogmortem cried out as more vines came. He had barely gotten the words out before a vine was wrapped so tightly around his neck no more sound could leave him. It was only a few moments more before he and his kin were splattered all over the clearing just as their leader had been.

There was no joy hiding in the shock twisting up Hagen's expression. Of course, the vile creatures deserved their fate. He would have given them a similar end. The blood didn't bother him. It was more the violence unleashed by the trees. He had always seen them as somewhat peaceful. The mess soaking the clearing up to his ankles was anything but that. The smallest hint of fear returned. It whispered a warning from the back of Hagen's mind.

The trees were sorry to have scared him. There was a stark almost childish honesty to the feelings oozing about their gentle humming. It was reassuring, but Hagen still failed to completely forget that tiny breath of fear. Even still, that fear seemed small next to the aching in his heart. A single tear perched on his eyelid.

"I am sorry for what you had to do," he smiled despite the tear, "I wished not for that end."

CHAPTER 2
THE CONQUEROR'S KEEP

The circular room at the top of the tower was the same as it ever was. The cyclopean stones piled on one another too perfectly to be as random and chaotic as they seemed were bathed in total darkness and then total light in such rapid succession, they seemed completely dark and completely light at the same time. It was almost as if the two conditions existed in one moment rather than a rapidly changing procession. The oddness of that condition of light giving way to dark which in turn gave way to the former so quickly no discernable difference could be perceived by any eyes save those of a god wasn't what had Ijilv's brows dipping toward his nose. It was the young man suspended between the obelisks emitting all the light and dark in such perfect and fast intervals. It seemed he was wearing a smirk. Ijilv had never noticed any sort of expression on the young man's perfect face at any of the many times he stood in the very spot he occupied and beheld the magnificent creature. Any expression would have been a bit disconcerting, but the smirk seemed especially troubling.

"You stink of fear, you pathetic thing," Kallum's voice groaned in his head.

"I love you, brother," Ijilv replied with as fake a chuckle as had ever been, "but you are nothing. What does the opinion of nothing mean to anyone?"

"False bravado is beneath you," Kaldumahn chimed in, almost giggling. "I can smell it too. You are terrified of visiting him in that false paradise you've created for him within his own mind."

"I am troubled," Ijilv granted the cackling fools, "That is not the same as fear."

"So, you say," Kallum laughed.

He protected the thought from his brothers, but they were correct. Fear coursed through him in that moment. Of course, there was no fathomable way they could smell it as Kallum had suggested, but they were certainly accurate in their assessment. It was that damned smirk. What could the boy be up to locked inside the fantasy he had concocted to trap him in his subconscious mind? As concerning as the idea was, he'd have to peek in eventually.

Geillan, the obelisks, the massive black stones, and both the light and dark melted away in favor of something far different than Ijilv expected. There were no fluffy clouds lazing about an impossibly blue sky filled with sunshine. Instead, the sky was pink. No, it was purple. Wait a minute. That sky was definitely orange. It suddenly occurred to Ijilv there wasn't anything wrong with his vision, nor had he forgotten how to properly identify colors. The sky was shifting. Not quite the chaos outside the tower where Geillan lay sleeping between those four obelisks, but not the orderly perfection he had left for the boy's mind to play in.

He was so intrigued by the sky that he failed to notice the absence of the lake. The last time he'd visited the boy there had been a lake there. It was gone, replaced by a wide field of unkempt purple weeds interrupted by the occasional bush. Those were hideous. Wild and rough with pointy, red needles nearly as long as a tree branch.

Geillan had obviously been busy manipulating Ijilv's creation, but how? Where did he get these horrid visions to speckle about the once beautiful landscape? The boy had never been anywhere but this place. He must have gleaned these haunting ideas from his mother before destroying her. What else had he learned while scanning her mind and soul? More troubling than anything about the new and odd landscape was the thought of where the young man might be hiding in the awful place.

Kallum strolled from a dark hole within a bright orange mound surrounded by grotesque blue trees. They weren't quite that, but it seemed they strived to be, twisted, leafless trees all gnarled up and sad. The trees weren't near so disturbing as his brother though. Him he had left in that mock prison, gray and defeated. The being walking toward him was nothing of the sort. He glowed with all the glorious light befitting a god.

"You look as if you have seen a ghost," Kallum boomed through a wide smile.

Ijilv felt as if he might vomit right there on the… It suddenly occurred to him that he was ankle deep in bright, yellow muck that only just failed at mocking the consistency of sloppy mud. Of course, there was nothing in him to vomit, but he remembered enough about the time before time to recall what it felt like. The perfect and horrible sound of Kallum's voice brought him right back to that place. How? The small and gravelly thing he had left him with was gone. Could Geillan have done that? He must have. Worse still, the boy must have reasoned a method to borrow Kallum's essence and his power.

He did his best to hide the shock and terror stomping about his mind when he finally replied, "You misread me, brother. Nothing happens in this place unless I will it."

"Is that so?" Moshat's voice boomed just as gloriously rich as Kallum's had been, "Is that to say you sent Geillan to free us from our cell?"

"Of course, he must have," Brerto laughed as he seemingly emerged from the scenery directly before Ijilv's face.

"I did not direct him to release you," Ijilv nearly stammered, "Nor did I command him to return you to your former countenance and glory. However, I did not prevent him from doing so."

Kaldumahn suddenly appeared beside Ijilv with his arm draped across his shoulders, "You did not prevent him from doing so, because you had no idea what he was going to do. You must do as you see fit, of course. If it were me, I would worry greatly over how he managed to accomplish the task."

"You have said yourself that he was under your complete control," Moshat agreed, "Could it be you are losing power over your plaything?"

"You convinced him to kill his mother," Brerto shook his head. "Tsk, tsk, what terror do you suppose he will unleash on you?"

Kallum approached quickly as if he planned to attack but stopped directly in front of Ijilv. "Kneel," he commanded as he raised his hand high above his head.

Ijilv chuckled at the gesture, "Do not fool yourself into believing this new freedom my son has granted you gives you any power in this place. You are still completely under my control."

Kallum's cheeks trembled slightly with effort. "Damn," he finally said before casually strolling off to stand near Moshat.

"I told you that would not work," Brerto laughed at Kallum before turning his attention back to Ijilv, "The boy told us as much. He freed us from your prison because he was bored, if I recall correctly."

"Yes," Kaldumahn smiled, "That is precisely the word he used. He was bored and wanted some company."

Brerto's smile fled as his voice lowered and deepened, "Brother, you might as well give up the charade. We can all see the truth weighing down your troubled brow as uncertainty bends your back. It is time. Whatever you have planned for that boy needs to happen now. It is only a matter of time before he solves your puzzle and frees himself. Perhaps he will look more fondly upon you if you release him before that happens."

"Fine," Ijilv finally sighed, "You are correct. There is no sense hiding it from you any longer. You are still helplessly under my control, but the boy seems to be wriggling out from under my grasp. Take me to him."

"I think we all might appreciate it if you would ask us nicely to assist you," Moshat teased.

"Please," Ijilv's voice remained flat as he acquiesced.

Moshat beamed as he replied, "Thank you for that. It felt good. Sadly, we are not completely sure where he is right now."

"This place is constantly changing," Kaldumahn complained, "I would imagine this is a result of your pet's boredom."

"Though we cannot take you to him as you so rudely commanded, we can help you find him," Brerto smiled, "Despite all you have done to us, I still feel an odd kinship with you. Furthermore, I think you truly believe whatever outcome you are reaching toward is the right thing for this world."

"As diluted as you are, I believe you believe it too," Kallum dryly offered.

It was an odd sensation warming Ijilv's chest. Emotions are so petty. Of course, he always told his brothers he loved them, but those were just words. They were useful tools he had always been able to exploit. They served their purpose well. Yet, it was something akin to love that he felt in that moment. As simple and dry as his brothers' proclamations were, they meant more to him than just words. Was it loneliness? Standing there exposed as near a fraud in front of his pious and pompous brothers, and they refrained from mocking him. He hoped the odd ideas tossing about in his mind failed to show on his face.

"What about that cave you emerged from?" he nodded his head toward the place where it had been.

Kallum turned toward the same spot and shrugged, "It is gone. Nothing remains constant in this queer place. It is like the lands surrounding your tower, chaotic and wild."

The sky flashed a translucent green off in the distance. A wild shriek rumbled over the land mere moments after.

"Is that a storm?" Ijilv asked.

"Near enough," Moshat answered.

"I think it would be wise to head in that direction," Brerto suggested, "The boy was toying with the weather while he played with us."

"What did he do to you?" Ijilv asked.

"Many things," Kaldumahn offered, "He brought the storms while he had us fighting one another in our animal forms."

"I finally got to battle the great eagle one on one," Moshat smiled.

"You cheated," Kallum complained.

"I did no such thing," Moshat shook his head, "It is not my fault you were cursed with a beak instead of blessed with glorious fangs."

"How did he know of your animal forms?" Ijilv asked.

"Probably from the brief moment he spent with his mother," Brerto shrugged, "Dragon's fire is more than just a mere element. Having access to it opens a man's mind to things other creatures simply cannot access. Who knows how much time he spent strolling through her thoughts and memories in that moment, as brief as it seemed."

Standing around and speculating about all these troubling thoughts brought him no closer to his goal. The sky flashed again in the distance. Ijilv nodded toward the spot where the bright green flash had occurred and led his brothers in that direction. The screech that followed came a bit quicker. Perhaps the storm was approaching. He wondered what rain concocted out of Geillan's mind might feel like. Would it be slimy, hard, or maybe just wet like any other rain?

The five brothers strolled through a forest of those blue things that seemed so intent on being trees along a trail that twisted, turned, and doubled back so often it was impossible to discern in what direction they headed. Despite that lack of direction, the storm remained in the sky. Though it was not a straight path, they appeared to be getting closer to it.

Then the trees disappeared, and it seemed they were in a cave. The walls radiated with a sparkly pink, iridescent glow. Mushrooms of all sizes and colors grew randomly on the walls and floor of the place as a stream of shimmering, green liquid oozed its curvy way through it all. It looked too thick to be water, and the odd creatures that occasionally broke the surface were able to walk upon it.

Those creatures were at least as strange as the water. They resembled frogs with legs a hair too long, but they had shells on their heads and two rows of blood red spikes lining their slightly yellow tinged skin.

"What are those things?" Ijilv gasped.

"Nothing I have seen in any reality," Kallum replied offhandedly.

"Nothing here occurs in nature," Moshat agreed.

"At least, not on our side of the Lake," Kaldumahn added.

"Where are all these ideas coming from?" Ijilv troubled.

"Perhaps they are not ideas, but malformed thoughts yet to be born," Brerto offered.

"You speak of the subconscious," Ijilv's eyebrows raised as he pondered the thought. It would make sense, of course. He dared not share the rest of the thought. He didn't want those ideas echoing in their minds. If Geillan had enough access to his own subconscious mind to bring his prisoners from one part of it to another, there is no telling what else he might be able to find.

"You have more to say…" Brerto began when the world around them began to swirl.

The colors went first, bleeding together on wind that seemed to originate from nowhere. Then the odd mushroom things were swept up, followed by the water, and finally the strange frog creatures with their formidable spikes. All of it whisked around the five of them until they were finally swept up in it.

Ijilv's eyes went wide with fear as he failed to control the things happening around him. A quick glance at his four brothers assured him all but Kallum were equally concerned about the chaos warping around them. Three sets of wide eyes drenched in terror stared back at him along with Kallum's dopey grin. The latter seemed to be enjoying the lack of control Ijilv had over a world he had created.

"You have crafted a nightmare for Ouloos over which you have absolutely no control," Kallum scoffed.

A tear perched on one of Kaldumahn's eyelids as he stared at Ijilv and asked, "Is this what you planned all along, to bring us all together so your monster could terrorize us before finally destroying us completely?"

The world just spun faster around them, colors and shapes bleeding together until it was all nothing more than a murky blur. Ijilv had to control it. He drew a slow, deep breath in through his nose. The air around them smelled like the instant immediately before a lightning strike. His face tightened around a scowl as he decided there would be no lightning. There would be no storm at all. He was done playing this silly game.

By the time his perfect mouth opened to respond, Ijilv had gained back enough control of his emotions to appear calm, even aloof, as he said, "Stop sniveling. The great silver lion who stalks the sky cannot be brought to tears by an illusion. Impossible. My son is having a tantrum. He finally had cause to use his great power to complete a horribly challenging task, and he is coming to terms with it. The boy killed his mother, burned her to ash with Dragon's fire. I expected it would take him time to process the act."

"This is a tantrum?" Kaldumahn lost the tear he'd been holding back as he spread his arms wide and glanced around dramatically at the swirling madness surrounding them.

"You failed to answer our dear brother's question, Ijilv," Kallum's smile slithered off as he continued, "Was it your plan to have the boy torture us before finally destroying us in this horrid place?"

Ijilv's smile feigned authenticity as he replied, "I have only had one singular goal since emerging from the Lake with all of you, watching the birth of this world. The mayhem surrounding us is merely a side-effect of my plan to achieve that goal. The birth of a world is no trivial thing. Billions of worlds fade from existence before ever achieving true consciousness. We must expect challenge and hardship if we hope to see this one to a different fate."

The impossible colors and gut-wrenching shapes swirling at unimaginable speeds suddenly ceased. Complete darkness replaced them followed immediately by complete light absent any hint of shadow. The darkness had been so pitch, and the light so bright, Ijilv could no longer see his brothers. He couldn't even see his own hands before him. Everything had been washed away. And then it was gone.

The world suddenly appeared less strange. Ijilv still stood with his brothers, but the sights around them appeared closer to the paradise he had created for Geillan. It wasn't quite that place, but similar enough that he could at least recognize a hint of his will remaining in it.

Geillan was there lounging on a flat, smooth boulder casually skipping stones across the frothy purple waves of a vast lake. The mountains surrounding the oddly colored drink were a burnt orange. The sky above was bright pink interrupted by smoky blotches of forest green that must have been clouds despite the way they darted rather than lazed about.

Ijilv didn't wait for Geillan to address them. "My son, you have trained in this paradise I created for you long enough. It is time for you to stake your claim as ruler of this world. The Dragons, Maelich and Cialia, will sense your power. They will come for you. Go to the Lake. You will destroy them and free Ouloos from their wickedness. You will be a conquering king. Ouloos will be reborn."

"I would prefer if you ceased giving me orders," Geillan's tone was nonchalant as he continued skipping stones without bothering to glance back at his guests, "Perhaps I like it here. Maybe I will remain forever in this place."

Ijilv ignored the sly smirk Kallum shot toward him as he replied, "Of course, you like it here. This place is a paradise. I made it for you to protect you from the horrors of this world until you were ready to overcome those horrors. You are ready, and it is time."

"You made me a prison perfect enough that I would never want to leave," Geillan remained aloof as he continued skipping stones, "I made this place. My mother's visit opened my mind to things I had never known, things you kept from me."

"Protected you from," Ijilv quickly corrected, "Your training required intense focus. Contrary ideas would have stunted your growth."

"So you say, but I remain unconvinced. I learned more about the world outside of this place in the brief moment I embraced my mother than the entire time I have haunted this prison," Geillan finally turned to look at Ijilv. There didn't appear to be any hate or anger or malice in his expression as he continued, "I am not a man. At least, I shouldn't be. From what I gleaned strolling about my mother's memories, no more than two summers have passed since you took me from her."

"Saved you from her," Ijilv again corrected, suddenly troubled by what other ideas the boy may have found there, "Time is an illusion meant to control the beings who occupy the lands on the other side of the Lake. It is necessary for them to have some method to gauge their progress as they journey through their physical experience. You are beyond such rules as are these lands surrounding us. No summers have passed since I brought you to this place, because there are no such things."

"I am uncertain if anything you have ever told me is true," the lack of expression on Geillan's face was more troubling than any scowl or glare could hope to be, "Your talk of time is interesting. Those moments I had with my mother were so brief and fleeting. Yet, it seemed I had a hundred summers to examine her thoughts. I penetrated her soul with my will expecting to find the malice and hostility you claimed she harbored for me, but it simply was not there. Her soul seemed pure. Of course, I know she was wily and powerful. Even knowing that, it troubles me that I failed to find even the slightest hint of wickedness tainting her intention. Even as I burned her to ash, I only felt love and sadness."

"Did you expect her to not defend herself?" Ijilv's tone dripped with mock shock, "She was wise and cunning. She knew her power could not match your own. Her only hope was to trick you into dropping your defenses. You failed to find her true intent because she hid it away from you. What you found was precisely what she wanted you to find, but you were not fooled."

"If I may," Brerto interrupted, "I have studied the minds of men for as long as there have been minds of men, and I am ancient. All that study has taught me that the minds of men are more complex than anything else in this world. Logic is easy. It makes sense. One thing is the result of another, each action has an expected result, etcetera. However, the minds of men are not ruled by logic alone. They are troubled by emotion, feelings, these illogical things that render expectations nearly fantasy. They can be used to sow doubt."

Of all Ijilv's brothers, Brerto was probably the wisest. He couldn't be certain what game the great, white tiger might be playing—he had always been as wily as he was wise—but he latched onto the assist. "That is precisely what she did to you," he almost blurted, "She hoped you would want to feel love from her, and she showed it to you, hiding all her other emotions deep below the surface while she toyed with your feelings and desires. It is only natural that logic would flee in the face of such an attack on your emotions."

Geillan's brow dipped toward his nose as his form deflated, "I suppose that is possible. Even as I sit here before you all trying to make sense of everything, my feelings are getting in my way. I am as uncertain what to think about anything as I am uncertain what I must do. I want to be alone. All of you may leave."

There was no gradual shift. One moment, Ijilv stood before Geillan with his brothers in a macabre twisting of the world he had created for the boy, and in the next moment he was looking down at his brothers in the cell he had created for them. He attempted to return to that place. It was a weak effort. Geillan was in an odd emotional state. It would be unwise to press him too hard at that moment. When the attempt failed, he resolved to give the boy a bit of time before visiting again.

"You still have control of him," Brerto's voice startled Ijilv out of his contemplations, "but you hold a terrifyingly light grip on the reigns."

"I know," Ijilv sighed, "I was surprised you came to my aid. You have always enjoyed games. I hope you are not up to one now. As you have correctly noted, the control I hold over Geillan is very weak at this moment. Your fate is tied to my own."

Kallum motioned toward Brerto with his head and said, "He is afraid of the boy."

"I am," Brerto agreed with a shrug.

"We all should be," Kaldumahn added.

Moshat cleared his throat dramatically and said, "It sickens me, but we must all work together. Ijilv may rule over us due to his treachery, but we will share in his fate. That boy is a powerful and volatile creature. I too fear the tortures he could concoct for us. If only you had left us to oblivion."

"He needed us," Kallum added soberly, "That is why he guided the events of this world to happen precisely as they did. He needed the twins to view us as enemies, so they would destroy us with Dragon's fire. He was not strong enough to control Geillan on his own."

"None of us alone would be," Ijilv agreed, "There are no more secrets between us. Maelich will realize Geillan is the reason for his precious Perrin's demise. Cialia will recognize the threat the child's power represents. The two of them will destroy the boy, and Ouloos can be reborn."

CHAPTER 3
CLOSURE

Consciousness was a cold monstrosity, heartless and vile. Sleep had been no better. Dreams of things that could never be. Alternate endings to things that should never have been. "Will this be my lot until the end of time?" Maelich wondered aloud.

The forest surrounding him offered no response save the quiet rustling of leaves motivated into a slow waltz by the slightest of breezes and the quiet babble of the brook flowing alongside the slab he leaned against.

The stone was cold against his back. The chill reminded him of the dead thing lying atop the altar. It wasn't his father who was laid out upon it. That much had become clear. Ymitoth had made his journey to the Lake at least… How long had it been? The thought troubled him enough to distract him from worse thoughts lingering in the dark corners of his mind. The amount of time which had passed since that horrible day made little difference. Whether it had been a few days, a month, or even a few summers, he had lost everything that meant anything to him while he slumbered in the waking world.

After a few moments chasing unknowable things, duty finally distracted him further from all he had lost. Though his father no longer resided in the shell lying just above him, his body deserved to be respected in death. He had failed to honor Ymitoth's memory when the titan had left this world behind. That was one failure for which he could atone.

Maelich shifted his weight to stand. His back had grown stiff seated against the cold stone as he slumbered. A quick stretch reminded him that self-care had been another victim of his recent delusional trek. He stunk. That wouldn't do. His father deserved more than a grimy wretch officiating his funeral.

The water in the brook was cool and fresh. Maelich rubbed his hands together briskly in the light current before splashing a big drink into his hair and scrubbing it down his beard. Then he stood and removed his clothes or what was left of them. He hadn't recalled them being so shredded and useless until just then. The mangled strips that remained were saturated in dirt and blood, and all manner of nastiness he could scarcely imagine just then. He laid down flat in the shallow brook and let the cool water flow over him until his lungs burned. Rising back up to his knees, he scrubbed his body so vigorously it seemed he might be trying to cleanse his very soul. It was a silly thought, but he scrubbed harder, nonetheless.

When he finally finished, it occurred to him he had no means with which to dry himself. Nor did he have any clothes to replace the soiled rags he'd been wearing. That wouldn't do. He could will himself a towel and some fresh clothes into existence, but he didn't want to use that power again. That is precisely the type of thing that sent him along this path of distractions. He had completely detached himself from his own reality to create a new one where his father still lived.

As he stood there dripping and thinking about what he might clothe himself in, Moluam stepped out from the trees. She didn't come as the black horse. Instead, she appeared as a woman with a wise countenance suggesting lifetimes of experience that somehow maintained an innocence both youthful and bright. Her hair was a glorious mass of wild waves and curls that seemed to slither and dance of their own free will. The black gown she wore did the same, dancing about in random flourishes.

"Is your game finished, black horse?" Maelich asked, "Is that why you come to me in your true form?"

"There was no game, Maelich," she frowned. "There was only your shattered spirit which needed mending. You were broken, and you were the only one who could fix it for yourself. I merely helped guide you to this place of understanding."

"I know you are not to blame. I am," Maelich sighed, "Still, I wish you could have just plainly told me how far away from reality I had fallen. Perhaps I could have saved them. Perhaps…"

"Perhaps your grief would have burned this entire world to ash," Moluam interrupted, "You wield a power great enough to destroy us all, and grief is a tricky thing to navigate. I had to take care not to interrupt that process."

Though he didn't like the answer, he conceded, "Your words ring true. I have made many mistakes. Most of them were born of emotion rather than logic."

"You need both to navigate this world. Emotions give us the reasons, and logic helps us choose our paths," she said with a smile so pure, it gave Maelich the briefest moment of something closer to joy than he'd felt in longer than he could remember. "Here," she finally said as she held out a bundle of clothes toward him, "I made these for you. You will tell me you do not deserve anything from anyone. That is not for me to judge. However, you feel you owe a debt to the man who raised you. These will help you toward that end."

Maelich accepted the bundle and dressed quietly as Moluam turned back toward the trees to leave the way she had come. "Wait," he beckoned with just a hint of urgency in his voice, "Please, stay with me as I see him off. There should be thousands of souls standing here right now to bear witness to the life of one so great as my father. He deserves more than just me."

"I think you would be enough for him," she smiled, "but I will grant you this comfort you seek."

"Thank you," he smiled back at her before adding, "and then I never want to see you again."

Moluam's smile never faded as she replied, "I expect not."

Maelich finished dressing and approached the altar alone. Heat began in his chest as he looked down at his father's corpse. That warmth quickly moved up to his eyes before spilling down his cheeks in fast rivulets of tears. It was more than just the loss of one who stood so tall in his eyes. Guilt also lingered. He was suddenly glad there weren't thousands of people there to send the mighty Ymitoth off to the Lake in a ceremony befitting a hero as great as the king of Havenstahl. He wouldn't want any of those people who looked up to the mightiest of men to see him in that state, bent, gray, and decomposed. If only he had been stronger, his father would have had the honor he deserved. Instead, the king who was loved by all would burn to ash quietly in a foreign forest far from his home.

Maelich's chest heaved as he fell to his knees and sobbed a fresh torrent of tears. Thankfully, Moluam kept her distance. It would be a shame to lash out at her for the crime of caring. It's easy to shift blame from oneself when scraping the lowest points of a lifetime. He didn't want her to suffer that for accommodating his request for company. She had done no wrong. He had.

Several minutes passed before the tears slowed enough that Maelich could gain control of his breathing. It was time. He gently slipped his arms under Ymitoth's shoulders and knees, cradling the corpse close to his chest as he carried him to the same brook in which he'd washed himself.

"Maelich," Moluam called out.

His wet eyes begged for peace as he turned to her in silence. She remained equally silent as she offered him a fresh cloth. That small part of him aching to shout at her to give him one moment to grieve in silence was glad a larger part of him kept any contrary comments from slipping past his lips.

He sat down in the shallow brook with Ymitoth on his lap as he washed his skin with the cloth. He gazed into those gray eyes trying to think of what he could say to his father. Of course, his father wasn't really in there, but maybe he would hear from beyond the Lake. Coeptus had said much about where souls go when they make their journeys home, but none of it was anything he could know. On top of that, Kaldumahn had assured him Coeptus were nothing that could be spoken to. Then, out of nowhere, a song came to his lips. It was a song Haleen had sung to him before he journeyed off to train with that vile betrayer, Brerto.

My lad, sweet lad, lay down your heavy head
My lad, sweet lad, forget the path ye've tread
Relax in mother's arms, let her soft caresses heal ye
Relax in mother's arms, let her soft caresses heal ye
Though the road behind be dark and the road ahead be hard
Never fear, for mother's love will be there to keep guard
When your journey be complete, and your task has been fulfilled
Mother's arms they will be waiting to keep your heart stilled.

He hadn't planned on singing that song. He wasn't even sure how he remembered it. It just came out. His cheeks reddened a bit when he sang the bit about relaxing in mother's arms. The slight embarrassment he felt about it fled quickly. Those could be the Great Mother's arms he sang about. Perhaps that is exactly why that particular song popped into his head instead of any of the multitude of songs Ymitoth had taught him over the years. Deep inside he hoped Ymitoth was finally resting in Helias' warm embrace. The Dragon had called him home. Hopefully, she would watch over him until the end of time.

He knew it didn't really work that way. It is not the Dragons' lot to watch over those who have already journeyed home. It is only their role to guide those souls to that end when the time for their journey comes. Facts didn't matter much at that moment. The song made him feel a bit better, and the idea that the Great Mother might be watching over Ymitoth made him feel better still.

Maelich built a pyre of sticks after cleansing Ymitoth's body, dressing it in silks from Moluam—she was a blessing—and returning it to the altar on which he'd found him. Then he carried his father from the altar to the pyre and gently laid him upon it. The corpse was so gnarled and bent, he couldn't lay his sword out on the warrior's chest as he would have liked, so he laid the glorious blade that had rescued so many souls from the evils of this world beside the great hero. Then he let the flame come. The base of the pyre caught quickly, and the fire slowly spread across the entire structure.

Maelich reached out and took Moluam's hand as he spoke, "I do not have the right words to say. Nothing that might leave my lips would be sufficient to describe how important you were to all who knew you, and I am unworthy of speaking them for all I have done. Still, you deserve something to be said. You were a legend in your own lifetime. Everyone across all the land knew of the great warrior and king, Ymitoth. All your exploits, the battles you won, and the people you rescued from whatever dire fate had befallen them were not the things I admired most about you. The things I admired most about you had nothing to do with your prowess with a sword or your mind for strategy.

"It was a command given to you by a god to train me and raise me as a hero. I was that before I faltered. You didn't just train me to be those things, to prepare me for the rest of my journey toward my destiny. You were my father. You didn't have to be that. You could have been cold. You could have only played the role of stern mentor. I promise you this moment would be so much easier for me if you had, but you didn't. My father was a Lake, and I know you truly believed my mother to be dead when you told me that lie spoken to you by another. You gave me that parent I never had. You chose to love me as your own. You taught me how to love. The gifts you gave me are things I can never repay, and even if I could, you would refuse the payment.

"Those are the things I love and admire most about you. You didn't have to do any of them, but you did. You are a better man than I could ever be, and you have shown me an example for which to strive. I will remain forever sorry for the vile way I treated you after the Lake called you home. You would never do something like that to me. I promise you now, I will do my best to be better. I will do my best to be more like you. Thank you for everything you have given me throughout my life. I love you, father."

Maelich fell to his knees as the last words left his lips. There were so many more things he wanted to say, but the tears refused him any more words. Moluam knelt beside him and pulled him close. It suddenly occurred to him, as this veritable stranger consoled him with kindness he didn't feel he deserved, that he had no one else. Had she walked away from him in this lowest of moments, he would have been completely alone. Everyone he loved was gone except his sister. What would she think of him if she could see what he'd become? His body shook as he wailed into Moluam's shoulder.

"Ashamed," Maulom's voice boomed above Maelich's sobs, "that is what he would be. The great and mighty Ymitoth, hero among men, raised you to be a hero and a king, a ruler of men, and you shrunk away from that responsibility like common vermin scurrying about the dirty ground. Pathetic. You, in your weakness, have destroyed Ouloos."

"Leave him be," Moluam hissed, "Give him one moment to grieve, you vile, selfish thing."

"I will not," Maulom shouted back at her, "He could have ruled this entire world. Instead, he sobs into the dirt like some lowly scrod."

Moluam's head shook violently back and forth as she admonished the white horse. "No," she cried, "You are the one who forgot your place, not him. He has only ever done what he thought was right based on things *we* told him. You were never meant to rule this place. You were merely a distraction. That was your role, and that was my role. You veered off the path. You are the pathetic vermin thinking you would rule some imaginary land by his side. You are the one who would have destroyed this world."

"Enough!" Maelich finally shouted as he quickly rose to his feet, "Both of you speak of me as if I am not here. I am here, and I need no one to speak for me. You have both tricked me and lied to me. I am finished with you. My destiny is my own, and neither of you will taint it any further." His tone softened as he looked deep into Moluam's eyes and said, "Thank you for staying with me while I said good-bye to the greatest man I have ever known. You gave me a gift I cannot repay because I will never see you again. Neither of you will ever speak to me again. I banish you from my sight. Never haunt my dreams or come to me in the waking world again."

And they were gone. Maelich was alone, his only company the dying fire smoldering about his father's ashes. It was an odd moment of peace. He didn't know what he was supposed to do next. For all his life someone had been telling him what to do. He needed to kill this thing or fight that thing. In this moment of silence, he had no idea where he should go or what thing needed to be done. He couldn't remember a moment when he felt so at peace.

Alas, the moment of silence could not last. He had left too much undone and failed in so many ways. The idea he might forget his further responsibility to the creatures of Ouloos was a farce. Despite not knowing what his next move should be, he had to do something.

Raya's perfect face jumped to the front of his mind. She would know what he should do, but she wouldn't tell him what to do. Perhaps more importantly, she wouldn't judge him for what he had done or left undone. He wasn't quite certain of the way, but he decided to find her.

His body grew lighter. Sounds became quieter. Light slowly faded to dark. And he was gone.

CHAPTER 4
DUTY CALLS

The sky was mostly clear that day. Of course, a completely clear sky is nice when the air is in such a state that the blue is pleasing and deep, but it isn't perfect. A random, fluffy cloud adds something to the grandeur of an exceptionally blue sky the color alone could never hope to compete with. There is something serene about that fluffy cloud lazing slowly across the blue that harkens to the most restful peace.

Cialia lounged on the warm sand feeling at least as lazy as the random puffs of clouds slowly moving across the sky above. She'd been resting there for days, baking in the warm sun, cooling her toes in the sand, and inhaling the sweet perfume of the Lake. It didn't smell like a lake at all, really. No hint of fish wafted on the perfect air. Not that it would have damaged the fragrance—the smell of a common lake had its grandeur after all—it simply wasn't there. It smelled sweet, not like fruit or honeyed wine or some kind of sugary pie, but it was sweet, nonetheless. Coupled with all the other aromas wafting about the air—earthly vines, hearty trees, and fragrant fruits and nuts—the air smelled delicious. She could scarcely imagine a sweeter smell.

Lameah lounged beside her, that tender soul. All the Dragons, her sisters, were perfect creatures born of a love so seldom achieved it seemed nearly a myth, but there was something special about her. Cialia couldn't decide if it was her gentle voice, the innocent sparkle in her eye, or the way she listened to any story no matter how common or mundane as if it were constructed of the most important words she'd ever heard spoken in the most perfect order and cadence.

Perhaps it was all those things. Whatever the reason, though she knew the idea of a favorite among her sisters was wrong, Lameah was her favorite. She loved that precious soul above all others.

"You have been here a while," Lameah spoke softly, "Will you stay with us for all time? Is the work finally done?"

Cialia looked up at Lameah's beautiful eye, so deep and massive whole worlds might live within it, and replied, "You expect me to say no like I always do."

Cialia had never seen a Dragon blush, but somehow the soft scales on Lameah's face reddened just a hint more as she confessed, "Of course, I do. I expect your work will probably never be done. I do wish for it though, that day when you find peace and decide to stay with us for the rest of time."

"You know me so well, sweet sister," Cialia smiled up at the Dragon, "but this time, I think you may be mistaken. Perhaps this time may be the time I tell you yes, I will stay. I will stay with my sisters for the rest of my days, even until the end of time, even until this body fails, and my soul slinks off to the Lake. Maybe this is that time."

"Please do not tease, my love," the Dragon begged, "You know my heart aches for you every time you leave us. The idea you might remain among us for all your days will have me soaring to the very heights!"

"Our sister does not tease, sweet Lameah," Helias offered, her voice as sweet as fresh rain, "She truly believes her words, but I wonder…"

"For one who never judges, your words often seem weighed down by judgement," Cialia sighed.

"What is it you wonder?" Lameah asked.

Helias smiled her perfect smile as she replied, "I have told you many times you will find no judgement here among your sisters. We love you more than you could ever know. However, that love is not blind, nor is it unaware. You have a restless spirit, my dear. You need a goal. You need people to protect and defend. How long could you possibly remain idle here in this place regardless how perfect it might be?"

Cialia cringed at the Great Mother's words, but she couldn't really fault her for sharing them. As always, Helias was correct. She did have a restless soul, but after a few days lounging beside the Lake, free from any feelings of duty to any creature besides herself, it seemed maybe she could forget that life of service to others. Perhaps she had done enough for the creatures of Ouloos. Maybe it was finally time for her to rest.

"You are right to wonder about such things," she finally said, "but in this very moment, there is no place I would rather be than right here with all of you. Right at this moment, I feel I could remain here among you as a true Dragon."

"I hope the way you feel right at this moment is the way you feel for all time," Helias' voice remained as sweet as her smile.

"As do I," Lameah quickly added as if the additional weight of her opinion could help make it so.

The air suddenly changed interrupting the contemplations about whether Cialia would in fact remain among her sisters or if duty once again would draw her away. It was a smudge on the scenery, a not quite white mist that carried an unmistakable coolness. Cialia reached up to stroke it as it hovered by, a small gesture full of love to share with a soul on its way home to Coeptus.

"Rejoice," Lameah gushed as she shivered slightly.

"Another soul has come home to rest after a lifetime of toil," Helias added.

"I love it when they come home," Cialia smiled as she laid her cheek back against the warm sand.

A darkness crept into Cialia's awareness distracting her from the sheer bliss of a soul returning to the sweet serenity of the Lake. It was like something in the back of her mind flopped out of whatever box it had been stored in and spilled directly into her consciousness. She saw Maelich's face. Tears streamed down his cheeks from puffy, red eyes.

"There it is," Helias' voice carried no malice or judgement, but Cialia assumed both to be present in the words the great Dragon used.

"No," Lameah lost a tear, "please, sister, stay with us. This is your home. Claim it. Be one with us."

Tears began streaming down Cialia's cheeks before she could think about holding them back. "I want nothing more," she cried, "but…"

"There is no shame, my love," Helias almost sung the words.

"But there is always a but," Lameah wept just as hard as Cialia, "You will not be staying with us."

"I said no such thing," Cialia nearly shouted.

"You do not need to say the words for me to know your heart," Lameah cried a bit harder, "Please know, these tears are not because you hurt me. I want you to stay, but I know you must leave us again. You are so brave and mighty. You could do nothing else. These tears are for you. You cannot allow yourself to enjoy the peace you deserve, because you feel it is your duty to stand for those who cannot stand for themselves. I admire you so, and I will miss you until you return. I love you."

"Maelich is awake," Cialia wailed, "I know where he is."

"And you will go to him," the sureness in Helias' voice was frustrating.

"I will not," Cialia shouted, "I will remain here with my sisters. I will be a true Dragon."

She held tightly to that idea for as long as she could, reasoning that her brother had made his choice. He chose to hide away from his duties. He chose to flee from his responsibilities as a hero and a king, and to turn his back on his family. As much as she wanted to confront him, to accuse him of all the things he'd done and left undone, he didn't deserve it. He deserved his pain. She could let him have that pain and remain with her sisters living that life they thought she could never allow herself to enjoy.

Another idea jumped into her head. It was a name, Raya. That name raced a circuit around her mind. It was a name she had never heard, but once it leapt into her awareness, she knew everything. She was the forgotten one, a god who tricked all her brothers into believing she never was. She had hidden away outside of their awareness while they executed her will. She was the vilest of them all. Everything those wicked creatures had done was a thing she had whispered to them, ideas they believed to be their own.

"How can this be?" confusion saturated Helias' tone.

"Did you know about her?" Cialia hissed, her question sounding more like an accusation than a query as it flopped inelegantly from her mouth. "Did you know this Raya was hiding herself away and guiding her brothers' actions while they remained unaware? I destroyed them. Did they deserve my wrath?"

"I remember now, but somehow I did not only a moment ago," Cialia wasn't sure she could believe the shock in Helias' voice as the Great Mother stammered about. That perfect Dragon was always so sure of everything, always knew everything. Was it possible she could truly have been unaware of this other god, this wicked thing?

Another name suddenly occurred to Cialia, Ijilv. He was another one who had hidden himself away. Those two were the ones who truly deserved her wrath. They were the ones orchestrating all the terror the others inflicted on this world. They would pay.

"I do not believe this Raya is wicked or Evil," Helias still sounded as if she were working through a dandy of a riddle.

"Hiding away and whispering wicked things into others' ears so your hands may remain clean of the evil things those others do seems viler than anything any of those gods I destroyed have ever done," Cialia stood up and faced Helias. Any whisper of joy that had tickled her countenance fled in favor of sternness as her cheeks flexed from clenched teeth.

"You will go to her and destroy her," Lameah sobbed, "My heart weeps for the darkness it will bring to your spirit."

"Good-bye sweet sister," Helias lost one tear as Cialia vanished, sailing on the currents of the air.

CHAPTER 5
MOURNING

The flickering fire cast an orange glow on the trees surrounding the clearing all the way up to the lowest branches of the canopy. The aroma of burning wood mingling with the earthy scent of a forest fresh from recent rains sent Daritus' mind back to happier times. Leaves dancing about a cool breeze rustled out a rhythm while the *hoo, hoo* of a handful of owls and the random croak of a tree frog added a melody. All of it should have had Daritus' spirit soaring high into the dark heavens. Instead, the weight of the forest seemed to crush him into the soft dirt.

He emptied the last swig of fairies' tears out of his waterskin and slurred over to Kantiim who was enjoying some conversation with a much less ornery group of travelers, "Hey there, toss me another skin of this stuff."

Kantiim didn't respond. He just kept along with whatever boring yarn he was spinning to those fools who hung on his every word with rapt attention like a pack of dull children.

Daritus attempted to rise to his feet but instead stumbled through the fire carrying embers with him as he lost his footing on the other side and rolled end over end a few times before finishing the awkward tumble on his back and shouting, "Did you not hear me? I said toss me another skin."

Kantiim paused his story, looked up toward the dark canopy, and hollered back, "If I were less of a friend, I might oblige your request as rude as it may have been, but it seems you've had enough."

That just wouldn't do. Daritus finally made it to his feet and stumbled toward the other fire. If his best chum in all the world wouldn't help him, he'd get his own damned skin of fairies' tears. It was a solid plan, but three unsteady steps were all he managed before tripping over his own heel and diving headlong toward Kantiim's fire.

The most ambitious flames were but an inch or two from Daritus' dangling hair when Kantiim leapt to his feet and saved him from falling right into the healthy blaze. He struggled as much as he could against his good chum's grip, but the effort failed to earn his escape from the unwanted embrace.

"You are a drunken fool. Take yourself to bed," Kantiim hissed in Daritus' ear.

"I am a fool," Daritus cried out as he landed on his rump after Kantiim released him, "She took everything from me."

"This again?" Kantiim sighed. "You are embarrassing yourself in front of all these men who see you as something more than the fool blubbering about things over which he has no control. My old chum never wasted a tear lamenting events he could not change. He controlled the things he could and left the rest to be what they may."

"Maybe I'm not that chum you remember," he slurred as he failed at gaining his feet once again, "Maybe after all I have lost, I will never be that man again."

The world dipped and swayed as he watched Kantiim approach with the kind of stern look a disappointed father might wear when preparing to scold a naughty child. He couldn't get his hands underneath him quick enough to get out of the way. A moment later, his angry friend was dragging him up by the collar.

It was a quick journey from his back to his feet, much too quick. His stomach complained loudly as queasiness swept in far more quickly than he could do anything about it. He thought it would be a burp. It was that, loud and deep, but it came with a bit more than merely a foul odor and a rumbling report. He spewed vomit all over his old chum's jacket. It was a shame. Kantiim had been so proud of the thing when he'd had the tailors at Havenstahl make it for him to replace the tattered mess he'd worn during the battle at Fort Maomnosett.

The disappointed look on Kantiim's face shifted closer to something akin to rage just before Daritus started laughing in his face. Chunks of his latest meal that hadn't already spewed onto that shiny jacket shot out with the laughter decorating Kantiim's beard with bits of slightly digested meat and bread. The sight only made Daritus laugh harder. It was obvious his old chum didn't find the slight near as funny, as that expression which appeared such close kin to rage melted into steaming, red fury.

"Sorry about that fancy jacket," Daritus slurred through the laughter.

Kantiim balled his fist up and cocked it back. His best friend in the world was going to punch him. That would be good. He had it coming. A good fight would be healthy the way he'd been feeling. Of course, it wouldn't be a good fight at all. There wasn't anything he could do to defend himself just then. Before that fist could connect with his jaw and send him off to sleep for the evening, he found himself back on his back looking up at the flickering canopy.

"I shudder to show you such disrespect after all you have done for me throughout my life, and all you have recently suffered, but get a hold of yourself, man," Boringas' voice whispered in his ear, "You drink to dull the pain you feel at your sweet wife's unfortunate demise. Have you thought at all about what she would think of you slobbering and vomiting all over yourself and your closest chum like a common drunkard?"

"Disrespect?" Daritus scoffed. The canopy dipped and swayed above him as he shot his eyes toward Boringas' blurry face before adding, "I would rejoice if all you had brought me was disrespect, but that is not at all what your vile lips spoke to my ears. Is it? No! You brought me nothing but respect as you told me my wife was dead at the hands of my daughter. You are so damned polite and respectful. I want you to be callous and cold, so I can feel justified in punishing you for failing to protect the one thing in this horrid world that meant anything to me."

"I am sorry for failing my queen," tears suddenly gushed from Boringas' eyes as he pulled Daritus onto his lap and spilled them onto his forehead. "If only I could trade places with her, if I could earn an audience with Coeptus themselves, I would beg they take my soul for hers and return her to you, but I cannot."

Boringas' words and tears were more than Daritus could bear. He struggled from the man's grasp, stumbled to his feet, and clumsily drew his sword. He nearly fell again as he turned to face the blubbering fool he had always viewed as something of a son. Once he had as much control of himself as he could hope, he slurred a growl through clenched teeth, "You did fail your queen. She was righteous and pure, and she put her faith in you to protect our city, our people, and her. For these crimes, I sentence you to die."

Boringas made no move to defend himself as a fresh batch of salty sadness poured forth from his puffy, red eyes and snot flowed freely to saturate his mustache. He only struggled to his knees, pulled open his shirt, raised his head to expose his neck, and wept, "No one could ever damn me more than I damn myself. I am guilty of these crimes, and I deserve your wrath. I do not expect ever to earn your forgiveness after I am gone. My only hope is that you someday find peace and can remember happier times we have had with fondness."

"This has gone far enough," Spang shouted as he strolled up from his spot at the fire and shoved Daritus to the ground. "This man has faithfully served your family for most of his life. You basically raised him and trained him to be an honorable man. He is that. Gods and a Dragon came calling. Do you think you would have fared any better against those odds?"

Gazing up at the great, green canopy bathed in the flickering glow of a dozen fires once again, rage managed to shove Daritus' sadness to the side. Even in his drunken state, he could find no fault with Spang's words. His old friend was quite correct in his assessment, but it didn't matter one bit. Someone needed to pay for his wife's death. He couldn't get his hands on his daughter, that vile thing he no longer knew, so Boringas would have to pay in her stead. Anyone who got in his way could taste the same fate.

"How dare you," he shouted with as much force as his phlegmy throat could muster while stumbling back to his feet, "That man's king has passed judgement on him. Do you stand in the way of Druindahl's justice?"

"I grew up in that place, long before your wife was its queen or you were its king," Spang shook his head, "This thing the drunken fool staggering before me wants to do does not resemble Druindahl's justice. Put your sword in its scabbard and your drunken ass in its bed before you earn yourself another thing to lament and regret."

A small, logical voice in the back of Daritus' head begged him to heed Spang's words, but there were too many ideas echoing around his mind that were far too loud to let it to be heard. He had no more words for his old friend. All he had for him in that moment was his blade.

He knew he would regret it when he woke, but the knowledge did nothing to stay his hand. His blade whistled as it sliced through the still, forest air straight down at Spang's head. The move must not have been nearly as crisp or tight as it felt, because that target was long gone before the shimmering edge of the magnificent weapon came close to sniffing even a hair on that head. Instead, it thudded dully into the soft, forest floor, and, after another quick and inelegant roll, there sat the canopy flickering in firelight above him once again.

"Damn," he muttered loudly before rolling as quickly as he could to slash at Spang's feet.

His blade nearly tasted Spang's ankle, but the last remaining member of the Dragon's Flame was far too quick for a sloppy slash from a drunken fool.

"Enough," Spang shouted as he stumbled over a log while lifting his leg to avoid the attack. "That was too damned close!"

Daritus used Spang's momentary lack of balance to get back to his feet. He planned to stab his old friend right in the heart. Just as he launched the attack, pain erupted in his elbow. It sent a searing tingle down his arm all the way to his hand. He had lost his sword and was stumbling back to the soft earth before he realized Kantiim had punched him on the outside of his forearm just below the elbow. A small part of him boiled with rage at the idea a seasoned soldier like Kantiim would interfere in one-on-one combat, but a much larger part of him was relieved he had. The mixture of shock, fear, and anger twisting up Spang's face had almost been enough to stay his hand. Luckily, Kantiim removed any possibility he could make such a dire mistake before he was able to execute it.

Daritus was face down with a mouthful of dirt when the absolute absurdness of his behavior finally sunk in. He pushed himself up to spit out as much of the moist soil as he could before a laugh rumbled up from somewhere in his gut. None of it was funny. He knew that, but he didn't know what else he could do but laugh. Then the tears came. They poured down his temples to soak his dirty hair that spread out around him in sweaty clumps. His body heaved as he fired words out in a choppy cadence among the sobs, "My own daughter has taken everything from me."

Then Kantiim was on him. One arm tightened around his neck as the other applied pressure from behind. He tried struggling out of the strong man's grip, but he had no energy left to fight. On top of that, Kantiim had rolled them over and wrapped his legs so tightly around his waist he would have failed to escape even if he wasn't riotously drunk on fairies' tears.

"Intent," Kantiim growled in his ear as he choked him, "Have you no consideration for intent? Do you suppose Cialia wanted to kill her own mother? Do you think she even knows that crime has been committed?"

"I do not care about her intent," he choked his response amid sobs muffled by a lack of air. He continued as the pressure loosened just a bit, "Regardless of the intent, my wife is dead. I will never again look in her eyes. I will never hold her hand in mine. I will never hear the sweet music of her voice or smell the delicate fragrance of her perfume. I will never again hold her in my embrace. All of that is Cialia's fault. I didn't even get to say good-bye."

"Do you suppose drinking yourself into a stupor every night will change any of those things?" Spang asked soberly.

"No," he shouted up at the darkness with clarity his voice hadn't boasted in days, "but she will pay. If a Dragon can be killed, I will learn how."

"I have had enough of you today, old friend," Kantiim whispered into Daritus' ear as he strengthened his grip on his throat.

The canopy above Daritus grew fuzzy and even darker than it had been as he struggled against his old chum's grip. He barely heard Spang say, "For Coeptus' sake, don't kill him."

"I'm not going to kill him," Kantiim growled back. "When the day comes that he is finally sober again, he is going to clean this jacket he destroyed. Then he and I will have a long chat about it."

"Chat?" Spang asked.

"There may be a fist or two involved," those words grunting from Kantiim's lips were the last thing Daritus heard before the world went black.

CHAPTER 6
THE GREATEST CITIES OF MEN

The castle halls were bustling with activity, soldiers dressed in full palace garb wearing shiny prang from their helms to their gauntlets marched their paces as their highly polished, black boots clicked away on the smooth stone. The orange glow of a sun just a few hours from setting warmed the air of the hall making it feel even more alive. Not much more than a week prior, that same hall had entertained little more than ghosts. Since Ymarhon and his massive host from all the great cities of men had arrived to chase those ghosts away, the place seemed as glorious as it had been before dead-eyed men had come to kill the king and a sad son had stolen his corpse.

Hagen paused before a set of massive wooden doors and took a moment to admire them. The craftsmen of Havenstahl and Druindahl truly had no equals in all the land. The two doors were massive and thick, each hand carved with the images of two sprawling trees in their backgrounds. In front of those trees just beneath the center of each door was a helmet carved with such impeccable detail, they looked as if they could be plucked right from the scene and worn on one's head. Leaping over the tops of those two helmets were fallon with thick necks and massive racks. Each looked as if it could leap right off the door and gore someone to death with their incredible antlers.

The newly young wizard smiled as he pulled the silky blue hood back from his face and ran his hand through his careless, brown locks. The castle had finally been fully restored to the glory it had earned before a god tore it apart brick from brick and stone from stone. Even more glorious than the castle was the fact that a king once again warmed the throne of the greatest city of men, and he was a king with a legitimate claim to that great seat he occupied, his grandfather a cousin of Ymitoth's father.

Just as he was about to use his mind to open those beautifully crafted doors and address the new and worthiest of kings, a darkness entered his mind. Maelich's face swam in that darkness. The boy was crying. He had finally accepted Ymitoth's death. This could be problematic. Maelich had just become king of Havenstahl when he abandoned his people to go on some escapade with a corpse. His wounded psyche had no place in any throne room. However, with his great power, no one could stop him if he decided to return and lay a claim to it.

As he stood there before the doors to the throne room, it became increasingly clear the Dragon king would be laying no such claims. He had no desire to rule over any kingdom, especially one that housed the memories of so many of his ghosts. He allowed his awareness to stroll about Maelich's emotions and intentions. The man was broken. A thought of Cialia danced by. She had found her brother, and both those Dragons were aware of one another. They were on a collision course to…

Raya, the name echoed in his head. How could he have forgotten? Of course, she had willed it so. Now that Maelich was aware, all would be aware. Cialia planned to kill that god, and Maelich would not allow it. That was a battle in which he had no desire to intervene. Hopefully, the Dragons could find a way to work out their dramas without destroying all of Ouloos.

"PETA," he said quietly to the two magnificent doors, and they slowly swung open.

He strolled into the massive hall. The room buzzed with life like it hadn't in so long. Dignitaries from all the greatest cities of men milled about discussing this and that. Hagen overheard a few words about a trade route from Belscythia to Valancer followed by a brief debate about which city's armed forces should protect the path. A small group admired the seals fastened all around the room just below the ceiling. Of course, the crest of Havenstahl held the place of prominence behind the thrones. That great fallon with its massive rack leaping over the helmet looked just like the symbols carved into the doors of the great hall. The others spread out from that central point.

The great fish of Belscythia had always been a favorite of Hagen's.

It wasn't that he held a great love for fish, even massive fish that burst through the water into the salty sea air. It was more a fond memory of the one who destroyed the beast when it became a menace. She had been a true champion. He missed that young hero, and her husband, that striving magician. Both held a place in his heart that ached more often than not. That was probably the saddest part of seeing more summers than a man should. Generations had come and gone as he haunted the great halls of Havenstahl. The ones he loved lingered in the quiet moments when he'd spare them a tear or two.

Hagen shifted his attention away from fond memories to the man standing behind the great table at the front of the hall. The crown fit him well as it sparkled in sunlight filtering through the stained-glass windows along the western wall of the great room above rusty waves that almost looked golden in the glorious light. Ymarhon would make a great king, and Hagen was happy to serve him.

He watched a few moments as the new king pointed to areas on a map that sprawled across the table, divvying up the spoils of a war none of them had to fight. The lack of a battle meant very little. Whether the dignitaries from all the great houses earned the land they were given or not, the coalition of those great cities was what truly mattered. There hadn't been such a coalition since Jorgon, when an angry and vengeful god sent his vile emissaries to cut that great king down. Not even Ymitoth, as well loved as he was, succeeded in pulling all those houses back into the fold. Ymarhon had managed it before even taking the throne.

"I come with glorious and heartening news," Hagen proclaimed during a brief moment of pause when the king had looked up at him.

"Those both sound like some of my very favorite kinds of news," Ymarhon beamed a regal smile. Hagen couldn't decide if it really was a deep fondness he felt for this new king, or if the warmth in his chest was merely the result of any king being in the throne room of Havenstahl.

"I think you will find the news I have to share quite pleasing," Hagen held his arms out wide, "All the remaining forces from across the Great Sea are dead or fled. Havenstahl is once again free from foreign invaders. These lands are ready for you to begin your campaign unfettered by war or strife."

The king shifted his smile to the sunlight shining in through the stained glass and replied, "That is heartening news. I must admit a part of me desired to ascend the throne as a conquering king, turning aside the monsters at Havenstahl's gate. However, there is a sweetness to taking control of this city with no loss of life. I am a bit saddened none of the folk who protected this place from those invaders remained to revel in their success."

"I did try to convince Daritus to remain, but he would not be swayed. He has suffered much loss. My hope is he will resume his place as King of Druindahl, and you can count another ally in the east," Hagen nodded as his smile faded slightly before returning as wide as it had been.

"He is one I would have liked to meet," Ymarhon frowned, "the killer of giants. One man standing tall against monsters. I wish to have stories so grand told of me someday."

"You have done something far greater than defeating an enemy," Hagen shook his head, "All the great cities have returned. I never thought I would see the day. That is a story the people will tell until the end of time. The history books will glorify your name as the man who brought peace and prosperity to the lands."

"And I want to be that, of course, but what man who has ever held a sword in his hand does not wish to have songs sung about his prowess on the battlefield," the king chuckled, "I sound like a small boy daydreaming about battles to come."

"You sound like a king to me. You have already done great things, and I expect your work is not finished. I leave you to it" Hagen smiled.

"Thank you, Hagen. It heartens me to know I have your support in my campaign to unite the great cities. Where are you off to?" Ymarhon asked.

"You are rightfully sharing your lands with the good people of our sister cities. Those lands are in horrible disarray at the moment. The vile beasts may have fled back to their homes, but the result of their attacks remains. I will return with a report once I have restored Havenstahl's forests, rolling meadows, and villages back to their former grandeur," Hagen bowed before turning to leave.

"Do you need men?" Ymarhon called after him.

A faint haze of lightning crackled across the ceiling of the great hall as Hagen raised his hands above his head and said, "I do not require the labor of men. A mind set to a purpose can move mountains. Magic helps too."

A sly grin slipped onto Ymarhon's face as he asked, "Move

mountains? Does that mean what I think it might?"

Hagen's blue robe fluttered dramatically as he spun back toward the king and replied, "Indeed. We lost many of our good friends from Alhouim when their great peak tumbled under the weight of gods and Dragons. Those who remain have no place in this world."

"But I have given them ample lands to farm and harvest," the king fretted, "Have there been complaints?"

Hagen answered Ymarhon's frown with a wide and genuine smile as he replied, "Of course not. The dwarves of Alhouim are grateful for all the gifts you've bestowed upon them, but farm fields are no place for the rough but nimble hands of dwarves. They need to dig, and we require the fruits of their toils. The men of this great coalition of cities can farm the land while our dwarf friends free the precious pord from the bowels of the mountain which was stolen from them. We can resume trade once their fair city has been restored to its former glory."

The king's eyebrows dipped toward his nose as he replied, "I am unsure how you might have missed this with your vast knowledge of all things, dear friend, but, as you clearly stated, that mountain you would have them mine has crumbled into a field off massive boulders. There is nothing left for them to mine."

"Leave that to me," Hagen chuckled.

"You cannot be suggesting you have the power to rebuild a mountain cracked apart by a god," Ymarhon's voice dripped with raw skepticism.

"That is precisely what I suggest," Hagen boomed before bowing low and adding, "I shall report back to you once each pebble has been restored to its prior place."

He left the king speechless and scratching his head. Of course, the idea would seem ridiculous to anyone who had never questioned the limitations of a physical body. There was so much more lying just beneath that surface. All one required to peer beyond that imaginary wall was a willingness to give it a slight scratch. Hagen had done much more than scratch the surface in his time. He had torn a hole in it and danced on through. Each of those stones haphazardly tossed about for hundreds of acres in any direction remembered from whence they came. Their edges longed to touch the edges of the stones they had hugged since the beginning of time. All he had to do was remind them how to get there. It wouldn't be easy, but the task was well within his grasp.

CHAPTER 7
DRAGON'S FIRE

Maelich drifted among currents that felt different than any breeze or gale. The stuff blowing at him hardly felt like any kind of air at all. It seemed as if he'd completely left his body behind to speed through a swirling kaleidoscope of colors propelled by some force which behaved like a great wind but wasn't quite that. Those colors swirling together like paint bleeding in heavy rains were at least as odd and amazing as the something forcing him through it all. Though he could plainly see them, they didn't occur to his eyes. It was like he knew them with his mind, all colors he had ever seen and even more that he had never imagined spun and twisted around him mingling with one another into a kind of smudge. Yet each color though blurred and muddy by the others was vibrant and distinct from all the rest.

Smells came and went as his awareness traveled this swirling corridor of light. Some were odd odors, unnatural and metallic in their oil-soaked heaviness, while others were fragrant and pleasant like daffodils dancing in a warm, spring breeze. Cooking meat and burning wood, forest moss and musty lake, all these scents occurred to his mind rather than his nose, but he smelled them just the same. One by one, they seemed to avoid each other, each wanting to be known without interference from the other odors drifting about.

It was almost sensory overload. He hadn't even considered all the things he was tasting. Some were sweet, some foul, and others he couldn't decide if they were one or the other. He probably would have been terrified if it wasn't so exhilarating. Despite his physical form seeming to have vanished, he was certain he'd be wearing a smile. He felt so at peace in that moment ideas like fear or uncertainty seemed impossible.

Then it was dark, pitch, the total absence of light. It was as if he had become nothing and yet was still completely aware of everything like some bleak limbo. The idea should have been even more frightening than the profusion of color and sound and feeling he had just experienced, but he felt just as peaceful as he had a moment prior. His mind had gone quiet, totally absorbed in the silence.

After a few moments or years, or even lifetimes—time made little sense as imaginary a thing as it was—bits of light began to penetrate the darkness. At first, they were just faint streaks of almost white painting shapeless reverse shadows on a black canvas. Then there were colors. Brief explosions of brightness evaporated as quickly as they came as if the light was trying to hammer its way through the void of darkness.

The battle lasted until the darkness finally melted away in favor of colors in shapes that made sense. Brown, thick trunks of trees stretched up into a vibrant green canopy. Birds flittered about in that canopy chirping out a chaotic chorus of songs while furry critters scurried about the mossy floor beneath them squeaking, barking, and grunting their replies.

As the forest materialized around Maelich—or he materialized within it—pleasing scents that made sense in the waking world wafted about a light breeze that felt like actual air on his skin. Wildflowers mixed with moss and decomposing leaves smelling like a natural cycle of birth and death. All those forest scents mingled and danced with the aroma of a small pond that almost smelled like fresh rain. He thought about diving into the drink when he noticed her.

Raya sat on a stone bench on the other side of the pond. The delicate waves of her dark hair danced calmly in the breeze as she gently stroked the neck of a pale, pink unicorn who stood beside her. The gidim raced about her head, brief streaks of light nearly too fast for a human eye to see. Maelich wondered if Jana or Jinky were among them. The idea all these creatures could exist in this world with no one being aware of them outside of myths and lore was at least as troubling as his first visit with Raya.

"You are finally awake, Maelich," the sweet song of Raya's voice was as beautiful as the first time he'd heard it, but this time it wasn't new. It was a song he'd heard before. Not that it failed to be equally mesmerizing, but his resolve remained undeterred from its goal. He needed answers.

"Eengurra was not real," he began, troubled by the shabbiness of his own voice compared to hers. He had to ignore it. The last time they had spoken she managed to convince him the answers he wanted were not what he really wanted to know. He pressed on adding, "You put that place and those ideas in my head."

Her smile was like the first rays of a glorious sunrise as she replied, "Eengurra was real for as long as you allowed. That was not a dream. You manifested that place based on memories you borrowed from me once you became aware of me. That place was a memory of mine from a time before time."

"You seem so wise, but you make very little sense when you speak. There is no time before time," frustration coiled around his words.

"Millions upon millions of worlds have lived and died without ever having been born, Maelich. Ouloos is only one of those. I lived a life before Ouloos, and I wish this world to find a different fate than that which befell mine."

He pressed into her awareness with his mind. The force he put into the effort seemed unwarranted. He had expected some kind of resistance, but there was none. She allowed his intent to stroll right into her thoughts unencumbered.

"I have no secrets," she frowned, "I do not expect you will believe that, but it is true. I also expect you will not understand what you find when you find it."

She was correct. As Maelich stumbled about her awareness invading her thoughts and memories like a raider tossing chests open looking for treasures in a stolen carriage, nothing he found made much sense. Much of it reminded him of Adapa, that strange and easy going fellow he'd met fishing along an unguarded trail. All his talk of technology and science was filled with such foreign and unfamiliar concepts they could be nothing less than magic. It all came from some other world, this time before time she spoke of.

Once he had grown tired of the search he asked, "What about the Shaiwah? Did I manifest them too?"

The idea he had spent who knows how long stumbling across a dry, cracked, and forsaken land with a soulless shell living and speaking with imaginary people as he led them to destroy more imaginary people was too much to process. How weak was his mind that it could break so easily?

"Your mind is not weak," Raya's voice remained like sweet nectar, "You suffered a great tragedy. The weight of that tragedy caused a crack. Maulom and Moluam took advantage of that crack and gave you a purpose to distract you from all the things you would battle to prevent. You have always been one to battle against things you do not want instead of striving toward the things you do want and allowing them to be. The Shaiwah were not imaginary. They lived and breathed. You gave them that life. You manifested them based on the story Maulom told you. He convinced you they were your purpose, that you were promised to them through prophecy, and you told the story of them which brought them to life."

"So, I can create worlds and creatures at my whim?" Maelich chuckled at the thought. There was nothing funny about the idea, but chuckling seemed a better response than sobbing. He'd cried enough while reliving the memories of all he had lost while entombed in the fantasy he had concocted for himself.

"We all create our own realities, Maelich," she replied softly.

"What am I supposed to do now?" he sighed, "Moluam told me I needed to wake up, and you told me the same. Here I am awake. What is different now that the fog has been lifted? I am powerless to change anything that has happened. Am I just to wallow in my grief as penance until my broken soul finally finds the courage to make its journey to the Lake?"

"You could explain to me why you fled your loved ones and responsibilities in favor of the company of a corpse," Cialia's stern voice arrived a moment before the air next to Maelich shimmered with dazzling light.

As her shape solidified within the light, Maelich moved to embrace her as he replied, "I would change it all if I could."

She pushed him away and nearly shouted, "But you cannot. While you cowered away, fleeing from your feelings, and nursing your wounded spirit with fancy and fantasy, only I remained to protect those creatures you left vulnerable and unguarded. You forced me to do terrible things."

"I know," a tear saturated with all the sorrow he felt formed on Maelich's eyelid as his voice cracked, "I am sorry for all the pain I have caused you and everyone else. Those are things I cannot undo. I also know your work is not finished. I cannot allow the thing you came here to do."

"Do not test me, brother," Cialia sighed, "You were trained to use and control your flame. You promised to train me just the same. Do you remember that promise? One more thing you left undone."

"I know you found your flame, and I know how you found your flame," Maelich lost a tear as he paused. He wiped his eyes before adding, "I am so sorry you had to endure that pain."

"I was too, at first. A part of me still struggles to reconcile these feelings, but those vile men were just like the gods. They may not have wielded the same power, but they exerted their will in the same fashion, lording over creatures weaker than them, taking what they wanted, and punishing when it wasn't freely given," Cialia remained stern and stone-faced as she allowed no emotion to bleed into her tone.

Maelich lost another tear as he replied, "It is not your place to judge any creature. I know I have been absent, and I have failed. But I am thankful for all I have learned while lost in that fog of sorrow and self-pity. Not even the gods deserve your wrath."

"You dare judge me for anything I have done," she scoffed, "Do not forget you were the first god killer. It was not my flame that cast Kallum to oblivion. That was you. You did that. Had you not destroyed that corrupt and horrid thing, I may never have entertained the idea I could kill a god."

"A battle between two Dragons with the capacity to wield their great power is nowhere I want to be, but I cannot listen to you accuse each other in silence. Neither of you are guilty of anything but being exactly what you were intended to be," despite the soft beauty of Raya's voice, Maelich cringed at the sound of it. He wasn't sure how he planned to distract his sister from passing judgement on her, but that was his plan. If only she had remained silent.

Cialia's head whipped toward Raya as she nearly roared, "And you are the vilest of them all. Once Maelich woke from his stupor, and I was once again aware of his thoughts, I became aware of everything. The other gods were pawns as you whispered your intentions into their ears and hid away while they exacted your will on the world I swore to protect."

"You know all I have done," Raya smiled back at Cialia's rage, "but you have no comprehension of my intent. Still, you must do what you must do."

"And now you have tricks for me," Cialia grunted in disgust, "I will not be disarmed by a pleasing smile and sweet voice like my brother. I see you for what you are, and I have judged you, Raya, god with no titles or fame who hides in the shadows. I sentence you to oblivion."

The smile never left Raya's face as Cialia's eyes glowed red as if the flame might seep right out of her. Maelich could feel the rage sparking off his sister's intent as it slithered toward Raya. The sensation was disarming. She had learned things about their shared gift he had never known possible. He expected flames to swirl around her arms or body in perfect circles she might launch at Raya to burn her to ash. What Cialia was doing at that moment was nothing like that at all. Her flame was contained within her will. She planned to inject her desire into each of Raya's cells and blast her to oblivion from within.

"Cialia, no," he shouted as he reached toward Raya with his own will and surrounded her in flame.

"Get out of my way, Maelich," Cialia sighed with far less concern in her tone than Maelich had hoped, "By now, you must realize, as I have, my mastery over the flame far surpasses your own. You are no match for me. Please, let me do what I must do, and then we can talk about what comes next for this world."

Spittle blasted force from Maelich's mouth as he fought against the force of Cialia's will. The sheer strength of her intention was incredible. He fell to his knees and gripped the ground in his hands as he pushed back against her with all his might.

"Will you do nothing to defend yourself as my brother boils his own blood in an attempt to save you from your fate?" The nonchalance of her tone was terrifying. Maelich knew he would fail at forming anything more than a labored grunt much less an entire sentence as he battled with her, and it seemed Cialia expended no energy at all. What could he possibly do to stop her?

"I cannot defeat you, Cialia of Druindahl, defender of all creatures of Ouloos. You are a titan. There is no force in this world greater than your will," Raya's voice remained as sweet as a flawless note vibrating off a perfectly tuned lyre, "Nor would I try if I could. You know my actions and the thoughts which guided them. Armed with that knowledge, you have sentenced me. It is not my role to interfere in the actions of men or any other creatures of Ouloos."

"But you have interfered," Cialia shouted back.

"That I cannot deny," Raya replied with just the slightest hint of somberness to darken the glory of her tone, "The things I have done have been done. I would not change them, and I cannot explain to you why they needed to be done." The god paused then and looked thoughtfully at the canopy above before adding, "I envy Dragons. I know envy is something to be avoided, but they are perfect. If I could be a Dragon I would. I cannot be that. I am not a god like you think I am, but I am a thing incapable of ever achieving that state of perfection. Still, I can do my best to be like a Dragon. That is what I choose. You must choose what is right for you."

"I choose to carry out the sentence I have spoken against you," Cialia sneered.

Maelich had slowly been gaining control of his breathing while Cialia and Raya danced around their fruitless debate. A memory occurred to him. It was one he would have preferred to ignore, but the result was useful as he wilted under his sister's unrelenting might. His mind went back to Ymitoth's death. The tear he lost to that memory seemed small compared to protecting a soul from burning in Dragon's flame, but it wasn't. The memory was as important as any of the ghost's haunting his mind. He recalled the physical effort it had taken to lift the empty shell that had once been the mightiest man he had ever known. Once he realized physical effort wasn't what he needed to move that body, the task became quite easy. Just as easy as it was to push back against Cialia when she pressed harder against his defense.

Cialia turned her eyes toward him and said, "Regardless of quaint memories about Ymitoth, your will is no match for mine. I have not abandoned this world, Maelich, and I will protect it from gods or any other beings who would do harm to its inhabitants."

Maelich had regained his feet and his composure by the time he replied, "I wish not to fight you, Cialia. I would prefer to embrace you. We have both lost so much. Please, abandon this mission. Your work is done."

"I will not," she scowled.

"And I cannot let you continue down this path," Maelich frowned as he pushed back harder against her will.

CHAPTER 8
MEMORIES

Things moved as they must, slowly. That was the problem for Ijilv as he stood atop his grand tower at the edge of time and reason gazing out at a macabre horror of chaos. Everything moved so slowly. Geillan was lost in his own world of self-discovery, scrolling through new emotions, feelings, and memories borrowed from his mother. That had been a risk for sure, allowing the boy to meet her. She had always been such a pure and righteous thing. Had the boy taken a moment to think, everything might have failed. Even after that success, the wire he walked was a thin one. Thankfully, the boy was so absorbed in his own thoughts, he had no time to attempt invading Ijilv's.

Gazing out at the grotesque skyscape and watching just how random and chaotic it was, Ijilv felt suddenly lonely. If only he didn't know the things he knew. If only he could forget his life before emerging from the Lake. Maybe then he could forget his ambitions and be one with his brothers. They were all catty and self-serving, but they could be his compatriots. He could engage them in their games, playing against each other in battles of wit and will. That would be something. Alas, it could never be. As long as he remained burdened with these memories of a time before time and his desire to author a different fate for this new world he occupied, he could never relent. He could never forget his plans or desires to succeed for Ouloos where he had failed Eengurra. Still, as slowly as things were moving, he certainly had time to entertain some folly with his supposed brothers.

Ijilv closed his eyes to the chaos erupting before him, that horrid play of colors that shouldn't exist in shapes scarcely possible, and opened them to the dingy, gray cell he had imagined for his beloved brothers. "Ah," he proclaimed loudly, "aren't the lot of you a sight for sore eyes."

"Save it," Kallum scoffed in a voice as gravely as it was before Geillan had plucked him and his fellow cellmates from their prison to cure his boredom.

"Indeed," Kaldumahn agreed, "The turned-up corners of your mouth masquerading as a smile cannot hope to hide the heavy dread weighing down your spirit."

Ijilv offered the most genuine smile he could muster as he replied, "On the contrary, dear brother, my spirit soars."

"Best not say such things in front of Kaldumahn, he would argue we have no souls. Considering what close kin souls are to spirits, he might argue with you for days on the topic. I promise you, it will be a fruitless debate," Moshat chuckled.

"And he would be correct," Ijilv smiled, "We are different than men or the other creatures occupying this place over which we rule. We have no souls."

"I told you as much," Kaldumahn shot Moshat a sly grin before casting his disheveled gaze toward Ijilv, "He argued that point with me for hours before finally relenting."

Ijilv was about to spout off another clever barb when something foreign grabbed his awareness and held on tight. It seemed a ghostly apparition at first, formless and white with blurry edges refusing to portray any kind of shape that might make sense in the physical world. The vision wasn't the thing that choked off the words that would have poured from his mouth. No, the smell did that. It was not a foreign smell. It was something he had known at one point in his life. It was a garden, a flower garden, but it was no garden on Ouloos. It smelled like orchids, but orchids had never occurred in this world.

"What is it, brother?" Brerto asked with genuine concern in his voice. Had Ijilv not been so absorbed in the confusing smell, he might have thought about how odd it was for any of his brothers to display any kind of concern for any of their brothers.

As Brerto's words reached his ears, a name occurred to him, Raya. Then it was like a flood. Memories crashed into his mind like an avalanche toppling a town at the base of a great mountain. It utterly crushed every idea or feeling scampering about his mind. She had loved orchids, tending to them in her garden and casting them about her office. Even her perfume carried their scent. That was mixed with vanilla and honey. The combination of scents danced dangerously close to being too sweet, but something about it drove him crazy. She knew it too, lingering too close while they worked over this equation or that.

Then her face slowly materialized on the canvas of his memory, like a painting that seems nothing more than a glob of colors until that one line or shade adds a point of clarity to make it look like more than just a smear of blended hues. How could he have forgotten? He was certain it was love, but she had probably been correct when she declined that unfortunate advance. That was the thing that ruined their partnership, and their friendship. The close bond they shared never fully returned. As much as it hurt to be rejected by the one person he had ever truly admired in that time before time, it wasn't love he felt for her. He admired her quick wit and unrelenting spirit. Even after all possible solutions to a problem had been attempted and failed, she would find that one idea no one else would think of in a million years. And he lusted for her form. She had told him that. "It isn't love raging in your pants when I stand close to you, dear. That is lust. I feel it too, but I promise it would ruin us," she said in that sing-song voice she would use when scolding him on anything. Even after she had told him that, he couldn't help himself. It had only been a kiss, barely a whisper of his lips on hers, but that was the end. She never stood as close or leaned in as tight again.

He suddenly knew the source of all the prophecies he had whispered into his brothers' ears. They were her words. She had whispered them to him so he could unwittingly whisper them to his unwitting pawns. Who was the pawn? He barely noticed the tears trickling down his cheeks to moisten the shock plastered across his face when Brerto interrupted his hopeless reminiscing.

"Incredible," the once great white tiger gasped, "How did she do it? How did she dupe you into senselessly doing her bidding while making us all forget she ever existed?"

"What is a skirt?" Kallum chuckled.

"What?" Ijilv hissed as he shot a fierce look in Kallum's direction while quickly wiping away his tears.

"You liked the way her skirt fit her rump," Moshat chuckled the same as Kallum until the two caught eyes and burst into laughter.

"That would be an unhealthy way to look at your sister," Kaldumahn smiled something devilish.

Brerto shook his head as he finished his brother's thought, "But she wasn't our sister any more than you are our brother. What is this time before time?"

"Get out of my thoughts," Ijilv stammered.

"What did she do to you?" Moshat shook his head.

"Pathetic," Kallum added with disgust.

"You are not one of us," Kaldumahn squinted, "You are not a god."

"No, he is more," Brerto began nodding slowly as he stroked his chin, "He lived a life with Raya, who held such sway over his emotions, in a world that died before ours was born. He is just a man, but he knows more about this place than any of us."

"Ha!" Kallum shouted, "That is how you did it. You are not stronger than the rest of us. You cheated. You knew of rules none of us even knew existed."

"Forget about that," Brerto's tone lowered to something ominous, "Tell us about the time before time."

Something else suddenly occurred to Ijilv. He was so rapt in memories drenched in sorrow that he failed to notice why he remembered them in the first place. Maelich was awake, and Cialia had found him. The two Dragons battled over his forgotten love.

"Tell us," Moshat piped up.

"Never mind that," Ijilv hissed, "None of it matters now. Everything that has been done has been done. The play has been set in motion, but she stole this moment from me."

"Finally, something you cannot control," Kaldumahn laughed.

"No," Ijilv nearly shouted, "You have no idea. If those two Dragons destroy each other, everything I've planned will fail. I have groomed Geillan to be pure evil. Those two Dragons must unite to destroy that evil. Whatever game Raya is playing, she has ruined any chance for that. This world will never be born."

"I disagree," Kallum shook his head, "You say you have groomed the boy to be pure evil. Is he?"

"He killed his own mother," Moshat shrugged.

Recognition sparkled in Brerto's eyes as he continued the thought, "But, he did that based on a lie you told him, Ijilv. Is it evil if he believed he was doing good? Kallum is wise in this. The two Dragons will occupy each other, battling over your lost love, while Geillan has a chance to prove himself as something truly wicked." He paused and looked earnestly into Ijilv's eyes before adding, "Do you have the will to see this through?"

"I don't know anything anymore," Ijilv slumped to the floor beside them, "Why would she betray me? We had a plan before we even came to this place, and she left. She gave me no chance."

"As you said, what has been done has been done. Do you have the will to see this through?" Kallum's tone grew solemn and serious.

Ijilv chuckled through tears that began flowing freely down his cheeks, "None of you would allow it now. You know everything. I have no more secrets from you. I can hold you here with me, clinging to your essence and power, but I have no control over you anymore. Any one of you could simply tell Geillan what I have done, and he would destroy me. I expect that end as soon as he calls us back to him to relieve his boredom."

"Stop sniveling, worm," Moshat grunted, "There are no more secrets between us. There never should have been. Now that we all know the game and the goal, we can move on from this place. You can be one of us, and we can see this world born. We are gods. Let us be that."

"Yes!" Brerto shouted, "The thoughts in my head seem crazy, but yes, let us rise up and be gods! All any of us ever wanted was to be worshipped, but this…this is something so…godly. Have I lost my mind?"

Kaldumahn laughed until his voice ran out and then said, "No, you have not, brother. I have never felt anything like this before. It is like a yearning. I want to make this be. I want this world to live."

"Even if we die?" Ijilv's tone grew solemn.

"We are already dead," Moshat laughed, "Let us be gods again, one god, all of us, together."

"I have always loved all of you," Ijilv freely wept, "I know my actions fail to convey those emotions, but you must know I always saw you as my kin. I feared I could not trust you with these secrets. I felt you would not understand. Ruling was always so important to all of you."

"Like you said, what has been has been done, and now we must do something else," Brerto's smile was as genuine as Ijilv had ever seen.

The gray, sweaty brick of the cell slowly faded away as perfect light filled the small dungeon. For a moment both brief and infinite, all shadow fled until no shapes could be discerned among the brightness. As it slowly faded, the four gods who had remained imprisoned for who knows how long within their brother's own mind found themselves in meticulously crafted, gaudy chairs seated around a circular table of equal stature. Ijilv gazed out at them all glowing in their unblemished perfection.

"Thank you, brothers," he smiled, "Let us begin."

CHAPTER 9
WHAT HAPPENS ON THE TRAIL…

Like a spike driving into both of his temples, that's what it felt like when his eyes opened to allow what must have been the brightest sunshine to ever touch an eyeball still dim from too many hours of sleep. Daritus groaned as he rolled over and vomited a sloppy pile of bile on the ground next to him. The sour smell of the mess made him want to vomit again. Rolling away from the stench didn't do any good. It lingered. It took him a moment to realize he'd never escape the rancid odor until he'd had a bath and a change of clothes. His beard and shirt were caked in it. How many times had he spilled the meager contents of his guts into the world? It would be tough to know for certain. His memories from the prior evening were sparse and blurry.

His throat burned like a vast, barren desert baking in the blazing sun. He needed water. After fumbling around his general vicinity for a few moments while opening his eyes to only slits allowing as little light in to add to his throbbing headache as possible, he finally came across a water skin. A quick shake of the thing assured him there was at least a small splash remaining within. His body heaved as soon as he uncorked the thing, fairies' tears. Normally, he found the almost sweet scent of the stuff quite appealing. After the last evening's shenanigans, he wasn't certain he'd ever find the aroma pleasing again.

"Water," he groaned. The simple act of speaking burned his throat and made his head throb even worse than it had been.

"It lives," Kantiim's voice was thankfully not much louder than a whisper, "I was unsure if you'd wake to see the light of a new day, or if you'd succeeded in ending yourself with copious amounts of fairies' tears."

"I wish I had succeeded," Daritus groaned.

"Well, I am glad you failed," Kantiim continued his loud whispering as he uncorked a water skin and handed it down to Daritus, "Here, start with this. Some water will ease the burning in your throat. Once you're able to keep some of that down, we'll fix up that throbbing in your head with some nice Dragon tea I'm brewing over the fire."

Daritus took a nice, long pull off the skin. The water felt cool on his throat. That was nice. The gurgling in his gut was less so. He curled up in a fetal position and covered his mouth until the urge to spew it all back up had passed. Then he took a slower, smaller pull that agreed a bit more with his belly.

The throbbing in his head hadn't eased at all, but it became a conquerable adversary. "I am embarrassed," he finally said after gingerly sipping a few more drinks of water.

"I imagine you would be," Kantiim grinned, "You acted a fool and mistreated a few folks who admire you and hold you dear. Personally, I'm finished with the whole affair. We have been through much worse than a drunken brawl and some harsh comments in our history. Your embarrassment is all the apology I need. Boringas, on the other hand, is a different story."

"How is he?" Daritus asked quietly. He couldn't recall much of what he'd said to poor Boringas in his drunken stupor, but what he did remember made him cringe.

Kantiim shook his head before replying, "I didn't sleep well last night. Every time I woke, I heard that poor man crying. You're like a father to him. You broke his heart last evening."

"I imagine I did," Daritus sighed long and deep before attempting another long pull off the water skin Kantiim had gifted him. His gut threatened, but he managed to keep it down. Once the risk of spewing that hydrating life saver all over his lap had passed, he continued, "I'll talk to him."

"I pray that conversation includes a very humble apology," the old titan nodded his head slightly, "You sentenced him to death and might nearly have succeeded if Spang and I hadn't intervened. And that dutiful soldier feels like he owes you an apology, like he somehow wronged you by being a faithful servant to you and your lovely wife, Coeptus bless her soul. I would like you to admit to me now that you understand Boringas is blameless for Leisha's death and your fury with him is misplaced. If you cannot do that, I will bar you from speaking with him."

Kantiim's words stung. If only he could remember more. He must have said and done some horrific things for his old friend to see fit to disrespect him like that. He shifted slightly to get his legs under him so he could stand. It was no easy effort with the forest around him dipping and swaying as it was, but before long he stood eye to eye with his old chum. His head could have exploded with all the pounding going on behind his eyes, but he managed to keep it together as he finally said, "I promise you I will make it right with that man."

"Then I will gladly stand aside and let you get to it," Kantiim offered a shallow smile as he stepped left and waved his arm toward a slumped figure trembling with sobs.

It would have been quite a bit easier to come up with the proper words to give to the weeping wretch who slumped under a tree before him if he could remember the words he used to drag that man to such a state of misery, but he could not. According to Kantiim's report, he had sentenced the dutiful soldier to die. Boringas was a righteous, pure, and loyal man. Being sentenced to death by your king must have crushed his spirit completely. He decided to start there.

"You did not deserve the callousness I showed you last evening," Daritus' voice sounded foreign to his own ears. It was hoarse, gravelly, and far too quiet, but it stirred a response from the sad lump sobbing before him.

That sad lump looked up at him with bloodshot eyes raining tears onto puffy cheeks and peering through hair drenched in those same tears. "I am sorry," Boringas' voice sounded as rough as his own.

His heart sank even further into depths of sadness he could scarcely comprehend. The man owed him no apologies, yet those words were the first to come to his mind. Though he couldn't recall the precise language he used to break the man staring up at him through tears which should have had no reason to be shed, the result was evidence of its callousness. "For what do you have to be sorry?" he finally asked.

"I deserved the sentence you spoke against me. You gave me a mission to protect my queen, and I failed. My queen is dead. Ouloos must go on without the brilliance of her mind, the softness of her heart, and the gentleness of her soul. That is my fault," he sobbed as he opened his shirt to expose his neck, "I beg you, execute the sentence you spoke against me so I might pay for my crimes."

Warmth behind Daritus' eyes heralded the coming tears as he crumbled to the ground next to the most loyal man he had ever known and draped his arm across that poor man's shoulders. "No," he wept the phlegmy proclamation through torrents of salty regret, "I was wrong, and I am sorry. You failed at nothing. I have stood before gods. The experience taught me many things. In this moment, the most important is the knowledge that there is nothing you could have done."

"No," Boringas nearly shouted as he struggled away from Daritus' grasp and opened his shirt to invite the killing blow once again, "My queen is dead, and I am not. My duty was to protect her or die in the effort. I should not be alive. Execute my sentence."

"I will not," Daritus' voice found a hint of authority despite its shabby complexion, "You deserve no sentence. I will not forgive you, as you are blameless in Leisha's death. Gods and Dragons, they represent forces beyond comprehension. No man could have done anything to stop them."

Boringas crumbled to the ground amid a fresh round of sobs. He curled up and wept, "If only I had the courage to take my own life. Then I might have the fate I deserve."

Daritus stroked the man's hair. The fact it was drenched in tears dragged his spirit even lower into the pit of misery it had been living within as he sighed, "I am no longer the king of anything, but you still see me as such. If that is true, then I have a command for you."

Boringas raised his eyes to Daritus' gaze as he replied, "Your will, my king."

"You will not take your own life. The gods drove my daughter to become this thing she has become, and she took away my wife. You are all I have left in this world," Daritus pulled Boringas closer until the man's shoulder leaned across his lap, and the two men wept together.

The idea had only just occurred to him as the words left his lips. Boringas was truly the only thing he had left in the world. He wasn't his father, but he had acted as such when the brawny man weeping in his embrace had been a boy. He'd been like a shadow back then, always following him around and doing his best to mimic his behavior. Perhaps the mission of helping this man forgive himself would be enough to allow him to follow his own command.

The sound of Kantiim clearing his throat was like a temple bell shattering the calm serenity of a quiet morning. Of course, there was work to be done. Leading a massive caravan down the trail offered little time for quiet reflection or even the mending of fresh wounds scarring souls.

"Give us a moment, please," Daritus didn't look up.

"Would that I could, old friend, but we've finished breaking camp, the wagons are packed, and we're wasting light," the lack of emotion in Kantiim's voice was frustrating but expected.

Kantiim paused as if he expected some form of response, but Daritus didn't have one for him just then. He didn't care about getting back to the trail or even when the large group he supposedly led would make it to their destination. All he really wanted to do in that moment was share a few sad tears with the only person in the world who could fully appreciate his melancholy. Kantiim could never understand. Duty stood above all else in that man's eyes. Spang maybe, but when he pledged his life to the service of the Dragon's Flame, he made a vow to never take a wife. Though he was more comfortable with things like emotions, he could never understand the loss of a soulmate. Boringas could understand. He loved Leisha and felt her loss just as strongly.

After a few quiet moments marked only by low sobbing, Kantiim continued, "There is one other thing. You have a guest, not really a mercenary or sword for hire. I have heard of him. The stories told are those of a traveler who rides under no banner but helps those in need. May I present Sanjo, the lone warrior of the wood, his…apprentice I suppose, Hasujo, and his pupil, Nothany."

Daritus paused his tears long enough to look up at his new guest. The name was familiar, but none of the three men standing with Kantiim fit the description he'd heard told in stories about the exploits of the lone warrior of the wood.

The tidy looking man immediately to Kantiim's right bowed to one knee and solved the riddle of which of the decidedly non-savage men standing before him was the legendary titan. His light brown hair and beard were neatly trimmed, and his skin appeared soft and youthful. If not for the light tan of his cheeks, it would seem they had never seen the sun. His clothes were just as tidy; clean leather trousers tucked into shiny black boots. His leather vest was just as clean as were the blowsy, white sleeves of his shirt. At least he wore a sword about his waist. Nothing else about the man suggested a fighter of any kind. Neither did the man's voice fit the description of a trail-hardened warrior when he said, "I am Sanjo, no longer a lone warrior of the wood. That fact should be obvious considering two men accompany me on the trail." He motioned his head toward the tall, soft man immediately to Kantiim's right and added, "This is Hasujo. He is not my apprentice. He might have been as much, but he boasts a kind soul and a squeamishness for things that slop out of bodies when you slice into them. He is my bard, well…he is learning to be my bard. We have been working on his voice and lyrical prowess." Then he tapped the young man kneeling next to him on the shoulder and added, "And this is Nothany. He is my pupil, a student of the blade. He will be a great warrior one day very soon. I give him two more summers at best before he is ready to range out on his own and earn the stories which will be told about him."

Daritus absently scratched his head as he attempted to come up with a response. It was a lot, a tidy warrior, a bard who cannot sing, and a lad learning to be a soldier. They all looked too clean. What on Ouloos would cause them to range into the wild and seek him out? Hasujo had scraggly, blonde hair peeking out from beneath a finely crafted, knit hat, probably lourng's wool. His beard was equally scraggly and blonde, but he still seemed somehow tidy despite the mess. His mandolin was equally clean and free from blemish. It would be a miracle if even one note had ever been played upon it. It had a rich, cherry finish that shined even in the dim forest light.

Nothany was a different story. The lad was fit despite a youthful roundness clinging to his cheeks. His brown hair was clipped short, an odd choice for a warrior, but it suited him. There was a seriousness about his eyes that seemed far wiser than a young man who'd seen so few summers, and his chin was only just learning how to house a beard.

After looking over his company for far longer than was probably necessary, Daritus finally asked, "Why are you here?"

"To find you. I have never ridden for any house or under any banner, because there was no man I found worthy of following. Then I heard about this killer of giants, a man who defended a city which was not his own against monsters from across the Great Sea. That is a man I want to follow. That is a man who can teach me something," Sanjo stood briefly to unsheathe his sword before kneeling back down, holding it aloft, and speaking a pledge, "I pledge my life and sword to you, Daritus of Druindahl, titan and king. I will follow where you lead, obey your commands, and battle beside you against all enemies until my soul returns to the Lake."

Daritus laughed as a fresh batch of tears rained down his red cheeks, "I am no leader, and I am no king. My city has burned to the ground, and I failed to protect the throne of my adopted city when a new king with a claim came calling. Why would anyone follow me anywhere?"

Boringas finally piped up after wiping tears from his cheeks, "I mean no disrespect, highness, but you are wrong in this. Anything good about me I learned from you. You taught me honor. You taught me duty. You taught me how to be faithful. You taught to me to be a man. You are a great leader. This camp is full of men and dwarves, even trogmortem and giants who believe the same. Even this legendary warrior has traveled a vast distance just to follow you. I have heard of this man, even tried to recruit him after you left for Havenstahl. The only person who does not believe in you is you."

Sanjo smiled, "I recall that time, Boringas of Druindahl. Please know I did not decline that offer because of you. You are an honorable man and a sturdy soldier. Unfortunately, the man sitting in the throne at that time was no one I could follow. Under different circumstances, I may have gladly donned the red of your great city and rode under the banner of the Dragon."

The compliment brought the slightest hint of a smile to Boringas' face. "Thank you for saying as much," he replied.

Then Sanjo looked at Daritus and said, "Your faithful general is quite correct in his assessment. You are more than you think of yourself at this moment. Things that cannot be replaced have been taken from you. You need time to process all the loss. But that does not change the man you are. My pledge remains just as I have spoken it."

It sounded like a scrod yelping when Hasujo plucked the first string. Apparently, he hadn't noticed how horrible was the sound as he just went ahead and plucked another and then another. It seemed he was working toward some form of a melody, but it wasn't that at all. The instrument obviously needed a good tuning as the horrid notes the bard relentlessly strummed out swirled together into a torturous stew of terror. And then the bard sang...

From the east one day there came a great man
Who stood against monsters from a faraway land
He cut down monsters and he cut down men

Then he killed a giant but he didn't stop then

"For the love of Dragons, stop that horrible sound," Nothany was the first to speak up.

"Nothany," Sanjo gently scolded, "speak gently. Hasujo is learning his art just as you are. While you study the art of the blade, he studies the art of making sweet melodies. Both take practice."

As horrible as the song was—both the lyrics and the melody—it was the tiny spark Daritus needed to feel something other than sorrow or rage. It wasn't quite a laugh which escaped his lips, but it was at least a good chuckle. He smiled fondly at the bard who couldn't write or sing and said, "Keep practicing your art, Hasujo, esteemed bard of Sanjo, lone warrior of the wood, and if you still see fit to honor me with it once it has been perfected, share it with me then."

Hasujo's cheeks reddened as Nothany shot a devilish smirk in his direction, but he allowed no disrespect to mar his tone as he replied, "Your will, my king."

"Thank you," Daritus offered Hasujo a genuine smile before turning his gaze toward Sanjo and continuing in a more serious tone, "You and your men honor me with your words and your songs, and the effort you put forth to find me in this disheveled and low state. I cannot promise you I will ever be the man whatever stories you have heard spoke of, but I will try. I will honestly try. My oldest chums and, hopefully, new friends who might become the same have offered me wise counsel. I would be the clumsiest of fools to ignore it."

The three men bowing before him barely had time to nod their agreement before Kantiim's voice tore through the quiet of the forest, "Mount up. We can finally get back to the trail."

CHAPTER 10
ACROSS THE COSMOS

Maelich was stronger than Cialia expected. They were together when they defeated Kallum over the Lost Forest. At the time, she had only the loosest understanding of Dragon's Fire or the power and control it took to wield it. After stumbling through the door to knowledge, she had learned much. Since then, her expertise had only expanded. Conquering Brerto's fantasy had been a test. Once she realized she was the only thing preventing her from growing beyond what she was then, the god presented no obstacle. Then Moshat and Kaldumahn battled with her more directly but still had their tricks. Once she saw past them, everything was in reach, even a deep grasp of her brother's weak comprehension of his power. He was no Dragon, not then nor in that moment as he stood in her way protecting the vile architect of all the horrors wrought by gods. He had barely scratched the surface of his potential, nothing more than a simple man playing with powers well outside his knowledge or control. Even still, he would have to be dealt with.

She pulled her focus away from Raya and directed all her intent against her brother, invading his mind and battering his senses. It wasn't malice, hate, or vengeance driving her to press harder and harder against him. After everything, she still loved him. Scanning his thoughts and even raw emotions, it was clear to her he believed in what he was doing. She almost felt sorry for him in all his weakness, duped by a conniving and manipulating god to do her bidding.

"Stand aside," she grunted a frustrated growl as she pressed deeper into his will. He should have broken by then, but he refused to yield. She could feel his pain and sense his doubt. Why wouldn't he just submit?

"This is not the way," he replied in a voice far less strained than it should have been. His tone should have been saturated in grueling effort, but he tossed the words out almost casually as his eyes begged her to relent.

"I do not want to hurt you brother, but I intend to carry out the sentence I spoke against this wicked thing you protect. Let me do what I need to do," she growled.

Her muscles tensed as she battered his will with her own. It suddenly occurred to her she was gritting her teeth nearly hard enough to break them under the weight of her jaw. She had to gain control. This battle required no physical exertion. All the strength she needed to defeat the fool standing before her and clinging to some silly ideal was in her mind. She took a deep breath in through her nose and released it slowly through her mouth. Her heart rate slowed.

Then she sensed it. It was almost a smell, musty and stale like the air in a hut that had been closed up for one hundred summers. He was afraid, but that dingy odor wasn't fear alone. Melancholy, maybe even hopelessness, mingled with the terror stomping about his mind. She felt the break, a small crack in his defenses, and she slithered through, stabbing into his awareness with dark intent.

His mind cried out in a horrid song saturated with an emptiness full of so much darkness it seemed a contradiction. How could something so empty be brimming with so much? But it was. The groaning note was a vast wasteland of nothingness full of hurt, dejection, and sorrow deeper than the Great Sea. She hesitated for only a moment. Her will would crush him into nothing and blast the meaningless bits which remained into oblivion. She didn't want to do that to him. It was the abominable thing behind him who deserved her wrath, but he refused to stand aside.

It happened so fast. In that tiny speck of a moment, she was distracted by her own thoughts. She questioned her own intent. Light like a desert sun filled her sight, but it was more than just her eyes blinded by the flash. It seemed any semblance of a shadow was chased away from her awareness.

Then she felt it. It was like he grabbed hold of her mind. There was no malice or ill intent in the squeeze, but she felt pressure like something physically gripped her brain. Then she was racing. A million colors flashed by all muddied up by one another and bleeding together into an unnatural blur of shimmering light. It ceased as abruptly as it had begun. The light, the sensation of racing into nothingness, and the colors were all gone. She was still for a moment surrounded by total darkness.

Cialia's tone vibrated with authority as she shouted, "Where am I?"

"A place where you can do no harm," Maelich's voice surrounded her in the darkness.

Then there was light. The sun blazed above in a vast blue sky unhindered by even the slightest hint of any cloud. A seemingly unending desert of dry, cracked earth expanded all around her in every direction. The landscape seemed almost orange in the relentless, desert sun, and there were no mountains nor any form of vegetation to interrupt the flatness of it all. He didn't say as much, but she knew the lands surrounding her were the same lands across which her brother had led a group of people he concocted from his own imagination on a mission to take back an imaginary place based on an imaginary slight while he hid from his responsibilities.

Maelich stood before her, his eyes still pleading as they peered past wilted locks sweaty with effort. "Please, take a moment to think about what it is you want to do. Do you even know your intention anymore or are you just acting out a thing you once believed you must do?" His tone carried the same begging quality as his eyes.

"This is not emotion driving me, Maelich," frustration seeped into her tone, "The gods have done unspeakable things to the creatures we swore to protect. Do you remember the vow you made? You did not speak it out loud to Coeptus, but you made the same promise to them that I did. Why do you protect gods when they are the very beings you vowed to protect all creatures against?"

"We did make a vow," he replied, "but you know it was not to Coeptus we made that vow. You are moving so quickly; you haven't taken a moment to think about critical things of which you are now aware. Intent. Have you even considered intent?"

It wasn't condescension. She knew that, but something about the words he chose troubled her to her core. He spoke just like the gods, admonishing her for doing what she knew was right. "I am not the simple girl you traded blades with beneath the trees of Druindahl, brother. I have traveled among the thoughts of gods, traversed time and space with merely a thought, and become one with our sisters. I require from you no guidance nor counsel. No decision I have made has been rash, nor has any action I have taken been impulsive. Everything I have done is a thing to which I gave more thought than it deserved. You are the one letting emotion lord over logical thinking."

"Yours is the most complex mind mine has ever touched," Maelich agreed, "but that doesn't mean you should never question answers on which you've already decided."

"I haven't the time for this," she sighed as she shook her head, "I have answered the questions and questioned the answers over and over again. I have struggled with and overcame the kind of doubt that can crush a soul into the dirt, and I am certain of my path. You stand in my way on that path. Remove yourself. I am done with this game."

She let the flame come. It wouldn't kill him. He was just as much of a Dragon as her. At least, she hoped it wouldn't. A Dragon could walk through flame, and no Dragon could kill another Dragon.

He looked too sure of himself as the flame swirled around her. She thought about lashing out and piercing his will with her intent, but that hadn't worked when he stood before and protected that evil creature, Raya. The flames coalesced into a swirling, raging ball above her head. It distracted him just enough, and she launched a streak of flame from her fists at his chest. The blast sent him sailing. At the very same moment, she opened up the cracked dirt to swallow him up and sealed it once it had.

"Ijilv," she said quietly as she gazed upon the ground she had buried him under, "that was the name of the pretender to whom we made our vow. It wasn't Coeptus, but at the time we believed it to be. I have considered intent. Our intent was to make a vow to Coeptus. It is a promise I intend to keep. The gods' intent was to subjugate and terrorize the creatures we protect to gain power from their worship. Protect your sweet Raya. I will return for her once I've destroyed the vile thing hiding at the edge of chaos."

She knew the makeshift prison wouldn't hold him for long, so she wasn't surprised when she sensed him escape it and give chase. She could feel his desire. It was like longing, but his want was so misplaced. Why couldn't he see how cruel and heartless the things he protected were?

Time evaporated. As imaginary as it was, she couldn't help but use the concept to track her journey as any simple creature who hadn't experienced the mysteries of Coeptus might. She had been one of those for long enough that the habits she formed remained. That's what was so jarring about it. The colors did what they did in whatever shapes they desired; smells smelled how they smelled, some pleasant some foul; the sounds vibrated the membranes in her ears in just the perfect rhythm and cadence to achieve both joy and horror in the sounds those vibrations represented; but the duration of it all was so wrong. Nothing in the natural world should happen so fast or take so long, yet that is exactly how it felt. An eternity experienced in an instant. She could have vomited the first time she split time. In this particular moment, she just felt a bit queasy. Then it was done.

The tower at the edge of time stretched further up into the chaotic skyscape than any other structure ever made by men. Massive, cyclopean stones piled one atop the other with such precision it was as if they existed only to contradict the randomness swirling and exploding behind them. There was something so perfect in the contrast of the two conditions.

The thought held her for just a moment. There is that time again, that meaningless thing which somehow manages to wriggle into the definition of any event. Time is not real. The thought seemed so elementary, yet she had to state it clearly to herself in her own mind. If only she could unlearn things she knew before her awareness had opened to the endless possibilities of reality. If she could do that thing, perhaps the massive, black structure towering before her would be ash floating against the cracked kaleidoscope of colors swirling behind it in ghastly combinations that should never occur in the waking world, but she could not. The nagging concept of time just refused to evacuate her perception of the world around her.

When she finally loosed her flame—a blanket of fire raining down from the sky like some blazing waterfall—Maelich was there to divert it. There was nothing elegant or elaborate about the effort. He shot a fireball at it. It was a massive one that somehow flattened out into a giant floating circle of flames immediately above the tower. The swirling mass repelled her attack and sent it flying back toward the macabre skyscape bopping and twisting like some kind of horrid art come to life in a drunken and confused state.

It was instinct more than cognizant thought which propelled the fireball from her hand. Had she taken the time to think about it, she'd have let it grow for a moment expanding enough to encircle him. As it was, it was no bigger than a large rock. Despite its small size, it did the trick. Too focused on repelling her attack on the tower, all his attention was trained on its top so high above them. It hit him in the back.

She knew the blast wouldn't burn his flesh, but she expected his clothes to catch fire. That might give him pause or at least distract him long enough so she could finish her task. However, his clothes hadn't caught fire. His own flame swirled around him like an instinct protecting him from the attack. Her flame hadn't touched him at all, but the force of the blast sent him sailing into the chaos churning beyond the tower. That was her opening.

She concentrated on the points where massive stone touched massive stone. It seemed impossible something so precise could have been built by men, yet according to all the stories told of the legendary place, it had been built by a man. She squeezed into those impossibly tight spaces with her will. After a few moments, her mind touched every stone while her intent filled every crack between them. Her flame slithered along that intention like snakes gliding along slick branches. She would blast the tower apart crumbling each stone in an instant with one swift flex of her will.

She dragged a deep breath focusing all her awareness on only the tower. Nothing else in the universe mattered in that moment. She was completely separated from everything but each individual stone making up the impossibly tall tower. When she released the breath, she would release her flame with all the power of the cosmos.

The flame came suddenly, but it wasn't her own. It sprayed out like a geyser around her as the force of it sent her tumbling across ground that seemed incomplete in the way it crumbled while constantly rebuilding itself. One hundred feet of that eerie landscape must have raced beneath her before she finally came to rest. It felt like a charging horse had trampled her.

"It hurts, doesn't it?" Maelich's irritating voice echoed through the suddenly thick air, "The flame doesn't burn us, but it still hurts. Now you know how it feels. Please, stop this. I don't want to hurt you, but I don't think I can stop you without doing so."

He was right. It did hurt. Her joints cracked and popped as she slowly regained her feet and replied, "So, I don't want to hurt you, and you don't want to hurt me. That makes our story rather sad. You refuse to remove yourself from my path, and I refuse to be turned away from it."

"Can we take a moment?" he begged, "Could we just talk, no fight, no fire, just words?"

"To what end, dear brother?" she sighed the query in utter frustration, "There is nothing you can say that would change my mind, and I am unable to convince you that removing the evil of gods from this place is the only way Ouloos will ever find peace."

"I could show you all I've learned while trapped in an illusion I concocted for myself born out of grief," he begged.

There was no humor in her chuckle, as she replied, "Five summers I waited for you to teach me what you had learned. It obviously wasn't important enough to you then. In your absence, I surpassed you. There is nothing left for you to teach, and the time for words is finished."

Her plan materialized as the words left her lips. She could not defeat him with flame. His own flame would not allow it, or perhaps it was his mind, some kind of instinct. Whatever the reason, he would remain protected. However, flame was not her only weapon.

She focused her will on his mind, her intent lashing out like tentacles encircling his awareness and holding him fast. She felt him struggling against the bonds, but she was too strong. The she thought about the Lake and her sisters. They would see her or at least sense her. They saw everything. Helias would have sad thoughts that would feel like admonishments, but she didn't care. Maelich had to be removed from her path. She would plunge him into the Lake. There would be no pain, and he would finally find peace.

An eternity of colors, sounds, smells, and feelings battered her senses for a moment so brief it seemed impossible it had even occurred. Maelich vomited. She felt his guts churn and even tasted the bile in her own throat. When all the colors and everything else vanished, they were both there floating above the Lake. Dragons filled the air around them.

Of all her sisters' voices crying out to her as she held Maelich fast with her will, Helias' came through as clearly as if they sat in a quiet room speaking to one another, "Your soul will not survive your brother's death if you are the cause. Your intent is cloudy, sweet sister. Please think about what it is you truly want in this moment."

The Dragon's words gave her pause. She had no intention of killing her brother, but achieving her goal while he lived would be difficult if not impossible. There were too many voices. She needed silence, a moment to think. That could not happen with all her sisters spewing their counsel at her. She needed a quiet place with no voices or distractions to pull her attention away from her goal. Up seemed the only logical choice. Space was quiet. She had never been to space, of course, not even any of the gods nor any Dragons had ever ventured into that vast darkness. However, she had experienced that deafening silence while her awareness stretched through it. It was lonely and beautiful while simultaneously terrifying. She had never felt so small.

A moment later she stood upon a vast, barren desert of what appeared to be sandy, dead soil in a crater that must have been at least a mile deep. The idea of what kind of object could make such a dent in something nearly stole her attention. How big would this thing need to be, and how fast would it need to be moving? She had no time for idle contemplation. She finally had control of her brother, and the effort required every shred of her focus. But then there were the lights.

Her feet sank slightly into the regolith as the darkness of space stretched out above and around her. Were they stars or planets, the shimmering specks of every color she could imagine stretching out to infinity? How far was she from this one or that? She could know. She could visit each one and spoil the mystery, if only this were any other moment than the one that would happen immediately prior to finishing her task of saving the creatures of Ouloos from the terror of gods.

Then she saw it spinning before her. Ouloos had never looked so enchanting while standing upon it. Floating there among the stars, it looked like a precious gem, a perfect sphere of white swirls covering blues, greens, and browns. She had always thought it was flat. She'd stood at the edge of it more than once. How could that be?

Maelich suddenly groaned, tearing her away from any question she might like to explore while enveloped in the tranquility surrounding her. He knelt before her in the center of the massive crater that nearly succeeded in stealing her attention away. There was no time for such pursuits. She finally had her brother under control. It was time to finish this.

His eyes rolled around in their sockets as if he were trapped in some kind of waking fever dream, but she felt no effort from him. Where was the struggle? His will had felt so strong only a moment prior, but now he seemed to be sleeping, completely at peace despite his wild eyes. She planned to build him a prison within his own mind. It would be crude, of course. There simply wasn't time to plan anything that would hold him for very long. A few moments would be enough. The rest of her plan would only take a heartbeat to complete once he was out of the way, but she needed to find him first.

She stared at her brother's wild eyes as her awareness slipped into his mind to find herself standing in some kind of hallway. Dull and unremarkable, gray brick stretched out farther than she could see in either direction interrupted by simple, wooden doors in random intervals. It seemed as empty as the vastness surrounding her while standing upon that moon. It was too quiet. Where were his thoughts? There wasn't as much as a whisper of an idea echoing down the hall. That seemed a trick. His eyes had been so wild. His mind couldn't be idle in that moment.

She walked up to the closest door. It was as simple and unremarkable as the bricks that made up the ceiling, floor, and walls of the place. There was no handle, just five planks of equal length. The wood felt cool when she pushed it. The room beyond the door looked like the inside of a hut, empty and barren. She only had a moment to consider the small room before pain erupted in her chest and she was ripped away sailing into darkness.

She saw the rock briefly as it careened away from her. Spinning out of control, she barely noticed Maelich was gone. It had been a trick. The entire time she thought he had been completely under her control, he had withdrawn and stretched out into the cosmos to find a weapon with which to attack her. Air seemed suddenly important as she sped sans control into darkness, but there was no air to breathe in space. The attack had destroyed her focus and made her forget the limits of the physical didn't apply. She was gasping.

By the time she gained control of herself, a massive orange planet loomed before her. Gas spewed out from it in eruptions exploding from the surface like geysers into the atmosphere. Maelich was there. She could sense his presence. He knew what she was going to do as soon as it occurred to her.

"Would you destroy the entire universe to get me out of your way?" he cried out to her. His voice sounded pathetic, like tears spilled for lost love.

"I would do anything to protect the creatures of Ouloos," she snapped, "I wish you felt the same."

Cialia focused her intent into the planet's core, piercing its crust with her will. Completely focused on breaking the giant thing into a billion pieces to pummel her brother into submission, she scarcely noticed a slight wind kiss her cheek. In that same moment, she was suddenly aware of Maelich's intention. He had stretched out his will and ripped a comet from its orbit to hit her with.

The giant, glowing sphere raced toward her spewing dust and gas behind it in a tail that stretched for miles behind it. She lashed out with flames hot enough to burn a planet to dust. It only took a few moments of the extreme heat to flatten the icy thing out before it exploded into gas.

The planet cracked in that same moment, blasting apart just like the comet had. Cialia remained connected to each of the billions upon billions of bits of massive rock and swirling globs of magma as they erupted. She dragged them all toward Maelich, pummeling him with a wave of destructive force.

The fear she felt from him made her soul weep. He had left her no choice. She watched as he defended himself with flames that swirled around him spinning faster and faster burning molten debris as it sprayed at him, engulfing his fire. There was just too much of it. His flames were insufficient to completely evaporate the largest chunks. They pelted him like stones thrown from an angry crowd, bruising and burning his flesh while cracking the bones beneath.

She lost a tear when he cried out in panic, "Please, Cialia, stop!"

Then something changed. Her eyes filled with white light brighter than any light she had ever seen, even brighter than Ijilv's robes had been when the false god had paraded as Coeptus to deceive them. Somehow the sound accompanying the impossibly bright light was even brighter. It made little sense, but sound had never been so loud in so many competing tones in any plane of reality. Her mouth filled with the taste of sorrow and loss. It was thick and metallic filling her sinuses with smells like the deepest pits of the darkest caverns of any planet. Icy cold froze her flesh at the same time.

The sensations lasted only a moment, and then everything was quiet and dark. It seemed everything became nothing in one horrible instant.

CHAPTER 11
A DRAGON OR A GOD

It was like a dream as Ijilv shot a quick glance at his surroundings. He had no recollection of arriving at the spot where he stood, nor could he recall any form of journey which led him there. The last thing he remembered was sitting around a grand table with his brothers after returning them all to their former glory. They had been planning, debating, and brainstorming over the best way to control the beast he'd stolen from Perrin as a baby and kept caged in a prison within the boy's own mind.

The area surrounding him resembled that prison only slightly. It had far more in common with the illusion after Geillan had made his changes, but it wasn't quite that either. The lake with its frothy, purple waves was gone, replaced by a fast-flowing river of red winding an erratic path through trees that made no sense together. There were balmy palms next to pines huddled beneath tall oaks sharing space with all manner of fruit trees. Oranges and apples, pears and lemons, and plums and pomegranates all mingled together with other tree-like things in a makeshift forest that made no sense. The smell of the place was as unsettling as it was overbearing. Any of the various odors swirling together would probably be pleasing on their own or combined with a smaller variety of scents. All the various flowers of impossible shapes and sizes didn't help adding a million other aromas to the already chaotic malodor of this supposed forest brook.

There was one scent in the hodgepodge of smells that stood out among the rest so much it seemed intentional. It was pleasing on its own. That one pleasing scent standing out amid the chaos somehow made the whole thing worse. More than that, the aroma itself was beyond concerning. In fact, it was terrifying if it meant what it must. The worrisome scent was unmistakably orchids. He hadn't noticed them among the wide array of flowers both known and unknown lining both sides of the river, but their aroma overwhelmed everything else. If Geillan knew enough about the importance of orchids, that meant he had access to Ijilv's mind. The thought sent a shiver through the god as he paused there beside the rushing, red rapids of a soundless river. What else had the boy learned?

Ijilv shifted his focus to his own mind. Where were his brothers? "Kallum?" he asked but received no reply. Then, "Kaldumahn? Brerto?" still nothing. That was even more troubling than the orchids. His brothers, or at least their essence, lived within his own mind. The imaginary world he occupied just then existed within Geillan's mind. When first he encountered his brothers in Geillan's prison paradise, he assumed it was a connection the young man had made between their two minds, borrowing the gods' essence while they remained within him. However, if he had stolen them completely it would mean he could pluck anything he wanted from his mind at will. The logic seemed impossible. Yet, if it were anything else, where were they?

He stood there for a bit. The amount of time which passed was difficult to ascertain. A minute? A year? The duration was probably unimportant. The one thing which seemed paramount in that bit of time—regardless how brief or lengthy—was how Geillan would react to whatever new knowledge he had gleaned since last they spoke. Immediately after emerging through the Lake with his supposed brothers at the very beginning of Ouloos, Ijilv had begun concocting various protections to keep his darkest thoughts from any who might pry into his conscious or subconscious mind. Since remembering Raya, he'd been vastly less meticulous. The boy might know everything. That could be catastrophic.

Despite the fear coursing through him while mercilessly battering his senses, standing there would bring him no closer to any goal. He would have to face Geillan at some point. It was a small step, that first one, but he took it, then another. He took one more before the slightest confidence entered his stride. The red of the water coursing rapidly along the river was a pleasing shade. The air was cool and refreshing. The mingling of odors that had so disturbed his sinuses when he first arrived mellowed to the point that he could pick out the various scents and enjoy them one by one. The thing that really got his legs churning toward whatever end laid before him was the memory of his original goal. He wanted Ouloos to be born. That result did not require him to exist.

The river continued on its twisty course, doubling back upon itself at least three times before following a straighter path into some wild-looking rapids. The red water churning about the rocks was a deeper shade. It almost looked like blood as it swirled and splashed down low dips and rises until diving among a misty fog. Distance was like time for Ijilv, never terribly important, so it was difficult to estimate how far away the waterfall was. However far, the rushing, red water poured over the edge of a cliff that seemed to be the end of everything in this place. There was nothing but a pink mist beyond what appeared to be the very edge of this world.

Moments passed. Time again, that troubling and meaningless thing, why was it so impossible to forget? Whatever the cause, the journey from first identifying the waterfall to standing at the edge of where it should have been wasn't terribly long. It turned out there was no waterfall, and the pink mist that had obscured anything lying beyond it was gone. The raging river that had become blood red was a much cooler and more pleasing shade again, but it really wasn't quite a river anymore. It was more of a brook flowing gently into an equally calm pond.

Geillan was there at the pond's middle sitting in a simple rowboat fishing and laughing with three companions. A chill perched at the base of Ijilv's neck for a moment before slithering down his spine amid a violent shiver when he realized who those companions were. Their mangy, orange mops of hair and equally orange and mangy beards were undeniable. Somehow, Geillan had gained control of the dead-eyed men and even pulled them into this dream world inside his head.

He thought of running away. It was a silly idea, of course, but it was the first thing that popped into his head. It would do no good. There was no place on Ouloos he could hide. That much was clear. Geillan's power had grown beyond any limits he could have imagined when he first plucked the boy from his mother's arms via those same dead-eyed things that now laughed along at whatever quiet jokes Geillan shared with them.

Just as Geillan's name made it to the back of his throat, that man who he had trained and groomed to be absolute evil snapped his gaze from the dead-eyed men to stare directly at him with eyes at least as beautiful and horrible as any god's. "Father," Geillan said in a voice that sounded like a chorus of beasts howling out a threat, "are you missing your brothers?"

"It hadn't occurred to me they were missing," he stammered, realizing immediately Geillan would see through any lie he spoke.

"You must understand all your secrets have been exposed," Geillan confirmed as if he were inside his head. "You were with them, your brothers," he chuckled something that sounded like death with teeth before finishing, "You all pledged your love for one another. Not in so many words, of course, but the way you all gushed made it clear. The lot of you are so petty and simple. Years of competition, distrust, and even hate washed away by a few kind words and the slightest hint of acceptance. Pathetic. Have you any morals or strongly held beliefs in anything?"

It wasn't fear gripping Ijilv's spine and stealing the air from his lungs just then. Fear was something he could manage, even overcome. This was something different, the kind of unbridled terror which steals the strength from muscles rendering them useless and causes a mind to crumble quickly into insanity. Then it was done. As quickly as that thing worse than fear had grabbed hold of him, it was gone. Geillan would destroy him. That was a foregone conclusion. Why fear something which is known? The pain of Dragon's fire? When he and Raya left Eengurra while it was dying, they had both been ripped apart and put back together again. Traveling from one reality to another was something that should not have been possible. A fact of which he was certain. However, Raya, with her cunning mind and relentless spirit, found the glitch. No program is perfect, not even a mind. The solution came at a cost. Could Dragon's fire be any worse than that?

"I believe Ouloos deserves to live," he finally said with strength behind his words, "Seeing that come to pass has been my only goal since arriving here."

"I know," Geillan smiled, "There is nothing in that simple mind of yours which is unknown to me. I was to be your pawn, your destroyer. Those fool brothers of yours would have helped you toward that honorable goal, but you have failed. I am not the evil you desired me to be. The lot of you have tainted everything in this place. Ouloos is the evil you pretend to despise. You have made it something that should not exist in any reality."

"You are wrong about that," Ijilv shook his head. Though he wasn't convinced the words he spoke were true, he managed to keep any hint of trepidation out of his tone.

The dead-eyed men laughed wildly as they shook out their wild mops of hair and slapped the red water to splash it all about the boat. Geillan laughed with them for a moment. Then he stopped abruptly and said, "You do not believe that any more than I. I will be the destroyer you made me, but not so this world can be born. I will erase any memory of the wickedness you and the gods have created."

It felt like a hole in his chest, the warmth which began there before moving up to his eyes. A single tear filled with failure, regret, and melancholy formed on his right eyelid as he asked, "Why? It seems you have access to all knowledge. You must know how precious this opportunity is. It is nearly impossible for a world like ours to be born. Millions, even billions of worlds just like ours failed, and trillions more will long after we are gone, not even memories, completely erased from existence. You are correct about me. I have done things I once thought I never would, but this world is innocent of my crimes. Why destroy it for things I have done?"

There was no movement, no flash of light, no visible cue that anything had changed, yet Geillan suddenly stood before him, his horrible and glorious eyes smoldering red like fire. The boat he had been lounging in was gone with his three companions. Nothing floated on the impossibly peaceful red waters where he had just been fishing. He didn't need to turn around and see them to know the dead-eyed men were spread out in a half circle behind him.

Geillan's voice was like a headache in his ears. Horrible notes which should never exist caroused with the most beautiful tones any vocal cords ever mustered. It sounded a godly chorus no creature's ear should ever have to endure as the god, Dragon, man, or whatever he was said, "I do have access to all knowledge. It is a sad gift to know the things I know. Most of it matters very little to me. What does matter in this moment while you stand shivering before me is what you have taken from me. You must know I am aware of your lies. You would have excelled on a stage, actor, faker, false god," he paused. There were no tears, but his face slumped into something that might accompany them as he continued, "pretend father. My mother was not the vile and wicked thing you convinced me of. She was pure. She loved me above all else in this world, and I destroyed her for it."

It was obvious no words he could muster would make a difference. There could be no more lies. The furious young man before him, his supposed son, knew everything, but he interrupted just the same. Perhaps it was hubris, some innate belief in his own powers of persuasion which prevented him from keeping his mouth shut. "Geillan…" he interrupted.

"No," Geillan's voice erupted into a crescendo of terror as flames flared from his shoulders, "you will listen. I have things I need to say, terrors which have been haunting my mind that I need to release. You have kept me trapped in this prison my entire life. I've had no one to share any ideas with but you. Therefore, you must hear my laments. You have earned them.

"You showed me love. I believed in you, even loved you. What you have done to me is unfair. It is the vilest, most wicked of things. You accepted my love, your adoring son. All of it was false. You disgust me. Even as you stand here before me in judgement, you are thinking of ways to persuade me toward your goal. I will not help you."

It felt like fire, the claws slicing into his flesh, piercing his muscles and digging into his bones. He had felt it before. On both occasions when he had unleashed the same three dead-eyed creatures digging their stony talons into his body, he remained connected to their victims. It was a strange fascination. Perhaps the scientist in him yearned to know how death felt. He needed to feel every poke of skin and every shredded tendon, even the last moments when the pain evaporated and gave way to an odd, satisfied peacefulness. In that moment, standing before his accuser with claws piercing his own flesh, he felt small, insignificant, a failure.

Physical pain was such an infrequent companion. He hadn't felt his own pain since emerging from the Lake. It seemed impossible. His body, whatever that was, wasn't even present, yet, somehow, Geillan gifted him the sensation. It wasn't any more real or excruciating as it had been when the pain belonged to someone else, and he was merely tagging along like a voyeur stealing another's experience. Still, somehow it seemed more relevant as two of those dead-eyed vessels that had for so long been connected to his own will stretched his arms out away from his body to the point it felt his ribcage might rip apart while the third dug claws deep into his cranium. Where was his body while his spirit suffered?

"The same place as mine," Geillan answered the wordless query offhandedly, "lying on the stony floor of that room at the top of your tower."

It suddenly occurred to Ijilv that no terror Geillan enacted on him in that place would affect his physical body. He would feel the pain, taste the blood welling up in his throat, even smell the putrid death of the dead-eyed things punishing him for their new master, but his body would remain unscathed. He was less certain about what might happen if Geillan unleashed his flame. Dragons' fire was different than anything else on Ouloos. It followed neither the rules of the physical nor the spiritual. Perhaps if his essence burned there within Geillan's mind his body would burn too. Of course, he wouldn't really burn. It would be just like what Maelich and Cialia had done to his brothers. He would be blasted to a billion bits and scattered to the wind.

"You are wise, for a god," Geillan prodded.

If only he could knock the smug look off the young man's face. He probably deserved the pain, even to be cast to oblivion, but he didn't deserve the condescension. "I am sorry for the things I had to do," he groaned, "but all of it was in the name of helping this world to be born. Destroy me if you must."

It sounded like boulders being ground up in a gear the noise Geillan made as the dead-eyed men pulled Ijilv apart. His joints burned as bone was separated from bone until the tendons snapped. As the pain gained intensity it seemed increasingly impossible that it could hurt any worse. Yet it did. With each new pop or rip, the searing pain soared ever higher. His soul wanted to cry out for mercy, but he refused to give Geillan the satisfaction of knowing how tortured he was at that moment.

"I can taste your pain even as you stand there pretending not to acknowledge it. Know that it is scarcely a shadow of the hurt you've caused me. My agony will remain with me until I burn up with this place," Geillan's voice had lowered to a dull growl.

Then the tension on his sternum was gone with a sloppy crack. He felt his body fall away in two halves from his head. That still had talons poking through it just deep enough to touch his brain. He mustered every shred of defiance which remained in him as he glared into Geillan's smoldering eyes and shouted, "This world will not burn. Ouloos will live. Your father and his sister, the Dragons, will blast you to oblivion, and evil will be dead on Ouloos."

Geillan's laugh was joyless and cruel, "You have made me too powerful. They are no match for me. I will destroy them, and you will be with me to watch this world burn."

Ijilv braced himself for searing heat as the dead-eyed beasts held different parts of his shredded body fast. It never came. Instead, he felt cold. It felt as if each of his cells froze individually all at once. There was a sound like the vibrating report of an explosion tearing across a flat, grassy prairie. It was deafening but somehow as quiet as a whisper at the same time. Bright light filled his vision, but it wasn't his eyes that witnessed it. It came from inside his mind and chased away all shadow from his awareness. And then it was dark.

###

The darkness slowly gave way to light that was much too bright, like the blurry first images spied by waking eyes between blinks. Nothing had any discernible shape. It was just a bunch of dull hues bleeding into one another like blobs of colors mingling in a formless void.

"Now you are truly one of us," Brerto's voice reached his ears a moment before he could make out the god's face.

The answer seemed obvious, but the question poured from his lips anyway. "Where am I?" he asked.

"In your destroyer's head with the rest of us," Kallum grumbled as he tugged hard on a fishing pole and added, "Hold on. I've hooked into a biggie here."

"You fish," it seemed a strange activity for former gods. Debating each other, pontificating on the mysteries of the universe, or lamenting the prison they'd been trapped in, any of those seemed more likely endeavors for his brothers than biding their time on idle pursuits.

"I hate fishing," Moshat complained as he leaned over to grab a worm. The boat they all sat in rocked and swayed as he shifted his weight.

"Then why do it?" Ijilv asked.

"We have no choice," Kaldumahn grunted as he cast out his line.

"No choice at all," Kallum agreed, "he told us to stay here and fish."

"Said he was tired of watching us battle each other," Brerto added.

Ijilv dipped his hand into the red water. The shade seemed as pleasing as it had when he'd first arrived to see Geillan fishing with the dead-eyed men. "Is this the same boat where Geillan fished with his pets?" he asked offhandedly.

"Difficult to know," Brerto replied.

"He had us walking in a circle forever just before he placed us here and told us to fish," Moshat added.

"How did he do it," Ijilv asked, "How did he pluck you from my mind and place you in his?"

"How, is difficult to know. He is powerful, but stealing thoughts seems impossible," Brerto scratched his chin before casting out his line again.

"I felt it though," Moshat began, "It was like being dragged down an invisible corridor, and then we were standing before him."

"He is so much more powerful than I expected," Ijilv sighed, "The first time I found you all in this place within him, he had only borrowed your essence. This time he stole you completely."

"And then brought you to us," Kaldumahn laughed, "Grab a rod and get to fishing."

The idea of sitting in a boat and fishing while Geillan prepared to undo all the work he had spent lifetimes toiling away at, influencing events and creatures so they would follow the exact path he had laid out for them, was ridiculous. They should at least try to put up some kind of resistance. The ideas were there, even the will to execute them. However, as the thoughts stomped around his mind, his hand gripped the fishing pole Kaldumahn handed him, and he cast his line out into the pale, red water of the pond.

CHAPTER 12
THE GREAT BEAST

Hagen felt each of the two-hundred and ten steps of the curving staircase in his quadriceps as he reached the secret back door of the throne room. Rebuilding a toppled mountain was difficult work even with the help of magic. The effort had him weary of both body and mind. It was a small price to pay to see his dwarf friends return to their homes. That first day when a small group of dwarves led by Alenaat—that former waste of a dwarf who'd had an epiphany since being strung up to the Sacred Pine by Maomnosett Ott for the crime of disrespect—whistled their way off to the mines, the song sounded sweeter to his ears than any he'd heard in as long as he could remember. It also marked the end of the work he needed to do to repair the damage done during the great war with those beasts from across the Great Sea. Ouloos and Alhouim were finally returned to their former glory.

He paused there in the darkness for a moment to collect himself before pushing through that secret door. No one in the throne room would see him until he stepped out from behind the gaudy and glorious chair the new king rarely took time to rest in. That was by design. The king and all his guests would think it was magic though his legs would know otherwise.

He took a deep breath, ran a hand through his light brown locks, crouched low, and pushed the door open. Many voices filled the room. Most echoed off the smooth stone of the walls and mingled together into a garbled chorus of shapeless noise, but two stood out. Both were unfamiliar. Judging by the nature of their complaints, they were minor lords from Valancer arguing over the usage of a pond they shared, the border of their respective lands running right down the middle of it.

One voice sounded far more agitated than the other. "He has ten sons, and all of them take at least ten fish a day out of that pond. How long until there aren't any fish left to be had. They don't even eat them all. They use them for sale or trade. I only take what I need to feed my family."

"Bah," the other one replied in a tone that ached with boredom, "you can't feed a family off pond fish. Fresh caught fish from that pond are a delicacy. You don't even fish that pond."

"Half of them fish you're selling are mine. I should get half your take," the first man snorted his retort.

"You deserve nothing," the other man groaned, "My family does all the work."

"Men," King Ymarhon finally stopped the argument, "you both have valid points, and you both have equal claims to that pond I allocated to you. I shall make a decree on this day. Squire, take this down. I, Ymarhon of the house Havenstahl, being duly sworn king of the free lands declare a five fish daily limit on Milner's Pond. No trout smaller than six inches may be taken from the pond, and no chooker smaller than ten inches. Should either house who have a claim to this pond sell or trade any fish they take from this body of water, they shall pay a twenty-five percent share of their profit, be that coin or grain, with the other house."

Hagen had heard enough. The things he wanted to discuss were far more important than petty squabbles over land. "SITTU," Hagen whispered quietly as he stepped from behind the throne. It was a simple spell to lull folks to sleep. The words weren't important. The words in any spell only served to focus the intent of the speaker. It was the will of the mind casting the spell that did all the heavy lifting. That he pressed into every mind but the king's. A moment later, everyone else in the room stood motionless and silent completely unaware anything around them was happening.

The king didn't turn around as he said, "Well, that is a new form of interruption. Though I appreciate your power and everything you have done to help me bring my new kingdom in line, I must remind you that I am the king of this place. You have sworn an oath to me. This feels like disrespect. It has been a very long day. Why have you overtaken my throne room?"

"Forgive me, highness," Hagen demurred, "but I have troubling news of the highest importance. Haste is necessary."

Ymarhon turned his stony expression toward Hagen a moment before the sternness in it cracked in favor of his customary warm smile, "What could you have to tell me that is more important than a dispute over chooker and trout?"

Hagen noticed a sadness hiding in the king's smile. "Does that crown fit the way you had hoped?" he asked.

"Hoped? No. Expected? Yes," he sighed, as his smile dipped slightly. "I barely leave this room."

"It is a very nice room," Hagen returned a sad smile. It was the same for all the men he'd coached and advised while they wore the crown of Havenstahl on their heads. They all wanted the power and glory of the throne, but none really knew the price until they were seated upon it. Bold proclamations belted out before crowds of adoring subjects with love swelling in their hearts, admiration filling their eyes, and cheers pouring forth from their mouths were the fantasy of romanticized dreams about what it would be like to be king. The reality was much more akin to squabbles about who owns which fish heard in the filtered light of a cold throne room. The title is a duty not a gift.

"It is a nice room," Ymarhon agreed as he glanced around it, "Sadly, it feels just the same as the room I left to occupy it. The light is far better. The polished stone of the floor shines much brighter. The décor is second to none. Yet…" he trailed off.

"Nothing has really changed for you," Hagen finished the thought for him.

"It has not," Ymarhon replied with a joyless chuckle, "The line of complaints for me to suffer through has just grown longer."

"That is the price of the crown," Hagen shrugged, "I expect that line will remain as long until the Lake grants you peace."

The king laughed, "You could have warned me."

"A thing I would never do," Hagen chuckled back, "You amassed a mighty force to come to the aid of a castle that was not your own, and though the rightful king of that castle was absent the weight of its crown, that king wields incomparable power. Bold. A king needs to be bold."

"I did not come to challenge anyone for a throne," Ymarhon shook his head, "I came to fill a void left by that great power you described."

"And fill that void you have," Hagen countered, "Whether you like it or not, you are precisely where you belong."

The king quietly strolled over to one of the stained-glass windows along the western wall of the room. The image it portrayed was a glorious if slightly embellished depiction of Maelich riding astride Helias and battling Kallum. He touched the brightly colored glass as he said, "Now, this is a story. A man, born of the Lake, rode the last Dragon and completely changed our history with one swing of his blade. I had only seen the inside of this room once prior to taking the throne. The history told on the windows then was vastly different than what I am looking at now. I was never close with Ymitoth. My father was his cousin, but that throne kept them from being very close. That kept us from ever being close. Still, that one time when I came to pay my respects and honor him as the rightful ruler of our house, it surprised me he hadn't changed them. Requisitioned a story like this to be etched upon them."

Hagen stroked his chin as he replied, "He talked about it more than a few times. Ultimately, he decided the history of Havenstahl should be presented as it happened. History doesn't change, so the story shouldn't either. He wanted his people to remember the wicked things men were capable of. No matter how great or honorable, men were just men."

"He was a wise man," Ymarhon nodded, "Had it been my choice, I would have shared the same sentiment. As it is, perhaps I'll have them replaced with something more fitting."

"You have some of the best builders in all of Ouloos at your disposal. They will see your will done," Hagen nodded back.

Ymarhon sighed deeply as he turned back toward Hagen and said, "I am certain you did not interrupt my court to discuss history or the wisdom of former kings. What do you need?"

"Indeed," Hagen agreed, "my rudeness was quite warranted. A great beast lies in wait at the edge of time and understanding."

"You speak of the place where the maps don't go," the king offered a wry smile, "I remain unconvinced of the stories, chaotic lands of inconsistent terrain where up is down and day can be night or day or whatever other random thing a man's mind could not possibly imagine beyond a Lake no man can see. What manner of monster dwells in this fantastical place?"

Hagen frowned as he replied, "Though I cannot speak to the

veracity of any story you may have heard, I can assure you it is what you describe and more, and this beast I speak of is a power like nothing this world has ever known. It is Maelich's son. He has been hidden away as a prisoner since Ijilv posed as Kallum and sent his dead-eyed priests to steal the baby from his mother. He is awake now, free from the shackles of the god he destroyed. He has the power of the gods and of Dragon's fire. He intends to destroy our world."

Ymarhon's brows dipped nearly to his nose as skepticism dripped from his tone, "I heard the story of those dead-eyed monsters stealing Maelich's son from his poor wife. I've never really believed in those creatures. I think men stole that baby. Maybe they died before they could ask a ransom. Whatever happened to them or the child they stole, I expect he is not anything to worry over. He can't have lived through more than two summers by this point."

Blue lightning crackled across the ceiling of the throne room as the light flooding in through the stained-glass windows dimmed. In a voice both deep and terrible, Hagen boomed, "NAM-LU-INIM-MA."

The sky above Ymarhon looked like no sky he had ever seen. Colors flashed in foreign hues he could scarcely understand in shapes that made his eyes burn and his head throb. His long hair whipped wildly beneath his crown, but he felt no wind. The air smelled like strawberries crushed into excrement and mixed with sulfur. The ground beneath his feet was no ground at all. It was flowing purple waves which behaved like water but looked like something else entirely. He cried out with all his might, but his voice sounded like a whisper in his own ears drowned out by a rumble that could have been a thousand horse hooves pounding against stone. His eyes slammed shut, but somehow all the horrid visions remained.

His guts wanted to heave when he finally saw it, a tower even blacker and taller than the thing he'd heard described in stories. It stretched up into the impossible colors and shapes further than any structure should be able to stand. It made no sense. Nothing did. He finally did heave, but the contents of his guts didn't spill out onto the wavy ground beneath him which had shifted from purple waves to jagged, green shards that looked akin to some kind of precious crystal. Instead, the bile fell upward before gurgling and dissipating into the macabre shapes above his head.

Fire swirled around the tower like a wall of protection. It didn't flicker or dance like the mesmerizing movements of flame in a campfire. It was fast, spinning like dust pulled up into a cyclone. The color was all wrong. It was red, almost like blood, but translucent enough that the tower of massive blocks behind it could still clearly be seen.

Then he felt it. Eyes watched him, but they didn't merely behold his trembling form shivering there in the madness. They peered into his mind and soul, tossing open his thoughts and rummaging through them like old, forgotten boxes in a cellar.

A voice rumbled across the landscape which had become orange swirls like whirlpools spinning in sand. "I am your reckoning. I am your terror. Your cities will burn, and your castles will crumble. None will be safe from my flame. I will destroy the wickedness of men. You have been judged. Ouloos has been judged."

"Help," he cried out as two opposing forces tugged at his will in opposite directions.

Then another voice cried out. He recognized it as Hagen's, but it sounded so much more powerful than he'd ever heard it. Vengeance and rage coiled around the words as they rumbled just as loudly as the first voice. "GI A-DA-LAM!" the wizard shouted.

It felt like he'd been yanked from deep within dirt, like the root of an ambitious weed once it's finally been torn loose from densely packed soil. Then he was spinning in darkness only occasionally interrupted by bright flashes of blue. Something chased him. He couldn't feel anything, but somehow, he sensed it, like icy fingers reaching for your back as you fail at running away from danger in a night terror.

Hagen's cheeks trembled with effort as he battled Geillan for Ymarhon's soul. It had been a horrible mistake to send the king there. The Dragon was so strong. Laughter rung in his ears as he fell to his knees, pressing into chaos with all his might and clinging tightly to his king's will. The child was toying with him, laughing at his effort. There would be nothing he could do about it if the monster wanted to keep Ymarhon. Spittle shot from his mouth spattering the polished stone as he reached the end of his strength. Then the resistance ceased abruptly, and Ymarhon knelt before him on the floor.

The king's eyes were wild as they darted about the room like they were chasing ghosts or sounds. The man was whimpering softly. It was the kind of sound a starving scrod might make while waiting at the door of a hut to which his master would never return.

Ymarhon's arms shot out like snakes, and he grabbed hold of Hagen's robe as he said, "Go to that place. Destroy that beast before he burns Ouloos to dust."

"Your will, my king. GESTUG," he whispered in the terrified man's ear. The command would make Ymarhon forget what he had witnessed. All he would remember would be sending Hagen on a mission to protect Havenstahl.

Blue lightning crackled across the ceiling as Hagen stood and shouted, "NGIR DU!"

The moment the words left his lips, the blue lightning crackling about the ceiling snaked down to the ground and swirled into a spinning circle. It was small at first, but it quickly grew until it reached from floor to ceiling. Then it gained depth. By the time Hagen stepped into the swirling mass, it had stretched into a long corridor.

Not much seemed different when he emerged from swirling, blue lightning on the other side of the portal. The throne room surrounding him looked like an old memory of the one he'd just left. All the important things remained, but some of the details seemed they had been forgotten.

"I wondered how long it would be until you came to call," Antopy's words danced about her sing-song tone.

"Of course, you did," Hagen smiled without looking back at her. Instead, he glanced about the room, this faded memory of the throne room at Havenstahl. It seemed such an odd thing for her to create. "Why do you waste your will on making this place resemble a place you despise so?"

She twirled her dress dramatically as she danced around to the front of him grabbing his hand along the way and twirling herself once more beneath it. "In the hopes my baby brother would pay me a visit, of course," she finally replied. She curtsied before adding, "I thought if I made a castle resembling that horrid place you love so much, you might feel a bit more comfortable here."

"Good story," he laughed as he spun his sister one more time, "but

I had no idea you'd decorated your world in my honor."

"You could have looked, but you're always so wrapped up in the comings and goings of those vile creatures on the other side of the Lake," she frowned as she danced away from him.

"They are not vile," he returned the frown she'd given him, "They are honorable men working their ways through this physical experience as best they can."

She held her gut as she laughed. He knew she was having a go at him. The laugh wasn't honest or good hearted. It was loud and dramatic, and she shook like she was nearly having a seizure as she belted it out. "You want to believe that," she finally said as the laugh faded, "but deep inside, you know it to be a fantasy concocted by your own mind, a dream of what you wish they were. You envy them in their simple-mindedness, striving toward clear goals with black and white rules where good is good, evil is evil, and there is no in between. You can never be that, because you know better than that. You are lazy."

Her words felt like a slap to his soul. She was correct, of course, but he couldn't accept the jab without defending himself. "Lazy?" he feigned shock as best he could while standing there accused of something he knew to be true, "I have spent my life toiling in the service of others, healing broken men and teaching them to be more than they ever thought possible. Grinding herbs and minerals into rare elixirs doesn't just cramp the fingers and tighten the joints, it takes the will of the mind opening to all possibility and urging those digits as they do the work."

"Oh stop, brother," Antopy put her hand up as if to block the words from her ears, "I am not suggesting you've spent your life lounging about snacking on berries. You have worked hard through more lifetimes than any man should, but you've been stuck in a cell of your own creation. I thought I had broken you out of that when I came to call and remind you of who you are. Apparently, I was unsuccessful. You are lazy because you have happily remained in that cell bound by the same rules as those men you serve. You could make any life you desired, yet you are happy to live within someone else's."

Hagen remained quiet for a moment. It was true, he loved the order given to men by the gods. Expectations were easy to meet when clearly known. Perhaps it was lazy, but it was what he wanted. Why spend energy on things not desired? It made no sense. Antopy was happy accepting whatever reality her chaotic world presented and shifting it on a whim when she desired something different. That wasn't something he'd ever wanted. He liked knowing what to expect. Why was that wrong?

"Perhaps it isn't," she sighed, "Perhaps it is unfair of me to judge you based on things I wish for you. We should all have the life we desire. I suppose I just wish you desired to be more. All I can see is wasted potential."

"I see it differently," he shrugged. A slight chuckle slipped past his lips before he added, "Stay out of my head."

"You know I can't do that," she laughed, "I also cannot help you on your quest. That is why you're here. I wish you had come to discuss the endless possibilities of this physical existence and challenge me with the things we could make from it, but you are too much like the men you serve, too much like mother was. You need to control the outcome rather than letting things happen as they will. You want to bring order to the chaos, force things to be what you want them to be rather than allowing them to be what they are."

"I do," he shrugged, "and I suppose I am as much like mother as you are like father. You are as hypocritical as he was, pretending to allow things to be what they will while you mold them precisely into what you want." He paused and sighed, "I am sorry for that. I didn't come here to debate with you or judge how you choose to live your life. Geillan will burn this world to dust. All the things you've said about me are true. I love mankind, and I want to protect them. I need your help."

He knew what her answer would be when he had decided to ask for her assistance, but he had to try. Though it wasn't her way, he hoped she might be swayed seeing him there and knowing what fate lay before him.

A tear trickled down her cheek as she went to him and cradled his face in her hands. "I love you, dear brother," she said as another tear chased the first down to her chin, "Geillan is going to destroy you. Deep down you know you cannot defeat the boy. His power is beyond comprehension. I also know you cannot turn away from the task you've chosen."

"You won't come with me to save this place?" His shallow smile hid the frown of his soul.

"You know I will not," she confirmed with a smile just as shallow as his, "What will be, will be."

"Perhaps I'm hoping for an alternative outcome. Perhaps I believe I can make a difference," he shrugged.

She shook her head as sadness clouded her eyes and she said, "Hope and belief are things you have when your expectations aren't satisfying. Good luck, brother. I hope you can make the difference you believe you can."

CHAPTER 13
COMING HOME

The air was crisp and fresh on the hill that morning. It was a small rise marking the last breath of the Edge Mountains which poured into the Forgotten Forest. Daritus thought they were both silly names as he glanced back up the hill to see the slow caravan of wagons and horses disappearing over the top of it. Three thousand men, dwarves, trogmortem, and even a handful of giants looked back at him with eyes full of hope. Those sparkling eyes seemed out of place beneath brows tight with tension and above frowns pushed down by memories of vicious battles and a grueling trek across the known lands. If only he could secure some of that hope for himself.

A brisk wind tussled his hair about. The dirty mess made his scalp itch as clumps flopped awkwardly about rather than dancing on the currents. He needed a hot bath and a long nap. After that, who knew? He hoped by the time his group had made it to this point he would have made it to a place where he wanted to be where he was, but that hadn't happened. There was no place on Ouloos he wanted to be. Nothing he loved remained. The Lake was what he really wanted, an end to a life which had never seemed his own. Now that it truly was his own, he didn't know what to do with it. He promised to try. The forest in the valley below marked the fulfillment of that promise. Watching the sun rise slowly over the trees, he decided the trial was over. He had tried, and he had failed to secure the desire Hagen and Kantiim, and so many others had wanted him to find.

There was a small part of him that wanted to be what they thought of him, to feel like the great leader of men they saw when they looked at him or told stories of his supposed exploits, but a larger part knew how misplaced their feelings were. He wasn't any different than any of them. His strategy at the Battle of Fort Maomnosett failed and thousands of men and dwarves died. He rebuilt a castle only to have it stolen from the king who should have sat upon the throne. His precious wife, a real leader, died while he was absent protecting someone else's castle from invasion, and she was killed by the flame of a daughter he trained to be a warrior. Obviously, he had failed to effectively teach her the necessary restraint to control her weapons. He killed a giant but barely survived the fight. It felt too much like luck to believe it had anything to do with his prowess in battle. Had Hagen not used magic to heal him, he'd be riding in one of the wagons behind him unable to walk out at the front of the caravan. He simply wasn't the hero they believed in. He was just a man who wanted nothing more than to be the husband of the queen who was stolen from him, and that was something he could no longer be.

Boringas jogged up and nudged his shoulder pulling him out of his trance. "It looks the same as every other time I've walked down this hill, but somehow it seems different. It looks empty," sadness lurked about in the man's tone as he gave voice to ideas that had been stumbling about Daritus' mind.

"It is empty," Daritus quietly agreed. Then he sighed and changed the subject, "I am sorry, but I don't want to talk about that anymore. My eyes burn from the tears I've shed. Even now they would be carving rivers through the dirt on my cheeks if I wasn't dry as a desert. Let's talk about the names of these places. This hill, for instance," he held his arms wide while glancing about in both directions, "the edge of Edge Mountain. Why do we call it that?"

"This mountain range marks the edge of the known world," Boringas shrugged, "I suppose I never really thought much about it, but it seems an accurate description."

"Is it though?" he asked, happily absorbed by the distraction, "Is this the edge of the known world? No, that name was granted by map makers who never journeyed farther out of fear of what lay beyond. That is precisely why our glorious forest was forgotten by the men occupying the lands west of it. We haven't forgotten this place. Why would we let men who don't occupy our lands name them for us?"

Boringas' chuckled as he scratched at his filthy beard and replied,

"Those are valid points. That is our forest, and we may as well lay claim to this hill as well. We should name them. What would you call them?"

"Good question?" Daritus glanced about again. The sun rising over the forest cast an orange glow on the very highest peaks that could still be seen over the hill. They almost looked like fire. "We could call the mountain range the Flaming Peaks."

"Mmm…" Boringas' face twisted into something disagreeable as he continued, "It isn't the worst name for a thing I've ever heard, but I think the name should have mountain in it. Something like Fire Mountains."

"I think that might be worse," Daritus laughed. It felt good to laugh. Then he added, "Perhaps we should enlist some minds more creative than ours to come up with a name for that range."

"Okay," Boringas began as he pointed down the hill toward the trees and continued, "how about the forest? The riders of Druindahl have stood in defense of Dragons since the beginning of time. What if we call this mystical wood, Dragon's Keep?"

Lito-Bi sauntered up to Daritus' other side, gave him a nudge, and said, "I have never seen anything like this place. We have no forests in my lands. Even trees are scarce. The land is beautiful when the bright sun blazes across it, burnt and orange with mountains and canyons offering views for miles in any direction, but this…" he trailed off as he spread his arms wide, "…this is breathtaking. When your man, Tarantian, invited Bom to visit this place, all I wanted was to go home. I only made this trek to honor my fallen friend. I am so glad I did. Not just for his memory, but because I would never have known how mesmerizing this world can be."

"There you have it, Boringas," Daritus smiled up at the awestruck trogmortem, "We can call it Breathtaking Wood."

Boringas didn't reply. He just offered a tight grimace and shook his head.

"The Forest of Fire and Enchantment," Lito-Bi gasped.

"That's a bit better," Boringas nodded.

"We'll work on it," Daritus decided.

The path down the hill was slow. The way through the forest would be even slower. By the time Daritus and his two companions made the trees, the very last wagon in the caravan was cresting the top of the hill. At the rate they were travelling, the woods would be dark by the time the last wagon made it into the trees, the last bits of sunlight the sky above the canopy clung to failing to penetrate the thick foliage.

Not more than one hundred yards of trail had passed beneath Daritus' aching feet when the feeling hit him. It started as warmth in his chest. He couldn't catch his breath. It felt like he'd just run ten miles at a steady clip the way he was fighting to suck air into his lungs. Then he was suddenly thirsty, but a dry throat wasn't the cause. It was like a hole in his middle that needed to be filled with something. The something he needed remained elusive. Water wasn't it, nor was food. This longing was deeper, like his soul was starved. Then he noticed the smell.

The forest was cool. Dampness hung about the thick tree trunks saturating the air between them. It amplified the muskiness of the moss clinging to the trees and rocks and mingling with fresh earth and decomposing leaves. The combination of those scents mingled with wildflowers that bloomed in the forest. It smelled like home, but none of those things were the culprit that had him gasping for air. It was a memory. Ignis bloom, a rare blossom that grew wild in the forest had a unique scent that stood out from all the other smells of the dark and enchanting place. It was like boiling dragon blossom mixed with fresh-baked sweet cakes, and it wrapped around them while slithering between them. It had been a favorite of Leisha's when she was young and Daritus courted her. She would tie up her hair in a loose bun and decorate it with those fire-red blossoms. The scent drove him crazy.

Suddenly, that thirsty feeling was gone, chased away by something like a vision. It wasn't quite that. It was just a memory, but it was so vivid and clear it seemed real, like something that was happening right at that moment rather than a reflection of a thing that happened long ago.

Leisha wore a white gown that fluttered slightly in the calm forest breeze. The most ambitious rays of blazing sunlight sliced through the canopy and danced off her golden hair. She glowed like a goddess in that perfect light. Nothing in all of Ouloos could ever have been so perfect as she danced between light and shadow, occasionally stooping to collect a blossom and slide it into the loose bun carelessly bouncing at the back of her head. She turned to look at him. He felt so shabby in his rough trousers and tattered cloak. He pretended it didn't trouble him at all that she was his queen, but during the quieter times, it did. He was nothing more than a sword in her army sworn to protect her and her city. She was so far above him. Dare he attempt reaching up toward those heights? The joyful smile that spread across her face as she ran to him almost assured him that her soft, brown eyes, so warm and welcoming, and yet, so wise, saw him differently than he saw himself.

"Daritus, my love," she nearly squealed when she jumped into his arms.

It felt more than he deserved as he spun her twice before gently setting her back to the ground and hugging her tight. Everything he wanted was in his arms casually stroking his hair. He never wanted to let go, but there was something he needed to do, a gift he needed to give her.

The idea of asking to hold her hand for the rest of her days was more terrifying than any other challenge he'd ever faced in his life. What if she said no? It would be the end. There were no other branches of his story. The only path he would tread led to her. The thought of waiting, of not asking the question that would seal his fate roared from the back of his mind. If he never asked, she couldn't say no, but then he would never know for sure if she felt the same things for him that he felt for her. He could walk beneath the canopy of the cool forest with her. He could enjoy a warm embrace every time they met or parted ways. They could talk together for hours on end about their goals and dreams. He could even enjoy the occasional, and always surprising, kiss on his rough cheek, but it would never be more than that unless he tried.

He clumsily fell to one knee as he fished the precious stone out of his pocket. She deserved so much more than the trinket he'd found while retrieving a dagger he'd lost in the shallow waters of a lazy brook while training, but he hadn't the coin for anything more back then. It was a beautiful stone, shaped like a perfect egg and roughly the same size. It looked brown in unspectacular light, but when the sun hit it, it blazed a glorious amber and cast tiny rainbows all about it. A ring would have been far more suitable, but it was the best he could do. He held the thing up toward her as his head bowed toward the ground.

The gasp she let out when she saw the thing didn't seem specific enough for him. Was it anxious shock because he'd overstepped his bounds, or was it joy that he had? The few moments which passed while he knelt there before her with his heart pounding wildly in his chest and his clammy hands as wet as a freshly caught fish seemed an eternity.

"Leisha," he finally found the courage to ask the question of which the answer he both dreaded and desired more than anything else, "would you…"

"Yes, my love, yes!" she shouted before he could finish, dragging him back to his feet by his collar with both hands before planting a deep but soft kiss on his clumsy lips.

They were soft, her lips, far softer than he had even imagined while admiring them as they would form words. As intriguing as the stories they told may have been, he'd get lost in them sometimes, those times when her delicate, brown eyes hadn't already enchanted him into a witless trance. Warmth began in his chest and raced through his entire body until he thought he might burn up right there in front of her as her lips lingered long on his.

When the softness of her kiss finally left his lips, she held up the stone he'd given her. Those same rays of sunshine bathing her hair in that golden glow, poured through the thing until it blazed like a small, amber star. "It is beautiful. I love it," she finally said.

"I am sorry it is not the ring you deserve," he mumbled quietly as he gazed deeply into eyes dampened by joy and brimming with hope for a future he prayed he could secure for her.

"Nonsense," she kissed him quickly again before adding, "My grandfather was the greatest smith in all of Ouloos before he passed. He was known for his swords, but I tell you, he could make anything out of precious metals and gems. I have a drawer full of glorious rings he left me. We can pick the one we like best, have it blessed, and I will wear it as a symbol of our love until my last breath and even beyond."

"They moved it," Kantiim's deep voice chased the vision away, and all that remained was the dirt of the trail beneath Daritus' crumbled form.

He would have preferred not to have streams of tears running down his cheeks when he raised his head up to reply, but he didn't wipe them away. They were all that remained from the vision that overtook him. He wanted to keep them for as long as he could. He left them alone when he asked, "Where?"

Kantiim trotted up on his horse until he was beside Daritus looking down at him. His eyebrows dipped toward his nose as he asked, "More tears, old friend?"

"I haven't been to this place in at least seven summers," he replied while doing nothing to stop the torrents from raining down his face to soak his beard, "She haunts these woods. I saw her there in the trees. I never got to say good-bye. I wouldn't expect you to understand."

"And I don't," the gruff old soldier agreed, "She was a gift. I've never experienced anything like what the two of you shared, but I do know what she meant to you. Your tears give me no cause to think less of you."

"Thank you," he offered his old friend a genuine smile before asking again, "To where did they move our city, and why? It was perfect where it was."

"I'd rather not say exactly why, but it would be impossible to rebuild it where it was. Construction is underway, further south, closer," Kantiim's gaze dropped to the ground as he answered.

"That new city is not my city," Daritus mumbled before adding with a bit more strength in his voice, "I want to see my city."

Kantiim's sigh along with the grimness which suddenly settled into his expression carried his message far more effectively than his words, but he spoke them anyway, "I beg you, don't do that. There is nothing but sorrow waiting for you in that place. You already have plenty of that oozing down your cheeks."

"I need to see it with my own eyes," Daritus replied as he stared off into the darkness between the thick trees, "I don't need a guide."

"Fine," Kantiim grunted his displeasure, "but I won't let you go alone."

His frustrated friend said more words, but he paid no further attention to them. There was some commotion while a horse was acquired for him, and instructions were given to some soldier to guide the caravan to the new Druindahl being built. None of it succeeded in drawing his attention from the darkness. Her eyes were there smiling at him. Her voice sung notes on the wind as it whispered through the trees. The perfume of her scent wafted on those same currents. The rest of it was nothing more than muffled commotion and blurs of muted color in his periphery.

After a time, he was on a horse trotting quietly down the trail beside Kantiim. It was an unfamiliar horse. Someone had mentioned its name to him, but he hadn't really heard what they had said. Kantiim made a few attempts at conversation but gave up quickly after achieving no replies. Daritus had no doubt it would have been small talk or more attempts to run him away from his goal. He had no interest in either of those, so he ignored them.

The journey through the forest was uneventful. Every time he'd thought about what his first return to the forest would be like, he imagined he would walk slowly down the trail savoring every color and scent, resting frequently to gaze out into the lushness of it all, listen to the songs and complaints of the critters in the brush and up in the trees, and maybe even camp under the canopy with the chill air cooling his skin. None of it seemed important anymore. He felt like he was walking into a graveyard, some forgotten dark place where even the ghosts hide in fear of the stark loneliness.

Then something caught his attention. It was small, maybe a couple inches square at best resting right in the middle of the trail next to a brown leaf decayed and a breath away from crumbling to dust. On any other trip he'd ever made down this trail, he would never have noticed something so small in the dirt, but this charred and blackened thing stood out to him like a beacon in the night. The burnt bit of wood was the first shred of evidence he'd seen of the horror which befell his precious city and took everything he loved from him.

He gave his horse a quick tap to the flanks to get the beast moving a bit quicker down the trail. The sudden need for haste made little sense, but he urged the horse on faster, nonetheless. There wasn't anyone to save. The only thing waiting for him at the end of this journey was sadness. He expected that to darken the rest of his days.

What he saw when he rounded the last bend of the trail that poured into the wide clearing which used to sit beneath his hidden city in the trees was more horrible than he'd expected. It was so bright. He expected it to be dark, like a sealed-up crypt. It felt like that, barren, desolate, and dead, but the remaining light in the sky from a sun nearly set blazed in. Most of the trees had burned to dust. The ones which remained looked like charred ribs jutting from burnt carcasses that had been ripped open from gizzard to gullet.

A quiet curse died at the back of his throat before it could be born into words.

"I warned you," Kantiim sighed, his sadness filling the quiet of the bright, dead space.

"Would that I listened, my heart would remain this cold, stony thing," Daritus replied, his words sounded foreign to his ears, "You are blameless in this, old friend. You did what you could. I would have found my way to this dead place one way or another."

"There is one thing here I think might lift your spirits, if only slightly," the tone of the man's voice betrayed his trepidation about loosing his next words into the world.

Daritus couldn't imagine anything that might bring even the slightest joy into his crumbling heart, but he asked anyway, "What is that?"

"There," Kantiim replied as he pointed toward what appeared to be a statue charred from fire.

The distance made it difficult to make out, but after a few moments of scrutiny he realized it was a stone Dragon that used to decorate Druindahl's vast library. The thing was crumbling and charred, the idea it had survived the heat of Dragon's fire did lift his spirits slightly. What lifted them even more were the brightly painted pots housing all manner of flowers surrounding it. There was something fastened to its front that he couldn't quite make out. It appeared some kind of parchment.

"What is that fastened to the Dragon?" he asked.

Kantiim finally smiled at him as he replied, "Move closer. Have a look. I would have preferred you to avoid this place completely, but, since you are here, you should see the one happy thing which remains."

Daritus hopped off his horse and approached the thing. It only took about ten paces before he recognized it. The colors had faded a bit, and the edges were charred, but those were his wife's eyes staring back at him from the small bit of canvas. It was a tiny piece of a painting gifted to her by a renowned artist who had no name that used to travel from city to city peddling his wares. The man had cried when he painted the thing and refused any coin for his efforts. He left well fed but no heavier in the purse.

Daritus had all but forgotten about that man. Staring at that gift he had left, a miracle to have survived flames which had burned trees to ash, he remembered what that man had said to him when he asked about the tears. At first the man wouldn't answer, but Daritus prodded. Leisha had gently scolded him to leave the poor man be, but he couldn't.

Finally, the artist frowned and said, "Your sweet wife and queen is a gift to this world. Someday, she will save us all."

"That's a wonderful proclamation," he had chuckled at the time, "Why shed tears for something so great?"

"Because," the man sniffled, "she won't be able to save herself."

At the time, Daritus thought the man to be nothing but an eccentric old fool. Most artists he had ever known had a less than close relationship with reality. However, after seeing the evidence of his clairvoyance staring him in the face, it was difficult to argue the point even with himself. Leisha had saved so many in her lifetime. Still, his proclamation that she would somehow, "save us all," seemed a bit of a stretch too far. Unless her story remained unfinished. She had birthed two Dragons, after all. Perhaps that's what the old fool meant. Maybe one of them would save the world. If he could get hands on either of those absent saviors in that moment, there would be nothing left of them to save anything.

"Care to give voice to the ghosts troubling your thoughts?" Kantiim's rough tone cut through the quiet like a herd of tubber trampling a market of glassware and pottery.

"Just memories of happier times, faded like a garment left out in the blazing sun. It brightens my heart to see they made a shrine to her. She deserves so much more, but somehow this charred thing speaks to me. It is perfect," Daritus replied quietly. His eyes were finally done with tears, but his soul continued to sob its silent laments. "I am glad I came to see this. My spirits are lifted. I am ready to see the new city and face whatever the future holds. My wife is dead of body. I will never hold her in my arms again, but she will live on in my heart, mind, and soul."

Daritus pulled a red ribbon from his horse sack and tied it to one of three clawed fingers that remained of the Dragon statue and then kissed the charred bit that remained of the painting fastened to its front. It was beautiful work. Those eyes captured Leisha's essence perfectly. Then he stood silently, mounted his horse, and nodded to Kantiim. Luckily, his old friend understood the gesture and kept any other words he may have wanted to share safely behind his teeth when he nudged his horse forward back toward the trail.

The very front of the caravan was arriving at the construction site by the time Daritus and Kantiim finished the trek. It would have appeared unbridled chaos to the untrained eye, but Daritus knew the purpose behind every step any of the many toiling under the canopy made. Young men formed in columns worked through sword techniques under the watchful eyes of grizzled veterans with years of experience carved into the lines of their faces. Laborers hauled supplies to load onto carts that would raise them high up into the canopy, so the builders could work their magic crafting an invisible city in the sky.

A bent old man beneath a simple prang crown strolled among the perfectly orchestrated movements with keen eyes trained on Daritus.

"The king has returned to claim his throne," the old man loudly proclaimed as he removed the crown from his head, slightly mussing up his grey locks.

The chuckle that flopped from Daritus' mouth as he shook his head was both joyless and dry as he replied, "This is not my city, and that is not my crown. I trust you to rebuild Druindahl and return this place to the glory my dear wife secured for it."

The man turned the thing over in his hands a few times. It glinted in filtered rays of sunshine but remained quite unspectacular. That was how Leisha wanted it. No queen nor king stands above any man. To her, the crown had been a mark of service not elevation. There was no need to adorn it with jewels.

When the man failed to share any further thoughts, Daritus continued, "Blancus, my wife entrusted you with that crown when we left for Havenstahl so many summers prior. She had faith in you. That crown belongs on your head. It is my wish that it remains there."

"I wish she were here with us," he chuckled as he continued turning the thing over beneath the filtered rays of sunshine, "This is such a heavy thing. If it is your desire that I wear this crown on my head and sit upon the throne of this city, I will consider it a command from my king. However, I do not feel I deserve the honor of this service."

A bit of sternness slipped onto Daritus' expression as he gently scolded the man, "You are the wisest among us. Your advice helped my wife become the great leader she was. You guided this city through one of the darkest chapters in her history. The throne is where you belong."

"I failed at that, didn't I?" Blancus' keen eyes grew misty as he continued to stare at the crown in his hands while he spoke, "My sleep is troubled by the terrors. Twice she came to call, the Dragon. The first time she was right. The look in Cialia's eyes when she removed me from the throne was somehow worse than the flames swirling in them when she returned to destroy gods. She was disappointed in me. I let our precious city fall to depths unseen. I was not a good king."

"And the fact you believe that is precisely why you are a good king. You could stand before all of us in this clearing and defend your time on that throne, but you are not doing that. You are humbly accepting responsibility for things you have done. Whether or not they are truly your fault is debatable, but accepting responsibility is what great leaders do. We all fail sometimes. The question is, will you accept defeat, or will you get back up and try again?" Daritus kept his eyes locked firmly on Blancus as he spoke.

Blancus dragged in a deep breath through his nose and blasted it back out through his mouth as he raised his gaze to meet Daritus' and returned the crown to his head, "Thank you. I have learned much, and I will do better. Druindahl will be reborn, and she will soar to the heights. I trust you'll remain with us. I can't think of a better advisor."

"I will not," Daritus smiled, "I told you this is not my city. No joy remains in this place for me. I need answers I will never find trapped in a city that holds nothing for me but the ghost of my lost love. There are good men and dwarves, even trogmortem and giants in that caravan. They will help you rebuild both your city and her army. I will leave with the dawn."

Boringas strolled up to the two men. Something about his posture had changed. He no longer seemed bent beneath the weight of the world. Despite each mile of trail being chronicled in the dirt caking his hair and face, he'd almost gained back his noble countenance. "I wish you would stay," he said to Daritus as he patted his shoulder.

"You could join me," Daritus embraced the man.

"I wish I could," Boringas' smile was filled with teeth that seemed too white against the grime, "but I know your goal. I cannot be a part of that. Cialia has broken my heart many times, but it still belongs to her. Though I understand what you must do, I don't want to see it. If you can kill a Dragon, I don't want to watch her die, and if you can't, well, I don't want to watch that either. My hope is the two of you find some kind of solace in each other and decide nobody needs to die as payment for Leisha's death."

"You're a much better man than I am, Boringas. You have a forgiving soul. It is a quality I once shared. That part of me is dead now, burned away by Dragon's flame. King Blancus is lucky to have you. Druindahl is lucky to have you," he smiled wide as he embraced the man. After a few moments, he sniffed a few times and added with a chuckle, "You are in dire need of a bath."

"Have you smelled yourself?" Boringas laughed back at him.

"Indeed. I am as foul as a stable which hasn't been cleaned in at least a moon. Sadly, I've grown used to the odor. A long soak will have us both back to form," he laughed back at him.

"Well, I will be joining you on your journey," Sanjo proclaimed as he walked up to the embrace. Somehow the man remained clean despite his time on the trail, "You can count Hasujo and Nothany part of your group as well."

"It heartens me to know my path will not be a lonely one," Daritus patted the man's shoulder.

Then Hasujo strummed a few notes on his mandolin. The attempt at a melody sounded more like a couple of scrods yelping in pain than any form of song. And then the bard sang.

When a tired old king rolled into town
He didn't want no throne or want no crown
Then an older king said he would step down
But the first king wanted to find a Dragon
So he could learn how to kill a Dragon

"For the love of Coeptus, stop that horrible noise," Nothany groaned.

"Nothany," the slightest hint of irritation tainted Sanjo's tone, "Are you feeling fresh?"

"I am," the boy shrugged.

"Feel like training?" Sanjo asked.

"Always," a cocky smirk spread across Nothany's face as he added, "I could teach these green recruits a thing or two."

"Get to it then, lad. Show them what you've got," Sanjo smiled as the boy drew his sword and walked away swinging through techniques.

"He'll be great one day," Daritus commented.

"He already is, with a sword," Sanjo smiled, "Training him to control his tongue has proven more challenging."

Then Daritus glanced over at Hasujo. The young bard's mandolin hung loosely in his hand at his side. The poor man was so deflated, he looked like a half-empty water skin. "It was a fine song," Daritus smiled, "Keep practicing your craft. Someday, you'll fill this world with beautiful notes. People will cry with joy when they hear them."

Chorindaal sauntered over to the bard. He was a gruff dwarf, shorter than average. He wore red bows in his thick, gray beard. They were tied to braids that were probably magnificent when he weaved them. After near a moon on the trail, they were ratty and disheveled. Despite all that, the diminutive creature carried himself with an air of nobility.

"I thought it was a fine song," the dwarf encouraged the bard, "Forget about them. Let's stroll. You can play me a tune about this adventure."

Daritus smiled at the exchange as he watched the bard light up. Whether the dwarf honestly enjoyed the horrible sounds Hasujo made when executing his craft, or if he was just being polite to lift the spirits of a downtrodden man, it was a nice gesture. As the two new friends strolled deeper into the forest, Daritus wished they would move just a bit faster. The squealing notes made him cringe.

"It appears you've added one more traveler to your troupe," Sanjo smiled at Daritus' as the horrible song faded into the trees.

"I'm blessed," Daritus smiled back, "Hopefully, those two take many long walks while the bard perfects his craft."

"You can add me to that count," Kantiim offered.

"I had hoped as much," Daritus smiled at his old friend.

"After everything we've been through, our stories are intertwined. I need to see where this ends," the old soldier smiled back.

Lito-Bi, the fiercest of trogmortem, and Hountmytall Moy, the tallest living giant walked up to the group. Both towered over the rest, but Moy had to duck to keep his head out of the lowest of branches.

"We would like to pledge ourselves to the service of your quest," Lito-Bi nodded, "If you'll have us."

"I am honored to share the trail with you, but I thought neither of you wanted anything more than to return home," Daritus nodded back.

Moy's voice was as deep as the giant was tall. It rumbled through the clearing as he said, "I wanted nothing more than to go home. Then I saw my kind rip each other to shreds. That isn't the kind I want to be. I've made friends on this journey, friends who are dear to me. They are my kind now."

"And we want to see Dragons," Lito-Bi added, his voice near a shout.

The proclamation earned a cheer from all in the clearing. Something swelled in Daritus' chest. It wasn't pride. It was something else. Hope, maybe. Whatever it was, a part of him felt it was misplaced. He dared not voice the idea. Everyone in the forest that day needed some happiness after everything they'd seen, but there was nothing noble or happy about his quest. His only goal was to learn how to kill a Dragon, a Dragon who happened to be his daughter. As petty a thing as vengeance was, he didn't care. But it was a sad thing not a reason for joy.

He shoved the ideas to the back of his mind and allowed the smile to return to his face as he pretended to swell with happiness, "We will see Dragons. This will be a journey for the ages. Go, bathe yourselves, rest, and prepare. We leave with the sun of a new day."

CHAPTER 14
THE RECKONING

Darkness surrounded Cialia. It was complete. No whisper of light existed to add any form or shape to anything. It was like being deep in a cave within the ground. Then things slowly began to come into focus. It was gradual, as if someone were gradually turning up a lamp. Shapes began to appear. There were trees. They could have been oaks, but their crowns were so high, and they were packed so closely together, they must have been something else. They formed a perfect circle around her. There was nothing in the clearing between them except a large boulder of which she could only see the very top. It was gray and surrounded by a milky, white fog that covered everything as high as her waist. She couldn't see her own feet beneath her. It was so thick. It swirled as she moved through it toward the edge of the trees.

Her armor clinked dully as she walked. That was strange. She had abandoned the suit once she learned that swords were no longer necessary for her goal. Yet, there they were. She tapped her hips and confirmed both of her blades dangled in their places within their scabbards. It had to be some kind of trick, a prison her brother had concocted for her mind. Apparently, he was no better than the gods.

She tried to slip past two trees when she reached the edge of the clearing, but they were too close together. She walked the entire perimeter of the space but found no break between any of the thick trunks. She touched one of the trees. The bark was too smooth. It felt like no tree she'd ever touched. As she moved her hand around the trunk into the space between two trees something stopped her progress. There was nothing physically there to hinder her, but something kept her hand from moving past the halfway point of each trunk. She repeated the exercise several times before giving up.

Then she walked over to the big boulder jutting out of the thick mist, flopped down upon it, and sighed, "What is this place?"

"This place is a clearing in a dense wood filled with mist and decorated only with a lone boulder to disrupt its simple perfection," a deep, though completely clear, voice which seemed to originate from no singular spot replied.

"Well, that seems an apt description," Cialia sighed, "Though it fails to tell me any more than I learned from a quick glance around it."

"It is a very precise description which explains this place perfectly. What are you trying to learn beyond that?" the voice countered.

"Where is it?" her voice earned a slight hint of frustration as she asked the question.

"Where is what?" the voice asked in return.

"This place," she threw her arms up above her head as her tone fully embraced the frustration she could no longer hide, "Where is this place?"

The tone of the voice grew genuinely confused as it replied, "This place is right where you are standing. The fact is elementary. Perhaps you have suffered an injury. You seem at least as intelligent as any other creature I have ever encountered, yet you ask questions to which you already know the answers."

"The rules of your game are becoming clear," Cialia drew a deep breath before continuing, "What lies beyond the dense wood surrounding this boulder I sit upon at this very moment surrounded by a thick mist?"

"That is not precisely how I would describe this place," the voice seemed thoughtful, "I would say you are surrounded by a dense fog rather than a thick mist, but I'll grant you they are close kin."

Cialia waited a few moments expecting more. When it became apparent the voice had completed the thought, she continued in as measured a tone as she could muster, "You failed to answer my question. What lies beyond the dense wood surrounding a dense fog which further surrounds the boulder I sit upon at this very moment?"

"This very moment," the voice began. The pause was nearly long enough to prompt Cialia to ask her question again, but it continued just as she opened her mouth. It said, "Time is such a strange thing. It means very little in this place. Have you ever thought about what is a moment, or why it even matters? Is there a difference between one moment or the next? How much time must pass before a moment is complete. How do you know when one moment ends and the next begins?"

"You don't know, do you?" Cialia asked as her head drooped, and she cradled it in her hands.

"I don't know what?" the voice asked earnestly.

"You don't know what lies beyond the trees," Cialia sighed.

"Why does it matter?" the voice countered, continuing its annoying dance of nothingness.

"Because I want to…" Cialia nearly growled before pausing. Perhaps she needed to take a different tact with this voice, who seemed horribly vague while pretending to be frustratingly particular. She thought for a few moments about the perfect question, and then asked, "How does one leave this clearing filled with a dense fog decorated only by a lone boulder and surrounded by a dense wood?"

"Which one?" the voice asked.

"This one. Me," Cialia shouted before counting to ten backwards quietly in her head and asking the question a different way, "How do I leave this clearing filled with a dense fog decorated only by a lone boulder and surrounded by a dense wood?"

"Well, that was excruciating," the voice sighed, "That was the question you wanted to ask in the first place. You must not be in a hurry to get wherever you're planning to go. You remind me of Maelich. He was terribly non-specific."

"You know Maelich?" she leapt to her feet. If only the disembodied voice had a body to grab hold of. She'd shake him until he told her where her brother was.

"I met him once. He liked to play games like you, dancing around topics and asking meaningless questions instead of getting to the point of what he really wanted to learn," the voice sounded as if it would be shaking its head if it had one.

She thought of arguing the point further with him, but it was obvious he enjoyed the struggle. It suddenly occurred to her that he was lonely. Whatever the place was, there didn't seem an easy way in. Whether Maelich had managed to trap her in her own head, or drag her into his, the voice she was speaking with probably didn't get many visitors.

"Please answer the question I wanted to ask in the first place," she finally said.

"Well, that is simple. You just follow the path directly in front of you," the voice replied in as elementary a tone as she'd ever heard.

As the words reached her ears, the fog split to expose a wide trail which led to an equally wide opening in the bank of trees at the clearing's edge. "That wasn't there a moment ago," she complained.

"Of course, it was," the voice was matter of fact as it replied, "You just weren't looking for it correctly. After speaking with you, it is obvious you are not completely certain of your goal."

"Perhaps, you are correct," Cialia chuckled at the overly particular voice, "My goal at this very moment is to end this conversation and bid you farewell. I hope someone else comes along to help ease your boredom."

"Who?" the voice excitedly asked.

"Well, I…don't…know," she stammered, "Anyone, I suppose. I hope anyone comes along to verbally spar with you in your never-ending game of unanswered questions."

"That is very non-specific. I expect nothing less from you," the voice complained, "You are just like your twin."

"How do you know I'm Maelich's twin?" she asked, a bit shocked this voice knew her.

"Everyone knows the tale of the twins," the voice's tone sounded like a shrug, "Good day, Cialia. Enjoy the rest of your journey, wherever your path leads."

"What tale of the twins?" she asked, "And how does everyone know it?"

She waited there for a moment, expecting a quick reply. It never came. A part of her was glad the voice had grown bored with the conversation, but another part of her was slightly offended that a being who spent their entire existence mostly bored would abandon any conversation. That meant she was even more boring than loneliness, at least to this being. Either way, it appeared the voice had nothing left to say, so she followed the path out of the clearing that definitely hadn't been there before.

The trail she walked seemed more natural than the clearing she had occupied with the annoying voice who seemed to know some useful things but only wanted to share ideas that weren't helpful at all. The trees were the same, too smooth and too close together to seem natural, but the fog had lifted. The dirt beneath her feet looked normal enough. It felt like a trail should too. There were no turns or bends, or forks of any kind for that matter. That was unnatural. It seemed like a long corridor instead of a forest trail through thick trees.

The light was gloomy, though ample. It seemed far brighter than it should considering the thick canopy above. There were no breaks in the leaves, but the trail maintained an eerie glow. The soft light had no apparent source. It was all around her.

There were no sounds or smells in the place. That was odd. Not every forest smelled identical to every other forest, but every forest had smells. It had to be something Maelich concocted when he cried out and filled her eyes with light. Perhaps he had trapped her in an illusion just as Brerto had when she faced him. Whatever the place was, she would defeat it just as she had that horrible god's.

The trail stretched on forever. Nothing changed. Each step seemed no different than the prior. There were no markers or any way to gauge how far she'd travelled. She may as well have been walking in place. She turned to see if there were any clues she might have missed on the trail behind her, but it was gone. The trail behind her ended not more than ten feet from where she stood. It wasn't real. She was done playing games, and she was done walking along a trail to nowhere. She would burn this false forest to ash.

There was no flame. The veins on her forehead bulged as her body tensed. She knew it was silly, but she refused to relent. The forest would burn. She battered the trees with her will, urging them to blaze. "Damn it," she cried out when she finally gave up the effort.

Maelich had obviously come up with some method of controlling her flame. It made sense. He knew he was losing the battle and came up with some trick to delay the inevitable. "You can't beat me with blades either, Maelich," she cried out at the trees as she drew her swords and slashed them through a few techniques, but the trees were suddenly gone.

The trail remained, but the trees had vanished. She stood in a field of impossibly green grass. It almost glowed. The cloudless sky above was blue and bright, but no sun decorated it. The light was just the same as it had been surrounded by trees, only brighter. It was perfect and equal but originated from no singular point.

Wind suddenly whipped around her. It blasted her hair straight back, but the tall grass surrounding her didn't move. Grass that long in wind that strong should have been bent, even flattened, by the force, but it stood motionless against the gale. She turned a complete circle looking for some clue of which direction her journey should take. The origin of the wind seemed to shift as she slowly spun. Her hair remained plastered straight behind her. That was at least as odd as the fact that her surroundings remained unchanged for as far as she could see in any direction. It was flat and green forever until she had completed her turn and faced the direction she'd originally been facing.

A horse stood before her, but not really. It was a light violet color, almost pink, and it had a twisted horn jutting from the center of its head. It wasn't spooked at all by her close proximity to it. It didn't stamp or whinny. The thing stood there motionless and staring at her. Its hair wasn't even blowing in the stiff wind. She reached out to touch it.

"Please don't," it spoke in a voice both calm and clear that sounded like a man wise with years, "I do not like to be touched."

It would be odd for a horse to speak, but this wasn't really a horse. It looked like a horse, aside from its color and the horn adorning its forehead, but no horse could talk. It had to be something different. "What are you?" she finally asked, immediately sorry she had used such non-specific language. If this creature were anything like the being in the clearing, the answer she received would probably be a question about what she meant or a complaint about how she formed her query.

Thankfully, the horse-like thing didn't complain nor question, it simply said, "I am a unicorn."

The answer wasn't terribly helpful. She had no idea what a unicorn was, so she asked, "What is a unicorn?"

"That seems a silly question. A unicorn is me and other creatures like me," he replied with a shrug.

The act was unsettling. She'd never seen a horse shrug, but this creature wasn't a horse. Horses lacked the ability to speak, and this thing obviously did not share the limitation. She had to stop thinking of it as a horse. That would be nearly impossible. A horse was her only frame of reference for a creature which looked like the thing standing before her.

"How many unicorns are there?" she asked.

"How should I know?" he shrugged again. It was at least as unsettling as the first time he'd done it.

It was a good question. "I don't know," she shrugged back,

genuinely unsure why she assumed he might, "I suppose I thought you all might live together."

"You are far less simple than that silly question," the horse, no…unicorn, snorted, "How many people are there? Do you all live together?"

"Forgive me, it was silly," she chuckled at the oddness of being politely scolded by a thing that wasn't a horse but must have been a horse, "I do not know how many people there are, nor do I live with them all. I suppose I don't really live with any people anymore."

"That seems both lonely and sad," the creature replied, "Are you lonely and sad?"

"I never really thought about it, but I suppose I am," she replied before shaking her head and adding, "I don't have time to worry over such things. I have a mission. It consumes me. It leaves little time for anything else."

"That does sound sad. I live with my herd. There are forty-one of us. And I love someone. She loves me too. Do you have love where you come from?" the unicorn asked.

The question made her pause. She didn't know what she loved anymore. She loved her brother despite all he had done. She loved her sisters, but it wasn't an active kind of love where she shared her thoughts and fears and joys with them. They were just there. She loved them, and they all loved her. It did seem at least as sad as the creature suggested.

"There is love where I come from, but I don't have time for it. Perhaps, when I finally complete this mission, I will rest with my sisters and explore what love can be," she sighed before asking, "You said you have someone you love. What is her name?"

"We have no need for names in my herd. There is no ego among us. We are individuals, but we are one," he replied.

"That sounds lovely," Cialia decided before changing the subject. "I have enjoyed speaking with you, unicorn, but I must be on my way. Do you know how I can get out of this place?"

"I do not," the unicorn replied, "I'm actually not sure how I came to be here. I was just about to pray about it when I noticed you. Would you like to pray with me? It seems we both need answers to the same questions. When I need answers, I find them through prayer."

Prayer used to be something she believed in. After everything she had seen and learned since finding her flame, it seemed a quaint distraction. Coeptus never had any answers. All the answers she had ever found were buried in her own mind. Thoughtful meditation could be helpful in her current situation. She could call it prayer if the unicorn saw it as such.

She folded her hands, bowed her head, and said, "Yes, unicorn, I would like to pray with you. Would you care to lead?"

The unicorn smiled. That was even more unsettling than the shrug had been, but Cialia ignored it as the creature began, "Maelich, creator of all things…"

"Did you say, Maelich?" Cialia interrupted.

"It is very rude to interrupt a prayer, but yes, a prayer could be to no one else. Maelich is the beginning and the end. There is nothing without Maelich, and Maelich is everything. But being you are part of everything, you should know that already," a hint of irritation swirled in his tone.

Cialia grew suddenly stern, "Maelich is my brother. This is an illusion. You are not really here. It makes sense that you are a creature which resembles something known to me but isn't quite that thing. He sent you to confuse me. Are we in his head?"

"I wonder if perhaps you bumped yours," genuine concern seeped into the unicorn's tone, "It seems you truly believe something as incomprehensible as Maelich to be your brother which displays a complete lack of understanding. Maelich does not have a physical form like me or you. Everything is Maelich. You, me, the grass, and the sky, we are all expressions of Maelich's will. He loves us. All things are possible through Maelich, and nothing is possible without him."

"He has found a way to control his subconscious mind," she said quietly to herself before looking back at the unicorn's eye and saying, "I need to get out of this place. If you need to pray to Maelich to figure it out, please do so."

"I will do this only out of genuine concern for your well-being. Please bow your head," concern remained in the unicorn's voice as he began his prayer again while they both bowed their heads and closed their eyes, "Maelich, creator of all things, beginning and end, help us in our time of need. I find myself in unfamiliar lands far from my herd or anyone who loves me, and this traveler with me has lost her way. She is distressed and confused. Please inspire us to find our destinations. Please…"

The unicorn kept praying, but his voice slowly diminished. When

Cialia opened her eyes to see if the creature was abandoning her, he was gone. Everything was gone except the unicorn's voice slowly lowering in volume as if he were walking away. Then it was quiet. It was as if the space she occupied just then was nothing, some limbo separated from everything. There was no light nor sound nor even odors. She moved to touch her own cheek. At least, she thought she did. She felt no motion nor any pressure on her cheek or finger to suggest any action had occurred. There were no inputs to any of her senses.

Then she heard something. It was kind of a chirp, but deeper and with more throat. Lights suddenly sparkled around her, light blue, almost white. At first, they seemed like stars, but they buzzed about blinking on and off in random patterns. They had to be some form of creature. Maybe an insect based on their diminutive size and random flight patterns. As she watched the lights zig and zag blinking on and off in no discernible pattern, other lights slowly came into being, giving shape to things that were familiar but somehow different.

They looked like trees, but they glowed rather than reflecting light from an outside source. The trunks were smooth and thick, and they radiated an amber color that pulsed like a heartbeat. Their branches curled up and out in massive crowns of leaves that glowed just the same. None of the leaves were green as she would expect them to be. There were red, fat ones with five lobes and saw-toothed edges, others were yellow and egg-shaped with smooth edges and pointy tips, and still others were deep violet and resembled the needles of a pine. They all glowed, pulsing with the same rhythm of the odd trunks.

A breeze tussled her hair before rushing through the trees to set all the different kinds of leaves in all their various colors dancing and swaying in a radiant waltz. The air carried a savory odor, like meat spiced just right and roasted over an open flame, but there were no fires about. The air just smelled that way.

Something brushed against Cialia's ankle startling her into a short scream. She jumped. The thing that startled her so seemed to laugh as it kind of slithered away. Its body resembled a short, thick snake, but it had legs, at least twenty of them. They were short legs, but the thing was definitely walking along the trail rather than slithering upon it. And it was furry. She had never seen a snake with fur, or a face that resembled a small scrod.

"Do you speak?" she asked, but the creature just kept chuckling as it slither-crawled away.

The sudden sound of water rushing behind her stole her attention from the odd, snake-scrod thing that had startled her so. She turned to see a small brook. It was narrow but seemed deep. The water glowed like the trees, but it was a milky pink. It seemed too thick, and the current seemed too weak for all the noise it made. Both banks were alive with all manner of flowers growing random and wild. Purples and oranges, pinks and blues, it was a kaleidoscope of colors all glowing and pulsing in various shapes and sizes.

She walked up to a red one with wide delicate petals and gave it a sniff. It smelled sweet but not like anything that should happen naturally. It was more like a cake. Perhaps she was hungry. Everything in the place smelled like food. Even the milky pink water of the lazy brook that sounded like rushing rapids in a wide river smelled like fruit. She cupped some in her hands, shrugged, and gave it a drink. It didn't taste at all like it smelled. It tasted like common water from any brook or stream.

A blazing blue streak of light raced by her face dragging her attention away from the common tasting water that didn't appear common at all. It was there and gone so fast, she couldn't really see what it was. Then an orange streak that seemed to originate from the water flashed by and disappeared the same way the blue one had. She saw this one a bit better. There seemed to be a tiny creature at the front of it, like the streak of color bled from the thing in a long trail of light.

"Who's there?" she asked, unsure if she had truly seen a tiny creature in the light or if it had been a trick of her eyes in the dizzying place.

Orange light streaked from high above her and stopped immediately before her face. It looked like a tiny person surrounded by sparkling light. The diminutive creature appeared feminine; the soft features of its face dominated by eyes that glowed an even brighter orange than the light emanating from it. "I am here," it said in a voice that was sweet like a song.

"Who are you?" Cialia asked.

"I am me," the thing's voice remained sweet, "That should be obvious. Who else would I be but me?"

"Of course, you are you. There would be no one else you could be. I am me, but people don't call me, me. They call me Cialia. Do you have a name?" she countered.

"Everybody has a name," the orange thing laughed.

"May I know it?" Cialia chuckled, far less irritated than she thought she might be. There was something endearing about the tiny creature that kept her from being annoyed by the game. Perhaps, it was some kind of enchantment.

"Sure, you can," the thing said with a wide smile.

"Will you tell it to me?" the game seemed to never end.

"I might," it happily confirmed.

Cialia laughed as she rifled through a stream of questions she could ask in her mind. The tiny creature seemed to be toying with her, but it hadn't lied, not once. Every answer it gave was a true statement, though not the statement she wanted. "What is your name?" she finally asked. It seemed as direct a question as she could give.

Unfortunately, it wasn't. "Same as yours or anybody else's," the creature shrugged, "It's what they call me."

"Her name is Oma," the blue light shot up like a streak from the milky, pink water's surface and stopped right next to the orange one. This one looked nearly identical to the first one, glowing and sparkling, though its features seemed more masculine. The only real difference between the two was the color of the light. This one was shimmering blue. The little creature inside added, "She won't tell you anything," while Cialia examined the tiny thing.

"I have told her everything, Zizy" Oma shook her head.

"Bah," Zizy threw his arms up, "You have told her nothing. You knew she wanted you to tell her your name, but you danced around her questions like they were piles of dung in a field."

"You're a pile of dug, and you're wrong," Oma countered, "She asked who was there. I told her it was me. She asked who I was, and the answer was the same. I am me, couldn't be anyone else. Then she asked if I had a name. Of course, I do. Everyone has a name. Then…"

"I met a pink unicorn with no name," Cialia interrupted.

"You can't trust unicorns. They don't know anything about anything, and I wasn't finished," Oma snapped. Then she continued, "As I was saying, she next asked if she might know my name. She could. How would I know if she did or not? Then she asked if I would tell her my name. I have no reason not to. Finally, she asked what my name is, and it is what they call me."

"You're insufferable," Zizy sighed, "You knew all along that she wanted you to tell her your name is Oma, but you played a game with her instead."

The argument was delightful, but it wasn't terribly helpful. "What are you?" Cialia finally asked.

"Zizy already told you everything. He is Zizy, and I am Oma. Are you dense?" Oma shook her head.

"We are gidim, but you would probably call us fairies," Zizy gave Oma a shove before adding, "There are millions upon millions of us in this forest."

"Stop shoving," Oma complained as she returned the shove.

"Millions upon millions, huh? Are they all as helpful as the two of you?" Cialia chuckled before asking, "I have never heard of gidim. I have heard of fairies, but I thought fairies were myths. What do you do? Do you grant wishes or something?"

"Wishes?" Oma laughed, "Of course, we don't grant wishes. We wait for weary travelers with lots of questions we refuse to answer, and after we get tired of them, we suck their insides out through their noses."

Zizy rolled his eyes at Oma before answering, "We don't suck anyone's insides out or anything of the sort. We help the forest grow by spreading our dust. I suppose it's a kind of an enchantment, but we aren't magic. Sadly, we don't grant wishes. I wish we could. I would grant all the wishes. Oma wouldn't, and if she did, she'd grant gross wishes that nobody wanted."

"You're gross," Oma scowled, "and I would grant the best wishes. They would be a billion times better than any dumb wish you would grant."

"Well, I guess that settles that, you don't grant wishes, but you do help the forest grow by spreading your dust," Cialia laughed harder at the two as she struggled through the conversation, "Is that like pollination?"

"Pollination? Do we look like bees?" Oma held her belly and laughed even harder before spinning two wild circles and blowing fairy dust all over Cialia.

"Ignore her," Zizy shook his head, "She'll just keep toying with you until you grow bored of it and leave. That's what she wants. Even though this is her favorite game to play. It is not like pollination, because pollination requires taking something from one place and spreading it about to other places. The dust we spread comes from us. It flows forth in a never-ending stream from our very pores."

"So, you sweat fairy dust all over everything to make the forest grow?" Cialia's face squinted up like she'd tasted something horribly sour.

"Yes! That is precisely what we do. We sweat and sweat and sweat our dusty goodness all over the forest to enchant everything," Oma loudly proclaimed before losing herself further to laughter.

Zizy looked like he wanted to scold Oma again. Instead, he shrugged and said, "It sounds gross when you say it like that, but it is kind of accurate. We don't sweat moisture like you. That is even grosser, but our dust does flow continuously."

"And you can thank us for all the brilliant colors in this forest. I bet things don't glow like that where you come from," Oma finally stopped laughing long enough to speak.

"You are correct, Oma," Cialia smiled at her despite how annoying the tiny creature was while teasing her, "Things where I come from don't glow on their own. They reflect whatever light shines upon them. There are times when things seem to glow, like the blazing orange of the mountains at sunset."

"It's not the same," Oma stuck her nose up, "It's better here."

"That may be the case," Cialia conceded, "but I still need to leave this place as wonderful and magical as it may be."

"Your world would be just as magical if that awful Kallum fellow hadn't cursed the place with no magic," Zizy offered almost offhandedly, "That's when she had to hide beings like us away."

"That's enough, Zizy," Oma nearly shouted. Then she turned back to Cialia and said, "He's a liar. You cannot believe anything he says. It sounds like he's telling you everything. You probably like his answers more than the answers I gave, but you can't trust them. I haven't lied to you once, and he has been lying constantly since you met him."

Cialia couldn't help but laugh nearly as hard as Oma had. The two of them were bewildering. It was interesting they knew of Kallum. Based on what Zizy said, it seemed maybe they once lived in her world. "How do you know Kallum? Did you come from Ouloos? Can you take me back there?"

"One question at a time," Oma scolded.

"Shut up, Oma," Zizy scolded her back, "You're a terrible host. She can ask as many questions as she'd like. All knowledge comes from Maelich. He shares all the histories and understanding with us, but not all of them belong to us. We know of Ouloos, but it was never our home. There were fairies in your home not that long ago. Your grandmother knew some, but we were never there. This has always been our home."

"Do you think I can find a way home if I pray to Maelich?" a bit of urgency seeped into Cialia's tone.

"Pray?" Oma laughed again before adding, "You don't need to pray to learn anything from Maelich. All you need is a desire to know."

"She's right about that," Zizy agreed, "Oma was correct when she said you can't trust unicorns. They aren't dishonest, but they really don't know anything about anything."

"The only way out of this place is the pit," Oma's voice deepened to something ominous when she said the last two words.

"But I wouldn't go in that place," Zizy added, "Nobody knows where it leads."

Cialia thought for a moment before deciding, "If that is the only way out, then that is where I'm going. Can you take me to this pit?"

"If that is what you really want," Zizy replied with a skeptical tone.

"I can't stay here forever. If this pit is the only way out, it seems my only choice," Cialia shrugged.

"You could stay here forever. There is nothing stopping you," Oma shrugged.

"I don't want to stay here forever," Cialia shook her head slightly as she replied.

Oma nudged Zizy with her elbow and said, "It's your fault. She hates you."

"I do not hate either of you," Cialia dipped her chin down toward the right, "You are both delightful, but I have a mission to complete."

"Nobody cares," Oma smiled as she flew past Cialia's face, hovered behind her and added, "Come. It's this way. Try to keep up."

Cialia followed closely behind Zizy and Oma as they quietly debated what seemed like a million topics. If ever there were a couple who argued more than the two fairies, it would be a miracle. She paid less and less attention to their conversation as the sights around her dragged it away from them. Something that looked like a bird was the first thing that caught her eye. It seemed to swim the currents of the air rather than fly among them. It was white with black stripes that looked like lightning. It glowed like everything else in the odd place. Even the black stripes had this kind of weird, negative glow. The thing's wings looked more like fins. They were long, wide and fleshy.

It had a massive mouth opened wide like an oval sucking in the almost white balls of light that must have been some kind of insect. It had a long and pointy tail that appeared to help steer it through the air.

A cluster of massive mushrooms were the next thing she saw. They smelled like some kind of berry and grew as tall as her waist. They had flat caps of all different colors with spots covering them that were different colors still. She touched one and was immediately surrounded in a cloud of spores that swirled in a sudden current like a cyclone.

"Watch what you touch back there," Oma hollered over her shoulder, "and don't breathe any of that in. You'll grow mushrooms in your guts."

"Shut up, Oma," Zizy scolded before looking back over his shoulder and telling Cialia, "They're harmless, but it would be best to keep your mouth closed and your hands to yourself."

"Are you two a couple?" Cialia asked before adding, "You argue like an old couple who's been together for a thousand years."

"Well, we're a couple of gidim," Zizy replied.

"Gross," Oma said before making some gagging sounds. Then she added, "She means like we're together."

"Oh, that is gross," Zizy frowned, "No, indeed. Fairies don't do that. We're different than unicorns or the like. That is another good reason not to trust them."

Then a massive animal leapt from the trees and sailed high over Cialia's head. It slightly resembled a fallon, but it was at least three times the size. The rack on its head was nearly five feet across and looked like two massive shovels with several points protruding from them. It had yellow fur that glowed almost like the midday sun, and that massive rack glowed just as brightly in a light purple. It bellowed as it flew through the air and touched down only for a moment before leaping over a bush. Then it was gone.

"What was that thing?" Cialia gasped.

"That was a moose," Oma sounded slightly shocked, "Have you never seen a moose before?"

"Moose are my favorite," Zizy added with the same kind of shocked awe that dripped from Cialia's tone when she gasped, "They are so big and majestic."

"We don't have those where I come from," Cialia's tone still echoed her awe at the massive thing.

"Good thing. They are disgusting. They crap all over the place,"

Oma said before adding a bunch of gagging sounds. Then she added, "You're lucky you didn't get trampled by that beast."

Zizy laughed almost as hard as Oma had laughed when teasing Cialia by the brook before he apologized, "Please forgive me. I know it's rude to laugh at a guest, but something just occurred to me. This mission you're on is obviously the most important thing in the whole world to you. Who will do it if you get hit by a moose?"

"Hit by a moose!" Oma shrieked before racing wild circles around Cialia's head only stopping to laugh at her again and ask, "What if you get hit by a moose?"

"Well," Cialia laughed back in Oma's face despite the slight, "I suppose the mission will be yours then. It must be completed, being far too important to ignore, and the two of you are the only other two creatures anywhere who know of it. If I get hit by a moose, you will have to complete the mission in my stead. That means you'll have to dive into that pit you're so afraid."

"I'm not going in that pit," Oma shook her head and zipped off to fly next to Zizy.

"She's right though. It does sound like an important mission. Somebody must do it," Zizy said to Oma before turning back toward Cialia and adding, "Please be careful back there. Don't get hit by a moose."

"I shall do my best," Cialia chuckled.

She was just about to ask after a strange shrub that glowed the most brilliant red she'd ever seen, and seemed to be breathing, when Zizy yelled, "Here we are. That's the pit."

"And the end of all your days, Cialia the traveler from some other world on a useless mission to nowhere that will never mean anything to anybody after you are ground up in the swirling pit of doom," Oma loudly proclaimed before melting back into laughter.

"That is terribly rude," Cialia frowned. Oma's teasing suddenly seemed less funny and just downright cruel.

"Is it rude if I think it's true?" Oma asked without ceasing her laughter one bit.

"It is," Zizy scolded before looking at Cialia and continuing, "but I agree with her. Forget getting hit by a moose. You're probably going to die in that pit. I can't watch. Farewell, Cialia. Good luck with the rest of your journey. I hope you don't die."

"I hope you don't die too," Oma frowned slightly before flashing a wide smile and adding, "Please come again when you have less time and fewer questions."

Then they were gone, flashing away as quickly as they had arrived. "Good-bye," she called after them, half expecting some cheeky response from Oma that would start another debate with Zizy, but they were really gone. She was alone.

She turned back to the spot where the two gidim or fairies, or whatever the tiny creatures were, had led her, but there was nothing there except a big circle of dirt. It would seem unexceptional anywhere else, but in this place, it was very exceptional. It was the only spot she'd seen that didn't glow some kind of color. It just looked like dirt bathed in the glow of the odd plants and flowers around it. It was a clearing for sure, but it wasn't any kind of pit. Perhaps Zizy and Oma had lied about the place, or perhaps she needed to do something to access the pit. Perhaps if she stepped into the circle, something would happen to open the thing.

Staring at the exceptional circle, which was only exceptional due to its dramatic difference from everything around it, proved rather useless. It hadn't done anything in the several moments she'd been standing there. She lifted her foot to step inside the circle, but something stopped her. It wasn't a premonition or anything like that, just a feeling. It was an odd sensation, nothing she'd ever felt before, but it held her foot fast just a few inches above the ground. She felt dizzy, like the ground beneath her swayed, but she was certain there was no movement.

It suddenly occurred to her that she was afraid. It had been so long since she'd felt anything like that for herself. She couldn't get her foot to budge, but she refused to put it down. A circle of dirt was nothing to fear. She'd fought gods and monsters and wicked men. None of those battles stole her breath and left her in such a tipsy turvy state as the unremarkable ground before her. As she stood there trembling with effort, unable to move her foot forward and unwilling to put it down, she realized why the thing seemed so terrifying. She didn't know, not what was going to happen or where she would end up if the circle opened to swallow her.

It took longer than she would have liked, but logic finally earned the upper hand on emotion. Perhaps it wasn't logic at all. Maybe it was determination. Whether one of those, or something else entirely, her foot finally began to obey her commands. It was a slow step after the thing finally budged, but moments later that foot was firmly planted just inside the very edge of the circle. Nothing happened.

She flopped down onto the dirt and with a frustrated laugh said, "Where is this horrifying pit of doom? I'd rather be ground up to bits than sit here with nowhere to go."

Orange light suddenly shined brilliantly before her. Oma's voice was sweet, as she said, "You are as dense as a boulder."

Zizy raced in beside her trailing bright blue light and scolded Oma, "You should be as quiet as one." Then he cast his gaze down at Cialia and said, "Have a look around before you give up."

Then, as quickly as they had arrived, they were both gone, and Cialia was alone again. She looked all around her. There was nothing. She had to be missing something. She leaned her head back and ran her hands roughly over her hair as she sighed. There it was. Directly above the circle in precisely the same diameter. It looked like a swirling mass of nighttime sky, stars spinning together in a whirlpool of space dust spinning ever higher into nothing. Perhaps Oma was correct, she was as dense as a boulder, but what kind of pit lies above?

She stared into the thing. It drew her gaze in until her eyes spun in unison with its movement. What had at first appeared to be white dots amid a perfectly black nighttime sky grew colorful. There could have been planets and moons and comets and even asteroids swept up and swirling in the whirlpool of space. Each separate sparkle was unique in color, size, and saturation like a rainbow blasted to tiny bits. Before long, she could see nothing but the parade of colors slowly spinning into some terminating point well beyond her sight or comprehension.

Then she was in it, no longer staring up into some colorful abyss but twisting like a helpless flower swept up into a whirling gale. Even as she spun helplessly among the stars, there was no fear. It seemed an odd thing. She could be racing toward some terrible doom, and the thought didn't frighten her in the least when only moments prior the prospect of stepping on some random bit of dirt had her petrified. The mind was such a troublesome thing. Despite everything she'd learned about herself and all the various dimensions of the world she occupied, she still couldn't understand or control emotion. No matter how enlightened she became, emotions remained chaotic refusing to be controlled or even remotely swayed by logic or understanding.

Her speed slowly increased until she was racing. She sped past stars burning like fireballs in blackness and vomiting massive, crooked arcs of liquid flame like lava. Comets spun past. Their tails curled by as they circled around her. It seemed the velocity of her own spin created some kind of gravity as it increased in direct conjunction with her speed deeper into darkness. She flew past rocky planets close enough to see the colorful stones and dust covering their faces. It all occurred to her in minute detail that seemed impossible as fast as she moved. Even the rocks—smaller than everything else but still massive—were so clear to her she could make out every lump on their surfaces as they slammed into each other in some chaotic battle of destruction, cracking one another apart and exploding into bits.

There were no sounds as she careened faster and faster into depths unknown except something which resembled a howling wind. It was difficult to know whether the wind existed on its own or if it were the result of her body racing through still air, but it steadily gained volume until it sounded like a living beast bellowing out some sad song of lament or some angry threat of violence.

Everything smelled hot. A heavy saturation of sulfur was the strongest odor which invaded her sinuses, but it wasn't alone in its assault. Something like burning metal molten in a forge occurred to her. Then the smell of nuts roasted on open flame swirled in to cavort with the rest. None of it was pleasing, but she was suddenly filled with an odd sense of joy.

Then it all ceased. The lights, the sounds, the smells, even the icy air freezing her skin all ended in unison, and everything was pitch. She closed her eyes briefly. When they opened, she was back in what appeared to be the clearing where she debated that overly particular voice about which words were the correct ones to use when asking a question or making a statement, but it wasn't quite that place. No fog or mist clung to the ground she found herself seated cross-legged upon. The trees looked natural with rough bark and light slipping in between their trunks. There were clouds in the sky and an obvious source of light.

"I wondered where you had gotten off to," Maelich's voice was calm behind her, "I was hoping we could take a moment to talk. It was more than hope. I wished for it. Can we speak?"

His gall was infuriating. Cialia slowly rose to her feet and turned to face her brother. He sat upon a giant boulder that resembled the one she had sat upon when she'd first arrived in this odd world, but it was as different as the trees were from that place. He wore his armor, and despite his casual posture, his sword was in his hand like he was ready for a fight.

"You couldn't beat me with fire, and your blade is no match for mine. You can't stop me. Get out of my way, Maelich. Release me from the prison of your mind," Cialia drew her swords as she spoke.

Maelich remained seated as he replied, "We're not in my mind, and I am just as trapped in this place as you."

"Don't toy with me," she snapped as she let her hands drop from a battle-ready position to her sides, "Everyone in this place thinks you're a god. Could we be anywhere else but in your head where you've exalted yourself to the position of the beginning and end, the creator, the everything, a formless consciousness without which nothing is possible? I feel sorry for you."

"I thought the same at first when I'd arrived, but this is not my own mind, perhaps an extension of it, but this was not my intention. I sought only to prevent you from destroying me and a moment to speak quietly with you," he shook his head.

Cialia's eyes narrowed as she pierced him with her gaze. If it were a lie he spoke, his expression hid the deception expertly. She pressed into his mind invading his thoughts. As she examined the ideas forming and floating around in there, she slowly realized he spoke the truth. If they were already in his mind, slipping into it wouldn't make any sense. Perhaps it could be possible, a mind within a mind, but simple logic suggested the contrary.

"I have no secrets from you, sister. This is not my mind," he stood up from the boulder he'd been lounging upon but made no move to attack as he spoke.

"Well, this is not Ouloos," she countered as she raised her swords back up.

"No," he shook his head, "That much is clear. Though I don't completely understand how, it seems in that moment of desperation as I was clinging to life against your fury, I somehow willed this place into existence."

The idea was ridiculous, but he obviously believed it. She'd know if he were lying to her as she strolled about his thoughts. It would explain why the creatures thought he was god. How long had she been trapped there? No more than an hour could have passed since she arrived in the place, yet it seemed the world around her had existed for millennia.

"I wouldn't travel too far down that path," he interrupted her thoughts, "Time is a tricky thing. Contemplating those ideas could drive you mad. What is the difference between a moment and eternity in a place where the rules you're familiar with don't exist?"

"On that we can agree," she finally conceded before asking, "Which one of us will remove you from my path? Will you release me from this place? I don't want to hurt you, but I have things I must do."

"I know," he frowned as he raised his sword, "The things you would do I cannot allow. I would not release you if I could."

"Fine," she'd finally had enough of his self-righteous meddling. Even knowing everything he knew about everything the gods had done to the world they had both sworn to protect, he defended them. It made him no better than them. She sighed deeply as she bent her knees slightly, assumed an attack position, and said, "Maelich, my brother, rightful king of Havenstahl, false Dragon, and failed protector of Ouloos, you know all the wicked machinations of the gods and their cruelty to the creatures you've sworn to protect, yet you stand in the way of their delivery to justice. You have proven as evil and callous as those vile things you protect. I sentence you to die. The next words you speak will be your last."

It was a joyless chuckle he gave her as his chin dropped to his chest and a tear perched upon his eyelid before he replied, "I have failed everyone I love, even you. I deserve no love or forgiveness, but I have found love. I love all creatures of Ouloos for what they are. Not because I have no choice but to feel this overwhelming emotion, but because I choose to give it freely without limit or condition. I love you, sweet sister, as you stand before me ready to execute the sentence you have spoken against me; I love the creatures who slither on their bellies through the muck and the creatures who sail the blustery gales high above the ground; I love men and dwarves, trogmortem and giants, even grongs and amatilazo; I love Dragons; and I even love the gods. I stand above none as I weep with all and implore you to change your mind about taking any further life from Ouloos. Please, sister, change your mind."

"I changed my mind when I decided to protect all creatures of Ouloos from gods you defend with your childish proclamations of love," she nearly growled through clenched teeth before adding, "It breaks my heart to do this. Good-bye, my love."

Her back foot was pushing off the soft ground before the last word even left her mouth, propelling her forward with speed and force.

Three long strides later, she shallowly slashed at the top of his head with her lead hand. It wouldn't have been more than a tap on his scalp, but it earned the desired result. He brought his blade up to block the blow while she slashed at his belly with her other sword. The tip of her blade narrowly missed carving into his flesh as he fell backward, curling his torso away from the attack.

"Cialia, please," he shouted as he stumbled back into the boulder he had been resting upon moments prior.

She ignored his pleas. She had given him more than enough opportunities to relent, and he had said everything she would allow him to say. She lunged at his chest with her forward hand before lunging with the sword in her other hand. He parried the first and spun to his right to avoid the second.

The effort to escape her blade sent him tumbling again, this time to the ground. She gave him no chance to recover, leaping high into the air after finishing her lunge. By the time he came to rest on his back, she was at the apex of her flight. She flipped both her swords in her hands to achieve a reverse grip on the handles and bore down on her brother's chest. He rolled right a split second before her blades would have cracked his sternum and pierced his heart. Instead, they sliced deep enough into the dirt that it took her precious moments to free them and slash with two backhands at Maelich's throat.

Maelich's downward slash began high above his head and ended when it connected with Cialia' two blades a moment before they separated. The move saved his throat and trapped her swords under the weight of his. They struggled there for a moment with their blades locked together. For everything her brother wasn't, he was strong. She pushed against him with all her might, but he held fast. Unable to overcome him, she dragged a deep breath in through her nose, centered her spirit, and called her flame. It failed to come. No fire swirled around her arms or her chest, and no flames rained down from the sky or erupted from the dirt beneath them.

"How are you blocking my flame?" she shouted the question.

"I'm not. My flame has failed me too," he grunted, "Dragon's flame must not exist in this world."

"Ridiculous," she growled back, "You can't steal my flame. It is a part of me regardless of what world or realm I occupy."

His resistance against her slowly diminished. She was breaking him down. She bent her knees and pushed against him with all her might.

In that precise moment, he stopped pushing completely, stepped to his left, and shot his leg out. Her momentum carried her forward two awkward and unsteady steps until her ankles connected with his. The ground came up to greet her as she rolled onto her shoulder and popped back up to her feet. Ten feet separated them by the time she righted herself and turned to go back on the attack.

"I don't know the rules here anymore than you," Maelich smiled as he slashed through a couple techniques that ended in a defensive stance, "I am certain our flames remain within both of us, but you cannot bend the rules until you learn them. My subconscious must have taken control, because I willed none of this."

Cialia dug her rear foot into the dirt preparing to launch herself at him and attack again, but she paused. As much as she hated to admit it, without the fury of her flame, he was stronger than her. She'd always been better than him with swords, but sheer force would be insufficient against him. It had been a time since she'd had cause to use her blades. She'd have to take a different tact. The plan materialized as she took her first step toward him.

She raced at him, covering the space between them in barely more than a second. The confident glint in his eyes proved he expected another brute force attack. Instead, she feinted with a thrust and planted her feet. Then she slashed at him with a backhand as he spun left just as she expected he would. His sword barely made it around to parry her blow. She followed with an overhand slash swinging down at the top of his head. He blocked that too. Then, instead of slashing again at his chest—a move she was sure he'd expect—she stepped toward him with her left foot and planted her right foot into his gut just below his sternum.

The blow knocked the wind out of him and bent him at the waist. She watched the confidence flee from his eyes as he slashed wildly to defend himself. Her mark was clear. She could have sliced through it twenty times before he could have done anything to stop it. A small part of her held that killing blow for just a moment. She didn't want to kill him, but he wouldn't stop interfering for as long as he was able. She flicked a forehand slash with her right hand.

A moment later, her brother's sword was flipping through the air away from her with his severed hand still gripping its handle. Her eyes slammed shut to avoid the blood that splattered her face, pulsing wildly from his wrist. She wiped the gore from her cheeks and forehead with her sleeve to clear her eyes and pushed him to the ground. He struggled against her, but his movements were random and uncalculated. He must have been panicking from shock.

"You'll live," she whispered loudly as she yanked the sleeve from his shirt, "but only if you calm down so I can wrap this."

She didn't expect it when his eyes went wide as two moons, and he sat straight up to move them immediately before hers. Then he took the hand that was still attached to his body, slammed it against her forehead, and shouted, "Wait!"

A moment later she could feel him stomping into her mind. "Where is it?" She heard him shout, but the sound came from inside her head. "Here," his voice called out again. It sounded like a door opening and everything before her changed.

Wind pushed the leaves of the trees high above her, motivating them into a fast waltz that played madness on the shadows they cast on the clearing below, but she couldn't feel it. She remembered the day, but details were missing. That wind had caught up her hair and tossed it about while ruffling her gown. She felt none of it. Nor could she smell the oddly pleasing mixture of moss, wildflowers, decomposing leaves, sweaty recruits, and oily metal. She could plainly see those green recruits clad in the red of Druindahl, that they had yet to earn, crashing those oily blades against each other, but she couldn't smell or hear any of it.

"Why are you showing me this?" she called out.

"So you can remember," Maelich's voice replied from no single point.

She was just about to push back against him and leave the memory behind when she noticed herself. Her back was to her. It was odd seeing herself like that. Was that what she looked like, or was her mind making up details to fill in things she couldn't possibly know? It made little difference. The scene would be the same as she recalled.

Leisha and Boringas stood before her. That had been a fruitless debate. They both would have been overjoyed if she would have just given up and given in to Boringas' desires. He was a good man, and she did love him. But she could never live the life he wanted.

They had implored her to leave Kaldumahn and Moshat alone as if those two were any different than Kallum and Brerto. They were all evil, using the creatures who worshipped them faithfully to act out their intrigues against each other. All they cared for was the worship of those poor souls. They held no love for them, nor did they offer anything in return. The protection they promised was a lie.

"If you're trying to change my mind, it won't work," she called out again.

Maelich offered no response. She thought of calling out again, but a bright flash distracted her. Once it dimmed, Kaldumahn stood before that memory of herself. She recalled how he attempted to counsel her as if she were merely a child with no understanding of the world around her. Of course, she knew now it had been a trap, but at that moment beneath her beloved city she was convinced she would destroy him.

The battle appeared different from this vantage point. His staff glowed with the same godly light, and his eyes swirled in their macabre and troubling way, but she appeared completely still with her arms out before her. Aside from a slight trembling from the effort of pressing into his awareness with her mind, it looked like she was just standing there completely still. She knew that wasn't at all what was happening. Her flame was slithering along her awareness like snakes gliding across wet branches, invading every shred of his understanding, even pressing into his cells. It would have burned him up from the inside had she released it, but the coward hadn't been alone. Moshat was there hiding just outside the spectrum of visible light to distract her.

She saw the flames swirl around her arms. Her mother had called out to her, but she couldn't recall the exact words she chose. Whatever those words had been, they didn't sway her. She saw the flames explode from her arms like winds of fire. Something had tugged her in that moment, pulling her shoulders back and ruining her aim. Moshat had materialized in that moment to whisk Kaldumahn away, and both the gods were gone. She had chased them. It looked like she stepped into some imaginary doorway as she vanished into the scenery.

"Why show me a memory still fresh enough that I recall every important detail about it?" she called out.

"This is not your memory," Maelich's voice surrounded her, "This is no one memory at all. It is a collective recollection borrowed from the very soul of Ouloos."

She was about to argue about the impossibility of what he'd just said when the canopy before her caught fire. It was immediate. The flames didn't grow out of a smoldering ember to creep slowly into a raging blaze, it exploded in an all-consuming ball of furious flame. The concussion of the blast knocked some men to the ground. Others watched in horror as their city in the trees burned. Madness settled into the clearing. Spooked horses charged off in every direction. One of them knocked Boringas to the ground and left him motionless. Her mother stared up at the blazing canopy for a moment before charging toward the cart that would lift her up to her burning city in the tress.

"No!" Cialia cried out, but Leisha boarded the cart anyway.

"You cannot change the past, Cialia," Maelich's voice surrounded her once again, "No one can hear you. Come. There is more."

She was suddenly in the flames high up in the canopy. She watched as her mother covered her mouth with a sleeve that was slowly catching flame as she ducked, crawled, and rolled across the smoking walkway trying to avoid the fire raging all around her. She found some children huddled up together and crying out in fear. Her mother led them through the smoke and fire back to the waiting cart that would lower them to safety and away from the blazing branches and walkways of Druindahl. There were so few with her, she wondered how many of the children had died from her flame. The realization of what Maelich was trying to show her suddenly sunk in as she watched Leisha send the cart down and turn back toward the flames.

"Go with them," she yelled in her mother's face, but saw no reaction to her plea.

Her mother returned twice with small groups of children. The first group made it to the cart. The second was blocked when a thick, blazing branch crashed into the walkway and smashed it to fiery bits. Tears rained down Cialia's cheeks as she watched her mother pull the three terrified children closer to her, hugging them tight and hiding their eyes from the terror before them. Her gown began burning first, then her hair. She didn't scream or cry out. Cialia couldn't hear the words her mother spoke, but her expression made it clear. She sat there soothing them as they burned within her arms. The few moments it took for the small group to burn completely to ash as Cialia sobbed before them unable to do anything to stop it seemed an eternity.

Then they were gone, all of them, the trees, the flames, and the ashes of children burned to nothing floating among currents heated by her flame; and she was back in the clearing sitting cross-legged and leaning against the boulder Maelich had sat upon before they battled. He sat before her in the same cross-legged manner. His arm had stopped bleeding. It wasn't any magic or the result of his power. It looked like he had fashioned a rude tourniquet out of his belt.

"I am done fighting with you and will interfere with your mission no more," Maelich said quietly, "I am ready to submit to the sentence you've spoken against me. I deserve death for everything I've done."

Cialia felt numb as she replied quietly, "I'm no better than the gods."

Her mother's perfect face jumped into her mind. It was an old memory back when her soft, brown eyes smiled with hope. If only she could go back to that place, back to her childhood in Druindahl when all she cared about was sword training and exploring the vast woods beneath her city, back before she had found her flame. As those smiling eyes widened in horror before drifting away like ash, other faces came. They surrounded her, all their eyes brimming with hope before bulging in terror and ultimately floating away, spent like dusty debris, victims of her flame, thousands of faces, and she could name them all.

"Is it finished?" he asked quietly.

"No one else will die in the name of justice," the words flopped from her mouth as her mind remained twisted up in the silent yet damning accusations those faces made against her.

"What will you do instead?" he asked. The forgiveness in his eyes turned her stomach.

She hadn't thought about that. What would she do when her mission was done? Perhaps she never truly believed she could do it. Had she perished in the effort, there would be no reason to do anything. But that couldn't be it. She hadn't planned to rule. Her only goal was to protect all creatures of Ouloos by destroying the vilest things ever created by Coeptus, the gods. She failed at both. Thousands died for her justice, and two gods yet lived.

"I will save Ouloos from the real terror darkening her dreams, me. I have judged myself in these few moments of clarity, thank you for that, and my sentence is to burn in the very flame I used to terrorize this world," she finally said, her tone as numb as her expression.

"Coward!" Maelich shouted, suddenly animated.

"How dare you!" she shouted back at him and his gall, "You call me a coward? You are the one who hid away from your responsibilities and left me alone to defend our world in your stead."

"I did! I am guilty of all that you say," he agreed as he spread his arms out wide losing some blood from his severed wrist in the process,

"It would have been easy to take my own life, and it would be a relief if you would judge and sentence me. But that wouldn't be the justice I deserve. Would it?"

"No," Cialia's gaze dropped to the ground as her tone dropped with it, "You deserve to feel that pain for the rest of your days."

"I do, and so do you," he pointed at her with the stump that used to house his right hand, "So, what do we do next?"

"Better," she mumbled as she crawled toward him and added, "Now, let's fix this hand."

CHAPTER 15

FIRE AND MAGIC

A corridor of blue light spun and twisted before him. It seemed to stretch on forever, but it didn't. It was just another illusion of time. Whenever he cut holes in reality to break the rules and skip a useless journey, no actual distance was traveled. He simply moved from one point to another. The sweet pungent aroma wafting about the swirling currents was no illusion. Messing with elemental rules and bending them to suit a purpose tended to mix those elements up and rub them together in unnatural ways.

The swirling corridor of blue light closed behind Hagen when he stepped out of it and into a world that looked like a warzone. Chaos reigned on this side of the Lake, but a spell cast summers prior by a magician whose powers rivaled the gods assured the chaos would constantly be challenged by the order he had forced upon it. The land which surrounded Hagen was a testament to that very fact. It appeared a dry and cracked desert, as unwelcoming a terrain as any man could imagine. It remained constant for a distance. Beyond that was a wild battle between the order forced upon a handful of acres and the unbridled chaos that reigned past its edges. It was almost a perfect arc terminating at the very edge of the world where a massive tower should have stood. All along that arc, the land crumbled as it was constantly replenished by a dead man's spell so strong even the gods couldn't break it if they desired.

Apprehension coiled around Hagen's spine as he gazed out at the macabre skyscape beyond the spot where a massive, black tower should have stood. It was impossible to tell if the heavenly bodies zigging and zagging about a kaleidoscope of colors that made no sense together were stars or planets or comets or some other incomprehensible things which should never exist in any reality as they smashed against one another and careened in directions which didn't fit their velocity or trajectory at all. Wild, windless howls occurred for no reason, at one moment sounding like a monstrous beast and the next like flowing water. There was no fire around, yet burning wood filled his sinuses a moment before oily leather which gave way to volcanic sulfur which was quickly overcome by wildflowers and wine. All of it combined to make his skin tighten into bumps. This was the very place where Merkhal had defeated him. Everyone who spoke of the battle he'd had with that magician sung his praises as if he'd won the fight, but he knew the truth. Merkhal broke him that day and killed magic for him until Antopy reminded him of who he really was.

The creature hiding in the tower he couldn't see just then made Merkhal look like a simple scam artist with card tricks and sleights of hand that could astound only the dullest of dolts. Geillan was a power like Ouloos had never seen. Of course, Antopy had been correct. He would lose, but he had to try. He couldn't explain it to her when she implored him to forget his mission. He couldn't even explain it to himself as he stood there trembling before madness. But he couldn't turn away. There had to be order on Ouloos. He had to try.

"PAD-E-ZE!" His voice was like a chorus flowing over the cracked land surrounding him.

The air before him shimmered. It seemed unremarkable amongst the chaos raging beyond it, but he could see the change. The tower slowly materialized before him. Oily, black stones more massive than any group of men or even giants could manipulate piled stone on top of stone with such precision it seemed to mock the incoherent mess exploding beyond it. It rose like that, perfect in diameter and shape further into the atmosphere than any structure ever built by men until it terminated in two pillars which sat atop the thing like massive horns. Each of them was carved from the same unnatural oily, black stone in one perfect piece that began wider on the bottom and slanted toward a piercing point.

It was overbearing as it loomed above him scratching a sky full of horrors. A gasp escaped his lungs as memories squeezed the air from him. The sky had been electric that day, purple lightning arcing out from the tower like spiderwebs to cover the dry, cracked land beneath it. The air would sizzle a second before a bolt of that same purple lightning would zig zag toward the ground to blow some suddenly helpless warrior to crispy bits of charred flesh. The bravest men Hagen had ever known shook with fear when faced with Merkhal's power as that old wizard stood brazen atop the same tower Hagen stared at with eyes consumed by the same kind of terror.

He hadn't been afraid that day, not for himself. Battling Merkhal had been a test he wanted back in those days, the only rival to his own power—besides his sister who cared very little to meddle in the affairs of men—hiding out at the edge of time and reality. When he stalked out onto that cracked landscape, the sky crackled with blue electricity. It hummed and sparked into a dome above those brave soldiers who fled like scared children at the sound of father's belt slapping a warning against a bureau. It only took moments for him to be alone on the battlefield when Merkhal's power surged against him.

He could have demurred and fled beneath the dome of protection he'd cast into the air like a net to save the riders of Havenstahl, but he didn't. Hubris. That's what it had been. He wanted the test. He wanted to prove once and for all that Merkhal was not the terror of Ouloos. It was him. He pushed back with all his might. Based on the energy pressing down on him, the power of his attack should have been enough to blast a hole in reality and topple that perfect tower into a pile of crumbling rock. That hadn't happened. Instead, Merkhal's power surged against him, evaporating his dome as quickly as he could reinforce it while he slowly lost ground.

The force of Merkhal's will wasn't what finally broke him that day. He liked to tell himself a different story, but he would have lost that day anyway, even without the horrid images that wizard showed him. Those were what broke him though. At first it was just gore, faces he recognized with pieces missing, a skull with snakes slithering in and about all the various holes. Those he could ignore as illusions, visions injected by a cheat who refused to battle him with nothing but raw energy and an expert control of the elements. But when the sounds and smells came, the stench of rot combined with the slurping and muddy crackle of bones and cartilage and tendons popping, ripping, and shredding made his stomach heave and destroyed his focus. The last was a vision of a Dragon standing victorious atop the tower with wings spread wide and belching fire into the sky. It was a premonition.

He'd known it then but failed to recognize it. That moment when his strength crumbled and he fled in the face of a power greater than anything he'd ever encountered, he was looking forward in time to the battle he was walking toward.

Geillan was that Dragon. Of course, that man wouldn't take the literal form of a Dragon and perch upon the tower, but that vision had been symbolic of this day. Somehow, Merkhal must have had clairvoyance enough to realize he would ultimately lose his life to powers greater than himself, but it hadn't been that day. That battle had been his greatest victory.

Hagen shuffled those memories to a dark place hidden in the depths of his mind, along with the fear which accompanied them. His eyes sparked with energy like flowing blue fire crackling amid a scent of ozone. He spread his arms wide at the same moment and that same blue energy sparked among his fingertips like lightning bolts arcing from digit to digit. A blue circle of the same energy swirled above his head as he shouted with a voice like thunder, "BARAQU!"

Energy surrounded the tower, blazing from its top to its bottom like chaotic flame and zig zagging toward it in crackling bolts to explode against it from all angles. The sky above lit up with that blue light brighter than even the boldest lights and colors blazing beyond in the macabre skyscape. Everything glowed a light blue that was brighter than a million suns. It blazed so brilliantly it completely chased away all shadow.

Hagen's cheeks shook as spittle formed at the corners of his mouth, and his body trembled with effort. He fell to his knees pressing harder and harder, reaching deep into his very soul to draw every speck of power the universe and even Coeptus had to spare for him. The tower stood strong.

"Now that looks excruciating," Antopy's voice sounded sweet like a herald of the dawn's first song of the morning despite volume great enough to overcome the crackling of energy, cracks of thunder, and the roar of elemental power blazing like fire.

"You could help," Hagen grunted in a choppy cadence while maintaining his focus.

"You know I cannot," she declined before imploring, "You also know it is not in my nature to beg, but that is what I am here to do. Please turn back, my dear brother. You have only just returned to me."

"And you know that is something I cannot do," he growled with effort.

"Please, come home with me," she asked again, "This will not be merely a demoralizing defeat like Merkhal. I mean, it will be that. It will be a defeat, and it will be demoralizing. But it will also be your end. You will not survive this. He will blast you to oblivion. He won't just kill you. You will cease to exist completely."

"I am unafraid," his tone remained beyond his control.

"Fine," the slightest hint of frustration marred the sweet melody of her voice, "Then just be reasonable. The destroyer must be allowed to find his fate. You risk everything. If you succeed, you doom us all to oblivion, and if you fail, you doom me to live out the rest of my days without you."

"I am sorry, sweet Antopy, I love you above all else in this world, but this is something I must do. The destroyer must be stopped," he relented just long enough to speak plainly to her with strong control of his voice, "Good-bye, sweet sister."

He smiled at the tear she offered, just one. It dribbled from her eye to rest on the softness of her cheek as she said, "Farewell, my love. I expect this will be the last time our paths cross. I hope whatever your outcome you finally find peace with whatever realm you occupy."

Then she was gone, and Hagen redoubled his efforts. The blue energy blazing like flame up and down the tower, the arcs of lightning, and random explosions bursting all about the length of it remained, but a swirling wind joined the chaos. Hagen's eyes grew as blue as the energy he battered the tower with as he called the winds to tear at the massive rock. The tower swayed ever so slightly, but no stone separated even the minutest bit from any other.

Geillan lounged in a gaudy, prang throne on a large raft of prang timbers. Both the throne and the planks of the massive raft glowed like smoldering fire beneath a red sun. The sky was like green foam above peaceful, purple water that seemingly extended forever in every direction. The dead-eyed men danced in a circle before him. Their movements were crude and grotesque, as they twisted their bodies into unnatural shapes to a horrific melody that boomed all about them with no logical timing or proper cadence. No instrument could make such a repugnant sound. It was like a million souls crying out in pitiable desperation.

It was boring. He was tired of it all. After destroying Ijilv and trapping that vile creature's power and essence within him, his first thought had been to cast out and destroy everything that supposed god had attempted to build and control, but something caused him pause. It was an odd and unfamiliar sensation. His heartbeat had quickened just at the thought, and he struggled to get a breath into his lungs. None of it made sense. He didn't even need to breathe in this imaginary world within his own head. His body remained safe hovering between the four obelisks at the top of the tower, the bed and prison Ijilv had built for him. Yet, in that moment of contemplation, he felt panic.

It took a great deal of searching, scouring the thoughts and memories floating about the ether to realize it had been the first time he'd felt fear. It seemed unfounded, even silly, as he sat watching his dead companions dance their horrid waltz of madness before him. There was nothing in all of Ouloos that could possibly match his power besides his father and that bastard's wicked sister. Even those two Dragons were no match for him. He had both the power of Dragons and the elemental knowledge and prowess of the gods. All would bow before him. He knew this. Yet, he still felt afraid at that moment and ever since. What if they burned him in the same fire with which he'd burned his mother. He felt her pain as he burned her to dust, mind numbing and terrifying. It was like ice and fire attacked each individual cell in unison, freezing and burning, while dull needles probed those same cells at the same time, like stabbing a nerve. It hadn't been torture. He had intended to kill her, to make her feel the fear his supposed father had felt while allegedly hiding from her at the top of his tower. It had all been a lie.

That lie deserved punishment. He had destroyed him, locked him away in his own prison, and stolen his power. Somehow, none of that seemed punishment enough. That wicked thing should feel every lie he ever told like a deep cut on his skin. He should feel terror akin to the fear he'd instilled in Geillan all those summers past, false fear, a lie about his mother. Ijilv would feel all those things.

Geillan waved his right arm in an arc over his head, and the dead-eyed men dropped where they stood, ceasing their dance immediately to lounge before him looking out at the calm, purple water. Then he reached out before him with his left hand and closed his fist as if he were grabbing something. Once his fist was tightly clenched, he pulled it back toward his face. A moment later, five gods stood before his raft above the purple water. There was no platform beneath them, just calm waves gently lapping their feet and moistening the bottoms of their perfect robes. Ijilv stood at the center of them with Kallum and Moshat to his right, and Kaldumahn and Brerto to his left.

Geillan offered a warm smile as he addressed them in a loving tone, "Dear father and my lovely uncles, how are you enjoying this paradise I've created for you?"

"You have created nothing. You are a child," Ijilv's tone suggested defiance, but Geillan knew it was fear dripping off his words like fat melting off a hunk of roasting meat.

He ignored the jibes as he continued, "Did you enjoy fishing? It seemed a fitting activity. My father kept me locked in this place with fishing as my only distraction. Did you hook into any that put up a worthy fight?"

"You are a coward, boy," Kallum grumbled, "If I owned the power you obviously possess, Ouloos would already be a memory."

"If you had that boy's power, Ouloos would be alive and well, and you'd be damning the name of whomever had outsmarted you," Brerto snapped at Kallum before turning his attention to Geillan, "Still, the moron has a point. You sit here on that throne with no one to worship you but soulless carcasses whose only thoughts come from your mind. You are completely alone. Is that why you're afraid?"

"He fears the real Dragons, Maelich and Cialia. You can almost taste it in the air as it oozes off him," Moshat spat in response.

"You are all old fools," Geillan measured his tone, but failed to completely hide his anger from them. Despite being raised by a liar, a vile wretch of a thing, he had no experience with dishonesty.

"Well, are you going to dazzle us with your brilliance or continue to dumbly stare at us?" Kaldumahn finally asked.

"I am in no hurry," Geillan's response was quick and short. Then he added, "I have much left to learn about the world I will soon destroy. One thing I have already determined, is that time is meaningless," he paused as the color of his eyes bled into a fiery red and he finished, "and I have more I want to do in this place."

Ijilv was the first to change. His arms flapped into mighty wings as his body grew until it had quadrupled in size and feathers covered it. Then his head stretched into a massive and mighty, hooked beak. A groan escaped him as he finished morphing into the beast. In two flaps of those mighty wings, he was racing away only feet above the purple water. He remained so close to it, a wake of frothy violet stretched out behind him.

The eagle was the next to change. Kallum slowly morphed just as Ijilv had and immediately gave chase. Then Kaldumahn and Brerto stretched and grew into the great silver lion and the mighty white tiger. Both leapt up into the quiet air before tearing into it with enormous and powerful paws as if it were soft dirt.

"You'll have us destroy him for your amusement?" Moshat asked before morphing into the mighty bear. Then he strained to turn his head back to Geillan, and added, "You should destroy him yourself, lazy coward," before tearing off into the sky in pursuit of Ijilv.

The great hawk had earned too much of a lead on his brothers—he was already the fastest among them, and he'd had a head start—so Geillan robbed his wings of the smooth currents they'd been soaring on and replaced them with a violently swirling gust. The hawk spun ever skyward as the great eagle closed the distance.

"He controls my every move," Kallum shouted as he raced by Ijilv slicing deep into his flesh with talons as sharp as they were strong.

Ijilv managed to snatch a hunk of flesh off the eagle with his beak before responding, "As he does mine. He will have you all destroy me for his amusement."

Brerto's jaws nearly snapped on the hawk's body, but Ijilv twisted out of the way while the white tiger tumbled by him. Ijilv hadn't time to recover before the silver lion raced by him, taking half a wing with him. The hawk cried out in pain as he spun wildly, barely able to maintain his flight. A moment later, Moshat, the mighty bear who lumbers about the north woods, pounded into the great hawk. The bear's jaws clamped tightly down on the massive bird's belly as his momentum carried them further up into a seafoam sky.

Lightning arced across the sky close enough to singe Moshat's fur. The thunderclap that followed was immediate and deafening. More bolts came until they spiderwebbed across the air above arcing out to blast the combatants as they helplessly brutalized the hawk. The silver lion was cast into the purple waves as Brerto was sent careening away from all of them only to be struck several more times as he toppled through the air.

"He toys with us," Ijilv cried out.

Geillan didn't bother responding. He didn't care what any of them thought, but the lightning was not his creation. Watching his supposed father battle his brothers was amusing. They all deserved every sweet morsel of suffering he offered them, but he would be the author of their pain. As pleasing as it was to smell their fur singe and hear their cries of agony as lightning stung their flesh, no one else should have any power in this place.

"Stop," he shouted across the water, his words booming and echoing above the suddenly wild surf. The moment the word left his mouth, all five gods battling above the never-ending waters of the lake abandoned their animalistic forms and returned to the spot where they had stood before him when he first called them. Strings dropped from the sky and fastened to their wrists and legs. "Dance," he said.

Dance they did as he commanded those strings to drag their limbs up and flop around like marionettes controlled by a madman. He smiled at them as he raised both hands before him, working his fingers wildly as their bodies contorted, bounced, and bent unnaturally. Lightning continued to torment them while they bounced and jumped about.

Geillan left them to their dance as he looked up into the seafoam sky and said, "I shall cower in this tower no longer. It is time."

The stone of the floor felt cool and wet against his back when he woke in the room Ijilv had prepared for him. The obelisks weren't flashing like they had the only other time he'd awoken in that place, that time he had killed innocence in his fiery embrace. No pain he could cause Ijilv would ever make up for the things that bastard had taken from him, but he intended to do his best to exact a fitting revenge. Lightning sizzling and crackling all about the ceiling reminded him his revenge would have to wait. Some power had obviously come calling to challenge him.

He closed his eyes and allowed his awareness to expand beyond the circular room, out into the chaos surrounding it. He knew the man as soon as he saw him trembling there before the tower. It was Hagen a sometimes wizard and sometimes healer whose understanding of Ouloos rivaled even the gods. He'd never met the man, but he immediately knew his entire history. It was much longer than any man's should be, but that wasn't the interesting part. The interesting part about this youthful man whose countenance failed to betray the vast amount of time he'd spent in his own physical experience and held sway over the very elements was that he had been broken once. Standing before the very tower Geillan occupied, that young wizard had battled against another wizard who was vastly more powerful and cracked. He became an old man after that, only recently remembering his former glory.

"It was a foolish thing to return to this place," Geillan allowed his voice to vibrate across the cracked lands surrounding the tower, "The man who defeated you all those summers past was just a man, and he nearly destroyed you. You stand before a god and a Dragon. What do you possibly hope to gain?"

He felt one last surge of power from Hagen, and then the attack ended. "I thought I might topple your tower," Hagen replied, "It is strong, but I can feel it cracking under my will."

"The idea is intriguing. What would you gain by toppling this tower?" Geillan asked.

"I am uncertain about my motives with this tower," Hagen's thoughts echoed the sentiments of his words. He really didn't know why he wanted to destroy the tower.

"It is a symbol of your defeat. Merkhal was stronger than you, but you refuse to believe that. You would have tussled with him again if given the chance, but a young girl succeeded where you…" Geillan's words trailed off as he gleaned more information than he'd expected to find haunting the young wizard's mind.

Merkhal had been a terror. He'd constructed the tower and earned the attention of Kallum. The god had made promises to the wizard that he never intended to fulfill, but he did grant the power that wizard sought.

"Kalia defeated your enemy after you had been broken," Geillan finally said, "All you could do is sit idly by and watch. How must that have felt for you? You admired her to the point of jealousy. She became a great warrior, and you shrunk into a bent old healer using recipes instead of any actual power."

"Perhaps, all that is true," Hagen's tone shrunk, "but I am not here to repay a debt to a dead man. I have journeyed across these chaotic lands to stop you from being a simple tool wielded by a false god."

Geillan ignored Hagen's words as he continued, "That girl, Kalia. She was supposed to be the mother of Dragons, but she preferred a warrior's life. Why didn't you press her toward that goal? Was it fear, jealousy?"

"Men should never have the power of Dragons," Hagen finally admitted.

"And yet, we do," Geillan's tone sounded like a smile, "Kalia gave birth to the mother of the twins who would save or destroy Ouloos. The stories you fools believe are fascinating. My father and his sister were never meant to save this world. They were meant to be destroyers, but fools like you and all the gods convinced them otherwise as you all worked to mold this place into what you wanted. The lot of you have succeeded in crafting something utterly vile, and your heroes have removed all the protections this world ever had. This place should not exist. I will destroy it."

"Please, there is beauty here. Help me cultivate it. Be more than the destroyer Ijilv has tricked you into being," Hagen pleaded.

"There is no beauty in your history nor your future," Geillan said as he stepped through swirling fire to stand before the wizard.

"BARAQU!" Hagen shouted as he vanished.

Lightning arced from multiple points in the chaotic skies. Eight bolts converged on Geillan, but none of them connected. He shook his head as he mumbled, "Fool. You cannot hide from me. I am everywhere all at once."

He could feel Hagen's shock as he spun his head to look directly behind him. The spinning head wasn't what earned the wizard's terror. It was the fact he had slipped into a different dimension running parallel merely one vibration right of Ouloos' physical dimension. That had been his plan, attack and hide, strike then flee, slipping from one dimension to another.

The wizard closed his eyes as blue energy flashed out in all directions from his body. In the same moment, he shouted, "NGIR DU!"

Geillan was surprised by the strength of the first attack. The force of it pushed him back. It was different than the lightning. It was more like a charging tubber blasting him in the chest. He slid backward unable to gain any traction on the cracked dirt beneath his feet, and then he was racing. The wizard had called some kind of doorway to rip a hole in the very fabric of reality. Then he was falling.

At first, it seemed Hagen's plan was to dash his body against the ground. It would have been a horrible plan. He'd learned enough about Coeptus and the universe at this point that he completely understood how meaningless the physical body carrying him around really was. It only presented limits if you believed they existed. He held no such belief. However, he quickly realized dashing him against the ground wasn't the wizard's plan at all when he fell right into another doorway swirling beneath him. He went through three doorways before realizing it was the same one. The entrance sat just above the ground while the exit rested one-hundred feet above it. He went in one side, came out the other, fell one-hundred feet, and then did it again. Each time lightning blasted him from all directions.

Only twice more did he allow himself to fall into that doorway before he ceased his motion to hover in the space between the two seeming holes in reality. He could feel Hagen trying to slip away again, but he didn't allow it, holding fast onto the wizard's will. "Enough," he whispered quietly, "I would let you leave to die with the men of your city, but I know you will not relent."

"RIMANIS IM!" the wizard shouted in response.

A wild cyclone of wind pulled up dirt to darken itself as it raced toward Geillan. He simply breathed at the wild gale, and it dissipated immediately. "I admire your desire to exact your will on the events of this place, but I have much to do," Geillan frowned as he released his flame.

He held no malice for the old wizard, so he didn't let the pain last long for him. The attack was quick and precise. He injected his will into each of Hagen's cells simultaneously and allowed them to explode in unison less than a heartbeat later. There was fear stomping about Hagen's mind in that briefest of moments, but his suffering wasn't lengthy, nor was he troubled for too long by the regret Geillan had found there fraternizing with it. One moment Hagen had stood before him locked in the greatest battle of that wizard's long lifetime, and the next moment he was ash floating off into chaos.

CHAPTER 16
A NEW HOME

Two days had passed on the trail, and Daritus' mood improved slightly with each sunrise that kissed his sleeping lids to herald the coming of a new day. He and his small group travelled on foot. Nothany had grumbled a bit about it, Hasujo outright whined, even Kantiim offered up a mild complaint, but everyone else in the group took it in stride. It was a logical choice. There were no horses in all the land that could carry the weight of either Lito-Bi or Hountmytall Moy, and none in the group knew if horses would be welcomed at the Lake. Even if they were, there was no guarantee they'd have adequate food or shelter. None of those reasons were what drove Daritus to decide they would make the journey on foot. Neither Lito-Bi nor Moy would have complained about walking while the men in the group rode, and by all accounts he'd ever heard, all creatures who sought and found the Lake were welcomed. The real reason was a bit more obscure and difficult to define. Part of it was probably about his goal. The more time which passed from learning about Leisha's demise—and more importantly the cause—the less certain he was about his vengeance. Cialia wasn't his blood, but she had always been his daughter. He grew less and less convinced learning to kill a Dragon was truly the point of it. There may have been a bit of nostalgia involved as well. It had been too many summers since his boots had kissed the soft dirt of his forest, and a slow walk through the towering trees seemed a fine distraction.

The sun was high in the sky, drenching the canopy in golden rays that had the green leaves glowing so brightly they were almost yellow.

The warmth of those rays on Daritus' face mixed with the cool though calm currents blowing through the trees were like a fond memory of much happier times. It almost felt as if he wasn't really there on the trail among the trees, just a specter haunting the wood and watching as life happened around him. His heart still ached. It felt like a brick in his chest weighing him down and slowing his stride. Yet, the fresh perfume of wildflowers mixed with moss and even the dirt of the trail all mingled together to make the air smell enough like home to bring the faintest hint of a smile to his face. The grin may have been wider if not for the hint of ignis bloom that coiled around everything else to add just a little more weight to that heavy brick.

"Why would you ever leave this place?" Lito-Bi asked loudly as he breathed in the delicious air, stretched his arms out, and leaned his head back as if he were speaking to the canopy above.

"It is something, isn't it?" Daritus asked as he smiled up at the trogmortem, "There was a time I never thought I would." His smile faded as he added, "Much has changed since then. Too many ghosts hide amongst these trees."

"That's not a ghost," Nothany said as he absently ran his left hand through his short, brown hair—that had earned just the hint of a few curls in the damp, forest air despite how short it was—while he drew his sword with his right hand and jogged a few steps out ahead of the group.

Daritus dropped his gaze back to the trail to see what had raised the young swordsman's hackles enough to draw his weapon. It was a man on horseback who didn't appear to be a threat to anyone who wasn't paying too little attention to a juicy hunk of meat or a sweet cake. The fellow was big and round, too round to be a warrior. His light brown hair seemed it might be blonde if a bit cleaner as it splashed about his red, pudgy cheeks in ratty curls.

"Nothany, hold," Daritus commanded, "This man presents no threat."

"Halt," Nothany commanded the weary looking traveler, ignoring Daritus' instruction.

"Nothany," Daritus' voice dropped to just above a growl, "I am the leader of this campaign, and I gave you a command. Stow that sword, boy."

Sanjo nudged Daritus on the elbow as he whispered in his ear, "I would never presume to question your leadership, but my pupil's instincts are serving him well. When is the last time you were on the trail?"

It had been a time before anyone other than Spang or Kantiim had challenged him, and they earned the right proving themselves time after time in battle after battle. The gall of this man to double down on his pupil's disobedience and defend it nearly had Daritus ready to draw his own sword. The correct words to express his frustration failed to come before Sanjo continued.

"The boy is not rash," Sanjo pressed on in a whisper, "Look at that man. His cloak is tattered and worn as if he's a simple beggar, yet he appears more than well fed. Then have a look at his boots. Those are finely crafted and fairly new. It would take a good bit of coin to earn a pair of boots like that if you didn't steal them. And that horse, where does a disheveled beggar get a mighty steed like that? Give him a moment. Call it training."

They were all valid points. Though the disrespect had him bristling a bit more than it probably should, he couldn't argue against any of the facts Sanjo had pointed out. "Nothany, continue," he finally grunted.

"State your name and what business you have in these woods," Nothany continued as he circled slowly around the man mounted on his mighty horse.

"The name is Brandovan," the man replied in a voice which sounded far cleaner than his cheeks, hair, or cloak, "Quite a few summers ago now, that would have been followed by, 'the fierce,' but I haven't been that in quite a time. As for my business in these glorious woods, I only seek some company and any generosity you might see fit to bestow upon me."

"There is the first lie," Sanjo whispered again into Daritus' ear, "Brandovan the fierce was a dark-haired titan from a small village on the low bluffs along the Sea of Sadness west of Belscythia who led a group of bandits who preyed on travelers along the road that ran from that same sea all the way through Pikan's Wood. He was killed years ago by the witch the simple folk from that area called Shellar."

"The she liar?" Daritus nearly hissed, his tone quite a bit louder than he intended. If the grubby traveler pretending to be that old robber recognized the name, it didn't register in his expression. Daritus continued in more measured tones, "I thought she was a myth."

"She was no myth," Sanjo replied still whispering, "From all accounts I've heard, she was killed by the very same king who was absent the throne while you protected his city."

"From where did you get reports of Maelich's whereabouts when I heard none? We had soldiers scouring all the lands and learned nothing of his conquests," Daritus replied, shock dripping from his whispered words.

"The trail speaks when you ask the right questions and listen intently for the correct answers," Sanjo whispered back offhandedly before changing the subject, "but that isn't important right now. Look, the boy is on to something."

"These horse sacks are of the finest quality," Nothany commented as he stopped at the back of the intruder's horse, "and very full. What have you got in them?"

"Oh, nothing of note, trinkets, old parts of things that don't work like they used to," the lie sprawled across the man's expression.

"That was lie number two," Sanjo commented quietly to Daritus.

"Agreed," Daritus mumbled equally quietly, "I saw that too. The man lies."

Nothany stowed his blade and began opening one of the sacks as he asked, "Mind if I confirm the claim?"

"I wouldn't go poking around in there, lad. Rusty old parts might give you a poke. An infection off something like that could kill a man three times your size without proper care," the man replied nervously.

"I promise to be careful," Nothany's smile echoed in his voice.

"Here it comes," Sanjo whispered as Nothany opened the sack.

The sun caught hold of the contents, reflecting golden sparkles all about the trees. Nothany pulled a coin from the bag and held it up for Daritus to see. Then he said, "This sack is filled with prang coins, enough to buy a small castle, and that's King Prian's face on those coins. This booty was taken from someone of some nobility from Balacyl."

Coins flew as the big man drove his heels hard into his horse's flanks and got the beast charging. Daritus shoved Sanjo out of the way before diving in the other direction to avoid being trampled by the massive steed. He hoped Kantiim, Spang, and the rest of the men in his group followed suit. It was difficult to determine much about what was going on around him with a face full of dirt, except that the big horse had continued galloping along the trail. Then there was a glimmer of hope that justice might shine that day.

"You're not going anywhere," Moy's voice sounded almost as big as his massive body as it filled the forest.

Daritus rolled quickly to his back to see the giant holding what would otherwise appear to be a massive man by his waist with one hand. Instead, the ample man looked like a fat child nestled within Moy's giant fist. The air grew foul when the vile thing shat himself in the face of the giant's roar. The poor bloke cried when Lito-Bi rapped him on the back of the head.

"You are unarmed and soft," the suddenly stern trogmortem growled in the man's ear, "You didn't steal that horse or that coin on your own. Where are your kin?"

"Judging by his smell and the massive trembling of those mighty cheeks, he won't be lying a third time," Sanjo smiled down at Daritus as he helped him back to his feet.

"There are four more in the trees a few hundred feet off the trail," the coward stammered, failing to disappoint.

Lito-Bi sniffed the air for a moment before saying, "I've got them," and charging quickly into the trees.

"I'm on it too," Spang grunted before sprinting after the big trogmortem into the darkness of the wood.

Sanjo dropped to one knee, bowing before Daritus, and said, "I beg your leave as the leader of our group to exact the sentence of trail justice on this one. His kin will get the same."

"You mean to execute him for theft?" Daritus frowned. The idea didn't sit well with him.

"No," Sanjo looked up at him, "I speak of a fair fight against my pupil. Nothany can use the training, and you do not want this man to continue down the trail to Druindahl and get up to whatever mischief he may."

Daritus sighed as he mulled the idea. He couldn't just let the man go, not in these woods. Tying him up to a tree would be unnecessarily cruel. At least he'd have a fighting chance. "What if he wins this fair fight?" he finally asked.

"He earns his freedom, and I mark him a robber by carving a cross in a circle on each of his fat cheeks," Sanjo shrugged.

"Well, fresh cuts on his cheeks will definitely grab Boringas' attention if the vile thing thinks of traveling to Druindahl. You have my leave. Exact your trail justice," Daritus shrugged back at him. Then he nodded toward Moy and said, "Please release him."

"It will hurt when I catch you if you run," Moy growled in the man's ear before placing him on the ground.

Daritus stepped back and stroked his chin as he watched Moy set the man roughly back to the trail. The poor bloke's eyes were nearly rolling in his sockets as his entire body trembled. For a moment it seemed he might attempt an escape, but it passed quickly. Fear is tricky. A man's response to it is even trickier. One man might flee without thought regardless the obstacles before him or odds against his success while another man will do precisely what the man quaking in fear before a boy with a sword and a troubling smile ready to take his life in the name of justice did.

"Wake up," Sanjo commanded the man as he lightly slapped his cheek and held out his sword toward him handle first, "You'll need your wits about you to have any hope for survival against my pupil."

It was difficult for Daritus not to feel pity for the man as he accepted the sword from Sanjo with a blank stare and quietly replied, "I am sorry for what I've done."

"And what have you done?" Sanjo asked. "Now is your chance to confess your transgressions, admit the wrongs you've committed, and wring the blackness out of your soul before the Lake calls you home. Depending on your skill with a blade, these may be the last words you ever speak."

"Please," the man cried out as he fell to his knees and grabbed a hold of Sanjo's cloak, dropping his sword in the process, "we didn't kill anyone. They didn't fight back. My men held them at sword point, and I gathered all worth taking from their wagons."

Sanjo's tone grew suddenly stern, "Remove your hands from me, and pick my sword up from the dirt."

The man stopped sniveling as acceptance washed over his face. He picked the sword up off the ground and slowly raised up off his knees. Tears began trickling down his cheeks as he quietly stated, "I didn't kill anyone."

"Really? You and your men took down a caravan of wagons and no one made any attempt at defending themselves? Did they have no guards?" Sanjo shook his head.

The man paused. For a moment, it seemed once again he might attempt to flee. Instead, he sniffled hard, and a soberness washed over his expression. He took a deep breath and replied, "There were two guards. They fought and died. They were protecting a duke, his family, and all their belongings. It was his wife and two small children. None of them were injured. It was dumb for them to range out without a proper force to guard them."

"They are not being judged right now. You are," Sanjo snapped before asking, "How many wagons?"

"There were three," the man seemed to slowly deflate as he spoke.

"The drivers didn't fight?" Sanjo's tone was cold as he continued to interrogate.

"One did. He died. The other two surrendered with the family," the man slumped even further as he spoke.

Daritus had grown increasingly agitated by the exchange. Everyone standing there listening to the line of questioning knew the man had stolen and lied. Based on the amount of coin weighing down his horse sacks, it was obvious enough that any guards would have been killed while defending their charge. That wasn't murder. They were paid to fight and die if necessary, and they had.

"Is this necessary?" Daritus finally asked. "This man is obviously a decoy for the real culprits in this deed. He is no killer."

Sanjo's eyes narrowed as he replied, "It is. Whether or not this man took any life from the trail, he is complicit in those deaths. He has earned an equal sentence, and trail justice commands a reckoning of a man's sins regardless of the crime."

"Fine," Daritus sighed before staring at the shabby man and asking, "What happened to the family? Did you let them go?"

The man didn't respond as his chin dropped all the way to his chest.

"What did you do to the family?" Daritus asked, the volume of his voice increasing to fill the forest.

"They tied them to trees," the man replied quietly.

"What?" Daritus hissed, "How long ago was this?"

"Must be three days now," fresh tears poured down the man's cheeks as he said the words.

Daritus didn't care much for the accusations laced about the look Sanjo shot him, but he couldn't disagree with his words when he said, "They'll be dead by now. Eaten by scarra or amatilazo. That is a horrible and terrifying way to die. Can you imagine? If it were amatilazo, at least it would have been over quickly. But if it were scarra or something else of the like..."

There was a numbness to Daritus' tone as he interrupted, "They would have started with the limbs. No, I cannot imagine how that would feel, not the pain nor the horror." Then he shifted his gaze to

Nothany and nearly spat, "Kill this scrod. Show him no mercy."

Despite finally being swayed to the idea that this man deserved the trail justice Sanjo had described, Daritus remained troubled by the casual smile draped across Nothany's face. Taking life was nothing which should evoke any form of joy. Executing any kind of justice was a duty not a pleasure. He recognized the hypocrisy of the thought immediately. There was a thrill that came with any battle. The idea of swords clashing while sparks fly from blades hardened and honed to razor edges that could effortlessly slice meat from bone would swell the breast of even the most seasoned warrior. This seemed different than that, but it wasn't. Nothany was simply feeling that thrill. Somehow seeing it saturating another's countenance helped clarify how wrong it was.

The fight was short. It could hardly be called a battle. Nothany more than lived up to the boasts Sanjo had made about him. The boy's stance was a bit more casual than Daritus liked, but his movements were fluid and smooth, almost like a dancer. The way he slipped around attacks wasting no movement was both elegant and effective. His opponent lacked sufficient training, but he knew how to swing a sword. The attacks were crude, but they would have had any seasoned soldier on the defensive. Nothany slipped around them as if the man were only swinging at him with air.

It had started with a thrust, almost a jab. Nothany barely moved to avoid the attack. He simply turned his body to allow the blade to sail past him. The follow up was a downward slash beginning from the left side of the man's face and ending at his right side. The attack never came close to the boy as he continued from his turn to spin toward the man's left side, arcing his back only slightly to avoid the blade. That was followed by an awkward spinning backhand Nothany easily avoided by stepping back. He hadn't even used his sword up to that point. When he finally did, it was only two moves. The man launched a forehand slash. It sliced the air toward Nothany's throat. The boy blocked it with a flick of his wrist and gashed the man's throat open with a backhanded slash sheathing his sword in what seemed the same movement. It was like watching art being made, gory and horrible art.

"Well played," Sanjo boomed, patting the boy on the back.

The smiles the two shared with each other while the mentor congratulated his pupil were horrifying juxtaposed against the macabre backdrop of a man gasping for air with his throat torn open and pumping blood all about the forest floor. It was somehow worse when Sanjo casually picked his sword up after the man dropped it to try holding his flesh together to stop the bleeding while gurgling through some ineligible proclamation.

"Finish," Sanjo finally said to Nothany as his sword found its way home into its scabbard.

The boy's smile remained as he drew his sword once more, placed his hand atop the dying man's head, slipped the blade into the man's shoulder just behind his collar bone, jammed it down into his torso, and said, "Justice has been served. May the Lake accept you with peace and wash away the filth of your existence."

A chill shivered its way down Daritus' spine as he watched the man flop to the dirt after his eyes grayed over. Something about it didn't feel like justice. It was more akin to misplaced vengeance. The man's victims would never know of the payment. No one probably would except the small group in the forest that day who witnessed a young boy training to be a warrior execute what he saw as the trail's justice. It seemed fair enough, but it still didn't seem right.

Sanjo must have noticed his unease as he asked, "What would have been a fair response in your estimation?"

"A cell, perhaps," Daritus shrugged.

The impossibility of it was obvious before Sanjo pointed it out, "What cell? Would you have us drag the vermin back to Druindahl to have him stand trial with nothing but his word as an accounting of his crimes? The man deserved his sentence."

Sanjo was correct. Daritus knew that despite struggling to justify it in his own mind. He may have debated the point further if not interrupted by what remained of the dead man's group struggling in the grasp of Lito-bi and Spang.

Both the prisoners had fight and defiance in them. They were painted across their expressions in fiery eyes and wild sneers. Neither appeared as dirty as the dead man who claimed to be Brandovan, and neither seemed a petty thief. Both carried themselves with the kind of swagger a man can only earn from years of battle. Lito-Bi held his man fast by the throat with stony claws threatening to puncture soft flesh while Spang pressed a dagger firmly against the throat of his.

"I thought there were four," Sanjo commented before asking, "Did the other two get away?"

"The other two are dead," Lito-Bi grunted.

"Shame," Sanjo complained, "I would have liked to see them suffer the trail's justice."

"They attacked. It was them or us," Spang countered, "and justice was served. Their guts decorate the ground, and their blood paints the trees. The beasts of the bush can feed on them."

"Nothing can be done about it now," Sanjo frowned at Spang before smiling at the two prisoners and adding, "Your friend told us of your crimes. You will face the trail's justice. Do you have any words you'd care to share before my pupil sends you off to the Lake?"

The man Lito-Bi was holding had nothing to say. He just spat blood from a split lip upon the ground. Spang's prisoner was a different story. He growled, "You can shove your justice. My deeds are my own business."

It happened quickly. As soon as the last word left the man's lips, his arm shot out. With a flick of his wrist, a small knife glinted through the air toward Sanjo. It was a good throw. Daritus would have jumped to avoid it had it been thrown his way. Sanjo hardly moved. Instead, he snatched it out of the air like a snake striking a mouse. A moment later, the same knife was jutting out of its owner's forehead, and Spang was holding a corpse.

Whether it had been a plan or the man whose throat was gripped within Lito-Bi's stony claws was merely taking advantage of the distraction caused by his friend would forever remain a mystery. As soon as the first one's knife was spinning through the air, the second one stabbed backward to drive his knife into Lito-Bi's shin. The blade barely penetrated. The man had no time to lament the mistake. A moment after he attacked, his head was off being crushed by the big trogmortem's powerful jaws.

Neither of the deaths was any less grizzly than Nothany's kill, but they didn't affect Daritus the same way. These two deaths somehow felt justified. The idea was troubling. The two men had as much chance of survival, yet their deaths seemed fairer. Unable to articulate the idea even in his own mind, he didn't bother to give it any voice. Instead, he asked, "Will you burn them now?"

Sanjo shook his head and replied, "No. They are vermin. Their bodies will feed the forest as any vermin who dies beneath her canopy would."

"Alright," Daritus nodded still a bit numb as he reckoned with Sanjo's trail justice, "Let's go then. This was a costly interruption."

Daritus remained distracted as he and his small group continued down the trail. His legs pumped with each step, but the movements barely registered in his mind. He may as well have been floating above the trail rather than treading upon it. Conversations happened all about his small group, but they were mostly lost on him. Spang asked Sanjo something about Nothany's training. Sanjo let Nothany answer. The young man's answer must have been a good one. It had both Kantiim and Lito-Bi laughing and cheering. He wanted to share that joy with them, but he couldn't bring himself to do it. He couldn't get the image of a smiling boy, not quite a man, beaming so happily over a dying man gurgling through his last breaths out of his mind.

Daritus sighed quietly as he dropped his gaze to watch the trail slip past him beneath his boots. It made little sense. Based on the testimony of the vermin who died in the forest that day, justice had been served. Perhaps he was getting soft. Perhaps too many summers in Havenstahl seeing too much blood and death and gore and destruction had sufficiently broken his resolve. Perhaps it was something different entirely. Maybe his heart was completely gone or dead, and he had nothing left for the world. That couldn't be it. Though he couldn't articulate his feelings about the slaughter in the forest, he felt something. If Leisha's loss had completely deadened his heart, the event probably wouldn't have him feeling so numb.

A twangy and unfortunate note pierced the air like the squeal of a dying pig. Despite the pain it caused in his ears, it might have been the most pleasing sound Daritus had heard in weeks. It was a perfect diversion from the thoughts troubling his mind, and it shifted the quiet conversations happening around him from muted revelry to loud complaints. Even though the poorly executed strum of that poorly tuned string would have undoubtedly led to an epic extolling the prowess of a young warrior dispatching a vile bandit, no one in the group would allow it to grow into something so grotesque.

"Why would you ruin the serenity of this pristine wood with that horrid note?" Nothany loudly needled the songsmith who'd crafted the disaster of a sound.

"I had hoped to honor your exploits with song," Hasujo replied crestfallen.

"There is nothing honorable about the sounds you make with that thing, nor the incoherent ideas which slop out of your gob to accompany them," the young swordsman sneered earning an uncustomary chuckle from Kantiim.

Sanjo, obviously less amused by the slight, scolded, "Nothany, a song sung in your honor is the greatest of gifts. Hasujo cares enough to spend his creative energy on you, and you spit upon his effort. On the sad day when the Lake calls you home all that will remain of your life are the stories people have told of you. A man with songs sung in his name never truly dies, but a man with no songs is quickly forgotten."

Nothany sighed and kicked an innocent tuft of grass that had managed to survive the thousands upon thousands of boots and horse hooves that had trampled across the trail as he groaned, "I am sorry for the slight, Hasujo. I am humbled you saw fit to honor me with song."

"That could have been more convincing," Sanjo frowned.

"Bah," Chorindaal grunted as he hobbled over to Hasujo and reached up to pat the downcast bard between his shoulder blades, "None of these talentless fools know nothing about art." Then he guided Hasujo's hand further up the neck of his mandolin and added, "Put your pointer there. Then this one there and put this finger there. Now give that a strum. And don't be holding back either. Get into them strings, lad."

It was a golden sound vibrating off the bard's mandolin. Daritus couldn't help but smile at the surprise on the young musician's face. He wished for a small piece of the joy oozing out of Hasujo's suddenly wide eyes. It would probably be a time before he could feel something close to that. Witnessing someone else's joy would be as near as he'd probably get. Still, his smile grew wider when the bard strummed again and created a note equally glorious.

"There you go lad, strum that out a few times," the dwarf beamed as he coached the novice musician.

"Thank you," Hasujo almost seemed to glow as he picked up the tempo, dancing down the trail while he strummed.

By the time Daritus and his group reached the point where the trail butted up against the great, red streak that ran as far north or south as the eye could see, Chorindaal had taught Hasujo two more chords and gave him some tips on creative fingering. The latter's cheeks were so plumped out above possibly the widest smile Daritus had ever seen they looked like they might burst as he transitioned from chord to chord strumming and plucking the strings to fill the air with a series of notes that actually sounded like a song. The bard's technique was a bit rough, but no one in the group was complaining.

Daritus pondered that great, red streak as Hasujo filled the air with melodies from his mandolin. No one really knew why the trees which had once stood there stained the ground red. Hagen had offered probably the best theory Daritus had ever heard. The souls of Dragons had been trapped within those trees. Hagen had postulated that the spirit of Dragon's fire being trapped within the haunted forest had leached out through the roots and deep into the ground to stain it red. It was as good an explanation as any.

Nothany was the first to touch the path of plain looking dirt which interrupted the red streak. It was the same path Maelich would have taken when he had journeyed to the Lake so many summers prior. Back then a forest still stood covering the red dirt which now occupied the space.

"Spirits haunted this place in summer's past," Daritus had warned the boy, but Nothany didn't hesitate. He dropped down to all fours and placed his hands directly on the dirt of the path between the two banks of red.

"It feels like any other dirt I've ever felt if not a bit looser than the average trail," Nothany smiled back up at him.

The boy then quickly crawled left to the very edge of the trail where the normal looking dirt met the red dirt running alongside it and reported, "This dirt feels the same." Then he looked up at Sanjo and asked, "May have leave to test this trail?"

"Maelich is the only man I know of who has ever tread that trail," Daritus commented, "That doesn't mean none other have, but his story was troubling at best. A spirit tormented him with horrid and terrifying memories that were as real as any of his own. He said the souls were drawn to the forest because they were drawn to the Dragons. He also said they failed to finish their journeys to the Lake until the Dragons were freed to return there. I can neither confirm nor dispute his account, but I would take care before venturing onto that path."

"Haven't you determined your destiny lies beyond this great scar at the Lake of Dragons?" Nothany asked, "It seems we have no choice but to try. I will test it."

"That is a sound and logical argument," Daritus nodded.

Nothany smiled, took ten steps out onto the path, turned, and said,

"I feel nothing any different than I felt a moment ago. There might be a sadness lingering around the air in between the two sides of this great, red streak, but it's hollow and empty. It feels more like the ghost of a recollection than anything so fresh as a memory."

Sanjo smiled at Daritus and asked, "My lord?"

"You're a brave lad, Nothany, and your report is well received," Daritus mustered a smile for the young man before turning toward his group and commanding, "This brave young man has shown us the way. Let's take this trail and finish our journey."

Hasujo with his recently pleasing mandolin was the first to heed the command. Chorindaal hobble-danced alongside him. "Play that riff again, over and over. I've a song a to sing," the dwarf hollered up at the bard who had found an exceptionally pleasing progression of notes.

Hasujo granted the request as the rest of the group made their ways onto the trail behind him. Most of them besides Chorindaal merely bobbed their heads along to the tune, but Moy added an odd shimmy and shake to his step that seemed almost comical enough to comment on, though no one in the group would dare the slight. A genuine smile spread across Daritus' face as Chorindaal began to sing. The dwarf's voice sounded as if he'd been gargling rocks since he'd been a wee lad, but there was something pleasing in how effortlessly he hit the notes with all the power he put behind them.

> A son of the wood, rider for no flag
> All wit and skill, only air in his bag
> Brave young man serving justice on the trail
> Bad ones tremble from wherever they hail
> When evil is among us day or night
> Nothany is there ready for a fight
> When a king without a throne gave command
> Answered but a boy, a man made his stand
> No ghosts nor ghouls could turn his soul aside
> Perk up all ye men for tonight we ride

Daritus hurried to walk beside Nothany as the bard kept playing and the dwarf kept crooning. He remained troubled by the pleasure echoed in the young warrior's smile after taking a life. Though a part of him understood it, an equal part wondered if one so young could truly appreciate what it meant to take a life regardless of the reason.

"Nothany," Daritus called out as he jogged the last few steps to catch the young man, "I'm quite impressed by your bravery. You're the greenest of the warriors in this group yet the first one to challenge this trail. I count it a blessing to have you on this journey."

"It was probably more curiosity than bravery," Nothany blushed, "I needed to see for myself. Besides, I knew my feet would be treading on this trail eventually. Seemed silly to put it off."

"And you're wise beyond your years," Daritus chuckled.

Nothany just shrugged. It didn't seem like a slight. Daritus was quickly learning it was just the boy's character. He expected things to be the way he wanted them, and they probably were more often than not. The old general tried to recall himself at that age, but there were too many summers between that trail and the hut he shared with the other recruits pledging to ride beneath the red of Druindahl in service of the Dragon. He remembered events, people, the faces of his friends, but feelings, even the way he saw the world then, were a bridge too far. Even still, he couldn't imagine he was nearly so confident at a similar age.

"Are you at all troubled by the life you took from the trail today?" Daritus finally asked, the volume of his voice dropping quickly.

Nothany scratched his head as he asked, "Why would I be?"

Daritus pressed on cautiously, "I understand the trail's justice. It makes sense. However, even though you were justified in your actions, a life is a life. Taking one seemed to bring you too much joy."

"That man will never hurt another soul because of me," the young swordsman stated as plainly as any words Daritus had ever heard, "I find no joy in taking life, my lord, but I do find joy in protecting innocents."

"Fair points," he conceded, "Forgive me. I mean no disrespect. I've only ever taken life from a battlefield. Those men chose to be there for the express purpose of taking lives in the name of someone's cause. I have no experience with patrolling the trail to bring vermin to justice. I know there is nothing any less honorable about it, but I continue to struggle with the idea. It feels more like revenge than justice."

"The purpose of this journey is so you can learn how to kill a Dragon?" Daritus didn't care for the smirk accompanying Nothany's words nor the obvious direction they were heading, "The reason you want to learn this skill is revenge. Even more, this Dragon earning your vengeance is your daughter, a woman you trained to be the most skilled warrior in the known world, a person you loved once."

"Your point?" Daritus allowed the slightest hint of frustration to color his tone.

"No point," Nothany offered another casual shrug, "I was simply stating facts out loud for you to consider. Your reasons are your own, and they are not my business. We all live with our own actions. I am proud of mine. How do you feel about yours?"

It felt like disrespect, but only because the owner of the words was so young. Daritus offered nothing further as he mulled the boy's statements. He was correct, of course. It was vengeance he sought, vengeance for his innocent wife, and vengeance for all the other innocent folks who'd died for his daughter's rage. She didn't mean to kill any of them. There was no intent.

He suddenly felt foolish as he strolled quietly beside the young man who had so plainly pointed out the fault in his reasoning. At least the man Nothany had killed intentionally committed a crime. Whether his actions warranted death was a fair point for debate, but his crimes were intentional. Though he hadn't been there when Cialia loosed her flames on the gods at Druindahl, he knew his daughter well enough to know she had only intended to hurt the gods she attacked. Everyone else who perished in her fire was a victim of fate.

Nothany remained mercifully quiet. It was as if he knew the struggles going on in Daritus' head. The boy truly was wise beyond his years.

The rest of the group kept on with their distractions dancing and skipping down the trail behind him. Hasujo kept strumming out the notes while Chorindaal kept belting out his growly song. Moy's dance became more animated as he went. Lito-Bi even hopped and skipped for a step or two while Spang and Kantiim bobbed their heads in unison. Daritus caught glimpses of their shenanigans here and there, but none of it could earn enough of his attention to drag him away from his torments.

Even as the trail spilled out into a lush landscape teeming with foreign vegetation splashed with colors like nothing on his side of the great scar, he remained distracted, absorbed in thoughts of things he still failed to justify. He could hear them describing the flavors of things they were eating and extolling the glorious odors of the place, but his mind remained separated from everything going on around him. Nothing really mattered but the Lake. They were so close. He could feel it. They could stumble upon Dragons at any moment.

"Hey there, Daritus. Try this," Kantiim called out before tossing something yellow at his head.

"I haven't the appetite," Daritus complained as he offhandedly snatched the curved thing out of the air before it smacked into his head.

"Well, don't eat it because you're hungry. Eat it because you're experiencing lands to which you've never been, and I promise you that wonderful thing is like nothing you've ever tasted."

Daritus grimaced when he bit into it. Kantiim's report was correct. The nasty thing was like nothing he'd ever tasted. It was almost like eating bark. There wasn't anything pleasing about it at all. "It's awful," he complained after spitting the nastiness out of his mouth and onto the ground.

"You've got to peel off that rind," Spang jumped in, "Delicious!"

He smiled after heeding the instruction. It was mellow and mouthwatering. A bit too mushy for his liking, but what it lacked in density it made up for in sweetness. He absently chomped away at the thing as he wound around random clumps of odd-looking trees, struggling to avoid the vines and shrubs that nearly covered the rest of the ground.

Someone complained about resting, but he paid them no heed. At that point, he didn't care if they were following him any longer. They could rest and chomp on the sweet treats they'd pulled from the trees if they wanted. He didn't have time for any of that. According to Maelich's account, he would see Dragon's any moment now. They were too close to the destination to waste any additional time.

After a long while of winding around trees and stepping high to avoid tripping over thick vines, Daritus finally paused. It was difficult to gauge the distance he'd traveled since leaving the trail that split the great red streak, but it seemed too far to not see any indication of the Lake or the Dragons who lived there. As far as he could see in any direction was nothing but more foliage. It was fragrant, peaceful, and beautiful, but it wasn't at all what he sought.

"Do you suppose we've gotten off in the wrong direction?" Kantiim asked around a mouthful of some sloppy orange thing he was slurping on.

"I don't know," Daritus sighed as he fell to his knees and continued,

"I don't know anything anymore. Based on the stories Maelich told of his journey to this place, we should have seen it by now."

"It was hidden from men hundreds of years ago," Spang interjected, "You know that as well as any of us, and you know why."

"The great campaign," Sanjo added quietly, a hint of sadness haunting his tone.

"Perhaps, you're not ready to see it. Perhaps none of us are," Kantiim added.

"I am unworthy of the Lake? Is that what you're saying?" Daritus asked quietly despite knowing the answer and not wanting to hear any more.

"Maybe," Kantiim replied somberly, "Maybe your goal of learning how to kill your daughter is the very thing that makes you unworthy."

The stark truth of all the words they had for him settled in and twisted like a knot in his gut. He knew it before embarking on the journey, but desire kept him from believing it. Heat behind his eyes threatened tears he would normally hold back. In that moment of hopelessness, he didn't care. They streamed down his cheeks in torrents as he wailed at the sky above. No one moved to comfort him as he pulled at his hair and clothes and cried out again and again at the trees and flowers and vines and even the air.

"Why?" he finally shouted, "What have I done to deserve this fate? All I've ever done in my life is serve and protect others, and everything has been taken from me. Why can I not have one thing for myself in this entire rotten world?"

The vines were rough beneath his cheek as he laid his head on the ground and sobbed. Thoughts of what the rest of his group might be thinking as he howled like a babe curled up on some foreign forest floor fled quickly. He didn't care what they thought, and he had no more direction to give them. The quest was a failure. He would never find the Lake nor the answers he sought.

Then it occurred to him. He knew exactly what he would do. As the tears continued streaming down his face, he resolved to remain there lying on the ground until his soul departed his body. Then he would be worthy. Then he would finally see the Lake.

"Fair Daritus, what dire cause earns your tears and laments?" a voice beckoned. It was strong but sweet as a song. However, he didn't hear it with his ears. Instead, the message seemed to occur directly to his mind.

"Who's there?" he finally raised his head, "Could it really be you, mother to us all, the Great Mother, Helias? Am I unworthy of your grace?"

"It is I, and you are worthy, Daritus of Druindahl. You have lived a life full of love and happiness but also pain and regret. It is an honor to have you at my door," the Dragon's voice remained sweet and strong as it floated about his awareness.

Then he saw it. The trees and vines and flowers and roots ahead of him all vanished, giving way to a prairie, vast and impossibly green. Massive Dragons lumbered about while even more soared the blue skies above. Straight ahead was the Lake, as magnificent and pristine as Maelich had described, a perfect circle of glassy calm water surrounded by an equally perfect circle of sand.

More tears came, but these were absent the sting of sorrow their predecessors carried down his cheeks to soak his beard. These salty drops swelled with joy and hope and awe and even relief. A thought fluttered through his head like a tattered flag torn loose from its mast cast about on a gusty gale. His journey wasn't finished. The Lake was just a stop. Vengeance was his final destination.

The sounds of his men reacting to the same vision which brought forth such torrents from his red and swollen eyes proved insufficient at dragging enough of his attention away from the glorious sight to identify who made them or if they were expressions of joy, sadness, fear, or some altogether other thing. Some wept, some laughed, and one shouted something like a war cry. This cry stood out among the rest. It carried no threat or malice or hate. Instead, it sounded like a celebration. One thousand voices cheering at some monumentally happy moment all at once together. That one voice grabbed hold of Daritus' attention and dragged his eyes to its source.

There stood Moy, the tallest and most terrifying giant Daritus had ever met, with the largest smile he'd ever seen strapped across his face. Tears flowed freely from the giant's eyes as he laughed and then hollered out with another joyous and booming cry. His arms were wrapped as far around a Dragon's neck as he could reach.

The Dragon was Lameah. Daritus knew the fact but couldn't reckon how. She was a kind soul. All Dragons are kind souls, but somehow, Lameah seemed to feel things a bit more strongly than her kin. She loved deeper, laughed harder, and grieved stronger than any of her sisters. There was no reason Daritus could know any of this, but he did. In that moment, he knew he loved her as if she were his own family, and she loved him the same.

As he stared at the giant hugging the Dragon with all his might, basking in her love and glory, things like anger and vengeance and hate seemed so small and useless. True bliss surrounded him. What could be more important than that?

"Daritus," Helias' voice spoke this time to his ears, "you have traveled a great distance. Is your journey complete?"

The scenery had changed abruptly. The Lake was gone along with all the green. No Dragons lumbered about or soared among the currents in the vast blue skies above. Those vast blue skies had fled as well, in favor of a high ceiling of rock glowing a dull red despite being shrouded in darkness. Even the grass beneath his feet had vanished in favor of something impossible. It looked like water that was just as still as the Lake had been, yet it held his weight without dampening even the soles of his boots.

He stood there alone save the giant Dragon crouched and smiling before him, her massive head with all its horns and those eyes smoldering red like embers waiting to ignite the next bit of fuel which grew near enough. It was Helias, the same voice which had spoken to his mind. He knew her just like he'd known Lameah. The how of it all mattered very little. Even why seemed a question unworthy of any care. He should have been terrified by her beastly form, but fear was not among the emotions he felt. She was beautiful to his eyes. All the love and joy and bliss he'd felt while gazing across a paradise sprawling out from that perfect Lake remained.

"What is this place?" he asked with awe dripping from his tone.

"We are beneath the Lake," she sweetly whispered her reply, "It was once a place to hide from the violent ambitions of men, but now it serves as merely a quiet place to speak. Is your journey complete?"

It wasn't, but somehow that idea seemed a lie. He journeyed to the Lake to learn how to kill a Dragon, his daughter. The thought seemed so bleak and dark as he focused on it, his intention. What kind of man seeks to destroy the thing he created? Of course, it wasn't his seed which spawned one of the most powerful beings to ever exist, but he raised her. Much of what she had become was directly because of him. "I am unsure," he finally said.

"Cialia, my sweet sister, and your lovely daughter is a force. She could burn this world to its core with a thought, but she bleeds the same as you," Helias' smile never faltered even as the meaning behind her words turned as bleak and dark as charred wood.

"You would help me destroy someone you revere as your own kin?" he asked quietly, barely a mumble. The idea seemed a farce, but no contrary interpretation presented itself.

"Help?" the Dragon's tone remained as sweet as it had been, "No, dear Daritus. It is not my place to help nor hinder. I am merely a guide. You came with a question in your mind, and I gave you an answer."

"And if I kill her?" Daritus' voice strengthened but remained barely more than a whisper.

"I will weep as hard for the loss of one so beautiful and dear as I will if she kills you," the Dragon's sweet tone remained as glorious as a song. After a few moments of silence she added, "Stay with us, you and your kin. Let the glory of this place wash away your sorrows. Then, when Cialia returns to us, and you look upon your daughter's face knowing all she's done, all she's ever done, you will know what you must do. I will love you both just the same."

"I will do what you say," it wasn't defeat in Daritus' muted tones, as he quietly added, "Thank you, Great Mother. I love you just the same."

CHAPTER 17
THE CHOICE

The blood had ceased, but the pain remained. It wasn't Dragon's fire that cauterized the wound Cialia had given him when her blade kissed the flesh of his wrist and sliced clean through taking his sword hand and the blade which made it useful in one expert stroke. Her technique was impeccable. With neither able to call their flame in this odd world that had sprung out of his desire, Cialia had gathered some wood and built a fire the old-fashioned way with a flint and some shreds of rope to get it started. It was a bit of a cheat, as she doused the hemp in fairies' tears to increase their flammability. Daritus would have been disappointed, but the wound needed tending.

He could still feel the hand even after she took a stick glowing orange with heat from the base of the fire and burned the spot. He had complained at first that he deserved the wound and whatever its result was his destiny. She shook her head when she told him, "That is a foolish sentiment. There is more work to do, and I cannot do it alone." She had been right, of course, but, as they sat discussing what the work to be done was, it quickly became obvious neither of them knew what to do next.

"My son is a man," Maelich said absently as he gazed at the wrapped stump causing all his pain. It had muted to a dull throb with the help of some dragon's blossom Cialia had used to coat the bandages and a few pulls of fairies' tears, but it still hurt. His palm itched. That might have been worse than the pain. The fact he couldn't scratch it was the most irritating thing he could remember. He would never be able to scratch it. He had tossed the hand into the fire after retrieving his sword from the severed thing, yet he could still feel it itching as if it remained connected to his burned wrist.

It was clear from the faraway look in Cialia's eyes her mind was elsewhere as she absently replied, "He is more than a man, more than a Dragon, more than a god," she paused as she picked a twig up from the ground, tossed it in the fire, and added, "More than us. He will burn this world."

Maelich shook his head, "That isn't what I mean. He should be barely more than a babe learning and babbling gibberish, only just putting meaning to the words he mocks. I know him now, since Ijilv allowed him out of his prison and his consciousness became free to explore the mysteries of Coeptus, but I still haven't met him. I've missed everything, and it is all my fault." The tear that followed the thought swelled with regret.

"Is that self-pity?" Cialia asked with none of the disgust her words might suggest slipping into her tone.

"No," the answer was honest as he shifted his gaze toward a deeply blue sky, "I feel many things. Pity for myself is not among them. Anger, even rage. I hate myself for the things I have done."

"As do I," a chilly numbness slithered about Cialia's reply, "I hate myself for all the innocent lives I've taken in the name of protecting those very same souls. I deserve to burn in the same flame that consumed them all."

Maelich offered a joyless chuckle before saying, "Helias would suggest hating any soul is unhealthy and wrong. Love the soul. Hate the action."

"And she's right," Cialia moved closer to him until her face was directly in front of his, "but how? I forgive you for all you've done. I mean that. I hate the things you've done, things on which I've blamed my own despicable actions. I no longer blame you for those things. I am the only one to blame for all my wickedness. But, somehow, I cannot forgive myself."

"I feel the same. I hold you blameless, but I cannot forgive myself," Maelich replied as he met her gaze and continued, "Time, I suppose. As imaginary a thing as that might be, I cannot think of a more effective salve or balm for a wounded spirit."

"Together," Cialia became suddenly animated, "Whatever we do, we do it together. We must stop dwelling on things which cannot be undone and turn our hearts toward things we can control. Let's be what we were meant to become."

"Dragons?" Maelich replied as hope brought a smile to his face.

"Yes," she nearly shouted, "Dragons! Let's swim the Lake, lumber about ripe fruits and fresh vines of the wild lands around it, and sail the warm currents of the vast and open skies above." She paused for a few moments as she pulled her brother close enough to lay her head upon his shoulder and added, "And let's love all the creatures of Ouloos with all our might."

"I want that more than anything," his lips drew into a wide smile beneath his faraway gaze, "but can we do that last bit? Can you love my son after he does everything we know he plans to do? Can I love him?"

"I can," she whispered confidently, her breath warm against his neck, "I have searched his soul since becoming aware of it. I know all the wicked things he plans to do. And I also know why. Everything he sees is evil. He is a bystander in this world with no opportunity to experience what it means to navigate it. He feels no connection to the souls occupying this place and no understanding of why they do the horrible things they do to each other. To him, there is no other option but to destroy this place and the evil which it is."

"I suppose you are correct," Maelich hugged her back, "And yet…"

"And yet," she agreed, "All we can do is try."

They sat there like that embracing, two tired souls who hadn't rested in far too long nurturing each other against all the pain and horror haunting the memories of the horrid things they had each done in the name of some cause that seemed so small and meaningless. Maelich couldn't remember the last time he'd felt so at peace. Everything was as it always should have been since the beginning, he and his sister working together, using the great power they'd been gifted by Coeptus and the Lake to show the creatures of Ouloos a better way, to teach them how to love like a Dragon. If only they could stay in that moment forever. Alas, their work was not done. The lessons they had failed to teach still needed teaching.

"I would like nothing more than to remain in this moment until the end of my days," Cialia whispered her response to Maelich's thoughts, "but you are correct. It is time for us to be the guides we were meant to be. Let's bring our people home."

Maelich chuckled dryly as he raised his head, looked around, and asked, "But, how do we get out of this place?"

"I thought you would know," Cialia raised her head off his shoulder to laugh at him, "You made this place. Isn't there some kind of secret door or tunnel somewhere to escape?"

"I wish I knew," he laughed at the perfect sky above them, "I didn't consciously create this place."

"Your flame?" shock dripped from her whispered words.

"I think it was protecting me?" his tone echoed his lack of understanding.

"It would make sense, of course," she shrugged before adding, "My flame has protected me without any conscious thought of my own on more than one occasion, but this is something so much more than blocking some malicious energy unleashed by a malevolent being. You created an entire world, like some alternate dimension."

"That's it," Maelich shouted, "This isn't some other world. It's like when we split time. It's just our world with different rules, like some slightly shifted reality running through the shadows and quiet places of our own."

"You're right," a sudden understanding flashed behind her eyes. "All we need to do is desire to be where we want to be."

"The Lake?" he asked.

"Yes," her expression grew serious, "but not yet. We need answers."

"Raya," Maelich muttered, "You no longer want to kill her?"

"I do not," Cialia's tone grew nonchalant, almost dull, "She has answers, and we need answers."

"Do we? Can we not just be what we were meant to be? Do we need to know why we must?" Maelich shrugged.

"We do," she nodded, "I don't know why, but I know we need to know."

Maelich closed his eyes and focused on that magical place where fairies swam about the skies and unicorns stooped to drink from the cool, fresh waters of a forest pond surrounded by trees and moss and wildflowers. So connected was he to Cialia that he sensed her will focusing on the same destination. They both stretched and reached, spreading their consciousness across time and space, slipping from one dimension to the next, breaking every rule ever concocted to keep a soul still where it stood. Raya knew they were coming. She flashed her brilliance like a lighthouse beacon over black waves beneath a midnight sky and helped guide them in. It was time.

The colors flashed the way they did. The sounds boomed in melodic choruses and screeched in horrid notes and mingled with odd variations of tones that seemed to account for every other auditory potentiality in between. It was cold, too cold, and then hotter than the most ambitious ember to ever glow. The air tasted sweet, then sour, then bitter, and then saltier than a big gulp of wide-open sea. None of it was shocking to Maelich. As awesome and unsettling as it was, it was the same as it had ever been. He could sense Cialia shared the sentiment. They were merely splitting time, a common thing they had cause to do on occasion, no different than walking down a hall or swimming in the cool waters of a lake. Then they arrived.

The scenery had only begun to materialize around them when Raya's voice danced through the other sounds to sing into their ears, "The twins return. Do you come as destroyers or saviors? Do you still battle for my soul?"

"You know we do not," Cialia allowed the slightest hint of irritation into her tone, "Why do you act as if you are unaware of things you obviously know?"

"Ideas are different than actions, dear Cialia," the smile between Raya's soft cheeks echoed in her tone, "Oftentimes, the things we plan are starkly different than the things we do. Logic and emotion, they remain locked in a forever dance. I think balance between the two is perfection."

"I suppose that is true, but my emotions are in balance with logic. I am convinced no other creatures deserve my wrath, and I wish only to love all things. I have returned merely to seek answers I believe you have," Cialia replied earnestly.

"But can you do that, Cialia, most vengeful of Dragons, can you love all the creatures of this world?" Raya's perfect eyes narrowed as her tone remained sweet.

"I hope so," the honesty in her voice nearly startled her, "and I hope even more you can tell me if that is what I'm supposed to do. Are these feelings correct?"

"That is an answer only you can decide," an odd sadness seeped into Raya's soft voice, "I know what I would like you to do, but only you can decide if you can truly do what you think you must do. I fear it might not be as easy for you as you expect. When you look into the fiery eyes of my great-great-grandson, can you love him the same way you believe you can love all creatures?"

Shock filled Maelich as he listened to the friendly debate. It seemed obvious now that he knew. How could he have missed it when he'd first met her? That's how those troubling gidim had known his grandmother. They lived with her mother.

"How could you be Kalia's mother?" Maelich blurted before adding, "You're like the gods. How could you birth anything from your womb?"

Maelich could sense the same shock from his sister as she asked, "And why would you leave her?"

"I am not a god," Raya smiled, "but I am more akin to them than I am to the men or other creatures who exist in this world. I exist outside the rules of this place. It took all my energy to present myself as a physical being in this realm. It took even more to carry her to term. When I *died* during childbirth it truly was the end of that creature I'd been for that short time."

"Were we part of your plan?" shock dripped from Cialia's words.

"No," the laugh Raya offered with her reply raised the hair on Maelich's neck. She continued before he could give voice to his displeasure, "I had planned for your grandmother to swim the Lake and become impregnated by it, but her true love was the trail. Her father was a good man: honest, trustworthy, loyal, and injured sufficiently that I knew he'd never again be able to heed the trail's call despite how much he might yearn for it. The only problem is that he trained his daughter to be the same. She was mighty. I thought all was lost until she found a companion. He thought he loved her. Kalia knew it was nothing more than a base need for companionship coupled with just enough lust to result in a pregnancy she never wanted. Luckily, Wendal was far less adventurous. He raised your mother to be a caring and loving soul, the nurturer you knew her to be. She swam the Lake accepting the mission her mother refused."

"I know the stories," Cialia nearly growled.

"I don't know them," Maelich muttered, "but it sounds like you never intended for us to exist. Part of me wishes I never had, while an equal part of me is somehow sad you hold no affection for us."

"But I need to understand why," Cialia continued, ignoring Maelich's interruption.

"Of course, you do, dear Cialia," Raya beamed, "You forever thirst for knowledge, but you are never satisfied with what you learn. As challenging as that may be for those around you, it is a gift."

"It feels like a curse," Cialia sighed, "but it is true. I cannot recall a time I ever felt truly satisfied. Everything always feels unfinished."

"And that is precisely why you feel so unsure about what you must do," Raya's tone remained as sweet as it had been as her volume dropped to a whisper, "I will give you my answer. You probably will not like it much, but it is the only answer I have. Then, if you continue to not destroy me, I plan to go to the Lake and spend the rest of my days yearning to be something I can never be."

"A Dragon?" Maelich interrupted.

"Of course, she means a Dragon," Cialia snapped at Maelich before turning her eyes back to Raya and prompting her to continue, "Please, tell me your truth."

Raya drew a deep breath in through her nose, released it slowly from her mouth, and said, "I think you've realized this by now, but Ijilv is like me. We come from another place, like this, but not quite the same. Our world died the same death this world will eventually die if we don't do something to allow it to live. We were scientists, a thing you don't understand. We studied our world asking the same kinds of questions for which you seek answers. We did this through observation and testing. Our population had split long before we were born. Maelich, the place you imagined was much like a part of that world. It was a paradise where everyone had everything they needed and contributed their skills so everyone else could have the same. However, there was another part of that world that thought how you did when confronted with things like the compliance pikes. You saw it as the evilest magic. The folks who defected from Eengurra saw it as a gross misuse of scientific knowledge which, in a sense, is the exact same thing."

"Men should have a choice," the words instinctively burst forth from Maelich's mouth without any need for thought.

"That is what we learned," Raya nodded.

"What does any of that have to do with Ouloos?" Cialia complained more than questioned.

Raya's smile faded slightly, "You believe—and I know this because Ijilv told you this while pretending to be Coeptus, a thing I told him to do, though he doesn't know as much—that Coeptus are some great, gathering of spirits swirling about in a lake waiting to be born into your world as some physical thing. That is not an accurate description.

Coeptus is a being, probably not dissimilar from you or me, and we are a part of that being. There are millions, possibly billions, of worlds that are almost exactly the same as your world, and my world before it died. We know very little beyond that."

"Why did your world die?" Maelich asked. He had so many questions, but most of the ideas he would question were so foreign he could scarcely come up with the proper words to ask them.

"We killed ourselves before we could even be born," Raya's smile remained despite the tear teetering on her eyelid, "It took generations, but we built what we thought was the ultimate utopia. I still fail to quite understand why, but things are so much more meaningful when you struggle to obtain them. Somehow, the pain, the strife, and the challenge render the reward so much sweeter. And choice. Some folks accepted the paradise we built for them, but many could not. They saw evil in every perfect brick of every perfect building and every sweet morsel of each meal. The strangest thing for me is, based on everything I've learned about Coeptus between both my world and yours, Eengurra would have died so much sooner if not for the mech wars.

"Ijilv and I saw it coming. Coeptus' gaze slowly began turning away from us. We had a portal just like your Lake. We studied it, found the patterns. They were like brainwaves. That was the key for us. We searched, and we found many other worlds just like Ouloos. I ran simulations, and this world was the only one that had a chance. Ijilv disagreed, but I saw it. You were early enough in your development that a push in the right direction could change everything. I convinced Ijilv that this was a world we could save. When I realized he planned to make essentially the same mistakes we made for Eengurra, I adjusted his understanding of me. In much the same fashion as the compliance pikes nudge a person's mind to a specific way of thinking, I erased myself from his mind."

"You loved him," Cialia blurted.

"Based on your idea of what that word means, yes, I did love him," Raya conceded before adding, "However, what I felt for him was akin to what you felt for Boringas. You called it love once, but I think you know it wasn't that. I felt a fondness for him. I even felt lust for him on occasion. He was my companion. I don't see that as love. Most see multiple kinds of love. There is first love, when you find that one person who swells feelings in you, maybe gives you butterflies when you think of them. Then, there is true love. True love is what you might call your feelings for Boringas if you would ever succumb to such a simple thing. There is no other creature in this world who might cause you to entertain such an idea. If you chose to submit, he would be your true love. There are random loves like a favorite meal or a particular smell you adore above all else, but the endorphins which make you think you're feeling love aren't even emotions. I see none of those things as any kind of love. For me, love is something you choose to give unconditionally. I love both of you that way, not because you are my kin, but because I love all creatures just the same. You could burn me with your irresistible flame or cut me down with blades, and I would die loving you for what you are."

"You could never be a Dragon," Maelich shrugged, "but you certainly sound like one."

"It is my greatest wish, but I can never be a Dragon," Raya agreed.

"Perhaps, it is enough to live like one," Cialia offered the slightest of smiles. "I have so many more questions, but I think I understand enough. We have a choice to make."

"We do," Raya agreed.

"Let's go to the Lake," a bit of confidence seeped into Maelich's tone. Though he wasn't certain of what choice he would have to make, the Lake was the only destination that made sense. After a bit of silence, he added, "All the banished creatures of this place will join us. This world belongs to them as much as it does us."

CHAPTER 18
A DRAGON COMES CALLING

It was a day unremarkable from any other day which had passed since Ymarhon had strolled into the greatest city of men and took another man's throne without incident. The massive and glorious room surrounding him was stuffier than most days. An annoying flock of sea owls had taken up residence in the ventilation shafts that normally brought fresh air into the throne room from outside. By the time anyone noticed, the shafts were stuffed with trash, twigs, and random bits of dried foliage those vile, rats with wings weaved into nests where they could lay their eggs and spawn new nuisances to crap all over the shimmering, stone walls of the city.

Ymarhon had removed his cloak hours prior, and his blouse, which had been a blazing white when first he'd dressed, appeared almost gray. It was drenched with sweat and stuck to him in places. He'd even removed his gaudy crown after the sweat on his forehead caused it to slip past his brow one too many times. Luckily, he had managed to keep from launching the thing at the wall and presenting a less than kingly image to the masses of subjects packed so tightly in the room with him. That would have been unfortunate. Instead, he grumbled quietly about its weight before gently setting it on the table behind him.

The two men standing before him droning on about some slight one perceived and the other saw as nonsense seemed equally uncomfortable despite both having servants fanning them with large feathers fastened to the ends of long poles.

"The beast breathed his last on my land," Ygardin of house

Varisghoul chirped in a voice that seemed miles too high for his bent form. Ymarhon knew the man was just shy of his sixtieth summer, but he carried himself as one who'd seen more than one hundred.

"But my son's arrow pierced the fallon's heart on my land," Grancyl, a wharf man from Belscythia who held no royal titles but carried stores of coin he was happy to share with the crown for favors like land and position, groaned as he shook his head.

It was nearly time for the midday, and Ymarhon had been listening to similar, childish squabbles since just after the sun had stretched above the horizon to kiss Havenstahl with the light of a new day. He'd had enough. "Who gutted the beast?" he interrupted.

"My son cleaned his kill as any good man would before he was abused and chased off of it by a handful of my comrade's righteous men," Grancyl replied, a bit of disgust coloring his tone for the last bit.

"And it was butchered by my boys immediately after," Ygardin quickly retorted while his arms flailed in what was probably intended to be a gesture that might add some sense of emotion to the statement but instead came off like some random spasm.

Ymarhon could scarcely care less one way or the other. The forests around Havenstahl teemed with fallon and hundreds of other types of beasts good for hunting and eating. Squabbling over one buck was beyond childish. He wanted to tell Ygardin to give his overzealous sons a good, sound thrashing and Grancyl to have his son go shoot another fallon on his own damned land, but he kept that all behind his sweaty brow. Instead, he said, "You both have valid complaints against the other. The meat has already been butchered and divvied up among Ygardin's kin. That doesn't seem quite fair. What would the two of you propose as a fair solution?"

"I think it would be fair to drag his sons to the courtyard and whip them for all to see," Grancyl snarled.

"And I might say the same about your trespassing son," Ygardin squeaked through a scowl that had his hooked nose looking even more like a beak.

"Oh, send these two away," an old man wearing a tattered, gray cloak that seemed even older than the form it covered bellowed in a deep and raspy voice as he shuffled past the line of complainants up toward the front, "There ain't no common ground to be had between the two of them. Meanwhile, you've got a witch in your midst probably brewing up a spell against the crown as we speak."

The man was unfamiliar to Ymarhon. He was no lord, nor anyone who had been granted any land. The only thing the king was certain of about the crooked and shabby old thing was that he had no business in his throne room. The heat must have had his security attachment lax in their duties. It was no excuse. He'd have a stern scolding for the lot of them before the midday. He tucked the idea in the back of his mind as he addressed the bold, old fellow who found it acceptable to interrupt the crown, "There is a line of people with concerns to bring before their king. Who are you to skip your place in line and place your claims of witches among us in front of all their concerns?"

"He don't belong in this room," Grancyl snorted, "His mind fled many summers past. His boy farms Ypholet's land just south of where Galgooth doubles back."

"My mind ain't fled nowhere, you twit," the old man complained.

Ymarhon ignored the babbling of both men as he fixed his narrow gaze on the older of the two and said, "There are no such things as witches in these lands or any other. Where is this supposed creature that possessed you to interrupt your king?"

"I am no witch," a young woman with bright, blue eyes nearly shouted as she rushed toward the throne on the other side of the long line of sweaty subjects earning loud grumbles from them and more than one hand on the hilt of a sword from the guards lining both sides of the room. The soft but firm curves of her face could not have been kissed by many more than twenty summers of sunrises, but the streaks of gray in her flowing, brown mane told a different story. She hiked the gray frock she wore up a bit to avoid tripping over the tattered thing as she continued toward the front of the room while loudly complaining at her accuser, "The things you say, father! You'd have me strung up by my neck in the courtyard while fair Gandyn toils away in the fields to put bread on your table which I clean for you."

"She is a witch," the old man trembled with agitation as he shouted at Ymarhon, ignoring the woman's defense.

The air seemed to shift slightly as the frustrated grumbling from the rest of the folks in line slowly gained volume. Folks who'd been not so patiently waiting in the stuffy, hot room to air their grievances grew steadily animated. One accidental shove or misplaced elbow of an arm flailing in exasperation could trigger an embarrassing event for the throne. The guards would react. Some, probably many, of his people would be killed or injured.

"Silence!" the king finally shouted, his voice bellowing over the crowd and filling the sticky room which grew instantly quiet. He drew in a deep breath and, in a much calmer tone, asked, "What is your name, old man?"

"Folks with a mind to call me anything address me as Crytan. My son, Gandyn, strong boy, works the fields for Ypholet, a fair lord who's always been keen to share his great wealth with the folks who've helped him build it and keep it," the old man replied suddenly calm and lucid as if he had just slipped out of trance.

Ymarhon nodded, shifted his attention to the young woman, and asked, "Is this man your kin?"

"She's a witch," Crytan grew suddenly animated again. His legs worked quickly up and down as if he were running in place as he shifted between waving his arms above his head and pointing at the young woman he accused of being a witch while continuing his accusations, "She lies! Bind her tongue before she casts an enchantment over this whole fair city and turns us all into pigs!"

In his head, it was a shout. However, the words leaving his lips were carried into the world by calm tones with even notes as he said, "Crytan, you have made your accusation. Please hold your tongue while I get the accused's side of the story. One more outburst like that, and I will have you removed from my throne room. Do you understand?"

Ymarhon stared at the befuddled old man for a quiet, few moments until the bent old thing finally nodded his agreement. Then he shifted his attention back to the young, would-be witch and asked, "Now, how do you know this man? Is he your father?"

Her head shook slightly as she replied, "My husband's. I look after him while Gandyn works the fields."

"She steals from me," Crytan complained, "casting spells to whisk my things away right from under my nose."

Ymarhon raised his hand up to silence the old man as he continued to address the young woman, "Is he always like this?"

"No," the soft features of her face twisted as tears began dribbling down her cheeks, "Most times, he's kind, loves to tell stories. He spent his youth as a wanderer. I'm not sure he's seen all he says, but I love his stories." The smile the memory earned fled quickly as she continued, "Other times, he forgets himself and everyone around him. I have two sons who fear him now. One moment he's kind, spinning yarns of wild adventure and sharing sweets, the next, he's punching and kicking anyone close enough to strike."

"Lies!" the old man shouted.

Ymarhon sighed deeply and turned his head to admonish Crytan for his outbursts once again. Before he could even open his mouth to speak, the most horrific sound he'd ever heard filled the throne room. On its surface, it sounded like the howl of a wounded beast, but it had more depth. It was like a chorus of tortured souls wailing in agony. Everyone in the room before him dove to the ground as if great fires raged above their heads. There was no fire, no apparent danger, just a loud and horrible sound.

A moment after the sound finally ceased, a guard charged in through the open doors of the throne room and shouted, "Havenstahl is under attack, my king. The king's army prepares for battle."

This was the moment, a moment he'd dreamed about since the throne of Havenstahl had emptied in the wake of Maelich's troubles. The long line of grumbling and unappreciative complainers could melt away as he charged off in glory to protect them with the greatest army in all of Ouloos at his back. His face tilted slightly toward the ceiling as he finally replied, "Ready my horse for battle."

The castle loomed above the valley, stone walls blazing white bathed in the bright rays of a midday sun. It stood like a beacon to the throngs of people milling about, trading coins or useless things for other useless things, or blabbering on about topics that seemed so meaningless. Geillan stood among them watching and listening as they tromped through dirt soft from recent rains. He wasn't certain if he hoped someone among them might give him some reason to think more of them or the awful place, or if he simply sought to confirm what he already knew.

He wore a plain, white robe. It was thin fabric, just adequate to hide his form while allowing the cool breezes sweeping through the valley to chill his skin from the warmth of the sun. No one seemed to notice him or care that he was there as they passed in front, behind, or along his side. He may as well have been a rock or a pole, just another obstacle to avoid as they moved on to whatever useless endeavor they'd be off to next. They were all so self-absorbed.

An old man approached guiding a horse dragging a cart nearly overflowing with bushels and bushels of apples. His trousers and cloak were clean despite the soft muck he stepped through.

"Good sir," Geillan beckoned the man as he removed his hood, "your bushels overflow with the riches of a bountiful harvest. Might you spare one of those ripe apples for a poor traveler weary from too many days on the trail?"

The man didn't look in Geillan's direction as he replied gruffly, "Ain't nothing on this cart for no beggars. If you haven't any coin, or anything to trade, I haven't any time for you."

"Of course," Geillan smiled. The response was precisely what he expected it would be. Ever since his mind had been opened, it had been like an avalanche of information poured in to fill it. Even the random thoughts and musings of every mind he touched with his awareness were selfish. And not just blatantly selfish but cleaned up and polished to parade as something pure and self-righteous. The ugliness of it all disgusted Geillan. It might bother him less if they were at least honest with themselves about their motivations. Not one was worthy of life.

He drew in a deep breath as he allowed his awareness to expand until it mingled with everything around him. The wind whipped first. It shifted from a calm and refreshing breeze to a wild and furious gale blasting through the valley. The mighty winds shook huts and tore tent fabric from poles as the people aimlessly milling about began pulling their cloaks up tight around their necks and seeking shelter.

As they hurried about, Geillan shifted his will to the mighty Galgooth rushing beneath the massive cliff at the top of the hill just before the castle. He drew moisture out of the river and pulled it up into the sky to swirl into dark clouds blocking the sun from the valley. It wasn't long before those clouds burst into a torrential downpour soaking all those self-absorbed people and their goods.

It was chaos as they ran all in different directions. No man helped another as they pushed and shoved any who got in their way. Geillan watched one man push a little girl into the muck as if he hadn't noticed she was there. Her blonde hair was streaked with mud when she raised her head to cry out for someone to help. No one did. They just kept charging around or over her. The one that finally sealed it for Geillan was a man who stepped twice upon the girl. He seemed to notice as his boot pressed down on her back, but he did nothing to help her.

The next step he took was on the side of her face, and it pushed her deeper into the muck.

Geillan had seen enough. He called the wind into his lungs and allowed his body to stretch until his head towered no less than twenty-five feet above the ground and his robe lay tattered upon the wet muck below. He stretched his arms wide as red scales grew to cover his naked form. His face remained as human as it had ever been as a Dragon's head grew from his torso. Though it was an extension of him, it appeared as a wholly separate being, growling and roaring and gnashing its teeth while its wild eyes rolled in their sockets.

The Dragon's head was the size of his own, but the jaw stretched into almost a beak full of fangs and horror. Two horns protruded from above green and menacing eyes. It let out a howl so mighty and terrifying that the sound alone was enough to force masses of fleeing folks to the ground. Once it had the attention of all the souls in the valley that day, it stretched to pluck the man who'd been blessed with so many apples he refused to share right out of the mud.

The man screamed as his bones cracked beneath the weight of the Dragon's massive jaws. It only took five chews to pulverize him into goo. Geillan searched his awareness for some inkling of remorse as the dying man's soul was squeezed from his body but found none. The only sorrow the waste of life carried with him to the Lake was sorrow for himself.

Geillan turned his attention to the apple cart. It exploded into flames with a thought. Then he shifted his gaze to another cart, this one full of weapons and other metal crafts. It exploded in the same fashion. The two men who'd been pushing the thing caught fire as molten metal splashed into the air. They spread the flame as they ran about in terror catching fire to everything they touched. Geillan called the dead-eyed-men to him as he continued to burn every man, woman, child, beast, and structure his gaze fell upon. He decided no one was safe, and none would survive.

The dead-eyed men fell from the sky. They appeared like brown streaks as they cut through the winds and rain to plummet to the soft earth. Surrounding Geillan, they removed their hoods. They all appeared copies of each other with wild mops of orange hair and equally orange and mangy beards. Their black, dead eyes grew wide until they appeared like dark moons as their mouths opened equally wide to roar out terrible howls that matched the deafening sound pouring forth from the Dragon's head jutting from Geillan's torso.

It was macabre and beautiful to Geillan. These self-righteous and self-centered, vile things fleeing in terror as all the useless stuff they cared so much about exploded to dust or burned in all consuming flame. The cries of those who hadn't burned were sweet songs of agony as they fought each other for even the smallest bit of shelter from the winds and rains and fire. Geillan's favorites were the ones who successfully battered their way through their kin to achieve those bits of shelter only to melt beneath their supposed protection as the Dragon burned it with his will.

A horn blast distracted Geillan from his art. He offered a smile to the thousands of horses and soldiers gathered at the top of the hill. Eagerness oozed from the group, most notably from their king. Dreams of glory danced about his head. It could be no better for Geillan. Fear would have been fine, but men confidently charging after glory fell so much harder.

Geillan raised his arms out wide to invite the king to battle. The dead-eyed men copied the gesture as the volume of their horrible howls increased tenfold. A sickening smile slithered onto Geillan's face as he pressed his will into the trees on either side of the valley and urged them into a massive and steady flame.

The king called his force to charge. Geillan remained motionless as they approached. Many in the valley who hadn't burned charged toward the force as if all those men and horses might provide them some protection. Unfortunately for those poor souls, the men on those horses were bound for war and glory. Not one of them let up in the slightest as they raced toward victory. Many of those seeking shelter found their ends trampled into the mud under the heavy hooves of charging horses.

The galloping horde was halfway down the hill when Geillan released the three. Those dead-eyed things launched themselves at the quickly approaching force, flying just above the ground like brown streaks of death. It only took moments for them to reach the mighty riders barreling down on them with visions of blood and slicing metal dancing about their minds.

It was a slaughter. Bloody pieces of armor with gore from parts of men which had been torn from other parts of men filled the air accompanied by equally bloody parts of their horses which sported equal amounts of gore.

None of the three terrors, those dead-eyed things, bothered at all with the king. Instead, they sliced through the columns of faithful soldiers charging behind him. Many of their victims, these supposed titans of the battlefield, lost their nerve as the riders before them or next to them were torn to sloppy bits. Those turned off their targets toward the flaming trees on either side of the path into the valley, or back up to the safety of that massive castle at the hill's top. Geillan burned them all slowly, allowing them enough time to panic and charge about spreading fire and chaos to their kin. It was like living art dancing before Geillan's eyes.

By the time the brave king leading the massive force on its charge down the hill reached the valley, that mighty force was gone. All that remained was blood and fire and gore, a smoldering sea of crimson slop.

Geillan's will slithered around Ymarhon's mind reveling in his thoughts of glory and grandeur. The poor king had no idea the army that had charged down the hill at his back chasing honor or renown or some other useless concept was gone. "I am Ymarhon, rightful king of Havenstahl, and leader of the mightiest army in all Ouloos. These lands and the men who occupy them fall under my protection. Today, you breathe your last," the king shouted.

Even without the benefit of strolling through the king's thoughts, Geillan could have surmised the poor fool completely believed the words trumpeting triumphantly from his mouth. The confident tone carrying his proclamation was proof enough. Geillan offered the king a genuine smile as he asked, "What men occupy these lands?"

Geillan's smile widened as Ymarhon's expression contorted from confidence to something more akin to unbridled fear. That was the moment he was waiting for, that moment when the mental protection of hubris and bravado melted away to expose a man's mind to reality. There is no glory in killing and death. There is only more killing and death.

A small part of Geillan felt bad for the disillusioned king as the latter glanced about the valley and back up the hill to witness the carnage. This was to be his moment of glory, the moment for which he'd waited his entire life, his destiny. Instead, it was his greatest disaster and the end of his pathetically short legacy.

"You are alone," Geillan whispered as he forced his flame into the cells of Ymarhon's horse. The beast didn't burn in noticeable flames.

It simply melted away to ash leaving the king to fall into the sloppy muck beneath him.

"None of us are alone in Coeptus," Ymarhon fired back defiantly though his thoughts betrayed his lack of belief in the words.

"I would be sad for you if you believed that," Geillan frowned, "but we both know you do not. You don't even know what Coeptus is."

It was both heartening and sad to see Ymarhon steel his heart and mind against fear and hopelessness while picking himself up from the slop. As the king leveled his sword at him, he wondered if he would do the same. He had nothing to fear from the small man with his tiny metal stick aiming up at him, as sharp as the shimmering thing may have been. He had nothing to fear from any of the creatures on Ouloos, not even the glorious and mighty Dragons. What if he did? Would he have the same resolve to keep fighting even when he knew he couldn't win? Would he even want to? It was folly to ponder things impossible to know without experiencing them, so he didn't do it for very long. Instead, he allowed the wind to stop whipping, the rains to cease their drenching downpour, and the clouds pouring all that water into the valley to evaporate into the breezes gently blowing about.

"Behold, your castle," Geillan boomed as two of the dead-eyed men grabbed hold of Ymarhon's arms and turned him round to look up the hill at the symbol of his power and legacy, "It is all you have left to defend. Why do you still fight to protect it?"

He could smell the salt in the king's tears despite not being able to see them moisten his cheeks as the broken man replied, "You could never understand. That castle is a beacon of freedom to all men. It has stood tall against all form of monsters and even gods. As long as it stands, more men will come to defend it and everything it means."

"I will not pretend to understand," Geillan's voice grew quiet as he troubled over the idea, "To me it is merely bricks upon bricks with no one living inside to give it life. Symbols are meaningless without someone to revere, admire, or fear them." He paused for a moment searching for some crack in the king's resolve or some change in his perspective. Once satisfied Ymarhon's mind would not be changed with words, he continued, "I will give you a gift on this day."

"You have nothing for me, and I want nothing from you," Ymarhon spat, "You are the vilest of things. All the innocent souls seeking only a peaceful life deserved none of the destruction you brought to them."

"It may not be a gift you want, but it is a gift I intend to give you," Geillan whispered as his eyes smoldered red like fire.

A moment later, the castle exploded. A sound like an avalanche of boulders shook the very air surrounding them though none of the heavy stones tossed up into the air like so many dandelion seeds blown from a child's wish lasted long enough to touch a blade of grass or spot of mud. All of them evaporated to ash consumed by a furnace of flames. It was precious few moments until all that remained of the greatest city of men was a smoking hole on top of a mountain.

Ymarhon cried out as the dead-eyed men turned him back around to face Geillan. He ranted some unintelligible threats in throaty, mucus-filled grunts. Geillan didn't need to hear the words meant by the horrid sounds coming from the tortured soul trying to speak them. His intention shouted clearly and loudly. All manner of curses stomped about the king's mind. If only he could lay hands on Geillan, he would rip him limb from limb.

Geillan offered the ranting man a sad smile as he said, "I give you peace."

It didn't appear the king's mind registered the pain his body must have been in as the dead-eyed men ripped his arms from his body and tossed them carelessly to the side. Neither did his angry shouts cease as the three pushed him into the mud and tore open his torso to yank out all the bits inside him. The furious and righteous man continued grunting out threats even after his tongue had been yanked from his skull. He didn't stop until he finally died. Geillan hoped the man ultimately found peace in that moment just before his soul departed for the Lake. If not then, the poor soul never would.

CHAPTER 19
PARADISE

It seemed intentional the way the hot sun warmed the skin as cool breezes tempered its fury enough to create the most gloriously comfortable environment Daritus had ever experienced. It was impossible to discern how many days had passed since he and his group arrived in the perfect place, home to Dragons, as nothing ever seemed to change. The sun was always there as if the time always remained just before midday. Dragons lumbered about flowing waves of green—which seemingly stretched forever in any direction—while others soared the cool currents high in the sky above, and still others lounged comfortably next to a perfect Lake of completely still water. One sat alone, magnificent as she perched atop a short peak at one edge of the Lake, her smooth, red scales glowing in the never-ending sunshine. All Dragons were beautiful perfection, but somehow, she seemed to shine a bit brighter. Daritus offered her a smile as his wide-eyed, happy gaze fell upon her, Helias, nurturer, and Great Mother to all.

The idea of time troubled him slightly as he smiled at that most perfect of Dragons. It made little difference, but tracking one day into the next, one week into the next, and so on had been of such vital importance prior to arriving in this place, the need somehow remained like a ghost clanging chains or howling softly in the night to keep from being forgotten. The trouble with tracking time in this place was, it didn't seem to exist at all. The sun never moved from its spot high in a glorious, clear sky of deep blue interrupted only by random tufts of clouds lazing slowly across the vast expanse above. They seemed like art, intentionally placed to add just a bit more texture and character to an already magnificent piece of work.

"Do you feel you've left things undone, dear Daritus?" Helias asked. The question floated on the soft notes of the Dragon's sublime voice despite occurring to Daritus' mind rather than his ears.

The query got him thinking, tossing through his thoughts to find an answer to something he hadn't considered in…he couldn't remember how long. After failing to find anything that might suggest he did feel he'd left things undone, he finally replied with his mind, "No. I have done all I sought to do in this life. I am whole. I wish only to remain in this place to protect it and the Dragons who occupy it."

"I am happy to hear that," her smile was joy personified, "yet, it troubles me that you feel a need to protect it. From whom do you feel we need protection?"

"From any who might cause you or this place harm," it seemed obvious to Daritus. How could a creature so wise and enlightened as the Great Mother fail to see it?

The sage response didn't come from Helias. Instead, it came from what seemed to be the most unlikely of sources, Moy. The giant was sitting in the sand stroking Lameah's head, gently dragging his fingers along the scales between her eyes and gazing out across the Lake wearing perhaps the most content expression Daritus had ever seen as he offered, "This place belongs to all and should be protected from none."

"Moy is wise," Lameah added, "All beings are born from this place to become what they will become and return once their time here is finished. It is a beacon to all."

It was the first time Daritus had felt troubled about anything since arriving. He failed at keeping a small hint of vexation out of his tone as he asked, "What about the great campaign when the men of this world hunted Dragons to the ends of Ouloos and left only you remaining, Helias? That is why Druindahl, my home for most of my life, even exists. I was trained from a young age to protect you Dragons and this place. What has changed?"

"The gods who gave that charge to you and the men of your great city are gone. It was them who battled over this place. Kallum and Brerto desired to destroy it while Moshat and Kaldumahn sought to protect it. Each had their reasons whether they were their own or ideas fed to them by Ijilv. None of it mattered or helped bring Ouloos any closer to any sort of goal. Their only accomplishments were bringing the fate of Ouloos closer to their own personal desires," Helias' voice remained sweet even as it carried words almost hurtful to Daritus' mind.

"Then what is the point of any of it?" Daritus' shock echoed in his voice as he said the words out loud rather than speaking with his mind to Helias.

The Dragon replied calmly with her mind, "Love, Daritus, unconditional love. That is love given freely with no expectations or requirements. There is nothing anyone needs to do to receive it. Do you understand that? Responding to violence with violence to protect something does not prove your love for that thing you protect. It only proves you desire a different outcome than that which you defend against."

"I am trying to feel what you describe for all creatures, but I cannot accept that there is something wrong with defending what you love. The idea is not justifiable in my mind," Daritus continued to speak with his mouth rather than his mind as his voice rose slightly with each word.

"You are not wrong, Daritus. Nothing is wrong. You are righteous and pure. However, a man's need to oppose things regardless of his reason for opposing them is why violence exists in this world. Sadly, those reasons are oftentimes the result of fear or a desire for revenge. You desire to protect this place for fear that it may be destroyed, and you will lose it. You came to this perfect place to learn how to kill a Dragon. That is revenge. Killing Cialia would do nothing to change your situation. Leisha will remain dead. The only difference for you is you would then have both a wife and daughter to mourn. Cialia did not intend to kill her mother, your sweet wife. That was a result of her need for revenge against the gods for their actions which she perceived as evil. Never and always are challenging concepts I prefer to avoid; however, I cannot recall a time when violence ever delivered the desired result for any man. Can you?" The Dragon's words were contrary to everything Daritus believed, but he couldn't find a suitable argument to them. It was revenge he sought when he had decided to kill Cialia, and fear, as much as it may have been disguised as duty, was the reason he defended Havenstahl against the forces from across the Great Sea and Druindahl before that.

Despite how much sense the Dragon's ideas made; they didn't sit well with Daritus. "So, I should sit idly by and watch if any creatures come to destroy this place? That stinks of cowardice."

"Of course, it does, in your mind" Helias countered, "Your entire life has been devoted to protecting beings and places from beings from other places, and you have become expert at that very thing. You see inaction as cowardice. However, I do not counsel inaction. Instead, I would suggest showing your supposed adversaries love. Receive them with open arms. Show them they are welcome in your world. Teach them how to do the same. I can think of nothing braver."

"And as they cut me down?" Daritus chuckled dryly at the thought as he shook his head in something just shy of disgust.

If Helias were at all troubled by the slight, her tone failed to express it, "Perhaps, you would have changed their minds. What a gift would that be? That is love, Daritus. It is selfless and unconditional. It is far greater than one man or one city. Change is neither quick nor easy, but it is necessary to become something more than what we already are."

This last bit was almost accessible as he mulled it over. It cast his mind back to every battle he'd ever fought, both losses and victories. Nothing much changed from one incident to the next regardless of whether his side won or lost. Perhaps she had a point. Of what use were his efforts if nothing were any better or worse for the men he protected? Victories in and of themselves were accomplishments, but what good were they if the result was nothing?

Hasujo's recently pleasing voice soaring over equally pleasing tones strummed confidently from his mandolin suddenly interrupted Daritus' contemplation. That bard sang:

A man bowed deep before a Dragon
She wondered the cost of all he'd done
Put down your sword and drop your shield
Love is all you need under the sun
That man and his heart they sunk so low
Did nothing he'd ever done matter
Don't fret 'tis not too late to begin
To talk of love is not a natter

Hasujo continued to drone on. His mastery over his craft was improving. The song sounded so triumphant, but the bard's words stung a bit. It was even worse when all in Daritus' group joined in with a chorus of Dragons to sing a refrain which celebrated actions which were near exact opposites of everything he'd ever done, everything he'd ever believed a man should do to be a man. Even Kantiim and Spang—two of the mightiest warriors he'd ever had the good fortune to fight beside—belted out the tune.

A sickening idea suddenly slithered into Daritus' mind. Was it a trick? Had the Dragons mesmerized his men with all their talk of love, acceptance, and community? Was it all merely a ploy to get them to lower their guard long enough for some kind of killing blow, one mighty blast of Dragon's flame to burn them all in some kind of unholy furnace?

"Daritus," Helias' voice broke through the song and became the only thing he could hear, "search my mind and heart. You can do that in this place. All you need is a desire to know. Look there and tell me if you find any form of malice or plans for some kind of trick. Your companions are happy. You should share in their joy. Be one with them."

"Even if I had any idea how to do such a thing, you could show me anything you wished for me to see," even as the words occurred in his mind, he knew they were false. Even if she hadn't shown him only love since opening his eyes to the grandeur of her home, both Maelich and Cialia had reported as much. Helias was love and honesty and all things pure. She was no deceiver.

Before he could voice as much with his mind or his mouth, he was distracted by a small band of grongs stumbling through the same foreign trees and reveling in the flavors of the same foreign fruits he and his group had enjoyed who knows how many days or weeks prior. The colors they bore on their armor suggested they were survivors of the great war between Havenstahl and the monsters from across the Great Sea. What cause did they have to venture so far east?

"They have the same cause as you," Helias' voice chimed sweet as a bell in his mind, "They seek love, peace, and a place to belong. You probably do not realize it, but your acceptance of this place has opened the awareness of it to all on Ouloos. More will come. My question to you is, will you welcome them with open arms or rally your troops to cut them down?"

"So, this is my test?" Daritus' tone was a bit sharper than he intended, "If I cut them down, I am unworthy of this place, and you will throw me out?"

"Sweet Daritus, your skeptical mind has always served you well, but you needn't keep your guard up in this place. There is no trick. There is no test. All are worthy of the Lake, and all are welcome. We Dragons will love you the same whether you receive our new friends with open arms or cut them down. We will all love you even as we weep for the loss of them," the slightest hint of pleading slipped into the Dragon's tone.

The malice he expected to feel was absent as he watched the grongs frolic about wrestling and laughing with each other. It occurred to him he'd never heard a grong laugh. It was a strange sound, something like a bag full of rocks being violently shook by a strong man. They seemed so happy. He wondered what they would do if he strolled out to greet them.

"They cannot see us, can they?" he suddenly asked.

"Not until we allow it," Helias replied, "I do intend to allow it, but it occurred to me you might struggle with that. I thought it wise to give you a moment to digest their presence before we welcome them in."

"May I go to them?" Daritus asked soberly. Even as he asked the question, he wasn't sure how he would address the group. Of the seven he counted, no less than four of them still carried clubs which were more than likely stained with the blood of men he'd sent to battle in defense of Havenstahl.

"Of course," Helias replied, "You are free to do as you wish."

"I am with you," Kantiim's voice startled him. He hadn't heard his old chum approach absorbed in such challenging concepts with the mother of all Dragons.

"When did you get so quiet?" Daritus laughed, barely succeeding in suppressing what would have been an embarrassing start. After the few moments it took to compose himself, he added, "I am happy to have you at my side."

"And I am equally happy to be at yours, old friend," Kantiim smiled as he patted Daritus' shoulder. Then he did the unthinkable. He removed his sword belt and laid it upon the ground.

"What are you doing?" Daritus nearly hissed.

"Exactly what these glorious Dragons would do," the old soldier smiled back at him, "Sadly, I fear I may lack the restraint they showed us. I am leaving my sword behind so I am unable to use it should my resolve falter."

"You are a brave man, Kantiim of Druindahl," Helias' voice echoed across the prairie surrounding the Lake.

The idea seemed ridiculous, however brave it might be. Nonetheless, Spang followed suit removing his sword belt as he walked up and said, "And I as well."

Daritus grasped the buckle of his belt as he glanced first at Kantiim and then at Spang. Neither man carried any doubt in their eyes or on their faces. Then he looked back at the small pack of grongs. They seemed so different than any grong he'd ever seen frolicking as they were. He was sure that would change as soon as they caught sight of him or his two chums.

The leather seemed so loud as he unbuckled his belt, held it up by his sword's scabbard and asked, "Are you both completely sure about this? We will be horribly outmatched without weapons."

"There will be no battle, old friend. We shall show our new friends love and hope they show us the same in return," Spang replied.

Daritus offered the most genuine smile he could muster at that moment while laying his sword down. He felt naked and exposed without the thing dangling by his side. He couldn't remember the last time he'd been out anywhere in Ouloos without it. "So be it," he finally said, "We will either welcome our new friends into our new home, or they will kill us and overrun it."

"I think you may be surprised by the impact a welcoming smile can have on a creature," Helias sweetly counseled.

"That is my hope," the smile which remained on Daritus' face as he said the words was absent any form of joy or happiness which might lift the corners of a mouth, like the ghost of some heartfelt expression haunting his lips. Instead, it stood like a flimsy shield hiding the trepidation coiled about his heart.

Daritus approached the happy band of grongs with Spang and Kantiim walking beside him. He glanced first at Spang and then at Kantiim marveling at the honest smiles they wore and wishing the false thing puffing up his cheeks was born of the same heartfelt emotion. Had he been alone, he may have slowed his steps and used the foliage to hide his approach until he was near enough to the brutish creatures to avoid any kind of attack they might unleash at the sight of him. The confident gaits of his two companions made the idea seem a bit silly. After all he had seen in his life, how could he be so afraid? He decided it probably wasn't fear. As much as he hoped to see them as some kind of kin, equal beings traversing a similar journey of life as his, all with wants and desires which may have been different than his own but no less worthy, he struggled to do as much. It occurred to him in that moment that his own thoughts betrayed his true feelings regardless of how different he might wish they were. He didn't see them as any kind of equals. He saw them as monsters, savages who would rip him to shreds if given the chance.

The weight of Kantiim's heavy hand on his shoulder dragged him away from his thoughts as his old friend counseled, "Best not focus on such negative ideas. Open your heart, old friend. Give them a chance before damning them as the beasts you believe them to be."

He couldn't quite do that thing Kantiim suggested, but he decided to get as close to it as he was able. "Friends, we welcome you. Please join us in the peaceful joy which is the Lake, beginning and end of all things," the sounds that filled the small clearing where seven grongs wrestled and laughed and ate all the marvelous fruits and nuts the trees had to offer were not the words that occurred to his mind as he said them. He didn't know many grong words—their language differed greatly from the common tongue with individual words describing what might be multiple sentences in the language of Druindahl and Havenstahl and all the great cities—yet the words carried into the world on his booming voice were words plucked directly from the grongs' own native tongue.

The grongs were obviously startled by the sudden interruption. It was apparent they hadn't noticed Daritus and his two chums until that very moment. Those grongs wasted little time. They charged quickly. There were no clubs swung at any heads, but it was mere moments before Daritus' arms—which were outstretched in the most welcoming of gestures—were roughly grabbed by two grongs and pinned tightly behind his back. He kept the smile on his face as he resisted the urge to struggle against his captors, even as Kantiim and Spang were accosted and restrained in the same fashion. Instead, he said, "Please, friends, we mean you know harm. As you can plainly see, we are unarmed and seek only peace with you."

"I am Slurg, chief of my people," the one grong who wasn't restraining any in the small welcoming committee replied. Though the sounds which occurred to Daritus' ears sounded like unintelligible grunts, their meaning was clear in his mind as the grong continued, "We seek the Lake, the beginning and the end of all things. The great one promised it to us in ages long gone by. The giants' war has ended. That was the omen, a great battle with men would decimate our numbers. Those remaining would earn the right to finish our days with Dragons. You bar our path."

Even as the two grongs holding Daritus fast tightened their grip and pushed him forward, closer to Slurg, he responded earnestly without any hate or desire for retribution, "We do no such thing. We come to welcome you to that paradise promised you. I fear I know very little about your beliefs. What I do know is that the Lake belongs to all of us."

"Please join us," Kantiim added, "We welcome you with love."

"They lie," the grong holding Daritus' right arm growled in his ear, "There are probably men hiding all about these trees waiting to pounce as soon as we drop our guard."

The ground beneath Daritus was alive with plant life. It was a blessing as a blast to the back of his knee drove him to the forest floor under the weight of the two grongs restraining him. His knees throbbed as he landed roughly on them. A hard-packed trail would have hurt much worse. Despite his gritted teeth, he maintained a calm tone as he replied, "There is no lie. Think about it. I know you have no reason to trust me, but why would we risk coming to you unarmed and vulnerable if our plan was to destroy you? I have left my sword behind."

"We stand before you with nothing to protect us but a promise of peace and the love in our hearts," Spang added before being roughly shoved to the ground in the same fashion Daritus had.

Slurg's expression softened as he looked to be mulling over whether to release Daritus and his men. It seemed he was about to command his grongs to do the former when the entire plan fell apart.

Daritus had no idea where the young swordsman had been hiding, but Nothany suddenly appeared behind Slurg with his blade resting against the side of the grong's throat. The authority in the boy's voice was surprising as he commanded, "Release my friends, or I will decorate the trees with your chief's blood."

"Nothany, no!" Daritus shouted even as he felt a grong's claw slithering up his scalp to grab a handful of hair and yank his head back, "These grong's are guests not adversaries."

"I would expect guests to more gracious," Nothany's reply sounded ominous as the volume of his voice dropped and its tone deepened, "I commanded you to let my friends go."

Daritus couldn't decide if it was defeat or disappointment flopping about Slurg's tone as the grong chief said, "There it is. Why give us hope we'd be welcomed if you only planned to cut us down?"

A tear followed the question. It traced a zig zag pattern between the scales of Slurg's face. Daritus knew the kind of feelings that could cause eyes to moisten so; hope dashed against the rocks of reality when you finally soften your heart to an idea only to learn you'd been duped into believing a lie. As he pondered the dark abyss which must have been forming in Slurg's heart, he couldn't help but feel pity for Nothany at the same time. It was obvious the Lake did not present the same promise to him that it represented for everyone else who'd arrived. He had trained for years to be a protector of lost souls with no one to stand for them against the horrors of Ouloos. All his efforts must have seemed a waste to him when the need for the skills he learned fled in the face of the same kind of inaction Daritus struggled with himself.

Despite the sharp claw poking against his throat while the grong holding him continued to yank at his hair, Daritus managed to keep his voice at a measured and calm tone as he said, "We do not need your protection, Nothany. Slurg and his group have come seeking the love and peace promised to them by the Lake. This is not your fight."

"And as these beasts bash in your skulls with their clubs?" Nothany nearly shouted.

"I don't believe they will," Daritus maintained his calm demeanor even as the grong holding him tugged his head back a bit farther, "But if that is my fate, it is a choice I made. It is unfair for you to interfere. I do not want you to save me."

It sounded like disgust when Nothany grunted something unintelligible in reply. Daritus knew it was more than that. There was frustration and probably sadness. From the young man's perspective, it probably seemed like Sanjo had told him to dig a big hole, and then Daritus had come along to tell him to fill it back up.

No one spoke as Nothany stood there still holding his blade against Slurg's throat while his face contorted into multiple expressions until he finally looked defeated and lowered his sword. "This isn't something I can do," he said as he slowly backed away from the group, "I will leave you to your fate, but I am not going back to that Lake. This is not my way."

"You have grown to be a good man, Nothany," Sanjo suddenly slipped out from behind a tree to stand next to the boy, "and a good man must choose his own path. There is little else I could possibly teach you. Let this lesson you learned for yourself be your last. Not everyone needs saving. Some folks want the fate you would protect them from. It is wrong to interfere with another's desires."

"Thank you for all you've given me," Nothany nodded slightly, "Though it saddens me to see what you've become, I wish you the best. I hope these grongs don't kill you, and you find the life you desire."

Then the boy was gone, slipping back into the trees to find whatever adventure would be his next.

"There will be no further threat to you or your group," Sanjo turned and said to Slurg after watching Nothany leave his life forever.

Slurg remained quiet for a moment while he glanced about the small clearing. Daritus could feel the throbbing of his heart all the way up in his ears as Slurg squinted his eyes while scrutinizing him and his companions. After a few tense moments, the grong choontah finally said, "I believe you. Release these men."

All the grongs holding Daritus, Spang, and Kantiim heeded the command except one. The one still clinging to Daritus' hair and pressing his sharp claw against his neck grew even more agitated as he nearly shouted, "Foolish."

"Glung," Slurg scolded the trepidatious grong, "The man you hold there could have instructed the boy to slit my throat. Instead, he convinced him to release me. It was the only leverage he held against us. Think about it. You know they have weapons somewhere. They could have taken us by surprise and cut us down as we lounged in this paradise. They did not do that." Then he turned his attention to Daritus and said, "I know you. You are Daritus of Druindahl. The brave general who killed Maomnosett Bok in one-on-one combat. These six grongs accompanying me are all who remain of the great force I sent to fight your armies in the great war. I know there are more, but they are scattered and afraid. I don't want to fight anymore. None of us do."

"You will find no fight here," Daritus replied earnestly remaining on his knees even after Glung released him in disgust.

Slurg nodded before continuing, "The stories I've heard of you suggest you are a noble and trustworthy man. I pray this is not an act."

As the last words reached Daritus' ears, Slurg's expression changed. The grong gasped as his eyes widened like two saucers of white with yellow circles at their centers that were flecked with brown. The black pupils running nearly from the top to the bottom of those yellow circles were like vertical black slits with two half circles at either side of them. All in the clearing turned with Daritus to see what vision had so amazed the grong.

There was the Lake at the center of a wide prairie of green with majestic Dragons dotting the countryside as well as the sky above. Daritus' smile was finely completely genuine as he said, "Welcome, friends, to the Lake of Dragons."

The sternness in Glung's tone fled as the grong fell to his knees next to Daritus with tears in his eyes and proclaimed, "This is the land promised us. I have no words to describe what my heart feels. I am whole, and we are one."

"Come," Daritus patted the grong's shoulder knowing exactly how he felt, "you must meet Helias, the Great Mother, and her sisters. They will show you nothing but peace and love as you make this place your home."

The walk to the Lake was as majestic as the first time Daritus made the journey. The smiles on all the faces accompanying him echoed what he felt in his heart. It wasn't just the sights surrounding him, overwhelming him with visions, colors more vibrant than anywhere else on Ouloos. As amazing as they were, they were equals with the clarity of sounds, each flap of a bird's wing or each blade of grass flowing in the calm breezes motivating them on a smooth wave with each other blade of grass in the wide prairie. And the smells. No lake smelled so fresh as the Lake at the center of it all, and no flower's perfume smelled so sweet carried upon that same gentle breeze. But, more than anything, was the way that breeze felt on skin warmed so perfectly by the glorious sun blazing above. It seemed impossible that any soul arriving in the place could feel anything but pure, unbridled joy. The sentiment echoed back at him from the expressions of all his companions.

"Welcome to your home," Helias' glorious voice sang out, filling the entire area with song.

Dragons, men, giants, and trogmortem all cheered together in response. Daritus' eyes welled with tears born of the truest joy he'd ever felt as he joined his kin in that cheer. If that was what it felt like to show unconditional love to a stranger, he wanted to share it with all. No other time in his life had he felt purer happiness. Even the happiest day he could remember—the day he pledged his undying devotion to his dear, departed wife—he hadn't felt a greater sense of hope than that which swelled in his breast in that moment. This was paradise.

It seemed impossible that he could ever feel greater elation until Hasujo set down his mandolin, walked up to one of the grongs, and embraced him. Daritus hadn't learned that grong's name, but he knew him to be Thok. Thok seemed tentative at first, but the trepidation didn't last. In moments, both Hasujo and his new friend Thok wept tears of joy as they embraced, like long lost brothers reunited after years apart. Others joined them. Before long everyone was singing through tears as they hugged and cheered each other for their good fortune.

Helias suddenly cried out in a pitiable song of lament. The sound stung, a stark contrast to the joyous proclamations filling the vast prairie surrounding the Lake. "They are arriving," she wept, "Havenstahl has been utterly destroyed with no souls left to remember the place or tell her stories. Geillan has passed his judgement on them deeming them unworthy of Ouloos."

The joy remaining in Daritus' heart seemed odd. He expected such news would have brought his soul crashing down from the heights, but it didn't. As horrid a thing as it seemed, all those souls would be coming home to the Lake. "Is that a reason for sadness?" he suddenly asked, "Because I feel none."

"It is not," Helias smiled through her tears. "I weep for the pain they felt as they burned in Geillan's flame, but I feel joy for their return to this place. They are coming home. I also weep for Geillan. He believes in what he does, but his actions will leave a darkness in his soul. No matter how righteous any creature feels about their actions, harming other creatures for any cause takes a piece of you away."

Those souls arrived before Daritus could respond. They came as a mist hovering close above the ground. He felt cold surrounded by them as they continued past him to the Lake. Memories from their lives all muddled together in discombobulated scenes that occurred to him as if they were his own memories. Some were happy, some sad, most were something in between those two emotions, but a few were born of extreme joy or lament. Those stood out among the rest like shouts in an otherwise silent cathedral echoing in Daritus' mind. He saw a baby girl being held up still glistening from being just born. Joy swelled through him as he looked up at the bright cherub seeing the world for the first time as if he'd given birth to her himself. In the next moment, that same girl was celebrating the end of her eighth summer. He couldn't fathom how he knew she was the same girl, but he did. Terror filled him as he watched her chase a butterfly onto a hard-packed trail carved with wagon ruts directly in front of a crazed horse who'd escaped its keeper. He hadn't seen the wild scarra who attacked the horse's corral and frightened the beast enough to knock down its fence and charge off along the main road into the town, but he knew the cause almost like a premonition within a dream. His heart flailed into a deep abyss of woe falling from the great heights it had achieved only moments prior while beholding that girl when she was newborn as he watched her be trampled to death beneath the unforgiving hooves of the crazed animal.

More visions like that came. He didn't need to see the faces of his companions to know they all experienced what he did as the mist continued its slow journey to the Lake. They became part of those memories rather than watching from outside of them. Daritus felt it all with them. He saw new life entering the world, lives being joined together with love and optimism for the future, moments of horror while loved ones were maimed or killed, and quieter moments of sadness with groups of teary eyes surrounding frail forms breathing their last. The emotions of those souls who shared them became his own.

Then the lights came. As the mist reached the Lake, bright lights fell from it into the calm waters. The Lake glowed as it filled with one after another. Each would dip below the surface before shooting up into the sky like a star falling in the wrong direction.

"How do you feel right now, Daritus? Will you leave us and seek revenge against Geillan for all the life he has destroyed?" Helias' sweet tones occurred once again to his mind rather than his ears.

He responded in the same fashion with clear thoughts, "I will not. I ache for the pain caused to the people in that place I once defended and called home, but my heart swells with joy at their blessed return to the beginning. I can think of no purer happiness than that."

"You fill me with hope, Daritus," Helias commended him, "You would make a perfect Dragon."

CHAPTER 20
THE TWINS RETURN

Pain. The idea seemed illogical, but it was a physical pain Cialia felt in her chest when she materialized in the cool sand at the very edge of the Lake. Heartbreak is not a physical thing. It is merely an expression hoping to describe something too difficult to define with simple words. Feelings were oftentimes like that, too abstract for an accurate representation that might help some other soul grasp what one soul felt. As silly as it seemed in her mind, Cialia's chest throbbed as if her battered heart might burst right out of her chest.

As much as she wished she could blame the perfect blue sky or the perfect, white fluffs of clouds slowly drifting about and decorating it, she could not. Neither could she blame the serene waters of the Lake or the cool sand beneath her bare feet. Though the sky, the water, the sand, even the warm sun cuddling with the cool air to swirl into the perfect temperature were the cause of her heartbreak, she was to blame. All the glorious sights and sounds, smells and tastes, even the perfect air on her flesh were flawless. They reminded her of what an imperfect thing she had become.

"Welcome home," Daritus' voice immediately behind her startled her. She braced for the killing blow to punch through her back and out her chest. She would do nothing to stop it. The sentence was deserved. She would simply slip off his blade into the Lake knowing that the quick death was a far easier sentence than she had earned with all the pain and death she had caused while seeking her revenge against the gods.

After a few moments, it was apparent her father had no intention of running her through, and she finally replied, "I do not expect you will ever forgive the horrible things I have done, but I am sorry. I am sorry for all the pain I have caused you and everyone else I love. I accept whatever punishment you deem fit."

"I spent many drunken days on the trail thinking of all the things I would say to you when I finally stood before you and killed you. None of those words are worthy of being spoken. After spending those days out in the wood and spending who knows how much time in this perfect place, I have learned what I've been missing in this life," the anger she expected to hear in his voice was absent as he replied in soft, happy tones.

Tears brimmed at the edge of her eyelids as she asked, "What is that?"

"Do you remember what you asked me when last we spoke?" he asked plainly.

She finally turned to face him, losing one tear down her cheek as she replied, "The last time I spoke to you was in my own mind, but yes, I remember the last time we spoke in the waking world. I disappointed you."

Daritus shook his head as he replied, "The man you disappointed in the tent that day is not the same man standing before you at this moment. You were equally disappointed with that man. You asked me where was my joy? On that day, I didn't believe I had anything to be joyful about. On this day, I know the answer to that question. My joy is standing directly before me."

More tears came. They rushed down her face like floodwaters washing down a mountain as she dropped to her knees in the cool sand and sobbed, "I am no one's joy. By this point you must know that my mother, *your wife*, died at my hands. I killed your wife. My father would never let a crime so vile go unpunished. I deserve your wrath and my sentence."

"I miss your mother, my sweet Leisha, every moment of every day. I smell her sometimes in the sweet perfume of the air. Her face constantly floats before me like an apparition. This world is a darker place since she is gone, but I do not blame you for that loss. You did not intend to take her from this world. You were trying to protect her. You were wrong, but your intentions were pure. I hold you blameless," his voice cracked a bit as the last few words left his mouth.

Tears were streaming down Daritus' face by the time she looked back up at him. The words stung. Part of her was relieved he still saw her as his own, but a larger part of her wished someone could hold her to account. "I do not deserve your forgiveness," she finally mumbled amid her sobs.

"Stand up," though Daritus' words sounded like a command, they were delivered more like a request.

When she obliged, her father pulled her close and hugged her tightly. Her mind raced back to a time when she couldn't have seen more than five summers. It was such an innocent time in her life. She had yet to witness the filth of the world. The memory was so vivid, she could have been living it right in that moment. She wept next to a baby fallon. Its leg was broken. She tried to pick the poor thing up, but the suffering creature began bleating so loudly, it sounded like babies screaming in the nursery. Father had found her there sobbing over the thing.

"This is a sad thing," he had said as he knelt beside her and put his arm around her shoulders.

"Where is her mother?" she cried.

"You might not understand this just yet, but men hunt these woods for food. The good men of Druindahl are bound to take no mothers for meat, but not all men abide by those same promises," his tone was the same then as it was standing there with her next to the Lake. In both instances, she didn't like the words he used, but his tone was somehow reassuring.

"I will be this fawn's mama then if she don't have one," exact details were a bit fuzzy, but she recalled stomping her foot as she made the proclamation all those summer's prior.

"Love," that was what he called her every time he was about to tell her something he knew she wouldn't like, "that fawn is suffering. You cannot fix it. As sad a thing as this is, we should end her suffering."

The idea seemed far less ridiculous in her mind thinking back on it than it did back when he had broken her heart with those words. In that moment she withdrew from him and nearly shouted, "The scarra will get her." As if on cue, a wild scarra howled in the distance. "See," she added.

She remembered his eyes more than anything as he held her by the shoulders. Sadness floated about in them. He hadn't liked the words he had to say any more than she had, but he said them anyway, "Scarra need to eat too. Life is one big circle. One creature's end means another's survival. This poor fawn will help feed that circle."

It made sense even back then. She loved scarra as much as she loved fallon. One of father's friends, Falingrid, had tamed one and kept it just like a scrod. It was so big and fluffy, and friendly enough to pet and chase. Scarra did need to eat.

She watched as father removed his knife from its scabbard, held the bleating animal close, and quickly slit its throat. Once it stopped moving, he laid it gently down upon the ground and hugged her the same way he had just then. Despite all the summers which had passed between those two moments, that reassuring hug was just what she needed.

She could have remained there forever, but a hug from her father could never erase all she had done. Luckily, Maelich's remaining hand—the one she hadn't removed with her blade—dropped gently on her shoulder. "I am to blame for all of this," his voice was quiet.

Daritus raised his head and replied, "We all have failed, lad. None of us is any better or worse than the rest of us. We have all done things we regret. None of those things can be changed."

"That is truth," Maelich's reply was so soft it sounded as if he were far away.

Cialia finally raised her head from Daritus' shoulder and asked, "So, what do we do now?"

There was something in his eyes that had been missing the last time she saw him. They almost glowed with pride and hope as he smiled and said, "We will be like Dragons and live the way they have been trying to teach us for all our days." He waived each arm one after the other as if presenting the landscape around them as he continued, "Look around you. It has already begun. There are men living with grongs and giants and trogmortem and all manner of creature. Look at them, talking and laughing, lounging and eating, and all of it they are doing together. We are teaching each other to be better. This place, this is love, Cialia. This is the beginning."

She did as he asked while he spoke words that seemed so foreign coming from the man who raised her. They had both changed so much since that day in his tattered tent where he desperately sought a champion to help him destroy the various creatures he now welcomed with open arms, and she left to kill gods. The activity around the Lake matched his description perfectly. She saw a grong excitedly discussing the petals of a blue flower with light-green flecks with a giant who seemed equally excited to hear all that grong had to say. He saw a man laughing with a trogmortem as they shared some sloppy fruit that seemed to bring them more joy than any food could. Everything was as she hoped it might someday be when she decided her role in this world was to defend all these creatures against the gods who taught them to hate each other, and yet, she couldn't find the joy they all shared in herself.

Helias' voice danced across the air like a song to her ears, "You know what is coming, my love."

The Dragon was as wise as ever and correct as usual. She did know what was coming, death and destruction, an end to this perfection that barely had a chance to be. "I do," she finally replied with looming sadness weighing on her words.

"What will you do?" the Dragon asked, "Will you protect them against the terror coming to burn Ouloos to dust, or will you embrace your nephew and show him the love none have shown him before?"

"The latter is my hope," her tone carried as much confidence as she felt in her heart. She truly wasn't sure what she would do when she finally came face to face with Geillan.

As Cialia struggled to add other confident words that might convince her she could do the thing she hoped, Raya spoke up with all the sureness Cialia was missing, "I will show him love. In my heart, I have already forgiven him for all he has done. It saddens me to think of all he's been through in his short time in this world, especially the loss of his mother. Though he was the tool used to destroy her, she was taken from him."

Cialia had all but forgotten Raya was there. Before she could formulate any kind of response, Helias' sweet voice boomed from the top of her low, rocky peak, "The forgotten one has been remembered, a wish of a Dragon that could never be. You have seen much I cannot pretend to understand. However, your motives are something I completely understand. It saddens me to know you have been hidden away, alone waiting and hoping for this very moment. Is it what you expected? Is this what you planned?"

"No, things haven't quite followed the path I intended," Raya's smile hid any disappointment she might have been feeling in her heart, "but I am hopeful we can still reach the destination."

"For Ouloos to be born," Helias' reply was unusually quiet. The mother of all Dragons had always been so completely sure of every word that left her perfect mouth, but her muted tone suggested doubt.

"You are unsure of this plan," Cialia blurted.

"I am," Helias conceded quietly.

"But you know everything," in all Cialia's encounters with the Dragon, she could not recall even one moment when the timeless creature failed to correctly predict an outcome. If the Great Mother was unsure whether they were doing the right thing, how could any of them be certain?

"I appreciate the confidence, dear sister, but I do not know everything," the bold glory of Helias' voice returned with her smile as she continued, "I know all the beings in this world well enough to guess how they might react to a given situation. That is not magic nor clairvoyance. I simply care enough to pay attention. Though I love Raya just the same, she comes from another place, a place I know nothing about. That makes it difficult for me to guess the path ahead."

"But this is our path," Maelich interrupted, "We have all followed different trails, but we have all ended up in this place. Regardless of our individual motivations, we share the same goal. Let's call everyone home."

"Maelich is correct," Daritus proclaimed with the confidence of a king, "Let us form a council of hope. Whatever might be our end, we can share the glory and peace and love we have found here with each other. Let us weep no more tears for sadness. Let love gush forth from our eyes as we marvel at the magnificence of our world."

It all sounded too easy, but Cialia came together with her father and brother and Raya, this foreign god from another world who knew more than any of them about what was coming. She still couldn't bring herself to trust that one. Hope is a wonderful thing until it is crushed. Still, she failed to find a better alternative at that moment, and the sight of giants, grongs, trogmortem, and even Dragons sauntering over to join the growing circle of this new council did fill her with something close to it. Dare she wish that Ouloos could be this, everyone loving and accepting everyone for being exactly what they were. Hope was all she could do.

CHAPTER 21
DRUINDAHL'S LAST RIDE

The air was cool and damp in the forest that day. It smelled like rain. Geillan troubled over the idea for a moment. He knew how a forest recently washed by fresh rains should smell, but he had never experienced the fragrance firsthand. It was more pleasing than he had imagined it might be. He chased after each muted note mingling together to create the perfection he breathed into his nose. Some were earthy, others musky, and still others sweet. Some were intriguing combinations of the three. He could identify the source of each whether they be a flower or decaying leaves or some random fungus thriving on the forest floor though he was smelling them for the first time.

His foot sunk a bit into the wet trail. The muck was sloppy and slimy on his bare skin. The sensation was initially troubling. However, a giggle escaped his lips as he pressed his foot deeper into the mire, and cool mud slipped up in between his toes. It was grotesque and wonderful at the same time. The slimy wonder of it had him imagining all manner of insect and slug slithering over his bare skin, yet he couldn't stop pressing his foot deeper and deeper with each step.

Leaves suddenly rustled deep in the thick brush along the side of the trail. A quick flash of brown was all Geillan noticed in the filtered rays of sunlight bold enough to break the thick canopy above. He knew it was a fallon. As he stared at the spot all the vibrant colors surrounding it came into focus. Wet leaves of the deepest green glistened with fat droplets of rain still clinging to them and bending the sunlight to cast tiny rainbows wherever a beam of light terminated. Sometimes it was the rough, brown bark of a thick trunk, and other times it was the delicate petals of a flower—those seemed to glow blue or purple, even orange or pink. Still other times it was just another leaf thick with droplets of water that would bend the light again and again.

"And you wish to destroy this place," Kallum's voice broke through the moment of serenity Geillan had found nestled deep in the peaceful forest.

Geillan hid the hint of frustration the interruption caused him as he casually asked, "Why are you here speaking to me? I thought I told you to fish."

"You did," Brerto's annoying voice droned in his head, "but I fear you may have forgotten about us. After several attempts to stop myself from fastening a fat worm to my hook and casting it out into the red waves you left us to drift upon, I was finally able to do just that. I set my pole down and suggested my brothers should do the same. Then we were free to roam about. You are having doubts about your grand plan to destroy this place."

The annoying god was correct. Geillan hid the idea from him and continued with a bored tone, "I know all, and I forget nothing. You fished for my amusement, and I no longer found it amusing. I have other things to occupy my attention than the pathetic lot of you."

"Son," Ijilv began.

"Do not call me that," Geillan snapped out loud. His prior responses had only occurred in his mind where those supposed gods meandered through his thoughts. "I have much to do right now, but I will put my full attention to torturing you until the end of eternity if you call me that again."

"Forgive me, Geillan," the god demurred, "I forget myself sometimes. It is strange, but I think I may have begun to see you as such. The creatures of this place are blameless. We gods are to blame for all you perceive as evil in this world. Do you not think it equally evil to destroy them for actions over which they had no control?"

Geillan smiled at the glowing canopy above him. They were correct he had forgotten about them while distracted by his pursuit to destroy the evil world they had concocted, but he still knew their thoughts. They wanted him to destroy these cities of men. Their attempts at hiding their motives were pathetic. Ijilv and the rest truly believed his father and his aunt, those false Dragons, could destroy him, and they truly believed wiping the wickedness from the face of Ouloos was evil. Perhaps they had haunted the spectral dimensions wrapped around the place too long to recognize just how wicked it truly was.

"When a tree becomes infested with ants or disease, you cut it down," he finally replied, "Ouloos is infected with your twisting of this creation."

"What will you do after you have burned this place into oblivion?" Moshat's deep voice bellowed through Geillan's mind. The idea grabbed hold of him for a moment. He had never heard any of them speak through his ears. Would they sound any different than when they spoke within his mind?

"It is a good question," Kallum added after a few moments of silence.

"Indeed," Kaldumahn agreed, "What will you do?"

"Will you just float about the emptiness when there is no world left to terrorize?" Brerto chimed in.

"Why do any of you care what I do?" Geillan's tone echoed his frustration as his voice raised while he continued speaking with his mouth instead of his mind, "None of you even exist anymore. You are all just ghosts haunting my head. You have no stakes in this. You have no stakes in anything."

"You are wrong about that," Kallum countered, "We are gods whether free to roam about or trapped within the prison of your twisted mind. We want to see this world live."

"Kallum, stop it. You say too much," Ijilv scolded.

"Oh, you stop it," Geillan shouted at the trees, "You have no tricks for me. I know you want me to be aware that you believe what I am about to do is evil. I am equally aware that you believe I lack the strength to face my father and his wicked sister. You are wrong. I will give this rotten place a fitting end, and I will destroy your heroes in the process."

"Do you need help?" a rich baritone asked from somewhere beyond the trees lining the trail.

"Why would I need help?" Geillan laughed at the trees squinting to see the owner of the melodic voice. It was a failed attempt. The rider did a magnificent job of hiding his form in the darkness of the forest.

"It sounds as if you are speaking to the trees," the rich, deep voice continued from somewhere surprisingly close to the muddy trail, "You look physically well, but it seems your mind might be troubled."

He probably did sound like a fool shouting at trees. How had the rider snuck up on him without him hearing?

"Probably the same way we escaped the torturous fishing excursion you had us on," Brerto chided with a chuckle.

"Shut up," Geillan fired back.

"Forgive me," the voice from the trees replied, "I seek not to offend. I only wish to help you on your way. These are sacred and protected grounds. Unless you have business in these woods, I would see you quickly pass through."

"As you noted," Geillan laughed, "I am a madman wandering lost in the forest shouting at trees. Please, fix my broken mind."

As Geillan teased the man, he gazed into the darkness of the forest with his mind. The owner of the deep voice wore a wavy mane of dark locks upon his head and an equally wavy beard upon his chin. There was wisdom in his dark eyes, but it was troubled by duty. What a challenge it must be for an inquisitive mind to blindly follow rules and orders. It was something Geillan knew he could never do. That was probably how he slipped from under Ijilv's thumb. Once he began to question why things were how they were and for what purpose they needed to be, the entire charade fell apart.

Geillan pressed into the man's mind. The pleasantries he offered were a ruse. The rider was merely working to assess whether the foreigner on his trail posed any sort of armed threat before he and the four riders accompanying him charged out of the darkness to capture him for questioning.

The man's name was Alamond. He was there when Cialia found her flame and burned all but twenty of Druindahl's riders. He had been nothing more than a soldier then. After all the loss the Dragon caused, he'd been elevated to the rank of general, reporting directly to Boringas. The four riders accompanying him were no one of note, names Geillan would forget shortly after burning them to ash.

"I can see you are unarmed, but I fear your mocking tone suggests you travel my forest with nefarious purposes. State your name and business with the house of Druindahl," the command from Alamond carried so much authority, Geillan imagined the fear a random traveler might feel at hearing it.

"Come to me and bring your friends," Geillan commanded back, "There are five of you traveling ahead of a caravan. All the souls of Druindahl tromping off to paradise and abandoning their homes. If only I had arrived sooner. I have only seen glimpses, memories borrowed from others. All those vivid recollections dripped with awe. I would have liked to look upon the place with my eyes before blasting it to oblivion. Alas…"

The ground rumbled as Geillan's voice trailed off. The canopy above quickly burned to ash as a massive fireball flew to the heavens roughly a mile north of where he stood.

The shock he had hoped to hear in Alamond's reply was missing as the soldier somberly asked, "It is gone, isn't it?"

"Indeed," Geillan confirmed as he stared into Alamond's eyes, all the shadow having fled with the ash of burned leaves floating on the breezes above.

Two of the riders with Alamond charged north. "Go," Geillan shouted after them, "fetch Boringas, your fearless general, to stand before me in judgement."

Alamond and the three riders who remained with him charged through the trees toward Geillan. The mighty hooves of some of Druindahl's finest horses only stomped the forest floor for a few strides before they were overtaken by dirty flashes of brown appearing like streaks of dark light rocketing through the charred forest.

The rider to Alamond's right was the first to go down. Geillan could tell it all happened too fast for Alamond to register the details. That was unfortunate. Still, the result was plastered across the young general's face. Blood and chunks of flesh glistened on cheeks stretched by his jaw hanging in shock.

"You know of the dead-eyed men," Geillan smiled, "They are vastly more effective under my command. Your rider's throat was torn out at the same moment his guts poured out of a gash in his belly. Then his horse was ripped in half and tossed up to coat the leafless branches above in gory glory. The same is about to happen to your other companion."

Geillan hadn't finished speaking when two additional brown streaks raced through the trees to rip apart the other rider who still remained with Alamond as well as that man's horse. "And then only valiant Alamond remained to battle the dead-eyed monsters," Geillan finally added as the back half of a horse landed directly next to Alamond who had ceased his charge a mere 10 feet from Geillan.

"Who are you?" Alamond's voice had lost all the authority it had boasted only moments prior.

Joy forced a smile onto Geillan's lips as he allowed his body to expand. His limbs and torso stretched until his head sat among the lowest branches of the charred canopy roughly twenty-five feet above the trail. Leathery red wings stretched from his back on what appeared to be long claws until they spread out from him nearly one hundred feet in either direction knocking down burnt and crumbling trees as they stretched. His back arched as a Dragon's head grew from his chest belching fire from a beak-like snout filled with razor sharp fangs. Its eyes smoldered as red as Geillan's as he proclaimed in a voice that rumbled the ground like an earthquake and toppled poor Alamond from his horse, "I am the Dragon."

Kallum's voice echoed in Geillan's head as the Dragon stretching from his chest roared, "They will fear you, but they will never love you. That is one thing I have learned with time to reflect on all I have done. Worship is not the same as love."

"Only one has ever loved me, and I destroyed her for it," Geillan shouted at the sky, "Everyone else has either abandoned me or used me to do their bidding. I know nothing about love. Fear will have to do."

"Geillan," Boringas' voice sounded small and far away to Geillan's ears, but it was as clear as if they sat together chatting in a quiet room, "I cannot understand how it can be, but I know that is you. Your mother loved you. Based on what you just said, I can only guess that you have killed her. You may have taken her from this world, but there are many others who loved you. Some probably still do."

"False," Geillan laughed as he allowed his body to deflate back to its normal size and stand directly before Boringas who, with the forty riders behind him appeared prepared to trample him into the wet trail, "There is no one in this world left who even knows me. Fawning over a bright-faced cherub fresh out of his mother's womb is not love. Almost everyone *loves* a baby though it isn't that tiny creature who really earns their affection. New life and hope and all that nonsense, misidentified emotions."

Then Alamond attacked. The faithful warrior charged from the trees quietly with no mighty war cry to accompany his hurried steps. What a strange thing to do after all he had just witnessed. As Geillan slithered about the general's mind, it was obvious the man knew he had no chance of victory. Some odd sense of duty propelled his feet forward as if he'd been given some silent command. It felt like bleak darkness in Geillan's chest when he allowed his will to expand and vaporized the charging hero to ash. It was quick, just a brief flash of pain, and he was gone.

"You are just like your aunt," Boringas grunted in disgust.

"And as callous as a god," Brerto whispered in Geillan's head.

Brerto's taunt didn't trouble him at all, but Boringas' words cut a bit deep. "She is a mere shadow of what I have become," he growled as he released his will into the forty riders accompanying Boringas. All of them exploded to ash that quickly swirled up into a cloud of darkness where a lush, green canopy once rustled in fresh, forest breezes. "Let me show you," Geillan finished with a smirk.

A moment later, he stood with Boringas further up the trail directly in front of a caravan of wagons and people walking. There were exactly five thousand two hundred and fifty-one souls huddled on the trail. Nearly one fifth of them were mounted on horses wearing soldier's garb and brandishing swords.

"This is all that remains of your legendary city in the trees," Geillan's smile echoed in his voice, "Is this the cause for which you fight? Do you even know why you fight?"

There was no fear in Boringas' voice, only disappointment, as he replied quietly, "You know, my father abandoned me too. I was young, not a baby like you, but he still left."

"So, you feel a kinship with me?" Geillan chuckled.

"No," Boringas shook his head, "I pity you. When my father left, I used that pain as fuel to be something better. I decided I would never abandon those who depend on me."

"Quaint," Geillan's voice dropped to barely a mumble, "You have made a vow to the gods or the Dragons or whatever silly idea in which you find meaning that you will remain steadfast no matter how lost the cause."

Boringas shook his head slightly as he replied, "I made a vow to myself. At the end of the day, I am the only one whose actions I can control."

"It is admirable, I suppose. You have kept your vow to these people. What has it gained you? I wonder," despite the mocking tone Geillan used, he truly was curious what motivated men to do the things they did when there appeared nothing material to be gained. Most were just vile and self-serving. This one, even some of his riders, seemed motivated by something else, some odd and twisted purpose.

Boringas didn't hesitate, "Peace of mind. I know I have done all I can to serve the souls who depend on me. In my mind, there is no higher purpose than to serve."

"Sadly, all you can do will not be enough," grimness seeped into Geillan's tone as the three stepped in front of him and Boringas.

The leader of the three paused and turned to face Druindahl's most dutiful general. He removed his hood exposing the wild, dirty, orange mop of mangy hair cascading from his head like some kind of twisted crown and his equally mangy beard. Menace twisted up his smile as he stared at the fearless general with black, dead eyes.

"Please," Boringas' deep voice trembled, "They are blameless. They mean nothing to you. Why destroy them? Take your hurt and rage and hate to those who do matter to you. Your father left you. Confront him. Punish him for his crimes against you. No one in this forest has done any wrong to you. Let them go find the peace promised to them."

"I will," Geillan whispered.

It only took moments. Wild screams of the most pitiable agony filled the sky, mingling with the rumbling roar of vengeful death bellowing from the soulless monsters exacting Geillan's justice. He didn't watch as his pets sliced through soft bellies, gashed throats open, and ripped limbs and heads from torsos tossing them up into the air in a thick cloud of bloody gore. By the time the slaughter was finished, all that remained of Druindahl was a sloppy pile of blood and indistinguishable pieces of flesh on the forest floor and coating the surrounding trees.

Geillan hadn't watched as his dead minions decimated Druindahl's population. Instead, he stared intently at Boringas watching helpless tears stream down the valiant soldier's face to saturate his beard and mingle with the gore splattering his cheeks. It brought him no joy. That was unfortunate. He expected to revel in the agony he caused these vile and worthless creatures when he had decided Ouloos needed to be cleansed. What he felt instead was close kin to sadness.

"Do what you will to me," Boringas spat, "There is nothing else you can take from me, and there is no pain greater you can cause me than what you have already done."

"I know," Geillan quietly muttered as he swiped a bloody hunk of meat from Boringas' cheek, "It almost seems unnecessary, but like you, I have made a vow. Thank you for articulating that so eloquently for me. I had almost forgotten my cause."

After a quick flash of flame, Geillan was alone in the forest with nothing but a pile of bloody flesh and organs and his soulless companions.

"You are pure evil," Ijilv's voice was quiet in the back of Geillan's mind.

"Precisely as you intended," Geillan replied with his mind, "Are you proud, father?"

"He will not admit as much, but he is," Kallum replied in Ijilv's stead, "You will make a fitting sacrifice to your father when he and Cialia blast you to oblivion and this world is reborn."

"This wretched world will die with their smoldering corpses," Geillan replied with no emotion animating his tone.

###

Ijilv sat with his brothers around a gaudy, circular table of shiny prang decorated with sparkling jewels about its legs and edges in a room glowing with bright radiance which seemed to emanate from every angle rather than one single source of light. They all glowed with the same pure brilliance as if they were gods once again rather than ghosts, prisoners in a violent child's mind.

"You say too much," Ijilv hissed at Kallum.

Kallum humphed and waved the idea off while Brerto responded to the accusation, "I disagree. He says precisely what needs to be said. Good and evil are nebulous things. We all have watched the creatures of Ouloos stumbling about their journeys through the physical representations of their souls long enough to know one man's evil isn't necessarily another man's. As much as we tried to make them see things as black and white, they never truly have. Killing a man to steal his treasure is somehow different to them than killing a man to stop him from stealing yours. Yet, the result of both is a dead man. Intent is what makes an action evil."

"Brerto is correct," Moshat chimed in, "Geillan must believe his actions are evil. Can they be evil if he believes he is doing good?"

"No," Kaldumahn replied.

Ijilv shook his head, "I refuse to believe you are the fools you pretend to be. You speak about men. Geillan is more than that. He is a Dragon and a god. The same rules do not apply."

"Intent is intent regardless of who owns it," Kallum shrugged, "Any mind can conquer the bonds of the physical. Intent is an expression of the mind equally unbound to the physical."

"This is a dangerous game," Ijilv complained.

"It has been since you duped us all into unwittingly playing it with you," Kaldumahn chuckled wryly, "It is no more dangerous now that it was when it began, and we have no choice but to see it through to its finish."

"On that we can agree," Ijilv slumped in his chair.

"Chin up," Brerto gleefully scolded, "Listen with your heart…"

"We do not have hearts," Kaldumahn argued.

"Ignore him," Moshat groaned.

"I will. Now is no time for fruitless debate," Brerto smiled, "Now is the time to pay attention. Whether it be with your heart or mind or will, or whatever you decide it is for you, we can feel Geillan's emotions here. We can know his intent. All we need to do is allow them into our awareness. He believes what he is doing is wrong, yet he continues his quest. That is evil."

CHAPTER 22
A DESOLATE SOUL

Green waves rippled in a vast ocean of tall and wild grass flowing beneath the currents of a pleasing breeze for as far as the eye could see in any direction. The sky above it was such a deep blue it seemed almost too perfect to be real. It appeared more like a painting exaggerating nature's perfection to make it seem even more magnificent than it was. The sun poured its brilliance on everything from the same spot it always did. The sameness probably should have dulled the effect the place had on Daritus, but it didn't. Every time he gazed out in any direction, he found some new and wonderful thing to ponder. On this day, it was a bird darting about against that perfect blue sky in such random patterns there could be no goal to the journey. Perhaps it was chasing bugs, filling up on creatures too small for Daritus to see.

The bird's random dashes from this place to that wasn't what sucked Daritus' attention away from an engrossing conversation he was having with Slurg, Moy, and Lameah. It was the detail he was able to easily see from nearly a mile away. The thing's body couldn't have been any bigger than his fist. At that distance, it should have been no more than a speck on the horizon, if he could even see it at all. Yet, he was able to make out every minute detail on the thing. Its body and head were bright red. Its wings were small and moved rapidly against the stronger winds that blew hundreds of feet above the ground. Despite their great speed, he could easily see pink highlights zigzagging across them. Those pink highlights matched a couple of small tufts of feathers that sat near the back of the creature's head. The same-colored highlights decorated its tail feathers as well. Its eyes, beak, and legs—which were drawn up tight to its pink belly—were all the deepest and richest black he had ever seen in nature.

Slurg seemed a bit offended as he frowned and asked, "Does talk of bygone battles bore you now that you've given up your sword?"

He had grown so entranced by the bird's movement, Slurg's voice breaking through the moment of silence startled him. He jumped a bit before chuckling his reply, "No, not at all. Please, forgive my rude behavior, but that bird dashing about so randomly stole my attention away. I can see it perfectly, but I cannot fathom why."

The grong Choontah looked out in the direction Daritus pointed and agreed with a hint of awe, "It is as clear as your face before me. My eyes are usually not so good in the bright light. They much prefer the dim light at dawn and dusk."

Lameah smiled and shared, "It is this place. It brings out the best in all who occupy it. It is more than just the calming sense it brings to your soul and mind. It also affects your senses, heightening them to perfection."

Moy, the tallest living giant, stretched and stood as he gazed out at the small bird who had earned all their attention. Equal awe colored his tone as he agreed, "That bird is only the beginning of the majesty of this place. Look there," he pointed toward a range of purple mountains maybe hundreds of miles from the tip of his finger, "Those mighty and rocky hills are so far away I should scarcely be able to see them at all. And yet, I can clearly see a smooth, white, polished pebble speckled with creamy green on a path between the massive rocky peaks."

"I see it too," Daritus gasped, "This is impossible, beyond perfection. No man's eyes can see so far."

"There it is, just as Moy described. Might be an illusion," Slurg suggested.

"Your awe brings me such joy," Lameah gushed with happiness glinting in her smoldering eyes, "Most who journey here have finished their time in the physical. They are drawn to the Lake, unable to behold the majesty surrounding us. It is no illusion. For as long as you remain, your spirits will grow until nothing that can be known is beyond your reach."

Lito-Bi sauntered up with Sanjo. They both chomped and sucked on some sloppy orange things, smiling as juice dripped down their chins. The former asked, "What is so interesting?"

"Well," Slurg began, "we were discussing why we battled at Fort Maomnosett prior to Daritus drawing us all into watching a bird fly about. Then Moy spotted a pebble, and here we are."

"I can tell you why I fought," Lito-Bi shrugged, "Prior to meeting Daritus, there was no man I liked very much. I cannot help it that I am more than twice a man's size or that my teeth and claws are more effective for tearing flesh than any sword ever forged. Yet, every man I had ever met before looked at me like some kind of monster, something to kill, perhaps a trophy for their wall. Most giants I know looked down upon my kind, but they never treated us like animals. When Bok made his call to arms, I had no good reason not to answer."

"It was the same for me," Slurg nodded, "that and greed. I have always liked the coins men and giants carry around, their treasures. I have no use for them. The land provides everything we grongs need, but we hoarded their coins when we could get them. It was just a small part of my motivation that seems so silly now. Being looked upon like a beast was what really got me. I suppose I had something to prove."

"Most men fear things they do not understand," Sanjo offered around the sloppy bit of fruit moistening his lips, "We are trained to battle and defeat our fears. It is no excuse, but it is often the cause that leads us to battle."

Daritus nodded as Sanjo's comment finally dragged his attention away from contemplating birds and pebbles which should be too far away to see, "That is correct. We are trained to view things we fear as enemies to be destroyed. I fought to protect a city that was not mine from invaders with whom I had no quarrel. In my mind, I saw it as duty. However…"

Pain erupted in Daritus' chest. It felt like he'd been stabbed in the heart. He had been stabbed more than once in his day and knew exactly how it felt to be pierced by a sharp blade. Though he'd never actually been stabbed through the muscle pumping behind his sternum, that is precisely how it felt. He fell in a heap.

In the same moment, Helias, Lameah, and thousands of their sisters, Dragons soaring high on the currents of the perfect sky or lounging about the flowing waves of grass, all cried out in unison.

"What is it," Lito-bi asked as he dropped his sloppy fruit to gently place his hand on Daritus' back.

"Druindahl is no more," Lameah wept.

As he lay there crumbling under the weight of sorrow, Daritus saw everything. He saw the faces of innocent folk twisted in agony as soulless beasts sliced through their flesh with talons sharp like razors and stronger than any metal smelted from any ore, even stronger than swords crafted from that ancient mountain that legend would have it fell from the heavens to be mined by dwarves. He heard their cries, unanswered songs of lament seeking some hero to save them as their bodies were twisted and limbs torn from them to be tossed about like dead leaves in a brisk autumn breeze. The coppery smell of blood quickly growing stale in the damp, forest air filled his sinuses thickening until it might choke out all his wind. He cried out, "No. I should have been with them."

"There is nothing you could have done," Lameah's soothing voice failed to ease the pain.

"Our sweet friend is correct," Lito-Bi's tone suggested he felt the weight of loss nearly as heavy as Daritus did as he consoled, "You would have merely died along with them. What good would that have done?"

"No," Daritus shouted at the sky as he struggled from Lito-Bi's grasp and charged toward the Lake to fall to his knees in the sand.

A mist rolled in to surround him. Individual bits of light fell from it into the Lake, glowing briefly beneath its surface before soaring forth from it into the sky above. There were thousands of them. He felt the fear they felt in their last moments. It remained heavy like a weight on his soul.

"Daritus," Helias' voice swam around his head like a soothing song, "this is no time for lament. Cry tears of joy with me for the glory of your people finding their ways back home to the Lake, back home to Coeptus."

"I can feel no joy when soaked in their pain," he shouted, his voice a tortured song of sorrow, "I should have been there with them to share their fate."

"That would have been a great loss to this world, and there is nothing you could have done for them," Cialia's voice behind him was nearly enough to drag him up from the depths.

"Nothing?" his shouts were muffled as he buried his head in hands. "I could have consoled them, gave them hope against the fear they suffered in those last moments. Instead, I lounged about, comfortable in this paradise." Then he turned his head to Helias and scolded, "And you, comforting smile in the face of distress, I am uncertain if you believe what you say about the glory of this place, but you are wrong. They will never know the peace I have known while basking in the majesty of this paradise. They take with them only the pain they suffered. That is not the same."

"I understand your pain," Helias' tone remained as calm and soothing as ever as she gave him words he didn't want to hear. "What will you do? Will you seek to kill the destroyer, the author of their terror and your pain?"

It happened so quickly that his mind hadn't fully processed what he planned to do until his feet were moving. It was only three short strides to the Lake through the sand, and then he was diving into the drink. He barely heard Cialia shout something after him, but the words and their meaning were lost on him.

Though it was a Lake he dove into, the stuff he floated in felt nothing like any water he had ever swum. It didn't even feel like liquid. It felt he floated in some kind of void. Time hadn't made any sense since he arrived at the place; floating there in the nothing, it made just as much. For a moment, there was peace, complete silence, darkness like a womb or cocoon surrounding him, protecting him from everything. That silence was replaced by a memory he had long forgotten.

He had barely seen the passing of his first summer and was maybe half again to seeing the end of his next when he crawled out onto a low grouping of slats outside the door of the hut he lived in with his mother and father until they were thrown out of the place in his sixth. His father enjoyed his wine a bit more than tending his fields. The crown frowned upon idle fields back then.

What his father lacked in motivation for plowing fields, he made up for in his ability to take a beating. He was a thin man, shorter than average. Daritus got his height from his mother's side. Her father was near a giant. His father's diminutive stature caused most men who were able with their fists and confident enough to put coin behind their boasts to underestimate him. As far as Daritus knew, that was always a mistake. No matter how bloody his father might have been at the end of a fight, he was the last man standing. Then he would spend his winnings on wine and bread. Meat was scarce in Daritus' hut in those days.

This particular occasion had been like most Daritus had ever witnessed. The distraction he caused earned enough of his father's attention to give his opponent an opening. The right hook that followed connected clean with father's jaw, wobbling his knees as he staggered away from the blow. After spitting a bloody tooth out into the dirt—there probably hadn't been much holding it in at that point anyway—he snapped his head quickly in both directions earning a crack with each and quickly moved back in close to the man who had only just failed to knock him out.

The punch that followed never had a chance. From the look on the man's face, he was certain that would be the end of it. Daritus' father had a different outcome in mind. He ducked beneath the blow and delivered a solid hook to his opponent's liver. The man's eyes went wide as he doubled over. The uppercut that blasted him under his chin snapped his head back as he stumbled in the same direction. A short uppercut to the gut to double the man over, and a left hook to his jaw later, and the big fellow was lying unconscious in the dirt at father's feet. They would have two loaves of bread in the cupboard that night, and father would be passed out from the wine long before the sun dipped below the horizon.

Father had no lesson for him. He just scooped him up, said, "That ain't nothing for you to see, lad," and carried him back in the house to play with a hunk of wood that served as his only toy. Sometimes it was a cart carrying soldiers to battle, and other times it was a horse galloping across open fields. It was always something different. Whatever happened to be in his head at any given moment.

Then it was gone. He knew he had been thinking of something, some long forgotten memory, but there were no details to give it any meaning. No matter how hard he focused, stretching his mind, reaching back through summers past to find that one thing he had just witnessed like a moving painting on his mind, it was simply not there. It was as if the memory itself had been stolen from him, stripped away like a soldier's innocence on the field of his first battle.

Daritus had precious few moments to trouble over where that memory had gone when another came. It was his seventh summer. This was one he thought of often; sometimes fondly, other times over a few tears. He was on a wide and busy road, halfway to Havenstahl from his childhood hut they had been thrown out of. Father hadn't had much luck getting anyone to throw hands for money with him.

The folk they encountered on the trail were far too well to do for such idle pursuits, and far too busy to allow their guards to entertain their egos in such brash fashion, so he had taken to begging. Luckily, those same folks who were too busy to brawl were generous and willing to share their bounties with those who were down on their luck.

Two riders approached. They wore brown cloaks and black leather trousers and boots. The boots shined nearly as bright as the sun. The men were thickly muscled, and so were the mighty, brown steeds they rode upon. Red ribbons fastened to their cloaks and horses flapped behind them. Daritus recalled wishing he could be one of them. The rider closest to him must have noticed the envy in his eyes. When father put his hat out toward that man, he ignored it. Instead looking directly in Daritus' eyes and asking, "Is this the life you want?"

Of course, it was not the life he wanted. At that age, he had no idea what the life he did want looked like, but he knew the life he had was not the one he wanted. He couldn't say that. It would have broken mother's heart. It probably would have bothered father for a time too. Luckily, father didn't give him a chance to answer.

"He likes his life just fine," father sneered at the man, "Come on down off of that horse, and I'll teach you how to show strangers the respect they deserve no matter what troubles they might be dealing with."

Most men Daritus had ever known would have bristled at a challenge like this, but the mountain of a man sitting triumphantly on his massive horse acted as if he hadn't realized it was a slight. That was poise. Daritus hadn't known what it was at the time, but he admired it. The man had some mission, and there was nothing that could sway him from it. The man continued to stare into Daritus' eyes as he responded offhandedly to father, "We are recruiting. I have no time to scrap with ruffians on the road and no time for idle chatter with the same. I will give you two thousand prang coins for the boy. He will be trained to ride and trained to fight. He will be well fed and taught from the great books of old. By the end of his sixteenth summer, I will count him equal, and we will ride for the same cause."

Father didn't even haggle with the man. Daritus had no idea how much two thousand prang coins was worth back then, but it seemed like a lot the way father's eyes glistened above the biggest smile he'd ever seen upon his face. Mother smiled too when she hugged him, but her smile seemed sad among her tears. He still wasn't sure if the tears were because she was happy for him or sad for herself. Either way, he never saw her again to ask. A moment later that big man who had just purchased him was hauling him up onto the front of his horse. The man's name was Harcon. He was the one who trained Daritus to ride and fight. And then, just as quickly as that memory had jumped into his awareness, it was gone.

Again, he was left knowing he had been remembering something but having no idea what that something was. There were no hints or clues to give any structure to the forgotten thing. It was simply gone like some thief had snuck in to steal it directly from his mind.

Then he was in the woods. The brush was thick beneath the trees. A ghost of the prior night's fire haunted the last few glowing embers still clinging to life. The bits of sky he could see through the thick canopy above him carried the faintest light of a sun threatening to rise. A light breeze rustled the leaves above as heralds of the morning chirped out melodies among them. He stretched the stiffness of a third night sleeping under the trees out of his back and neck before shuffling closer to the dying fire to chase the morning chill from his bones.

The prior night had been the best he could remember at the time. Harcon and Morlun had so many adventurous stories to share. Some were funny, some chilling, and others were kind of sad. The one thing they all shared was the detail with which they were told. Daritus could almost feel a mighty steed galloping hard across the field beneath him while he gripped a sword tightly in his raised right hand. At one point in one of Morlun's stories, he became so entranced that he shouted out a war cry. The outburst sent his two companions tumbling over with laughter, and he laughed right along with them. It was the most fun he could recall having up to that point in his life. He was just another adventurer on the trail heading to his new home and a new life.

Once the last chuckles had fled, Harcon offered him a waterskin and said, "Here, lad. Give this a go. This is what men drink. Take heed. This is serious stuff, better than what keeps your father skinny and weak."

Daritus skeptically sniffed the open skin. There was a muted sweetness to the aroma that mingled with woody notes. Something else lurked about beneath the rest, a familiar scent. It took him a moment to place it. It was something he smelled on a spice peddler's cart. He had only gotten a quick whiff before the rude man yanked the bottle from his hands and told him to piss off. Dirty children have no coins. Whatever concoction was in that bottle smelled just like that other scent hiding beneath the sweet and wood. "What is it?" he had finally asked.

"You might not be quite ready if you need to ask," Morlun winked as he chuckled out his response.

He shrugged and took a long pull off the waterskin. That was a mistake. A sip would have been sufficient. It felt like flames might shoot right out of his mouth. "That is horrible," he laughed despite the pain.

"I cannot believe you kept that down," Harcon laughed as he tossed him another skin and added, "Here, chase it with this."

The water helped cool the fire. Douse it was probably a more apt description. He chugged nearly half the skin of water before pausing to suck in a deep breath and chugging the rest. His two companions shared a hearty laugh at his expense. He shot them a look of defiance as he tossed the empty waterskin back to Harcon and took another long pull off the other. It burned just the same, but he refused to let the confident smirk leave his face.

"You will make a fine soldier," Morlun laughed as he patted him on the back, "Now give me that skin."

He had three more pulls off the waterskin that night. Harcon told him his head would ache in the morning, and hurt it had. It felt like a fat fallon stood above him stomping directly on his forehead. It hadn't really started until he sat up and made his way over to what was left of the dying fire, but when it came, it stormed in without mercy. Rubbing at his temples didn't help. Water was what he needed. When he looked around for a skin, he realized he was alone in the camp. Harcon and Morlun along with their horses and all their supplies were gone.

"Hey there, lad," the gruff voice was far too loud, "Them men you been riding with, where have they gotten themselves off to?"

It felt like someone drove a spike into the top of his head when he turned it to look up at the man, so he didn't look very long. All he could tell was that there were four other men with him, and they all wore shiny armor decorated with blue ribbons streaming from their pauldrons and helms. He hadn't known it then, but these were soldiers from Havenstahl.

"Boy, this man asked you a question. You'd best answer," another equally gruff voice commanded.

"I only just woke," he mumbled without looking up at the man, "They were gone when I did."

The trail suddenly rumbled with the sound of horse hooves. One of the men dragged him up by the collar and held him fast in a loose choke while Harcon and Morlun charged down the trail sounding like a column of riders. The other four men drew swords. The battle was short. Three of those men were trampled under mighty hooves while the other was stabbed in the heart. It was an expert strike that Daritus would remember and use later in life. Harcon spun his sword, so the blade was pointing toward the ground. Then he raised his arm up high and slammed it down. The strike was carried out with such force, it seemed impossible he would hit his mark, but he did. That sword slipped in just behind its victim's collar bone and drove straight down until half the blade was in the man. It came out just as quickly followed by pulsing blood that decorated the tree trunks in crimson.

The point of a blade against his throat dulled the throbbing in Daritus' head. The only man left wearing the blue of Havenstahl was using him as leverage. He thought of crying out. That wouldn't do. He had gleaned enough from his trail mates' stories to learn his first real lesson about being a soldier; a soldier never shows fear regardless of how furiously it might be running through his veins.

"Release the boy," Harcon commanded the man as he leveled the point of his sword at him.

"I'll be doing no such thing," the man spat after his reply.

It was at that moment as the point of the dagger pressed a wee bit harder against his neck that he remembered the gift Harcon had given him on their first night in the forest. It was a dagger, glinting sharpened metal with a meticulously crafted handle decorated with a Dragon at its base. He slowly slipped the thing out of its scabbard.

Pressed as tightly as he was against the man's belly, he could feel the break in his armor between his chest plate and his fauld. He slammed his hand back. There was only the slightest resistance before the blade sliced into the man. Then he slashed away from himself to leave a gash from just right of the man's belly button to his side.

The attack wasn't immediately fatal, but it did cause the soldier to loosen his grip. Daritus dove to the ground. He didn't see Harcon's blade crash through the man's eye and out the back of his skull, but the awful noise the attack made was enough. Bones make a distinct sound when cracked apart. Then there was some sloppy gurgling, a thud when the body dropped to the dirt, and finally silence.

Then it was gone. Just like the other two memories, empty sacks of ideas with no details to give them life. More came. He remembered training and drinking, spinning yarns around fires, and galloping hard down trail after trail with the wind wildly whipping his long, brown waves behind him. When they came, they were as vivid as if he were living them again, but when they left, they were gone for good.

And then Leisha stood before him. It was the first moment he had ever seen her. By that time, he had developed a bit of a swagger. He was strong and fit and easy on the eyes, as his lady friends would say, and he had plenty of charm to redden their cheeks and quicken their heartbeats. None of that mattered when those deep, brown eyes caught hold of his. There was a smiling softness to them so enthralling he thought he might be trapped there; lost in a prison he would never want to leave. None of the slick words he might use to cause a young maiden to swoon were accessible as he stared dumbly at her. Even if he could have found some clever thing to say, he dared not. It would have been beneath her.

The child in her arms suddenly babbled some gibberish. Daritus hadn't noticed her until just then, a bright faced cherub with red cheeks and golden curls peering at him with blue eyes as innocent as they were bright. That was the moment the two of them stole his heart away from the Dragon's Flame, and Spang took the call in his stead. They became his mission from that point on.

It was almost as if he were living his life again, but it was nothing but a collection of scenes and feelings that vanished once consumed by his awareness. And then there was nothing but darkness. It suddenly occurred to him that he could no longer recall his name. He knew he had one right up until he had no recollection of what a name was. And then Daritus of Druindahl, husband, father, king, general, and defender of Dragons was gone. All that remained was empty stuff, food for Coeptus.

CHAPTER 23
A HOME FOR ALL

The sky was glorious as ever. The sun warmed the skin from its constant spot in the sky while the cool breezes offered the perfect amount of chill to keep it comfortable. The scents dancing among those currents were wildflowers and fresh rain. The smell of rain stood out to Maelich. As far as he knew, it had never rained there. In fact, he had never noticed any more than two or three fluffs of clouds in the brilliant blue above.

"This place gives your senses precisely what they want, Maelich," Helias' musical voice sang in Maelich's head.

He glanced up at the most perfect of Dragons perched upon her peak across the Lake from him. The sight of her filled him with awe. It was the same way he felt the first time his eyes beheld her and every time since. He felt so small and insignificant standing there shabbily before her. She would gently scold him for seeing her as anything more than anyone else or for seeing himself as anything less. He couldn't help how he felt. It seemed strange that anyone could look at her and see anything short of perfection. Still, thinking back to the first time he ever saw her all those summers prior, the wonder that filled him then had been fueled by fear. That had been Kallum's great trick, or Ijilv's rather, one using the other as a pawn, both unwittingly acting out Raya's plan.

"I am unsure how I feel about that," Maelich finally responded with his mind, "It reminds me of the prison where Eana held the Shaiwah after her guards had used their compliance pikes to convince them that what they wanted wasn't really what they wanted. It seemed wicked to me."

"There are no bars keeping you here, Maelich," though the Dragon continued speaking with her mind, her tones remained like a chorus in his head, "You have a choice. It will break my heart if you leave us again, but you are free to go if you must."

The fact was something he knew. There was no place else he would rather be than standing there at the edge of the Lake, gazing out at the glory surrounding him, and curling his toes in the cool sand. And yet, something just didn't seem right about it.

Raya strolled up beside him. He knew the pleasing scent which followed her around was wild orchids expertly blended with vanilla and honey though vanilla and orchids were both things he had never smelled before meeting her. "Sit with me," she said with a voice nearly as sweet as Helias' as she took his left hand and led him gently to sit cross-legged in the sand.

"Look at me, Maelich," she held his cheek after gently turning his head to face her, "You still seek the trickery in every soul you meet. Nothing is hidden from you. Why do you refuse to believe all the things you know?"

"Training," Cialia offered as she sat beside him on his other side, "The same reason I am unable to completely give myself over to this place. There is nothing I want more than to let it all go and be here, completely in the moment, free from any doubts or fears, but I cannot."

"It is a wise thought, Cialia," Helias offered, "Despite everything you have seen, you still question everything. No questions remain unanswered. Yet, you continue to look for something more, seeking to battle against anything you find that fails to fit your idea of what is right."

"All questions have not been answered," Maelich finally pulled his gaze away from Raya's. "I was with Daritus when he swam the waters of the Lake. He became nothing. Everything which made him the individual we all knew as Daritus was stripped away like layers of chipped and peeling paint scraped off an old door to prepare for a fresh coat. Ever since Ijilv tricked me into believing Coeptus was some being with whom I could converse and share ideas, I have been preaching the mysteries of Coeptus and the Lake as if together they were some promised paradise."

Then he turned to Cialia and said, "You were there with me, watching, reliving those memories with him as they were stripped away one after another until he no longer existed, until he was nothing. Is that what you expected?"

The smile Cialia offered was genuine but sad as she replied, "Mostly, it was. I think if you search your heart with an honest mind, you will find you expected the same. Perhaps that is why we fought so hard to keep the creatures who looked to us for protection from finding this end for as long as possible. We knew it meant the end of who they were when they lived."

He wished her words weren't so damned accurate. The story Ijilv had given them when he paraded as Coeptus was less than completely truthful, but it bore enough of an essence of reality that Maelich should have expected exactly what he found. If only he didn't know all he knew. The heaven Kallum promised was so much grander, an eternity of peace seated at god's side. Of course, it was a lie. As he shifted his gaze back to the glass-like water of the Lake, he wished he still believed the lie.

"What about hope? That is the question which troubles you," Raya held Maelich's hand a bit tighter as she continued, "You see the Lake as an end. It is that for those individual souls, but it is so much more for this world. It is a chance to become something more than it has ever been, something my world failed to achieve. Ouloos can be reborn as a place of love, the same unconditional love the glorious Dragons of this place show all creatures, the same unconditional love we all should strive to share with one another. That, dear Maelich, is paradise. Look around you. It is already here. All these creatures living together in love, caring for one another like the closest of kin. And this is only the beginning. There is no end to the peace and glory we will find, all of us together as one."

Maelich followed Raya's hands as she gestured in each direction all around them. Hordes of men, dwarves, giants, trogmortem, and all manner of creature poured in. Group after group and one after another they came. It seemed impossible all those souls would fit in the lands surrounding the Lake, but they did. It seemed the place expanded with each new being who joined them.

"It is a miracle, I know. All these beings who have spent their lives hating each other all coming together in grace, listening to our message of unconditional love and acceptance, and living it with us," Maelich sighed, "Why does it feel like a beautiful prison?"

"A restless spirit has found its way home," Helias replied softly, "I feel your pain, and it breaks my heart, Maelich. It is the same sorrow I have always felt for your sister. The two of you are like us in every way except you come from men. I fear you will always struggle to find peace within yourselves while you believe you are sitting idle. Your belief could not be farther from the truth, but you fail to see the act of showing another creature love as any kind of action. You will probably always feel as if there is something else you should be doing."

"We are trying," Cialia found the words more quickly than Maelich, but he would have said the same. He was trying as best he could to believe what they were doing meant something but failing to convince himself.

Maelich squeezed Raya's hand a bit tighter as he rested his head on Cialia's shoulder, "I hope someday to be able to do these things. I fear my resolve might falter when I finally see my son's face with my own eyes. Can I feel satisfied I am doing all I can simply by showing him love if he comes to destroy all these souls who have finally made it home?"

"I plan to try," Cialia spoke quietly.

"As do I," Raya agreed.

Maelich hadn't noticed Hasujo and Chorindaal saunter up until the latter cleared his throat. The former seemed a hair too tall carrying his tiny mandolin. The fact he was accompanied by one of the shortest dwarves Maelich had ever met made him seem even taller. Both were thicker about the middle than average, and neither appeared to care a lick about it.

Once the two reached the edge of the sand, Chorindaal asked in a voice far gruffer than that which belted forth when he sang, "Might the lad and I offer up a song to help sort out that what you sit pondering?"

Maelich chuckled something that sounded like pure joy and replied, "Please, a song of peace or joy or triumph over darkness and pain is just the thing my spirit needs right now."

"Then we have the perfect ditty for you," Hasujo bowed dramatically before plucking a few pleasing notes that grabbed the attention of all within earshot, "It's a song my good chum and I have been working on since we arrived. This one is new for us. Most of our songs have been about quests and battles or failures and triumphs. This one is called, *A Home for All.*"

As soon as the final word left Hasujo's mouth, his fingers tore off into a melody that raced to the heavens like an arrow shot straight up from the ground from a bow tight enough to propel it to the stars before gracefully floating back to the soft sand beneath Maelich's rump. Each note built on the prior, and Hasujo strung them out masterfully. Then the dwarf sang in a sweet voice that was just rough enough around the edges to bring a soulful tear of joy to more than one eye watching the two perform:

Magic
That's just how it feels
It seems like magic
But we know its so much more

It's a home for me
It's a home for you
It's a home for those who want it
It's a home for all
It's our home

Love
That's what she promised
And yes this is love
Now that word means so much more

It's a home for me
It's a home for you
It's a home for those who want it
It's a home for all
It's our home

Hope
To chase away fear
We're all filled with hope
Our hearts beat with that and more

It's a home for me
It's a home for you

It's a home for those who want it
It's a home for all
It's our home

This is paradise

Where the Dragons soar
And there's food galore
And drink and friends to share
Who could want for more

We will laugh and love
'Neath the sun above
Safe in our home for all
That's what I call love

It's a home for me
It's a home for you
It's a home for those who want it
It's a home for all
It's our home

More and more voices joined the miniscule dwarf and his tall friend in their joyous hymn until all creatures sung together. Even Cialia added her voice. All had grown connected to all while basking in the glory of the Lake. It was exactly as Maelich had hoped it might be. Yet he struggled to give himself over to those feelings everyone else willingly embraced.

Then a giant dove into the Lake. Soon after, three grongs, a trogmortem, and no less than twenty men all dove in after him. It was different than when Daritus gave himself to the Lake. He had been full of regret and lonely for his kin. This group brimmed with joy, so wrapped in the sheer bliss of their connection to everything that they wanted more. It was almost like greed or addiction. A small taste of belonging to something so much greater than themselves had them yearning for a bigger taste, swept up in a desire their minds were ill equipped to process. They were all with Daritus as everything he had been in his life was stripped away, food for the collective mind that was Coeptus, and somehow, they wanted to be part of that, connected more deeply than any could while existing in their physical plane of reality.

Something suddenly occurred to Maelich. What if this was the trick? What if this was how Ouloos would end? There would be no struggle and no war. One by one, every living creature would simply give themselves to the Lake freely forfeiting their individuality to become part of the one. The Lake was like a potion concocted by some wicked enchanter. It didn't feel like a choice.

"But they did make a choice, Maelich," Helias' calm and sure voice danced into Maelich's head sounding as sweet as ever while the Dragon continued to sing and rejoice with the rest of the group scattered about the lands surrounding the Lake.

The truth seemed less black and white to Maelich as he replied also with his mind, "Was it a choice they made freely, or were they convinced by the magic of this place?"

"There is no magic here. You know that," the Dragon's sure tone remained like fresh nectar to a dry throat, "We Dragons have been here since the beginning. We were first. We have always been one with each other, Coeptus, and all things. This fact has not stripped us of our individuality. We are all one being while still maintaining our own thoughts and even desires."

She was correct, of course. He did know that. Perhaps it was just that individuality she described which kept him from fully accepting the glory of the moment. "I fear I am unable to quiet these questions troubling my mind," he finally replied, "The best I can probably do is refrain from interfering with anyone who can."

"That is the best any of us can do, allow each individual to be who they are meant to be," Helias' words sounded like a smile.

Maelich sighed deeply before raising his voice to join with the chorus swirling around him, "It's our home."

CHAPTER 24
THE LAKE OF DRAGONS

The forest was unusually quiet. Wind rustled the leaves high up in the canopy like it did, but there were no birds chirping out melodies or other critters adding any squawks, barks, howls, or anything else to accompany the sound. Geillan knew all the creatures who may have added any melody over the rush of wind above had already completed their journey to the Lake or were well on their way. His flame hadn't frightened them from their homes. They had obeyed the call. It was the same call beckoning him to come home.

That seemed strange. His intent was clear enough in his mind, and he made no effort to hide it. He wanted all to know he was coming. The odd thing was that it seemed they wanted him to make the journey. The Lake wasn't what pulled so strongly on his awareness. It was the millions of souls who had already made the journey welcoming him to join them as if he might run to their embrace. As he focused on this queer idea, it occurred to him that they all knew precisely what he planned. Fools.

"There it is, the great scar," one of the dead-eyed men strolling with him down the trail commented while pointing at the great, red streak which marked where the Lost Forest had stood tall for so many summers, a prison for Dragons slain by men urged on by a violent and vengeful god.

Despite knowing the dead-eyed vessel who had spoken to him was merely voicing words Geillan had filled him with, he replied, "The men of this place are so dramatic with their names despite their complete lack of anything close to originality or wit. That name was meant to sound ominous, but it doesn't."

"What would you have called it?" another of the dead-eyed things asked.

Geillan had grown tired of talking to himself, so he refused to answer. At first, it was a fun game to distract him from his loneliness on the trail. It quickly became a chore, controlling not only their every movement but also managing all ends of every conversation. His father had spent more than a summer controlling his grandfather in the same fashion. Of course, the former had completely lost his mind during the course of his journey and, after a while, had no idea he was totally in control of the latter's every thought, word, and movement. It still seemed like an immensely boring chore.

"I am done with the lot of you," he finally said.

The three immediately crumbled to dust. There was no gradual transition from animated thing to rotting corpse. They were simply there walking beside him in one moment and gone the next with no evidence of their existence aside from soot floating up toward the canopy to be swept away by the currents rustling the leaves above.

As he watched the remains of his former companions drift away in the wind, the leaves caught his attention. He couldn't recall when those leaves had returned, but it had to be several miles from Druindahl. His flame had burned all the leaves away from a wide swath of trees. It was probably a bit excessive. There was no real reason to burn an entire forest. He could have focused his intention more directly to only burn those things he wanted to destroy.

The more he thought about it, the sillier his behavior seemed. Of course, it had been theatrics. Ijilv had counseled him on his dramatic and unnecessary displays of strength. Their only purpose was to intimidate. Unfortunately, the souls who might revere his great power and look upon him with awe were all destroyed. No one remained to tell any stories, not about his greatness nor his might. No songs would be sung, and no epic tales told. No one would ever know he existed.

A small part of him wished he hadn't just obliterated the dead-eyed men. He suddenly felt like arguing with someone about why his logic made sense. He would still be debating with himself, but somehow hearing his words from another mouth might help convince himself of his own ideas. As it was, he just grew steadily more doubtful about his plan.

"Nonsense," he finally said out loud to no one, "there are none in this world whose worship means anything anyway. Who cares what any of them think?"

"I think you're vile," Nothany's voice made it to the path a moment before he slipped out from behind a tree to stand with his sword pointed toward Geillan's chest. "I've been listening to you as you spoke with those things. You must be this Geillan everyone is so worried about."

The boy's sudden presence took Geillan by surprise. He hid the start as he laughed, "Trail justice. I know you. You are as bad as the rest at your core, but there is something about your method I quite enjoy. It's almost like a game. You give them a fair fighting chance. I like that. I think I might let you live a bit longer," Geillan paused and absently stroked his chin for a moment before adding, "Of course, a bit is all you'll have. I intend to burn this entire world to dust. And I must tell you, the trail is quite barren of late. It seems most have heard the Lake's call and have answered."

"I seek no souls but yours," the boy's confidence was at once intriguing and frustrating as he stood there loose behind his sword, "I offer you the trail's justice. I know what you have planned, and I have no intention of allowing you to execute that plan against the creatures there who will welcome you with open arms. You are a dirty and vile thing."

Geillan feigned sadness as he replied, "It seems you think far less of me than I of you. It saddens me a bit. I would rather not kill you in such a personal way as this. It would be much more pleasant to think of you as a sacrifice to the greater good."

"Do you have a weapon to defend yourself?" Geillan marveled at the young pup's poise. He was so focused on his mission, toying with his emotions wouldn't work. He was simply carrying out a duty.

Despite the fact his jibes had yet to earn a reaction from the young soldier, Geillan continued to tease, "I've never used a sword before. I myself am the most powerful weapon this world has ever known. It never seemed prudent to learn how to wield one. I like you though. I'll humor you. Let's see how this goes."

As Geillan finished the taunt, a beautifully crafted sword materialized in his hand. He reached back into Ouloos' memory to find the essence of a man who'd been taught by dwarves to craft the finest weapons from a star which had fallen from the heavens. That is what the myths said about the mountain that ancient tribe of dwarves mined so long ago. It wasn't a star at all. It was a just a very big rock that fell from space and managed not to blow up before it pounded into the ground and caused a great deal of damage when it did. Thousands of summers passed before anyone mined anything, but when they finally did, the metals they crafted from the ore extracted from that mountain were stronger than any others on Ouloos.

He felt a bit nostalgic as he held the thing up in front of him. That man whose essence helped him in imagining that perfect sword to life had been his kin. He would have liked to know that man. He was probably as awful as everyone else, but he had quite a skill. On top of that, he would have been Geillan's great-great-grandfather, Agrimon. They called him titan and sang songs about him. Geillan knew he would leave nothing of the sort behind, but the sword was certainly nice.

Geillan marveled at the confident smirk behind the blade whistling through the forest air toward his face. It was a lazy attack. He would have never known that as difficult as it was to raise his sword in time to block it, but he pulled the knowledge right from Nothany's thoughts. The move was only intended to get his sword arm above his head to expose his chest. He was also able to glean that the next blow would be quick and crisp. It was. The blade punched right through his chest and out his back.

The pain numbed his mind for a moment as he stared dumbly into his attacker's eyes. There was no emotion hiding within them. Cutting him down in the forest was just a job to the boy, a task to complete. Neither the throbbing in his chest nor the casual method in which the young swordsman bested him was the worst thing about his first sword fight. It was how quickly he lost. He knew exactly what the boy was going to do, and there was nothing he could do to stop it without cheating. The only skill he really had was burning things with fire. At that he was expert, but Dragon's fire is unstoppable. The only force that can match it is itself. As he stood there watching Nothany's serious expression slowly shift to concern before quickly earning just a glint of fear, he wondered if his own mastery over flame was equal with the boy's mastery over the blade. Would he feel as confident when he went to battle against his father as that boy had been during their brief skirmish?

His laments only lasted a few moments, and he shoved them to the back of his mind. Then he smiled at the boy gripping the blade that had run him through and said, "You must be wondering why I'm not dead."

He continued to stare into Nothany's eyes as the sword running through his chest and out his back vaporized to dust. The boy's eyes widened in shock, but he stood his ground. That was impressive. He expected the boy to flee, but the young swordsman's resolve remained as strong even without a sword in his hand. Even more surprising was the fist flying at his face. The child knew he would lose, and yet he continued to fight.

As much as Geillan wanted to experience how it felt to be punched, he'd grown bored with the battle. It was a nice distraction, but the journey had become a chore. He just wanted it finished. He let Nothany's fist nearly reach his face. It was a mere half an inch from his jaw when he took control of the boy's mind and stopped the attack.

The child had at least as much confidence in his fists as he did his sword. It would not have gone as he expected, but Nothany's thoughts suggested the blow would cause Geillan's knees to buckle. He would have followed that up by grabbing the back of Geillan's head and pulling it down while he quickly raised his knee to smash his nose. On anyone else, the attack would have worked brilliantly. The boy's skill was impressive.

Nothany remained fearless as he stood there unable to move and grunted, "Will you burn me now?"

"I could, but I don't want to," Geillan shrugged, "I admire your skill. I don't believe I've ever felt jealous in my life. It's an interesting feeling. I have incomprehensible power, but I cannot beat you in a physical fight, not with swords nor fists. It is completely barbaric, but I want to be the best at everything. I could make myself appear to be the greatest swordsman to ever roam the trails, but it would be a lie. It wouldn't be pure skill. I could read your thoughts to know your next move and will my body to respond appropriately. Anyone who saw would think me a master, but I would know the truth."

"Why do you care?" Nothany's tone remained tight as he continued to struggle against Geillan's will.

Why indeed? Geillan wasn't sure. He'd only been walking about the *real* world for a short time. Everything was new. "Of that I am unsure," he finally replied offhandedly. Then he looked up toward the canopy and added, "What I am sure of is that you will join me for the rest of my short journey. You can continue to struggle if you'd like, but you'll be far more comfortable if you don't."

Nothany finally lowered his fist and moved to stand beside Geillan. His movements were not his own as Geillan forced the boy's muscles to flex properly to move his body where he wanted him to stand. It was just like controlling the dead-eyed men. The only real difference was that he didn't have to control this one's thoughts. They could have an actual conversation. The boy refused to speak anymore, so Geillan strolled about his thoughts to amuse himself. The exercise wasn't interesting. Some of Nothany's memories were rather epic, but most were quite mundane: traveling, training, eating, and washing. It was horribly boring.

Geillan's plan had been to walk with the dead-eyed men to the path across the great streak that his father had trekked when charging off to face the Dragon in the name of his false god. There was no good reason to do that. The dead-eyed men were gone, and the replacement he had found for them was no more fun than they had been. He was ready for the end. The Lake was just across the great red streak no matter where one crossed it. It was time.

"This is your moment," Ijilv's voice rang in his head. The tone carrying those words almost sounded triumphant, like a mentor preparing his pupil for battle or some test of skill.

"I am your captor, not your pupil," Geillan replied offhandedly, more relieved he had someone to talk to besides himself than annoyed that the vile god had the gall to speak to him again.

"I didn't say anything," Nothany offered a queer look, "I know you're my captor, and I know you'll eventually kill me. I have accepted my fate."

"I wasn't talking to you," Geillan snapped.

"You know you sound insane when speak to us out loud," Kaldumahn's voice sounded like a laugh in Geillan's head, "Do as you see fit, but know this. Good advice is good advice regardless of the station or rank of the being who offers it."

"And it is your time," Ijilv continued, "You have made a vow to yourself to destroy this place and all the creatures and life who inhabit it. However, I sense doubt in you. You have the potential to create and destroy entire worlds, yet you lament about a lack of skill swinging around a sharpened stick."

"And the boy, why let him live?" Brerto asked.

"You fear your father. You should. The man is a titan, and his sister might be even more powerful. She has explored her abilities far more deeply than Maelich," Moshat added.

"And you have to contend with them both," Kallum chuckled.

"I know exactly what you are doing," Geillan struggled to keep his frustration out of his tone, "It will not work."

"I have done nothing," Nothany sighed and shook his head, "I can't. You control my every move."

"I told you I am not speaking to you," Geillan's frustration bled from his words.

"But it is," Brerto replied quickly with a wicked twinge to his tone dragging out the s until it sounded like a hiss. He paused only a moment before adding, "We can all feel it. As powerful as you are, you have very little experience."

"You're barely more than a babe, an angry toddler stomping about and having a tantrum," Kallum chuckled through his words until finally bursting into laughter.

"Shut up!" Geillan shouted at the trees. "There is no reason for me to hurry. There is no reason I could not wait to destroy this place and take centuries to torture the lot of you."

"You could do that," Kaldumahn agreed, "but you will never defeat your father and his sister. They are too powerful."

Flames shot up from Geillan's shoulders as the tone of his voice deepened until it shook the ground beneath his feet, "They will welcome me with open arms, and I will burn them out of existence. There is no force in this world that can resist me. I am god here."

The other four gods laughed at the outburst as Ijilv calmly counseled, "Your inability to maintain control will be your downfall. Maelich and Cialia are skilled at their craft. Raw force will not be enough to overcome them. You are not good enough to defeat them."

Geillan closed them off from his awareness, locking them in their little room while they sat about their gaudy table pretending to be gods. The sudden silence was nice. He needed a moment to think without their annoying distractions. His breathing slowly steadied as he knelt upon the hard trail. As much as he hated admitting it, the fools were correct. Raw power and emotion would not be enough against two Dragons with access to everything their flames represent. He needed precision, focused and accurate strikes. He needed control. But how?

Nothany's voice trembled slightly as he asked, "Are you feeling alright? It seems you speak to folks who aren't here."

In his frustration, Geillan had almost forgotten the boy was there. Knowing someone witnessed his outburst made him feel small. It took a moment of rifling through information in his mind to understand he was embarrassed. He didn't like the feeling.

"There are gods living in my head," he finally replied, "They are insufferable and annoying, and they will not stop speaking to me."

The riotous laughter Nothany offered as a response made Geillan feel even smaller. No one looked up to him, and this one didn't even fear him. The boy just laughed and laughed. As bad as that was, it was worse when the boy ended his laughter with a jibe of a question, "You have gods in your head who speak to you? What do they say? Do they tell you you're great? Are they mad you couldn't beat me with a sword?"

"I don't think I like you much anymore," Geillan's reply lacked any of the emotion his words suggested, "I would like to kill you now, but I think I have something better for you."

"Why wait? Just do it. I'm not afraid of you. No one is," defiance coiled around Nothany's reply.

"They will be," Geillan scowled, "I will take you before your master and you can watch me burn him to ash. Then you can watch me burn every other living creature crowded around that Lake except those two vile Dragons, Maelich and Cialia. They will be last. They can watch me burn you before I destroy them with rest of this pathetic world."

The fear Geillan hoped to see on Nothany's face was absent as the boy quietly replied, "I have had many fights with many different opponents. With all that bravado, you sound like someone who knows he is going to lose. You fear those Dragons, but you won't stop because you want some kind of revenge."

"I don't want you to speak anymore," Geillan sighed as he forced Nothany's jaw shut.

It wasn't fear. There may have been some doubt, but he was sure it wasn't fear. Maybe it was. Maybe all the voices tormenting him knew more about him than he knew about himself. They all had more experience dealing with emotions. As much as tried to pretend he felt nothing for his father, it was a lie. He could tell the annoying boy and those petty gods haunting his mind that he felt nothing, but he couldn't fool himself. There was a tinge of fear slithering about his mind, and it was rage buried deep in his gut to fester and ooze like an open wound riddled with infection driving him toward the Lake. It was true that Ouloos was a vile and horrid place that should never exist in any reality, but if he was honest with himself, Ouloos was not the focus of his goal. It was merely the method through which he would hurt the man who hurt him first. Maelich loved Ouloos and the vile creatures who inhabit it. Destroying it before his eyes would hopefully hurt him as much as it hurt to know he had been abandoned.

Geillan took a few deep breaths, and he was ready. He gazed up and down the great, red streak. It was a strange thing. The rules of the place made little sense most of the time and made absolutely no sense some of the time. This red streak made no sense at all to Geillan. The stories men told each other about the lad of the Lake freeing Dragons from their prison when he obliterated a god suggested the ground had been dyed by the essence of Dragon's flame leeching out from them. That seemed a perfect description for a mind with access only to what it has learned and remembered for the brief moment it had spent in the physical, but it seemed a stretch when all knowledge ever known was accessible.

Geillan stepped onto the red streak with Nothany. His bare foot sunk slightly into the loose dirt no other foot had tread upon at least since the men of this place had attempted to kill all but one Dragon. Another strange thing that made absolutely no sense. Men physically killed all those Dragons with swords and spears, but none of them returned to the Lake. Instead, trees sprouted along this strip and their souls were trapped there. Then Maelich killed a god—who also didn't actually die, his essence was merely scattered about for Ijilv to slurp up like soup—and all the Dragons physically returned, spewing forth from the Lake like a geyser. Regardless of who actually died or didn't, the dirt was loose enough that his foot sunk into it a good inch. It felt cool on his skin. It might have been psychological, all the ideas about the place floating around the ether impacting his mind's ability to process what it was feeling, but he didn't think that was the case. The dirt probably just felt cool.

The sensation continued with each step he took, but nothing else was any different than the trail he had left to step upon the odd thing. Then something changed. It had nothing to do with the dirt beneath his feet. That remained constant. It was a feeling. It felt like it should have been dread like the overwhelming fear that overcomes a soul just before they feel the impact of whatever calamity is about to befall them. It should have been exactly like standing on the edge of a high cliff, losing your balance, and realizing you are too off kilter to correct it. Death would be imminent, and there was nothing you could do to stop it. But it wasn't that at all. Instead, he was suddenly overwhelmed with sadness but not for himself. This sadness faced away from him.

A tear trickled down his cheek as tangible pain tore through his side. He felt larger in that moment, and his desires seemed different than what he thought they should. The world around him was suddenly replaced by something else, a different landscape entirely. A small man stood before him with vengeance and hatred oozing from his wild eyes not more than five feet from his snout. He tried to snap at the man with his powerful jaws before realizing they weren't his own. It was a Dragon's memory as clear as if he were living it. As the realization settled in, he finally understood the sadness he felt. It was sadness for the author of the pain the pathetic Dragon who owned this horrid memory felt as that vile man mercilessly stabbed it again and again with a bloody spear.

He could sense that Nothany was experiencing a similar vision, but it affected the boy differently. He seemed to understand the sadness the Dragon felt. To him it made sense that the Dragon would feel compassion for the hurt the man who killed her would feel instead of sadness for herself at the pain the man caused her. It all seemed backwards and insane to Geillan.

"Enough," he shouted at the sky.

The sadness fled along with the pain and the vision. Dragons were pathetic. All the power trapped within their hideous forms, and all they could do was weep for the pain the creatures who killed them would feel when the Lake claimed their useless souls. Was that unconditional love, caring for a thing above all else as it destroys you? It was a disgusting thought. Those Dragons deserved their prison. They deserved to be destroyed.

"That is love, Geillan," Helias voice chimed in Geillan's head like a lullaby. "It is the same love all creatures in this place feel for you. This is your home."

"And I am your doom," Geillan whispered as he closed his eyes. When he opened them again, he was a giant standing beside Helias who perched upon her stony peak as if she were some kind of queen resting upon her throne. A Dragon's head stretched out from his chest as his eyes smoldered fiery red. Nothany vomited. The quick jaunt through time had twisted the boy's mind and jarred his equilibrium enough to urge the meager contents of his gut all about the perfect ground. Distracted by the mother of all Dragon's, Geillan had little attention to give to his new companion. Otherwise, the event might have given him a good chuckle.

There was nothing funny about the tear that fell from Helias' eye. That was as infuriating as her words. Both served only to stoke Geillan's rage further. "My heart weeps for what your actions will do to your spirit," she cried, "Everyone here loves you. I know you feel justified in what you are about to do, but I promise it will break your heart."

"It breaks my heart you refuse to defend yourself," he sighed as the Dragon's head jutting from his torso opened its fiery mouth to belch flame at the supposed mother of all Dragons.

The flames engulfing Helias' face and head failed to earn even a hint of fear. That was frustrating. He wanted her to cower before him. He wanted to hear her beg him to cease her suffering and allow her to die. Then it suddenly occurred to him that his flame had failed to singe her scales in the slightest. That was unfortunate. It made sense. A being composed of Dragon's flame could not be destroyed by it.

"You can destroy me, Geillan, but you will take no joy from this," the Dragon begged him, but she still refused to grant him any fear. All she felt while weeping before him was sadness for him.

"This is exactly what I felt when strolling across the prison every Dragon save you spent hundreds of summers trapped in," he growled, "That is why you will be the first to die. You did nothing to help the sisters you claim to love. You did nothing to help them when men hunted them down and cut them to pieces. You are no queen perched upon that throne. You are a coward."

Scales grew over the Dragon's mouth so she couldn't infect the air with any more vile ideas. Unfortunately, it didn't stop her from speaking to his mind. "I love you," was all she said.

"Love cannot save you," he whispered as he forced his intention into her mind and her chest simultaneously, driving deeper and deeper into every physical cell of her body while completely overtaking her consciousness.

He held her there like that for a moment as brief as the flap of a fairy's wing before allowing his will to expand in all directions. Her body exploded from atop her stony mount sending bloody hunks of scaly flesh up into the sky to quickly vaporize to dust.

"No!" millions of voices cried out in unison. Sadness dripped from the lone word, but it wasn't only for the Dragon the owners of those voices so adored. There was also sadness for him.

One voice seemed just a bit louder than the rest. It was Lameah. He knew everything about her the moment he latched onto her awareness. Somehow, her sadness seemed just a bit deeper than everyone else wallowing in their pathetic emotions, but it still was mostly saved for him. Why could these pathetic creatures not feel anything for themselves? Would none stand before him and defend anything they believed in?

"I believe in you, Geillan," Lameah suddenly hovered before his face, her smoldering, red eyes oozing emotion like a leaky wound, "I believe you can be one with us, freely receiving and giving love like all souls deserve."

"And I believe you might be the most pathetic soul ever to haunt this horrid place," Geillan sighed in something just short of defeat. A moment later, Lameah was ash slowly drifting away in a damnably perfect breeze.

All those same voices cried out again in another pathetic melody of sadness. Finally, one stood out that seemed it might hint at something more than blatant inaction. It was the one voice he really wanted to hear. Finally, a challenge.

"Stop," Maelich's voice boomed above the rest.

Then the world suddenly changed. The Lake, the vast and sweeping fields of green, the bright, blue sky, and all the poor souls weeping pathetically at the loss of lives they had convinced themselves they loved were gone, swept up into a swirling corridor of color. The air was suddenly pungent like weeks old flesh rotting in the sun. Then it was sweet like a cake fresh from the oven. Then it was something else entirely that Geillan failed to identify as a loud booming erupted in his ears. The sound lasted only a moment on its own before it was joined by a wild cacophony of discombobulated sounds.

It seemed he was racing though his body felt as if it were standing still with the wild kaleidoscope of colors melting and blurring around him. It had to be some kind of trick. He reached out with his will searching for his coward of a father. "Where are you hiding?" he mumbled.

"I am not hiding," Maelich's voice spoke directly to his mind.

The moment the statement finished, it all stopped. The colors ceased swirling; the shifting smells dissipated; and the horrid sounds that had been pummeling his eardrums fled in favor of silence. Even the icy chill that had pulled his flesh into tight bumps seemed to evaporate away until the air felt like nothing against his skin. Only darkness remained.

Little streams of light slowly began breaking tiny holes in the darkness like needles poking through cloth. They came faster and faster until the darkness had been completely overcome. There still was no detail or depth to anything. It was just light, plain and unremarkable. "It sure seems you are hiding or playing some form of trick," Geillan finally complained.

"I am not hiding," this time he heard Maelich's voice with his ears.

And then the man was there, seated directly before him on a large flat rock. His hair blew behind him as if motivated by a brisk wind, but the air wasn't moving at all. The world surrounding Geillan was completely still. The air smelled like it wanted to carry the pleasing odor of a forest, but it wasn't quite right. The moss was off. The wildflowers were fragrant, but somehow smelled like a potion some disturbed healer might concoct in a dark cell deep beneath an old castle. Even the rotting leaves smelled like something brewed rather than born into the world to live, die, and decay.

The trees surrounding him seemed real enough. The leaves were painted in the correct shade of green, and the trunks protruding beneath them an accurate enough brown. Everything seemed a bit too smooth, like just a hint of the details were missing or forgotten. "Where are we?" Geillan finally asked. "The trees surrounding us seem more like someone's memory of a forest rather than a real place."

"It is a memory," Maelich replied, "A place I apparently made up while trying to process my father's death. I'm still not certain if I truly made it up on my own, or if it was the result of a suggestion made to my subconscious mind by another. This head has hosted many unwelcomed visitors."

"Is that what I am?" Geillan flashed a devious smile before offering a humorless chuckle, "Am I an unwelcome guest in your broken mind?

"Quite the contrary," Maelich shook his head, "I want you here."

Geillan shrugged as he asked, "To what end? You must realize you cannot keep me in this place."

"No, I cannot," Maelich agreed, "You are far too powerful. I just wanted a quiet moment to speak with you, away from all the noise. I know your thoughts. You don't hide them. But I don't know you. I have never met you. That breaks my heart."

"It breaks your heart that you were absent and unable to steer me toward whatever destiny you had in mind for me. You deserve that. You chose to leave me. It will break your heart even more when I destroy everything you love," Geillan remained aloof as he spoke. He even snatched up a blade of grass that felt a wee too slippery and began methodically shredding it into smaller and smaller strips.

"I hope to convince you that this path is not yours," no tears accompanied Maelich's words. His puffy eyes suggested they might have run out.

Geillan dropped the last bits of the shredded blade of grass from his hand and laughed, "Of course, you do. That is the one quality of yours I am depending on. Though you have almost convinced yourself to succumb to the Lake's charms and completely given up your individuality in favor of this nebulous concept of unconditional love, you will still try to protect them. You know how this ends. You will watch as I destroy every being you swore to protect, and then I will destroy you along with this horrid world. Because I know you know this, I know you will not be able to sit by and watch that happen. This is your first attempt to interfere when you promised Helias you would not. It saddens me slightly that she won't be here to witness you break that promise. My gift to her."

"You are correct," Maelich conceded as his eye mustered enough moisture to offer another tear, "I am interfering, but only to ask a question. Would you please take one moment to know this thing you are so eager to destroy? I love you. Everyone here loves you. Take just a bit of time to feel that. It is good. Then, if you decide you still want to destroy me and everything else, do as you see fit."

"You love me?" Geillan's laughter grew heartier. It took him a few moments to compose himself enough to continue, "That is rich. You said yourself you do not even know me. Your love is meaningless. There was only one person who ever truly loved me the way you and the fools who followed you to your Lake claim you do, and I destroyed her for it. I should never have had to make that choice. That is your fault. You are weak and undependable. Nothing you could say to me will make a difference."

He stared intently into his father's eyes waiting for the next bit of gibberish the pathetic thing would offer. When no more words came, he stood and said, "Come. Let me show you."

In an instant, he was back at the Lake standing next to his father. He nudged him gently with his elbow and said, "Watch this," as he pointed at a Dragon wailing and weeping as she slowly floated on the brisk currents high above. As soon as he was convinced Maelich's gaze was aimed in the right direction, the Dragon burst into ash.

Maelich fell to his knees beside Geillan crying out in some pitiable wail that sounded more like a wounded animal caught in a trapper's claw than a man. Another Dragon exploded and another. Maelich howled that same pathetic cry with each Dragon who erupted.

Seeing his father's form quivering in the sand sent a wave of disgust through Geillan, "Get up and fight me, you coward. Will you just lie there in the sand like some impotent thing while everything you love is destroyed?"

Maelich offered nothing but more sobs in reply.

"Thank you for showing me what you truly are," Geillan spat, "I am grateful you abandoned me. You may have molded me into the same kind of pitiful being who could sit by in idle lament while the creatures who depend on them are tortured and destroyed."

As the last words left his lips, a grong began screaming. There was no visible reason why the creature would be in distress, but the poor soul wailed like he was being ripped apart by amatilazo.

"See that?" Geillan asked. He nudged Maelich's shoulder again before continuing, "I'm burning him from the inside. His liver smolders while his intestines burn to ash. You could stop his suffering."

"Geillan, please," tears streamed down Cialia's cheeks as she ran to Geillan and stood immediately before him, "Your father has failed you. I have failed you. But these creatures have done nothing to deserve the pain you are causing them. I love you. We all love you. Take your vengeance on me, not them."

"This is…" Geillan began but was interrupted by Raya.

Her brown waves danced on the breeze as she reached out to Geillan and gently held his cheeks in her soft hands while interrupting him, "I am the author of all your pain. I am the reason Ijilv used you the way he did. Take your vengeance out on me."

"Ah, the forgotten one," Geillan's delight swirled around his words, "You are the vilest of them all. Your betrayal destroyed Ijilv. I think

I'll keep you. You can speak with him about it."

Geillan's mouth expanded as Raya slowly vaporized into shimmering bits of light that looked like ash glinting in the bright sun. However, the light was not a reflection. Each bit shined with its own glory as if fragments of her essence were trapped in each one. Geillan breathed in deeply and sucked each bit into his mouth. A few moments later, there was nothing left to suggest she had ever been.

The creatures surrounding him continued crying out. Some wept for those already lost. Others wailed in brief songs of agony as they exploded to ash or slowly burned from the inside out. Still others wept for him. Those were the most pathetic of the bunch. Maelich and Cialia were among them. They were the worst. They had the power to do something about it, but they refused to challenge him.

Finally, Geillan stretched out his awareness to latch onto Nothany and Sanjo. A moment later, they both stood before him. Nothany remained motionless, but Sanjo wrapped his arms around the boy and hugged him tightly.

"I should never have let you leave," the pathetic old soldier cried into the boy's shoulder.

"Pathetic," Geillan grunted at Sanjo in disgust, "You view this boy as a son, yet you trained him to be a cold killer. He is that, and quite expert at his craft." Then he turned his attention to Nothany and said, "I almost forgot my promise, damn Dragons. Look at this man who sees you as his son."

As the final word left Geillan's lips, Sanjo's arms stretched out wide. The man's boots slid across the grass as Geillan dragged him away from the boy with his will. Then he turned Nothany's body to face the man who'd acted as a father to him, forcing his eyes open as he did.

"Behold," he said as he launched a small fireball from his finger. It was a tiny thing, but it blasted Sanjo to sloppy bits when it struck him in the chest.

"No!" Nothany shouted as tears poured forth from his eyes.

"Finally, the cool-headed swordsman shows some emotion. That is all I wanted. You may go now," Geillan smiled as he forced Nothany's cells to split apart from each other in an instant. The result was an explosion of blood like a wave splashing out in all directions.

Then he turned to stand over Maelich's cowering form and growled, "Can you look at my eyes as I cause all this suffering around you, and tell me you love me?"

His father surprised him. He raised himself up until he was sitting on his knees, wiped his eyes, smiled, and said, "My son, I do love you. Nothing you could ever do would change that. Search my heart. Search my mind. If you do, you will find my words are true. You can destroy this world, and I will love you for what you are despite all you have done."

Then that vile Cialia did the exact same thing before adding, "And I love you, Geillan, for who you are. There are reasons why you must do what you must do, and I know you believe what you are doing is right. I would love you the same even if you didn't believe that."

"You all disgust me," Geillan's voice remained a growl as he continued, "You are both destroyers. I expected you to do something."

"We are doing the most important thing," both Maelich and Cialia replied in unison, "We are showing you the love you deserve."

Something about the air suddenly changed. It wasn't a smell or taste. Nor was it any adjustment in the velocity of the breezes blowing about. It was nothing which occurred to any of his senses, but something changed. It was troubling enough that he chased it around his mind. He couldn't define this thing that was different. And then he knew.

Maelich and Cialia both began changing before him. Their skin flushed pink before deepening into a fiery red that quickly turned to scales. Horns began growing off their heads as they stretched and elongated into jaws filled with teeth. Their eyes smoldered like embers while their limbs stretched, and claws grew from their fingertips. Two Dragons sat before him.

"No," Geillan shouted at them, "You do not get this prize. I will not allow it."

He lashed out, driving his intention into every shred of their beings, and blew them apart. Damn it. He would have preferred them to suffer. They were supposed to be the last ones to die. He would have held them there after every other soul on Ouloos had been obliterated, and then he would have tortured them until he tired of it. Only then would he have blown Ouloos to bits and died along with it. They ruined everything.

Then something equally troubling happened. A feeling of hope oozed out of every cell of every creature remaining there. Even the ones who suffered through the pain of Dragon's fire oozed this misplaced emotion. It stomped all over the fear he'd been relishing from them. That would have to change.

He expanded his will, reaching and stretching, focusing on each of the thousands upon thousands of souls still living until he was connected to them. It was as if he were one being with them, one being who was about to die. He closed his eyes and released his flame.

In that same moment, something like a swirling wind began from the Lake. It appeared like a cyclone, but it wasn't wind. It was some kind of force belching forth from the calm waters to grab all around it. It expanded until everything was swept up into it. He battled against it with his will even as his cells were exploding along with every other creature he had just executed. The force was too strong. He was helpless against it as he swirled into everything else.

And then it was dark.

CHAPTER 25
AWAKE

Aphegeta stood before a bank of monitors mounted on the wall five across and four down analyzing data points on charts as they slowly drifted across each screen. The room around her was as white, sterile, and quiet as ever. A faint hint of bleach danced on the still air, a memory of the morning's cleaning. The soft whir of computer fans was the only thing disturbing the silence. The sound was so constant, she barely registered it most of the time. However, the volume had just increased. One of the dreamers must have had a nightmare.

After a quick examination of the monitors, she found the one that had caused the closest thing to commotion that ever happened in the lab, the sudden increase in fan volume. A red light flashed on the monitor three from the left and second from the top. She swiped as many times left and then as many times down on the digital pad she held loosely in her left hand before pushing her glasses up to her brow only to have them immediately slide halfway back down her nose like they always did when she looked down. She needed a new pair. Then she brushed the few strands of light brown hair dangling before her green eyes back behind her ear. She could never get that particular curl to remain in the loose bun at the back of her head.

"What is it?" Boethus asked as he peered over her shoulder at the monitors, his chin nearly resting on that same shoulder. He was a close talker who smoked too much. The odor of stale tobacco was bad enough, but mixed with the mint he failed to cover it with was somehow worse.

She rolled her eyes slightly and took a step forward before responding, "It's Coeptus. He had a flurry of activity about five minutes ago."

"Nightmare?" he asked, stepping in closer to look over her shoulder again.

"I don't think so," she sighed while stowing the tablet in the large pocket of her lab coat and walking over toward a bank of containers aligned in the same layout as the monitors mounted to the wall, "This spike in activity was much bigger than any nightmare I've ever seen."

Aphegeta had never liked the new containers much. The old ones had really been nothing more than repurposed EEGs. Unfortunately, the dreamers kept waking up and spoiling the research. Some geniuses had come up with a method to keep them sleeping for the thirty days they remained under observation. It was effective, but she didn't like it. She liked it even less that this batch consisted of children. The children were placed inside of containers that resembled stainless-steel coffins with small windows reminiscent of ship portholes. They were sedated. Sensors were attached to their bodies and feeding tubes were installed. Then the containers—or dream pods, as the board liked to call them—were sealed and filled with a gel that was intended to mimic amniotic fluid. So far, everything was working as expected. After twenty days of monitoring, none of the dreamers had awoken. Until now.

The light hazel eyes staring back at her from the porthole were wide with terror. The world slowed as those eyes locked onto hers, pleading with her for relief, seemingly still as the child's head thrashed wildly about. "Holy shit. He's awake. Get this damn thing open, now," she hollered at Boethus who had occupied himself with recording the spike.

"What?" he hissed. The screen of his tablet cracked when it hit the floor. Aphegeta had complained about the cheap cases the institute had purchased for their tablets, but no one ever listened to her.

"Coeptus is awake. He is panicking. Get this damned thing open before he goes into cardiac arrest," her tone remained pointed even as she did her best to appear calm and in control of the situation.

"Okay, shit. Give me a minute. We've only simulated an emergency response. I didn't expect any of them would actually wake up," Boethus replied as he fumbled with his cracked tablet, furiously tapping the screen for a few tense moments before giving up, "This one's done. It's broke."

"Well, fire up another," she shouted, "and hurry."

Boethus was correct. This was the first actual run for these new pods. Though each test had only lasted a few days, none of the test subjects had woken. The emergency response protocol had only been simulated with empty pods and no one's life on the line. It was just another thing she had complained about. She had wanted full, thirty-day simulations with paid volunteers who understood the risks. It was another request the penny pinchers had overruled her on.

There was nothing she could do about all the failures the bureaucracy had caused in her work. Lamenting it wouldn't help the poor child thrashing about, trapped in the result of their cheap impatience. She touched the earpiece in her left ear and said, "Relax, Coeptus. I am here with you. You will be fine. Just breathe normally, and we'll get you out of there."

The child calmed only slightly. His eyes remained wild, but he seemed to understand the instruction. It wasn't enough. The *123* blinking red on the small monitor just beneath the porthole only dropped to *121* and then remained steady, "Let's go," she hollered over to Boethus, "He's tachycardic. We're going to lose him."

"Got it," he finally yelled back just as the seal around the edges of the pod released with a hiss and a quick blast of vapor.

Coeptus continued to thrash about as the lid of the pod rose too slowly.

"Get over here and help me," she shouted as she slid the top half of her body between the lid and the container, soaking the sleeves of her coat when she reached in to lift him out of the slop and hug him.

Boethus fell as he attempted to hurry. The new tablet he'd been carrying smashed against the floor and slid as he did the same, moron. He obviously wasn't going to be any help. What good is an assistant who doesn't really assist with anything?

Everything was covered in slime as she raised her head up until it bumped against the lid which was still rising too slowly. She couldn't see the trigger on the massive, black hose which controlled the feeding tube. It took a moment of fumbling to find the release button. She sighed quietly once she finally found the damn thing to push it. That kicked off a string of events. Monitors began popping off the boy, hissing as they fell away from him. Simultaneously, the feeding tube was slowly removed from his esophagus. Once it had fully retreated into the hose, it withdrew into the bottom of the pod.

"Help," Coeptus choked, his voice hoarse and crackly.

"I'm here," she whispered as calmly as she could, "I've got you."

"What can I do?" Boethus asked, late, as usual.

"Check his heart rate," she snapped.

"Mmm…ninety-five," he replied as quickly as he did everything else, which wasn't very fast at all.

"Good," she replied as she was finally able to raise her head up far enough to look in Coeptus' eyes. She brushed the boy's hair back and said, "You're going to be alright. Let's get you out of this mess and clean you up. We'll get you a nice candy bar and a pop, and you can tell me what happened to get you so distressed."

"Ouloos," he whispered before falling back to sleep.

The sky was the same color that wanted to be purple—but was somehow more purple than any other purple—as it had been since the UV dome was installed long before Coeptus was born. He had never seen the sky before then, but father had shown him pictures. Apparently, the thing glowed that color because of the UV light it blocked. He didn't really understand it. Father tried to explain it to him, but it only sounded like, "Science, science, science," to him. Mother did a bit better. She explained that the UV rays were trapped for a bit before bouncing back into space, and they bent all the other light to make everything look purple. He still didn't understand exactly why, but that was how it was.

He sat just inside a sloppy waste tube. He'd have about thirty minutes to watch the rockets take off. Then he'd have to hurry back through the tube to avoid the release that happened every four hours. Father would be furious if he found out. He had caught him once because of the slop on his shoes and grounded him for a month. Coeptus had been careful to clean them thoroughly before going home every time after.

A slight tremble signaled it was almost time. It slowly mounted into a rumbling in his chest even before he heard any of the noise. The mounting roar came a few moments later as the valley below filled with smoke and flames shooting in every direction. This was it.

The rocket rose slowly at first. Gradually gaining velocity until it looked like a bright ball of flame racing toward the deep purple sky. Then he saw it, a bright blue flash in the purple dome above. A tiny fleck of real sky, a hint of what the world looked like before the dome. That was what he really came to see. He'd seen images of it in photos and paintings, but he yearned to see how the sky would look if that tiny blue speck spread across the entire purple dome.

Then, suddenly, he was riding his hoverboard over sand, racing right along the shore of a lake. Both were perfectly round, a circle inside of a circle. The wind whipped his hair straight back behind his head as he crouched deeply into the board, leaning forward to earn just a bit more speed. He felt completely free. Then he noticed the sky. It was the same blue as that speck of sky he could see when the portal had opened in the dome to let the rocket escape from the atmosphere.

He had only just begun troubling over how he'd gone from sitting at the end of a waste tube watching a rocket launch to cruising on his hoverboard around a lake he'd never seen when his chest began to rumble. It felt just like when the rockets launched, and a similar deafening roar followed. This one was so much louder. The sand beneath his board began to quake. Then the water in the Lake, which had only a moment prior been completely still, suddenly became agitated like water slopping in a bucket being violently shaken.

The earth beneath him bucked and sent him sailing off his board. He curled up bracing for impact, but it never came. Instead, a massive and swirling gale flung him up toward the blue sky above. His body spun sideways in a circle as if he were hovering in one spot, but he wasn't. He was being whipped around an ever-expanding cyclone of water rising higher and higher above the lake.

And then there were dragons. Thousands and thousands of them raced out from the lake spinning and swirling in the cyclone of water with him. He knew their names. He knew their thoughts. He knew everything about them. More creatures came, and men, all of them swirling together in the great, howling cyclone. Some of them looked like monsters. Things he'd seen in his worst nightmares. Some were giant. Some had fangs and scales. They were all grotesque and terrifying to behold, but he knew them too. They were not monsters. They had names and thoughts and desires just like everyone else.

An entire history raced through his awareness like a blur. Yet, he saw every detail, tasted every flavor, smelled every aroma, heard every sound and every word ever spoken, and felt every pain or pleasure every being who had ever existed in this history had ever experienced. He even knew their thoughts, ideas, and intentions. He knew everything about this place called Ouloos. But there was more, something else, an outside influence that brought with it remnants of some other world which existed before.

Then he fell, plummeting from the heights as lifetime after lifetime of experiences bled into his awareness. He tried to cry out, to howl in terror, but no sound would come from his open mouth no matter how wide he stretched it or how hard he tried to yell. It seemed as if he might fall forever, but when he splashed into the water of that lake, it felt like he had been tossed right into it from his hoverboard. Time is strange like that sometimes.

It suddenly felt like he was drowning, gasping for air as water poured into his throat with each breath he attempted to take. He tried to swim, but it was no use. Something was dragging him down and down, further into the dark depths. He thrashed wildly about while his body convulsed.

And then he was awake. For the briefest of moments, he felt relief. It had all been a dream. But he was suddenly drowning again. His body was covered in water, but it wasn't quite that. It was like some kind of slime. He tried again to breathe, but there was something jammed down his throat. He could feel it. He tried to move his arms, but there were things connected to him. He felt pokes every time he moved. The brief bits of pain it caused failed to stop him from thrashing about. He knew he was going to die.

Then he saw her face peering down at him from a bright circle of light above. He recognized her eyes. Her name was Aphegeta, but she looked almost as terrified as he felt. He suddenly remembered everything she told him before he went for the long sleep. This wasn't at all what she explained. Something was wrong.

He barely registered her arms wrapping around him as he felt things snapping off what seemed like every spot on his body. Then he felt whatever was stuck in his throat sliding out. He gagged multiple times on it as he tried to breathe through his mouth. It didn't matter that his lungs weren't burning at all. He must have been getting air from somewhere.

She pulled him out of the muck and held him tight. He felt safe in her embrace. She said a bunch of things, but he couldn't make out her words. It sounded like nothing more than a bunch of mumbling. Then he had a sudden urge to tell her about this place he had just learned so much about. He needed to tell everyone. "Ouloos," was all he managed to whisper before everything went dark.

CHAPTER 26
A TALE WORTH TELLING

The room Coeptus sat in was sterile, unwelcoming, and small. The walls were some kind of metal. There were a couple monitors on the wall next to him with charts slowly trudging across them. Beneath those was a small sink that looked like the same metal as the walls. The clear, plastic chair he sat upon felt cool against the backs of his legs. Boethus sat facing him on a short stool with wheels, the only other piece of furniture in the room.

Boethus was annoying. He thought he was funny, but his jokes were worse than Father's. The only way Coeptus could really tell that Boethus was telling a joke was a slight tick the man expressed which he had picked up on. Boethus would brush his hair back and flash an awkward sideways smirk after he'd made some comment or asked a silly question. That meant whatever he had just said was supposed to be funny. Once or twice, his comments had been, but most of the time the chuckle Coeptus' offered was merely to be polite.

Finally, the door slid open with a *whoosh*, and Aphegeta entered worrying over the tablet she held in her left hand. The door slid quickly shut behind her with the same kind of *whoosh*. "Well?" she asked Boethus. Based on the mild annoyance in her tone, it seemed she felt similarly about Boethus as Coeptus did.

"I think our patient will live," Boethus winked at Coeptus when he answered. Then he brushed his hair back and offered him a sideways smirk.

"So, all his vitals are normal?" Aphegeta's tone remained humorless

261

and direct, ignoring the unfunny joke.

"Yes, boss," Boethus saluted dramatically when he answered. The smirk never left his face when he turned back to Coeptus and added, "Keep it serious, kid. I forgot to mention this is a joke free zone."

"Excellent. Let me know once you have logged your observations," her tone remained dry with Boethus. A bit of sweetness crept in when she turned her attention back to Coeptus and said, "I am terribly sorry for the distress you experienced upon waking. That is not supposed to happen. We have a standard process to wake dreamers once they've experienced something like what you did. However, we have never seen one that strong. Ideas born into your conscious mind from your subconscious are typically complete. There seems to be some foreign concepts infecting this one."

"Does that mean there is something wrong with me?" The idea of something infecting his mind sounded kind of scary.

"Not at all," she smiled, "If what I think is correct, there might be something very right with you, but I need your help to confirm my assumptions. When you woke, you said *Ouloos*. What is that? Can you describe it for me?"

"It's a whole world that is thousands and thousands of circuits old, but they don't call them circuits like we do. Even though they have all the same seasons we do, they call their circuits summers. The reason is kind of weird, but it has to do with when things grow," Coeptus shrugged, "The really weird thing is I know everything about them. I understand concepts I never have before. It's like they taught me things."

"That is unsurprising," her tone grew more serious again, "Our subconscious minds can make connections to things our conscious minds simply cannot. That is the whole point of this exercise. Well," she paused, "mostly. It is what I am trying to understand. How do these concepts swirling about our subconscious minds, which I believe are all connected, jump to our conscious minds? How are ideas born?"

"Why?" he asked. It seemed a useful thing to know, but there were so many other problems to solve.

"Because, we are running out of them," she shrugged, "They aren't coming fast enough. Our world has been dying for years and years. Our efforts have slowed our inevitable end but not enough. The purple dome, for instance. For all the good it has done us, it has caused us a multitude of problems. We need to come up with another solution.

What if that solution is out there somewhere, swirling about in someone's subconscious, but is never born into an idea? If we understand how ideas are born, perhaps we can extract them."

"That sounds crazy," Coeptus' head was spinning, "but it kind of makes sense."

"It does," she agreed before adding, "Perhaps we'll get some answers from your story. Were you able to determine the point of it?"

"I think so," Coeptus nodded, "unconditional love."

"Are you sure?" Aphegeta looked like she'd just bit into lemon, "Yahweh's going to hate that."

"What's wrong with love?" his face twisted until it felt like hers looked.

"Forgive me," she smiled, "There is nothing wrong with love. Yahweh's story was more about fear and worship. Love was something a few of his predecessors convinced him to add after the first time it almost died. It was obviously an add-on that didn't fit the rest of the story. Now, it has become so convoluted that everyone in his world seems to believe something different than everyone else."

"That sounds horrible," Coeptus sighed.

"It is. Now, tell me more about Ouloos," the slightest hint of impatience tinged the edges of her otherwise friendly tone, "Did anything in this world seem out of place, like it didn't belong?"

"Yes, Raya and Ijilv," he continued, nodding more rapidly, "I only know bits and pieces about their world. It seems like it was a lot like ours. They were scientists, but everyone on Ouloos, even the gods and Dragons, thought they were gods. I think it was their plan that allowed Ouloos to be born. Raya had a baby named Kalia with Agrimon. She was supposed to…"

"Stop, stop, stop," Aphegeta shook her head slightly as she waved her hand back and forth, "We don't have time for all this right now. I think we might be on the verge of a breakthrough. Two concepts from an idea that died before it could be born latched onto another idea to help it be born," she scratched her scalp several times with all five fingers as she ran her hand through her hair that had fallen out of its bun.

"If that's what they are, it seems like you're right," Coeptus shrugged again.

"I know you are the next storyteller, but that isn't my decision. I need to take you before the council. I don't know why they are the ones to decide, but they are. You'll tell them the entire story," Aphegeta grew increasingly distant as she spoke.

Everything was moving too fast. He needed a moment of quiet to process everything. "What if I don't want to be a storyteller?" he finally asked.

"Why wouldn't you? That is like the best job you can get," Boethus chimed in, winking and making that stupid face again, "You will be the thirteenth storyteller on the thirteenth council. Everyone who came before you is famous. When their stories end, they get whatever they want and go wherever they want whenever they want."

"He's right about that, Coeptus," Aphegeta agreed, "You'll be a star."

"But I want to ride the rockets to space," he groaned, "I don't want to be trapped inside a room with a bunch of stuffy old guys who think they know everything. I want to visit all the outposts and see all the different colored skies. I want to see the purple dome from the other side."

"Unfortunately, we don't get to choose where we serve," Aphegeta seemed sad about the news she shared, "Your brainwaves suggest storyteller is the correct job for you. Had you not had your breakthrough, you would have gone back to the academy until you reached the proper age for your next best job. That is just how it is."

"This is horrible," he slumped, sliding down his chair until he nearly fell out of it, "Father will be furious."

"Well, if it's any consolation, he would have been equally furious about your next best fit," she tapped her tablet a few times before reading from the screen, "He wanted you to be an architect…"

"Ooh…that would have been a good one," Boethus interrupted, "You could have designed the next outpost."

"Or the next public toilet house," Aphegeta's tone echoed her irritation with the conversation, "The point is, you would not have been an architect. You would have been a teacher. However the story you tell ends, it will be the only job you have. You can do whatever you'd like after that. I would recommend entering this program, but that's a conversation for another time. Right now, I need to take you before the council. You can tell your story, and I can do some more analysis."

"Come," she said as she took his hand and stood, "Let's grab a bite, and I'll coach you a bit on how to address the council. They are very particular."

He took her hand and allowed her to guide him toward the door. It slid open with a *whoosh* when they got close to it. It felt like she was leading him off to be executed as they started into a long hallway together. Maybe he could run away.

"Calm down. You seem awfully twitchy. There is no place for you to run, so don't even think about it," she glanced down and said to him before looking back over her shoulder and telling Boethus, "Get a few of the trainees to help you wake the rest of Coeptus' group. Follow the correct protocols so there isn't any further drama."

"Will do, boss," Boethus saluted dramatically before looking at Coeptus and adding, "Hey, kid, if she's right, and she usually is. The work you do will be more important than anything anyone has done before you."

It was the first time Boethus didn't add the silly smirk and wink to enhance his statement. He seemed to earnestly believe it. Coeptus wasn't sure if he could believe it himself. He just hoped the council wouldn't tear him apart.

CHAPTER 27
THE COUNCIL

It seemed the hallway stretched forever, a bland corridor of shiny metal walls that matched the ceiling. Both were only interrupted at 10-foot intervals with thin, recessed lights that somehow managed to keep the place just a hair brighter than was comfortable on the eyes. The floor was equally boring, but at least it was different than the walls, consisting of large, dark gray tiles pieced so tightly together they appeared one long slab. Whoever designed the place was intent on keeping it as humdrum as possible. They hadn't even left space for mortar. Maybe that's why father was so intent on seeing him become an architect. The folks currently doing those jobs had no concept of character.

Aphegeta had been droning on and on the entire length of the hallway. Unfortunately, Coeptus had reached the end of his attention span shortly after she'd led him out of the lab and into the boring hallway. By that point, his mind was sailing up toward the great, purple dome, racing to space in a rocket. He didn't even realize he was interrupting her when he asked, "Where does this hallway go? And why aren't there any doors or windows?"

She was a bit rougher than he liked when she stopped abruptly to grab him by the shoulder and spin him toward her. "Have you not heard a word I've said?" her head shook rapidly from side to side as she sighed. "This is critical. They don't have to like you, but they must at least not dislike you. I may not have made this clear enough, but the members of the council are quite full of themselves. They've been acting as gods for their collections of stories so long, I think they see themselves as such. You need to conduct yourself properly to have any hope of getting them to listen."

"I'm sorry," he shrugged, "This is all really boring."

"No, I'm sorry," her tone remained tense despite the apology, "I forget you are still a child. This must be dreadful for you. We've passed several doors. They are just designed in such a way that you cannot see them. As for the lack of windows, the view is less than spectacular. Here," she tapped the digital pad she still held in her left hand a few times before continuing, "You might like this better."

The hallway was suddenly alive with life. It looked like he was standing in the middle of a jungle. Colorful birds with blue backs and yellow bellies raced from limb to limb in the highest branches of some of the tallest trees he'd ever seen. All manner of primate climbed, jumped, and swung from those same branches while a big spotted cat crouched on large branch appearing ready to pounce at any moment. It was a much better scene than the boring metallic smoothness it replaced, but he knew it was a simulation. It reminded him of another one he'd seen when father took him to a special exhibit at the museum called *Under the Deep Blue Sea*. That one was just as fake, but it really seemed like he'd been walking on the bottom of the ocean with every kind of fish and sea creature imaginable swimming all around him.

"It is better," he finally conceded.

"Good. Now, pay attention," she continued her rant after turning him back in the direction they'd been heading and motioning him to continue down the hall, "I need you to grow up very quickly and listen to me."

Her voice continued to drone on and on. He did his best to listen, but it was a lot. She told him all about the members he'd meet on the council and what things he should avoid saying to this one or that. He missed most of it. There was an intriguing sloth barely climbing up a tree not too far from a hungry looking jaguar who hadn't noticed the slow-moving mammal. It seemed it wouldn't be long until one was no longer hungry, and the other was simply no longer. That was way more interesting than Neith or Enki or Marduk. He did latch onto a couple of things she'd said. Gaia seemed interesting. Most of the others presented themselves in their stories as entirely separate beings who created the planet on which all their subjects lived, but she actually was the planet itself. Sadly, it sounded like her message got at least as convoluted as the rest when her world grew beyond the story she intended.

"Will my story fall apart like the rest of them?" he finally blurted.

Aphegeta rolled her eyes as she replied, "You haven't been paying attention to anything I've said, have you? I'm sorry to spoil this for you, but the jaguar never notices the sloth. He will eventually run off."

Coeptus' cheeks grew a bit warm around the sheepish smirk that slipped onto his face when he replied, "I didn't even notice that jaguar. I was listening. I like Gaia's story, but it sounds like they all fall apart eventually. Will mine do that too?"

Aphegeta's expression lacked any hint of optimism as she replied, "I hope not. You are the thirteenth seat on the thirteenth council. If your story fails, we won't have to worry about having our funding pulled. Our world will be a memory."

"So, the world will die if I do a bad job?" his voice trailed off as he replied, the weight of it all finally hitting him.

It didn't help when she repeated, "I hope not."

"Okay," he said as he rubbed his eyes and focused intently on her, "I'll pay attention."

"Good," she forced a smile, "The only one you really need to worry about is Yahweh. His story has continued far too long with no resolution. There have been moments of progress, but those moments have been far too brief stuffed in between long periods of regression. His world would have destroyed itself at least one hundred times if the entire council was not actively intervening to keep it alive. Even though he knows it is long past time to let his story end, he will not want to let it go."

"What if they say no? What if they don't think my story is good enough?" he squeaked. As the words left his mouth, he wasn't completely sure which end he'd prefer. The bits and pieces he'd retained from Aphegeta's description of the council didn't sound like anything he wanted to be a part of. On the other hand, if she was honest about how important his story might be, he should probably tell it.

"Just do you your best," her smile seemed only slightly more genuine as she stopped him in front of the biggest orangutan he'd ever seen in any book or on any screen eating bugs off a slightly smaller orangutan, "We're here."

The scenery playing out on the walls of the corridor vanished as a door-sized panel in the wall slid into itself with a *whoosh*. She directed him inside.

The room was mostly dark. The walls looked like space. Millions and millions of tiny lights flickered in all directions above and below. A massive blue sphere slowly rotated in the center of a long, circular table that ran completely around it. It kind of reminded him of the Lake with its perfect circle of sand surrounding it. There were lights on the sphere, and long swaths of clouds. It looked like a giant marble floating there. It dimmed as he watched it until he could see through it to the other side of the table.

Seated around the table were three women and nine men. There was one empty chair at the opposite end of the table from where he stood. He knew them all, knew their stories. None of them looked like he expected they would. Most of them presented themselves as brightly shining beacons, or at least, that's how the beings in their stories understood them. They all just looked like regular people. None of them wore robes or anything, just loose-fitting comfortable-looking regular old, gray clothes like the outfit his dad wore on the rare occasion he'd go off to run the circuits.

Neith was first. She sat in the chair immediately to the right of the empty chair he knew would be his if they accepted him. There was something regal about the way her chin tilted slightly toward the ceiling. Her brown eyes seemed less skeptical of him than some of the other eyes staring at him from around the table. Her story was interesting. It was packed with an entire pantheon of gods she birthed on her own without the assistance of a male counterpart. The worshippers in her story changed things about her to their liking over time adding to the list of things she had done. They came up with this idea that she reweaved their world daily on her loom. He wondered what something like that might look like, billions of threads twisting into trees and lakes and mountains and people.

Seated immediately to Neith's right was Ninhursag, Enki sat next to her. The two looked like they might be related, they were the only members of the council with a shared story. It seemed their story was as twisted by their worshippers as Neith's had been, so much so that their original intended story couldn't easily be interpreted. The important thing which stood out to him was the idea that neither actually created the world in their stories, just the people. They found all the other creatures as if they'd come from somewhere else. They also seemed more mischievous than almighty, constantly competing with one another and the multitude of other gods they added to their story over what seemed to Coeptus to be wholly childish things.

Ra sat to the right of Enki. He basically stole Neith's story and changed her from being the creator of all things to his mother while taking that title for himself. Despite the apparent theft of ideas, he was adored by his creation. In his adaptation, he created all forms of life. Most notably, he created humans from his tears and sweat. However, despite how much he was loved by his creation, they too managed to destroy themselves.

Brahma came next. His story wasn't much different than the others. He included other beings in his narrative who worked with him to sustain and ultimately destroy everything. The intrigues and dramas among the various gods he added over time were different than the intrigues of the gods in the stories who came before, but ultimately, the result was the same. He created the universe and everything in it for some reason that isn't adequately described, possibly boredom or loneliness, Vishnu, as part of his trinity, sustained this everything Brahma had created, and the final piece in his trinity of creation, life, and destruction was Shiva, whose role was precisely as it sounded, to destroy. There were a couple truly interesting things about his creation. The first is how he was eventually supplanted by other gods to the point that he became an ancillary character known but not worshipped. The other is how the beings he created seemed to believe they could achieve some kind of enlightenment or oneness with him through some nebulous exercise of meditation and looking within. It reminded him of the Dragon's Flame, those warriors who believed they could actually become Flame through meditation, introspection, and knowing oneself. None succeeded in his story. Some in Brahma's believed they had.

Then there was Gaia. She was quite robust and looked like he thought she might. Her hair was wild, brown curls, and mingled in with the caring tenderness of her blue-eyed gaze was a kind of innocent freedom, not dull or aloof by any means, but wise. Something about the way she looked at him reminded him of his mother; he missed her. Gaia's story was at least as intriguing as her eyes. It differed from the others, because she was the world her creation lived upon. It was an active creation. She lay with the sky and gave birth to everything that came after, the oceans and mountains, and everything else. They were titans who were later supplanted by gods, each generation battling against the prior. The other thing about her story that differed from the others was that she didn't actively create the beings who worshipped her. That was a character who came generations later in her story.

Zeus and then Odin came next. Their stories were very similar. Zeus stole Gaia's story and never created anything, and Odin seemed to take the root of that story and changed it enough to make something almost original. Both presented themselves as father figures, but Zeus only ruled over another character's creation which stemmed from Gaia's older story. Odin actually created his earth and sentient creatures who populated it with the assistance of his siblings. One other notable difference was in how they presented themselves in their stories. Zeus was an often-violent storm god, while Odin seemed more interested in knowledge. That isn't to say the latter shied away from ideas of violence or war, it just seemed less a focus in the origins he presented his worshippers. As with the prior stories, the roots they laid down were twisted by their creation until they bore little resemblance to their source.

The large hairy man sitting opposite Odin from Zeus was Pangu. His story differed from theirs inasmuch as he actually created everything rather than simply ruling over something created by someone else. That being said, his story was equally convoluted. It began with nothing where the universe was in a formless state. Somehow, this formless nothing coalesced into an egg for eighteen thousand years where these concepts he came up with called yin and yang—opposing forces which starkly resembled the order and chaos of Ouloos coalescing into the Lake, a perfect balance between the two—became balanced. Pangu popped out of the egg, cleaved the yin from the yang to form the earth and heavens, and then took another eighteen thousand years to spread them apart and thicken them up. It was all very strange. Perhaps the strangest part was, then he died. The world he created was born out of his dead, hairy, giant body. His breath became the air, his eyes the sun and moon, his head the mountains, etc. The grossest part of that was where the creatures who populated the place came from. They were the fleas who fell from his fur. Hopefully, there weren't any fleas crawling all over him still.

The man sitting beside the large and overly hairy Pangu was Ahura Mazda. His story had a similar beginning, effectively taming chaos into order for some intangible reason. However, the difference between his and most of the other stories was how he presented himself. He came before all else, the beginning and the end. Every thought, feeling, and physical thing was a representation of some aspect of him. Of course, there came a pantheon of beings, some good, some bad, but they were created by him and therefore still part of him which differed from the characters in the previous stories. He was the one true god, and his story revolved around doing good in the world through positive thoughts and actions while fighting against evil.

And then there was Marduk. His story was similar to some of the older stories. He didn't present himself as existing before all else. He was merely one member of a vast pantheon of gods born of the coupling of older gods, Tiamat and Abzu. Abzu became frustrated by all the noise the younger generation made and decided to kill them. This younger generation kills him first. The act motivates Tiamat, as a representative of chaos, to wage war on her children. None of them are brave enough to face her save Marduk. He agrees to go to war against her and her minions in exchange for effectively being elevated to the position of king of the gods. He goes to war against her and the monstrous offspring she's given birth to for use in her war, defeats them, and carves up her body to fashion the earth and heavens. It didn't get much better from there.

Seated between Marduk and the empty seat Coeptus knew he would occupy if the council accepted him, was Yahweh. His jaw remained tense as he stared across the table at Coeptus. There was no joy hiding in his narrow eyes or tight expression. The rest of the group seemed rather aloof, almost bored. Yahweh appeared tired and defensive. His story contained elements of all those who came before. Like Ahura Mazda, he presented himself as the beginning and end, all-seeing and all-knowing, but the ideas seemed discombobulated. It also seemed his story had changed several times tweaking the narrative and making it difficult to follow it to any kind of logical ending that didn't include the destruction of everything.

Coeptus glanced up at Aphegeta and asked in a hushed tone, "Why do I know everything about them?"

Her smile was genuine as she replied, "I think because you are supposed to be here. Let's find out if they agree."

Then she turned back toward the council seated before them and said, "May I present Coeptus as a candidate to take the thirteenth seat of the thirteenth council? He has a story to tell." The nod accompanying her words almost seemed like a slight bow.

The tension tied up in Yahweh's expression finally let loose as if he'd been eagerly awaiting a challenge. He abruptly shook his head, pounded the table, and said, "No. My story has not yet met its end."

Before Aphegeta could muster any kind of response, Enki chuckled, "Your story ended more than two-thousand cycles ago. It will break my heart when the tale ends as it always does, but it is time to let it die."

"Oh, but dear Enki, lest we not forget about his son who was actually himself but somehow different while still being the same," Ninhursag laughed, "That changed everything."

Aphegeta took advantage of the distraction to whisper to Coeptus, "It sounds like Enki and Ninhursag will be on our side. It's difficult to tell how the rest will fall."

"What is this disrespect?" Zeus asked with a hint of agitation in his voice as his wavy, white locks bounced and his cheeks shook slightly when he turned his head to continue, "What is that you're whispering about?"

"Forgive me," Aphegeta replied, "I was helping Coeptus to understand the workings of the council to ensure he shows you the proper respect. It is worth noting that he knows all of you, and he knows everything about your stories just by walking into this room. I think that is meaningful."

"Indeed, it is," Odin said as he turned to look at them. "Tell me, what is the point of your story?"

"No. We don't need to know the point of his story, because his story will not be told. My story is not yet finished, despite what some of my colleagues might think," Yahweh complained.

"I think you've been wrapped up in your own story for too long. We all have," Neith seemed sad as she gently rebuked him.

"I disagree," Yahweh grew more and more agitated as he spoke, "This story, my story, is the one. Despite all the times my creation has reached the precipice of destruction, they have always managed to keep progressing. They are not done."

"Oh, my dear," there was pity in Gaia's smile as she continued, "we all felt our stories were just that, the tale to end all tales, a world where they would finally break through to a level of enlightenment where they could achieve this paradise we all described, and yet, they all ended just as yours must."

Marduk looked up toward the dark and starry ceiling as he added, "Not to mention, your story was just a blatant plagiarism of every story that came before. You haven't had an original thought in your life."

"How dare you!" Yahweh fumed as he slammed both his fists against the table.

"Plagiarism might be a bit much, but your story does seem strikingly similar to the stories which came before," Brahma shrugged.

"In fairness to Yahweh, all our stories came from our subconscious minds which, if you believe as I do, are all connected to the same collective. None of our stories have been all that different from any other stories. The details change, but the core remains the same. We've all shaped order out of chaos," Odin offered.

"I want to hear the point of the boy's story," Ra leaned forward in his chair intently, "Then we can decide if it is a saga worthy of telling."

"Unconditional love," Coeptus blurted, quickly covering his mouth after the words had come out. He immediately regretted interrupting the debate, but they were talking in circles around each other.

None of them complained about the interruption, but Marduk laughed. "That will never work," he finally said once he composed himself.

Coeptus' cheeks grew warm as he glanced about at the handful of council members who laughed along with Marduk. The ones who weren't laughing offered sad, patronizing smiles as if they felt sorry for his lack of experience and understanding, as if his quaint idea was a child's dream. Of course, it was. All the stories ever told had at one point begun as a child's dream. A small, defiant part of him wanted to shout something back at them about the silliness of all their stories, counsel them on how simple and egotistical their need to be worshipped really was, and point out the hypocrisy in their messages of love only given in return for complete subjugation and adoration. They all tried to shove love into their stories. It never fit because it wasn't really love at all. However, a much larger part of him wanted to shrink away and slink back out of the room. He only made one small step backward when Aphegeta grabbed a tight hold of his collar and held him fast.

She dropped any shred of respect from her voice when she said, "Coeptus will be heard. The lot of you are not the great and mighty forces you present yourselves as in your stories. You have a job to do like everyone else, and this your job."

"She's right," Pangu sat up a bit taller in his chair and glanced about the table until everyone who had been laughing finally stopped. Then he looked over at Coeptus and said, "Go ahead, boy. Tell us how unconditional love saves the world."

The eyes staring back at him as he struggled to find the words weren't welcoming. It felt like they all peered through him like they would hear his words but not really listen to them. Despite how small and naked he felt as they scrutinized him, he couldn't just stand there dumbly staring back at them. He had to say something.

He drew in a deep breath, stood as tall as he could, and said, "Unbridled emotion is chaos, like the unformed and violent, swirling mass with which most of your stories begin, even the ones which borrow an origin from others. Emotions only gain true meaning when shaped by logic, when they are given by choice."

"You cannot choose to feel something," Gaia's eyes narrowed skeptically, "Feelings are different than thoughts."

"But you can choose to feel something," Coeptus countered feeling more and more confident about the words leaving his mouth, "Isn't that the goal of meditation, to manage or control our feelings through a deeper understanding or enlightenment? Isn't that the point of all these stories? The goal your creations have failed to achieve is that perfect balance between unbridled emotion and stifling, logical reasoning. One shaping and guiding the other. The point of my story is a person learning to choose to show all creatures unconditional love because they understand that every being has a purpose and worth, and every action is taken for reasons you may or may not understand. The key is that you do not need to understand. You only need accept that your lack of understanding of a thing or its actions does not diminish its value or make it unworthy of love. You all have focused so intently on good and evil, light and dark, opposing forces where one is right, and one is wrong. I say there is no wrong. Both opposing forces are necessary. That is the point of my story."

They all stared back at him in silence for a few moments. Enki mumbled something to Ninhursag as she nodded. Yahweh slowly shook his head as he looked up toward the ceiling. Odin whispered something to Zeus who shook his head and laughed. But none of them gave Coeptus any kind of reply.

After a few uncomfortable moments of random mumblings and

occasional nods, Gaia finally smiled at him and said, "I want to hear your story." Then she glanced about the table, raised her voice a bit, and proclaimed, "I vote to welcome Coeptus to the council. I'm not certain his is the final story, but I think his reasoning is sound."

All but Zeus, Marduk, and Yahweh agreed. The latter refused to pull his eyes from the mock sky decorating the ceiling. A brief wave of pity warmed Coeptus' eyes. He didn't shed any tears, but their essence was painted across his heart. Hopefully, he wouldn't find himself in that same position at the end of his story, attempting to save the thing he'd created, but there were no guarantees the beings who populated the world in his story would find the end he hoped for them.

There was a brief bit of silence after the vote had concluded. Tears streamed freely down Enki's face as he stared at the globe rotating at the center of the table. Somehow, Coeptus knew he wept at the end of every story. Some of the others shed a few tears, but Enki seemed to take it the hardest.

Neith finally spoke up, "Come, Coeptus. Take your seat at the table. You are one with us now." Then she turned to Yahweh and said, "It is time. Let them go."

One tear trickled slowly down Yahweh's right cheek as he clenched his eyes tightly together. It looked more like anger than sadness settling into his expression as the globe lit up with bright flashes all about it. The blue parts grew agitated as they overcame the green and brown parts. The spectacle only lasted a few moments before everything went dark. None of the false lights that had been sparkling on the surface remained.

As Coeptus eased himself into his chair, Yahweh gave the command, "Initiate the cleansing protocol."

A glass cylinder lowered slowly from the ceiling. It lined up perfectly with the inside edge of the table encompassing the globe—which had stopped spinning at its center and sat still like a dead thing—and continued until it clicked into a rim that circled the floor. The glass cylinder filled with water. It poured from the ceiling to the floor like a cleansing shower until it was full. It remained like that for a few moments until the water quickly drained.

"And now I am the destroyer," Yahweh whispered as he slouched deeper into his chair and stared back at the ceiling.

Enki's sobbing slowly subsided as the glass cylinder retracted back into the ceiling. Then he looked over at Coeptus and said, "Go ahead, tell your story."

This was it. Coeptus glanced at all the eyes staring back at him and then began, "Before there was anything, there was thought, unfocused and random, a swirling mass of incomplete and malformed ideas. After a time, some of these ideas coalesced into an intention, focused and complete. This intention manifested itself as a Lake, a doorway, a path for other ideas to be born. Then came Dragons, thousands and thousands of them and with them came their Flame. Helias was the first. Her sisters all looked to her as the Great Mother, first and wisest among them. Together, they were unconditional love given freely and without choice. Their Flame was the greatest power that would ever exist in the universe, all knowledge that would ever be and the power to create or destroy, but their nature prevented them from ever unleashing it. They were the guides to the Lake and all understanding, a beacon to any seeking the mysteries of the universe and all creation which was Coeptus.

"Next came the gods, Moshat, Kallum, Kaldumahn, Brerto, Ijilv, and Raya. They despised the chaos swirling about the Lake and resented the Dragons for having all the power of creation but failing to use it to tame the wildness surrounding them. They saw the love they oozed as weakness. Two among them, Ijilv and Raya, were interlopers, left over ideas from a time before time, a world that had lived and died without ever being born into awareness. The other gods failed to recognize it, but these two were different. They knew things about the nature of Coeptus yet unknown by their contemporaries. They knew how to work outside the rules governing the other gods. Using this knowledge, they concocted a plan to use the other gods to help this world Kallum dubbed Ouloos to be born.

"More ideas came through the Lake. Each time a gathering of ideas swirled into an intention, it was born through the Lake into physical existence. Before long, all manner of beast and man walked the lands, living and dying, learning. The gods save the two interlopers craved worship. They competed with one another for the adoration and worship of the sentient beasts including man. They told their own stories to these creatures blessed with reason and understanding, stories which they believed gave these creatures purpose. They slowly tamed the chaotic lands until order ruled all of Ouloos west of the Lake, but to the east Chaos remained. The Lake became a barrier between them, a perfect balance between these two opposing concepts.

"Every material thing which lived, worshipped, and died in this physical existence would return to the Lake with a lifetime of experiences both good and bad, drawn there by Dragons, those beacons of love and hope to be stripped of those experiences and feed the cycle of life returning to the source to swirl once again as part of the whole."

As Coeptus continued his story, everything he said played out in the suddenly empty space at the center of the table where he sat with the rest of the council. They listened and watched with him as his words manifested before them. The land looked different than the globe it replaced when it finally came. It was a flat, circular disk instead of a round globe. The lands on one side of the Lake at its center were wild and untamed while the lands on its other side grew more and more orderly as he spoke.

CHAPTER 28
OULOOS LIVES

The Lake sat at the center of all creation, a perfect circle of dark still waters surrounded by a perfect ring of soft sand. The sun warmed it from a clear, blue sky free of any cloud which might seek to hinder its brilliance. Despite the bright sun shining down upon it in all its radiant glory, the glass-like surface of its waters bore no reflection. Neither did the cool breeze blowing across it cause even the slightest ripple.

Green upon green sprawled out from the Lake for miles in every direction, trees of all kinds and types clumped together dotting the landscape and bearing all manner of fruit and nut good for eating. Bushes and shrubs surrounded these clumps while vines stretched across the grass separating them as if they were some kind of cable connecting all living things together in one network of being.

Maelich sat in one of the grassy clearings. He crouched with his back legs curled beneath him. His horned head sat twenty feet above the smiling faces peering up at him from the grass below. The sweet scent of wildflowers danced upon the cool breeze gently caressing his scales. A scrod rested all curled up within the curve of his tail coiling behind him.

Cialia sat beside him. They were identical in every way from the horns atop their heads to the tails coiling behind them except for their right hands. Maelich's was missing, a reminder of darker days in a time before time, a time before enlightenment, a time before two Dragons learned to lose the shackles which had bound them and love all creation for what it was meant to be.

They were the first to step through the Lake and the only ones to remember that time before time. The beasts came next, born from the ground as if they were made right from the soil. The people came last arriving in the same fashion, they grew up right out of the ground as if the soil itself had spoken them into existence.

Of course, Maelich knew the soil wasn't creating anything. Coeptus' words echoed in his mind urging him to teach these empty vessels how to live fulfilling lives, loving each other and all things, and allowing all things to be what they are meant to be without hindering them. He knew Cialia heard it too. They remained connected even while they were being destroyed and after. They were the only ones who remained after the rebirth, and they were connected to everything born into Ouloos.

One of the one hundred faces staring up at him was Daritus. Cialia had named them all as they grew up out of the soil. Something about this one reminded her of her father from that time before time. She had told him about his namesake first, asking, "Would you accept the name of this man who meant so much to me in a time before time?" He was honored by the gesture and proud to bear the name.

Daritus' light brown eyes oozed with innocence as he looked up at Maelich and asked, "Would you tell me about the time before time again?"

They all loved the story, but Daritus asked to hear it daily. "Of course, I will," Maelich smiled down on him before glancing at Cialia and asking, "Would you like to begin?"

Cialia inhaled deeply while she closed her smoldering eyes and began, "In a time before time, pain and suffering, fear and uncertainty, and all manner of terror and violence ruled the hearts of men. Thousands upon thousands of Dragons tried to teach them love, but the gods turned their hearts cold and urged them on to fight against one another to take what they wanted and protect what they had. They only loved those things they could control. Even fair Maelich and I were wrong. We were like them."

Maelich continued when she paused, "The Dragons tried and tried again and again to educate us about how to love all things, but we proved stubborn and hard to teach."

"They never gave up on us, our sisters, those embodiments of unconditional love," Cialia added.

"Not once," Maelich agreed, "No matter what wicked thing we did, they loved us just the same, never condemning nor forsaking us. They were perfection, and they showed us how to live."

Cialia picked the story back up when Maelich paused again. It was how they told the tale every time. Every soul in the clearing listening to them speak was swept into the tale every time even though it was told every day, sometimes multiple times in a day.

There was one soul who didn't care for the story. That soul didn't exist in any of the bodies seated before them. It was separate, slithering about the trees like a phantasm searching for a vessel to inhabit. Maelich knew it was Geillan, but he was unable to speak to him. Unlike every other being on Ouloos, he couldn't connect with that one. He could only sense aspects of his nature. Rage, sadness, and fear were all wrapped up in it. If only he could have a moment to speak with him.

Geillan slipped about the crowd of people staring up at those Dragons and listening to the same story they told over and over again. It was all a bunch of lies. They had the facts correct, but the way they stated them twisted them into something false. The Dragons they elevated to such heights by giving them credit for making some great sacrifices were the exact opposite of the heroes they described. They did nothing, and somehow their inaction became some great accomplishment. He would give them an accurate account if he could, but they couldn't hear him. No matter how loud he shouted, they didn't even know he was there.

"Why do you haunt that place?" Brerto's voice droned. He always had something to say, some unwanted opinion he just couldn't help but spew out into the world.

"This place shouldn't even exist," he snapped, "I destroyed it."

"But you didn't destroy it," Raya's sweet voice was like a dagger in his head, "Your actions allowed it to be born. You saved it."

"This is all wrong. This world should not exist. We all should have died, and here I am paying some penance by being trapped, a specter unable to tell these dull creatures the truth."

"Perhaps now you understand how we all felt trapped within another's mind. You are a ghost like the rest of us now, nothing but the memory of a life which once was," Kaldumahn sadly added.

"I didn't do that to you, your beloved brother did that," Geillan's tone remained sharp, "I wish he hadn't. Silence would be lonely but better than suffering the lot of you."

"We all have to suffer each other," Ijilv grumbled, "Even Raya is with us now. We are all unwanted company for the rest of us."

"This can't be the end," Kallum scoffed, "There is a reason we are here."

"Yes," Moshat agreed, "Though I remain unable to understand what that reason might be, nothing happens without a reason."

"Perhaps we're meant to rule this place," Kallum offered.

"Have you learned nothing?" Raya sighed.

"Shut up, you vile thing," Geillan snapped. They were all insufferable, but she was the worst. She was the reason he ever had to exist, tricking the rest into doing her bidding. Everything was her fault. Regardless of that, he did exist, and Ouloos had been born. Lamenting the fact would make no difference.

Kallum had a point worthy of exploration. Why else would they exist. Of all the living creatures on Ouloos he destroyed, only Maelich and Cialia, those wicked things, survived. Everything else had been destroyed. Why had he remained? The Dragons had a purpose. Perhaps he did too.

"Perhaps we were meant to rule this place," he finally replied, "I can think of no other reason for us to remain."

"But how?" Ijilv asked.

"The same way we ruled before," Brerto's words were quietly ominous, "We need to study this new world and learn the rules governing existence."

"And then we can break them," the words felt like a smile as he said them, "Come. Let's get to work."

The End

Author's Note

Welcome to the end. I hope you enjoyed riding along with the characters who inhabit this world as they grew and learned things about themselves while conquering the challenges laid before them as much as I enjoyed sharing them with you. Ouloos will live forever in my mind, and though she has more stories to tell, this one is finished. This trek has taken nearly twenty years to complete. Thank you for trusting me to lead you through this small bit of Ouloos' history. It has been my supreme honor to serve as your guide for this journey.

This adventure began as somewhat of a tool to deal with struggles I had with my faith and beliefs. Some of those questions have been answered. Others may never be. One thing I have learned is that no matter what you believe, everyone's journey is a personal one. For me, I intend to allow folks to be who they will, doing my best to live by the mantra I've adopted, mind your own <expletive> business. In the end, the only person's actions you can truly control are your own. I am not a religious person, but I do believe in the power of prayer—or for me, positive vibes / thinking. Here is one I recommend that I'm sure you know. I consider these words to live by:

<Insert deity or concept here>, grant me the serenity to accept the things I cannot change, the courage to change the things I can, and the wisdom to know the difference.

As I mentioned earlier, Ouloos has more stories to tell. She has a rich history to draw from with complex characters whose lives and adventures amount to tales worth telling, and I do intend to tell them. That being said, these stories are from her history and not her future. Someday, I may endeavor to share the tale of Ouloos' future, which would undoubtedly be tied to the fate of Coeptus' world, but right now I would rather not. For now, I leave the fate of Ouloos with your capable imaginations. After all, the Lake of Dragons is a home for all.

ABOUT THE AUTHOR

E. Michael Mettille is the author of Kill the Dragon (Lake of Dragons Book 1), Kallum's Fury (Lake of Dragons Book 2), Kill the Gods (Lake of Dragons Book 3), The Forgotten One (Lake of Dragons Book 4), and Hell and the Hunger (as Mike Reynolds). He has also written numerous short stories and poems. Mike has spent the last twenty-five years in direct marketing, print, and communication. He is fascinated by history, belief systems, the human condition and how all of those things work together to define who we are as a people. The world is a wonder and, based on the history of us, it is a wonder we have a world left to wonder about. Mike lives in Franklin, WI with his wife, Shelia, and their two dogs, Ziggy Stardust and Lady Stardust.